"Southern fiction full of small-town charm, second chances, and fierce family love. It's one of those rare books that leaves the reader smiling through tears and longing for a trip to June's."

—Audrey Ingram, *USA TODAY* bestselling
author of *The Summer We Ran*

"*Good Hair Days* is a story as heartwarming as it is heartbreaking and is told with a heavy Southern accent and an even heavier dose of charm. The love between sisters is 'brighter and sparklier' according to Walz, and the connection between Junie and Georgia is a palpable one that encompasses forgiveness and hope and everything in between. Throw in a hair salon, a large family of women, a long-lost love, and a devastating legacy and you've got the kind of book you won't want to put down."

—Karen White, *New York Times* bestselling author

"With plenty of Southern charm and juicy family drama, a second-chance romance with her lost, teenage love, and a mystery surrounding the identity of Mack's father, this appealing novel sits nicely alongside other southern fiction focused on women's lives, like the novels of Kristy Woodson Harvey and Mary Alice Monroe."

—*Booklist* for *Southern by Design*

"With this Charleston-set debut novel *Southern by Design*, Grace Helena Walz has taken her place among such treasured Southern novelists as Dorothea Benton Frank and Anne Rivers Siddons. Her stories and her voice is one readers are bound to adore."

—Mary Kay Andrews, *New York Times* bestselling
author of *Summers at the Saint*

"Fans of interior design, Southern secrets, and good, old-fashioned family drama will flock to Grace Helena Walz's page-turning tale. A story of second chances and long-lost love as atmospheric as the Lowcountry itself, this is a positively charming debut from a stand-out new voice. Add it to your TBR list immediately!"

—Kristy Woodson Harvey, *New York Times* bestselling author of *A Happier Life*, for *Southern by Design*

"With bright, snappy dialogue, characters so real they jump off the page, and a Charleston setting to swoon over, *Southern by Design* is a sparkling debut! Walz is going to win fans with this sweet story of big dreams, to-die-for design, and real love."

—Lauren K. Denton, *USA TODAY* bestselling author of *The Hideaway*

"What's not to love about a humid Southern setting, a second-chance romance, and a family full of secrets? This debut novel sets Grace Helena Walz up to become an instant favorite for fans of Karen White, Kristy Woodson Harvey, and Patti Callahan Henry. *Southern by Design* is pitch perfect for book clubs, and just the right amount of sweet."

—Kimberly Brock, award-winning author of *The Fabled Earth*

"*Southern by Design* is a refreshing and lighthearted read that beautifully captures the charm of Southern living while delving into the complexities of single motherhood, family dynamics, and second chances. Magnolia 'Mack' Bishop is a relatable and humorous protagonist whose determination to succeed, both professionally and personally, makes her journey one you'll want to follow. The story's blend of witty dialogue, unexpected twists, and heartfelt moments keeps you hooked from start to finish. If you love stories with strong, resilient women and a dash of Southern charm, this debut novel is a must-read!"

—Jennifer Moorman, bestselling author
of *The Vanishing of Josephine Reynolds*

"This charming debut has it all—second-chance romance, a balmy Southern setting, and plenty of long-held secrets that kept me turning the pages. As easy to imbibe as a glass of cold sweet tea on a hot summer day, *Southern by Design* is perfect for fans of Kristy Woodson Harvey, Karen White, and Mary Kay Andrews."

—Colleen Oakley, *USA TODAY* bestselling author
of *The Mostly True Story of Tanner & Louise*

ALSO BY GRACE HELENA WALZ

Southern by Design

GOOD
HAIR DAYS

A NOVEL

GRACE HELENA WALZ

THOMAS NELSON

Since 1798

Good Hair Days

Copyright © 2025 Grace Helena Walz

Published in Nashville, Tennessee, by Thomas Nelson. Thomas Nelson is a registered trademark of HarperCollins Christian Publishing, Inc.

Thomas Nelson titles may be purchased in bulk for educational, business, fundraising, or sales promotional use. For information, please email SpecialMarkets@ThomasNelson.com.

Publisher's Note: This novel is a work of fiction. Names, characters, places, and incidents are either products of the author's imagination or used fictitiously. All characters are fictional, and any similarity to people living or dead is purely coincidental.

Any internet addresses (websites, blogs, etc.) in this book are offered as a resource. They are not intended in any way to be or imply an endorsement by Thomas Nelson, nor does Thomas Nelson vouch for the content of these sites for the life of this book.

Library of Congress Cataloging-in-Publication Data

Names: Walz, Grace Helena, 1987- author
Title: Good hair days: a novel / Grace Helena Walz.
Description: Nashville: Thomas Nelson, 2025. | Summary: "Two sisters, a failing family business, and a whole lot of hairspray—Good Hair Days is a modern twist on Steel Magnolias with a little extra Dolly Parton flare"—Provided by publisher.
Identifiers: LCCN 2025001427 (print) | LCCN 2025001428 (ebook) | ISBN 9781400345663 trade paperback | ISBN 9781400345670 epub | ISBN 9781400345687
Subjects: LCGFT: Southern fiction | Novels
Classification: LCC PS3623.A4555 G66 2025 (print) | LCC PS3623.A4555 (ebook) | DDC 813/.6 \$2 23/eng/20250414—dcundefined
LC record available at https://lccn.loc.gov/2025001427
LC ebook record available at https://lccn.loc.gov/2025001428

Printed in the United States of America

25 26 27 28 29 LBC 5 4 3 2 1

For my sister, Alice.

A NOTE FROM THE AUTHOR

GOOD HAIR DAYS IS A story about sassy Southern women pulling together in a series of fun hijinks to save their family beauty shop. However, much like life itself, the story also includes heavier elements to which some readers may be sensitive. If you are a reader who prefers to go in blind, please stop reading here, as below I will list trigger warnings.

This story contains cancer diagnoses, cancer treatment, and discussion of genetic testing related to inherited illness. Cancer has touched the lives of many people, all of whom are at different points in their reckoning with it, so it is important to me to make note of this content so folks can be advised before jumping in.

CHAPTER 1

GEORGIA

I BELONG TO A GENERATIONS-OLD LINE of hairdressers, women who snipped and sprayed and teased each head of hair to perfection in our small-town beauty shop. Well, I did belong until I was lovingly cast out. Nevertheless, salon blood runs in my veins. And since I can't go home, I visit local salons like a meditation, like a pilgrimage, like a desperate grab at the life I wish I could've had. Even when my bank balance hovers around zero, I never regret an appointment. Not for a sniff of that life or the family I miss most.

Because good hair is not negotiable.

Not in my life, and not in my heart.

The floral perfume of the glossy, high-end salon wafts over me as I step inside, despite the fact that I absolutely, positively cannot afford it. It's my first time here, and the familiar scent of tea tree oil floats by, pushed my way by the warmth of a blow dryer. It's like a reminder that everything just might be ok. The music, a soft pop track, plays at a pitch-perfect decibel. Every employee is well-mannered, unruffled. Without question, these folks are professionals.

A blonde woman with pink streaks and a nose ring introduces herself as Sadie and wraps a towel around the back of my neck. I know the drill, and as she lifts my thick red hair like a velvet curtain from my back, I recline into the washbasin, my breath pouring out in a sigh as the water rushes over my crown. I was raised between the basins, under the feet of my mother, my aunts, and my grandmother, two hours north of here at June's Beauty Shop. It's the best hair salon in north Georgia—or at least in our small town of Whitetail—and it's the most wonderful place on earth.

Well, to be entirely transparent, it's also an outdated, hole-in-the wall shop slathered in Dolly Parton memorabilia. And there is no guarantee that the June's staff is always on their best behavior—even if they try. But we cut folks a break when they're out of a job, or down on their luck, or their transmission just quit, and we get by. With a little help from the occasional gambling tables we set out after hours.

June's is where the women of my mama's family have worked and lived and loved for generations. June's is the reason every firstborn daughter in the family is named June. It's the reason every June grows up to run the beauty shop, with the other women by her side. What can I say—we take our traditions seriously.

"Water a good temp?" Sadie asks. She's definitely a hair apprentice, the person who will sweep and take out the trash until she's a full-fledged stylist.

"Great," I tell her.

I close my eyes and hear the quick squish of shampoo being pumped from a commercial-size bottle, and the tension in my neck unwinds as Sadie's fingers begin to massage my scalp. Being the person in the chair feels like tossing someone else the keys, a break from the responsibility I've assigned myself. A chatty young woman sits down at the basin beside me, smacking her bubblegum loud enough to punctuate the music. She launches into a detailed account of her recent promotion and the vacation to the Bahamas she and her fiancé have planned. *Must be nice.* Still, I shouldn't compare. I'm at the beauty shop; I shall savor it.

"Cutting the water back on," Sadie announces, then starts to rinse.

Look better, feel better. That's what my mama always said about a good hair day. June Louise Scott was the fourth June of her kind, and she died when I was only thirteen. Those of us left behind—me, my sister, and our maternal aunts, Cece and Tina—follow her mantras like a beacon, like a ritual of love.

Sadie turns off the water with a clunk when she's finished and says, "Let's get you back over to the chair."

With a towel wrapped around my wet hair, I follow her across the shiny tile floor, past the mirror-lined stations where expensive-looking clients clutter the seats. Sadie clips me into a cape and heads back to the wash station as my stylist arrives.

"Hey there, thanks for coming in. I'm Jaxy." She has a short-cropped Afro and is wearing a skintight denim jumpsuit I could never, not in my wildest dreams, pull off. "What can I do for you today?"

I have the script memorized. "Only a trim, please. I'll keep the long layers and not too choppy around the face."

She nods. "I hate it when it looks all clunky when it's pulled up."

"*Yes.* You're reading my mind," I say, and I know I'm in safe hands.

Jaxy flashes me a pearly white smile, then gets down to untangling and cutting my hair as professionally as she represents herself. I feel myself loosen up with every stretching comb and quick snip, and eventually my eyes close.

The office where I work is right above us. One of many offices stacked on top of the retail spaces at street level, like this salon. Mine is a customer care center where phones ring incessantly and are answered in far-too-loud voices, almost as if the company's success is measured by volume. I'd be lying if I said it was my dream, but it's not all bad and I do my best to be a top-notch performer. I'm an executive assistant to the boss, the VP of customer support, Felix. I manage his schedule, his calls, and occasionally his moods, and my well-organized brain and take-charge attitude are well-suited to the job. I remind him about appointments, flag his documents for spelling and grammar mistakes, and generally cover his rear when he gets flustered.

Which isn't infrequent.

I open my eyes, and in the mirror, Jaxy looks laser focused as she measures and trims. Before long she reaches for the blow dryer, and I let myself sink into the white noise and warm air surrounding me.

Now this is what life's about. Hair nirvana accessible only from a premiere service.

Even if I'm doing fairly well as a secretary, *this* is where I want to be—in the salon.

Well, June's Beauty Shop specifically.

Jaxy takes my thick red hair in sections, curls it, and rakes it into waves with her fingers once it cools. She hands me a mirror and turns my chair to give me a 360-degree view. "What do you think?"

"It's exactly what I wanted. Thank you," I say. "You're a killer stylist—and that's coming from a fifth-generation haircare family member."

Jaxy's cheeks flush. "Well, hopefully I'll see you next time."

I assure her that she'll be my first-choice stylist for next time, but in my heart I know *next time* will be a long time coming.

I *should* be someone who can afford it, and if anyone were to ask my family back home in Whitetail, they would assure them I could. Because I am a hometown hero, the class valedictorian and varsity athlete, sent to college on a full scholarship. A Star Child who worked her way up to a job as a VP of customer support in only eight years. Or at least, that's the lie I let them believe.

After Mama died, I was something they could point to that was going well. I gave them something hopeful to look at, something to brag about around town. Something to tack up on their fridges and the beauty shop walls in pride. Something to assure their friends that their lives had a silver lining. How could I tell them it all went wrong?

That the family superstar had burned out? It would mean laying hurt and embarrassment on them. And I couldn't do that.

Jaxy walks me to the checkout desk, and we say goodbye. I settle up my tab—on a credit card—and leave a generous tip.

I push out of the glass storefront into the thick, warm summer air. I hear the rumble of Atlanta traffic stopping and starting on the main road adjacent to this side street. It's evening rush hour, which seems to last most of the day in this city with our overloaded highways.

I turn the corner and extend my badge to unlock the entrance that leads to the floors above. In the vestibule I press the button to call the elevator down. When it arrives, the doors opening with a friendly chime, a small group of colleagues empties out.

"Georgia!" Mercedes, an early-twenties bundle of energy, calls out. "A few of us are heading down to Russo's for happy hour. Want to join?"

I smile as I brace an arm across the elevator door to hold it. "Thanks, but Felix doesn't have anyone for Sophie, so I agreed to keep her."

Mercedes shoots me an impressed look. "You really go the extra mile for him. He's lucky to have you."

I playfully look left and right, then whisper, "Don't tell him, but it's for *Sophie*, not for him."

Something about Felix's daughter reminds me of my little sister, Junie, the person I love most in this world. I step inside, and once the doors close, the elevator zips upward lightning-quick, making my insides flip-flop briefly.

I love home, and I love June's. But I love my sister, Junie, in a way I'm not sure I've ever loved anyone or anything else. It's probably a good thing, considering she got the name. In our family, every firstborn daughter is supposed to be named June—except when it came to me.

Mama bucked tradition. Well, she tried. She only made it halfway until, for some mysterious reason, she changed her mind and named her second girl June. And in naming her so, Mama also gave Junie the rights to June's Beauty Shop. It was tradition after all. In her typical fashion, Mama put a good spin on it for me. I was the star of the family. I was destined for more. I shouldn't be chained to the rickety old salon unless I chose to be. So she gave me a new name and an open door to any possibility. It was a dream I believed in too. Even if I couldn't quite outrun the small but constant tug June's had on my heart.

Since I didn't get the name I was due, my consolation prize was my middle name, Louise, Mama's maiden name, the last name her sisters Tina and Cece still held. Tina and Cece always called themselves Louises, and as girls Junie and I joined in too. As a group we are Louises. It was a sliver of proof of my belonging among them.

Any way I dice it, my name should've been a revolution. A ticket to an enviable life beyond the shop.

Until I couldn't make good on the version of myself Mama planned for me. Until I didn't turn out particularly glittery. Until I came to resemble a fairly average person. And the eagerness to please Mama's memory turned to guilt inside me.

The elevator doors open and my mind clears as the sprawling open workspace appears in front of me. Most of the desks are empty since it's after five. I snake through the rows and rows of low cubicles in shades of greige to my perch, in similar bland neutrals, outside Felix's office. The door clicks open as I approach, and I catch sight of Sophie. She begins to bound out but corrects herself into a slow walk when she presumably remembers she's a preteen now and a bit too cool to be excited about a strange woman in her thirties.

I raise a hand, trying to look cool. "Hey, Soph."

She walks up and slouches on my desktop.

"You're stuck with me again, huh?" I say, setting my bag on the desktop and pulling out my phone.

"Can we do a massive fishtail that goes all the way down like a French braid?" she asks.

It's my favorite thing about hanging with Sophie—and probably one of the bigger reasons she reminds me so much of Junie—her love for hair. We've done every variety of French braid, mastered the fishtail, executed peak early 2000s butterfly clip styles, and even experimented with temporary hair colors (with her dad's permission). She once asked me to cut it, but that was where I had to draw the line.

"Of course." I smile and reach into my bag, then pull out my jumbo case of rainbow hair ties, clips, and every other hair trinket a girl could dream of. "I came prepared."

Sophie squeaks and claps in excitement.

A tight part of my insides unfurls with relief. I've been waiting, expecting the moment when she decides she's too cool for me. Because along with the inevitable polite *"No thanks, I'm not into that anymore,"* Sophie will close this magical window in my mind that allows me to go home for a bit, to see Junie, to revisit the moments we were closest.

Felix comes out of his office, pulling on a sport coat and finger combing his hair. "Thanks again for this, Georgia. You're always Sophie's first choice."

I squeeze a quiet smile. I must admit babysitting isn't exactly the picture I had of a Friday evening at thirty-two, but this is different. Sophie's mom has been in and out of treatment facilities for her addiction and the mental health problems that have sprung from it like tendrils. I don't know the details—they aren't really my business anyway—but I feel a special desire to show up for Sophie. She's eleven years old. The same age Junie was when our mom died. I did my best back then to step in and be there for Junie, to do whatever seemed like a "mom job" and to do it exceptionally, but I know it wasn't a fix.

Just like my hanging out with Sophie won't fix her missing her mom. But I know what it's like growing up without a mom around, and if I can make the girl happy for even a few minutes by braiding her hair, saying yes is a no-brainer.

"You guys good?" Felix asks as he turns to go. He grinds to a halt, slaps a palm to his forehead, and groans. "*Dinner.* I didn't plan dinner. Georgia—"

"I've got it," I say, cutting him off.

Sophie grins and shoots a look my way. "We seriously always get the same thing. Pizza. Next to the hair place."

Felix nods rapidly. "Of course. Yes, of course you do. Again, *thank you.*"

I wave him off as an exasperated Sophie chimes in, "*Dad,* just go. Georgia is, like, the most responsible person I know. And we've got plans."

Felix throws us a final wave and disappears toward the elevator, and Sophie wastes no time in pulling up the YouTube video she found demonstrating the braid she wants me to execute. I watch it a few times to make sure I've got it before she settles on a makeshift pillow at my feet and hands me her brush.

"Braid first, then pizza, right?" I ask as I pull the brush through her brown waves.

"For sure," she says.

We have a routine: braiding at the office, then pizza downstairs, and last, YouTube or TV on her tablet. It's never made sense for us to sit in rush-hour traffic for the drive to their house that's in the opposite direction of my place. Plus, Felix keeps these work dinners short, saving what he has of his single-dad energy for outings with true friends. Or at least that's what I assume; we aren't particularly close, to be honest. I have to admit the arrangement suits me, being able to help Felix out without having to go to his house. The last thing I need is people gossiping at the office about the nature of our relationship.

Sophie is quiet as I braid her hair, only making the occasional comment about shows she's watching or something a friend told her that she wants to fact-check with me. I'm almost to the end of the braid when my phone rings.

I look over and the screen is lit with Junie's smiling face, the photo I have saved for her.

"Hang on, Junie," I tell the phone. "I'll call you right back."

The phone rings off then immediately buzzes back to life on the desktop.

"You can get it, you know," Sophie says. "She's calling twice in a row—maybe something's wrong."

I reach for the phone, thinking the same. Ever since our mama died, even all these years later, I expect the worst every time Junie calls. As if losing Mama, a force of nature, was so baffling that the only possible explanation is that we are cursed. It's a never-ending limbo, waiting until the next catastrophic thing happens. Other bad things have to happen; statistically it's the case. But I've dedicated myself to being diligent and practiced and organized and efficient enough to minimize whatever ill arrives on our doorstep. If I can hold it together, it could make all the difference. If the ship goes down and I've trained long and hard enough, I'll be a strong enough swimmer to save them, the whole family. Maybe even myself too.

I click to accept the call. "Junie."

I'm met by a quiet sniffling that crescendos into a deep, heart-wrenching sob.

The braid slips from my fingers as I rise to my feet. "What's happening? Where are you?"

I hear the sound of her breath that she's trying to catch, the inhale caught on the sorrow reverberating inside her. "It's—" She blows her nose. "It's bad, Georgia. Can you come home?"

"Yes, of course, I'll leave first thing in the morning, but what's wrong? What's happening?"

"I'm so sorry," Junie says.

"Have you been in a car crash? I'll call 911." I turn and reach for the landline on my desk.

"No. Don't. There's no crash. I'm at June's."

I wait for her to go on.

"I've really messed it all up, Georgia," Junie says. "Like always, with everything I try to do, I've messed it up. And this time it's the shop. June's is in trouble."

CHAPTER 2

JUNIE

JUNIE TUCKS THE PHONE INTO the back pocket of her jeans. She promised Georgia they'd hash out the details in person. Junie drags the tissue under her nose and looks up from where she stands in the middle of June's Beauty Shop.

Or what's left of it. The maroon carpet that once ran under her feet—under their mama's feet—is long gone, ripped out and tossed in the dumpster out back. The drywall is halfway gone, the storage cabinets that lined the back ripped down to the studs. Aunt Tina's wig wall is boxed up and gone, now stacked in her guest room.

It's demoed.

And Georgia doesn't know.

The entire situation reminds Junie of the time she brought home the class gerbil, Pumpkin, in fourth grade, back when Mama was sick and they were mostly in charge of themselves on the weekends. Daddy sat at Mama's side like a sentry until she needed something. Even when she shooed him away, he never went far, hovering instead on the outskirts. Thus, it wasn't unusual for Junie to find herself bored and unsupervised, and this day she had decided to give the pet a bath in the kitchen sink. Ron Horowitz had told her that gerbils could swim and that he'd watched Pumpkin do it during his weekend to keep her.

Junie filled the sink, cooing at Pumpkin through the wires of her cage about the fun awaiting her. But when Junie lowered Pumpkin into the full basin, she spooked, scrambled out of the sink, and made a mad dash along the counter. Junie chased her, scattering cups and stacks of mail in an attempt to catch the gerbil as she neared the open door to the backyard.

To this day, Junie can feel the panic, the searing sensation of fear seizing her chest. She was doing something nice for Pumpkin, and horrible fates weren't supposed to await people acting in good faith. It never made sense how good intentions didn't count for squat. She'd realized that difficult truth as little Pumpkin hightailed it toward the door and the unfortunate fates beyond. It was like a twisted pre-requisite to enduring her mother's eventual death.

In that moment Georgia had spun around the corner in a flurry. *"Junie Scott, what on earth?"* Her long red hair whipped behind her as she skidded to a stop. Georgia's eyes landed on the fluffy rodent as Pumpkin disappeared out the door.

Junie froze. Her big sister paused, snatched the Cheerios from the pantry, and tiptoed outside after Pumpkin. Junie didn't act. She didn't follow. Her brain hadn't even considered that anything else might be required of her.

Georgia had returned a few minutes later, Pumpkin gnawing on a mound of Cheerios in her palms, and efficiently slid the gerbil back into the cage, dusted off her hands, and said, *"Let me help you get her out next time."* Then she exited the room as quickly as she'd arrived.

At the time, Junie was flooded with admiration for her sister, and frankly, she was also flushed with relief knowing she wouldn't return to school on Monday with an empty cage. But as the years passed and Junie watched her sister remedy situation after situation without breaking a sweat, the contrast between the two sisters was drawn so starkly in Junie's mind, it was as if it defined her. Georgia was competent, a fixer, organized, and proactive. Junie made messes, rushed in, and didn't think things through.

Georgia knew better.

Georgia *knows* better.

Junie runs a hand over the hair chairs covered in drapes. They were supposed to get dolled up as part of this whole thing too. Recovered, perhaps, in a modern fabric, something that would hold up and didn't feel like a plastic tablecloth from a corner pizza restaurant.

It was another part of the plan, part of this big agreement Junie had reached with Goldilocks Haircare as a part of their "family-run salon investment project." In exchange for Goldilocks covering part of the cost of a renovation and allowing the shop to purchase products at a discount, June's Beauty Shop would feature a display of Goldilocks products, as well as various branded signage, in a prime location.

Junie had asked Daddy, who manages the accounting for the shop, and he told her the funds required on their end were available. Now Daddy claims otherwise, that he said some version of *"probably"* or *"maybe"* and *"I'll need to look into it further."* If Junie is completely honest, she might've stopped listening after he said, *"It probably won't be an issue, but . . ."* How could she not? The excitement at the possibility, *the opportunity*, of seeing June's brought into a new chic era.

Junie did her best to be responsible, checking with the accountant, crossing a decent amount of t's before charging on, but at heart, she is a girl obsessed with hair and seeing stars over being close enough to touch one of the trendiest haircare brands on the market.

That brand alongside June's Beauty Shop.

The heartbeat of the family.

The only physical piece of Mama left.

The door of the shop scrapes open with a muted jangle of the oversize bell attached to the knob. Even the bells are choking under construction dust.

Junie turns. Aunt Tina comes first, a compact woman at barely five feet two with her neat, shoulder-length strawberry-blonde bob. She's flanked by her boyfriend-slash-dependent, Randy, and behind him follows Aunt Cece.

"Alright, Tina. Ten minutes, tops," Randy says briskly. "I'll wait in the car."

Tina turns, opening her mouth to reply.

"I've got darts tonight, and I won't be late because of you girls having some chitchat," Randy says, and then the door shuts behind him.

Tina lets out a quiet, practiced sigh.

Cece scowls at the door. "Son of a—"

"*Cecelia,*" Tina cuts in.

Junie stifles the snicker that erupts, despite the circumstances.

Tina cocks her head from side to side, as if she's trying to come up with some defense for Randy. Eventually she says, "His soft skills need some work, I'll agree to that."

Cece tuts, making her disagreement clear, then lets it go.

Tina crosses the room to Junie, takes her hands, and squeezes. "We'll get this figured out, sweetie." Tina's voice is as small as her physical presence. "I spoke to my Tuesday appointments, and they're ok to keep things hush-hush."

Junie pulls Tina into a hug, wrapping her easily in her long arms and standing a full head and a half taller. Even if she is small, Tina makes her love known in a big way. She is Junie's hairstylist partner at the salon and the woman who kept the shop open and running after their mama died. Sure, other hairstylist friends tagged in and out to help, and their appointment capacity fluctuated as Tina, ever the people pleaser, subbed at other small businesses around town. *"Tina, you've got your sister's beauty shop to run. Why are you waiting tables on Thursdays?"* Cece once asked. Tina might not know how to tell people no, but without her, June's would've shuttered. Years later, the place was humming along, waiting for Junie as she finished cosmetology school, got her license, and took her spot behind the hair chairs.

Junie releases Tina, who begins walking slow circles around the open floor, taking it all in.

Aunt Cece examines the interior as well, but she is painstaking, covering every surface, her jaw clenched tight, eyes flitting as if she's taking mental notes. Cece is the tallest among them, pushing six feet, and she long ago let her dirty-blonde hair fill with silvery streaks. It came as little to no surprise; Cece shrugged off the whole haircare industry after a short-lived term at June's washbowl. Junie knows Cece cares—even if she is a little snappy sometimes—because she continues to show up, even if Junie suspects Cece might be ok with the shop slipping away into oblivion.

"At least the construction crew mostly cleared out behind themselves," Cece says. Her face says the rest: *"But look at what's left."*

Junie squeezes a hopeful smile and nods, but despite her efforts, tears fill her eyes. "You're right. Yup, that is one positive. But—I'm sorry, y'all." Junie lets her face fall into her palms.

Tina rushes over and stands between them. "Nonsense, Junie, it was an honest mistake. We all know Rich isn't always the best communicator. Not that I'm saying it's your daddy's fault—just to be extremely clear—y'all don't tell him I said that. Promise? Gosh, I don't want him to think I'm *blaming* him."

Cece swats the air. "Stop. We know what you mean." She turns to Junie. "And as for you, it's no help getting upset now. We've got to focus on what we can do next."

Cece is practical almost to a fault, as if her right mind can override her heart. How could Cece not want to wring Junie's neck for ripping apart her twin sister's salon and proceeding to immediately drop the ball?

"I might feel better if you yelled at me, Aunt Cee," Junie says. "Just real quick."

"Not interested in that," Cece replies.

"Well, I know we probably shouldn't, but what if we kept doing hair?" Tina asks, shoulders curling in on her in self-doubt. "Should I have suggested it? Was that awful?"

Junie crosses her arms and opens her eyes wide. "We'd have to be careful."

Cece lets out a slow, pressured breath. "I hate to say it, but I'm not sure y'all have much choice."

"One thing . . ." Tina drops her gaze to her toes. "Misty Prince."

Junie lets out a groan.

Misty Prince is the town busybody. She wishes Whitetail had an HOA that governed every building, so she could run for president and send people notices for an off-center shingle, a tired flower bed, or a lawn measuring half an inch too high. Misty's sunglasses always ride low on her long, slim nose (one that legend states was certainly bought and paid for) so her eyes can be in other people's business without barrier. If it were a little glossier and a little less bureaucracy and paperwork, she might just run for local government. Misty seems to have it out for the Louise women, or maybe it's June's Beauty Shop where her issue lies, but whichever it might be, there's no mistaking none of them are on her good side.

"Misty might be a piece of work, but she knows better than to mess with June's," Cece says.

Junie frowns. "Really? Since when?"

Tina clears her throat. "Sorry, Cece, I don't mean this the wrong way. I love you, but I have to agree with Junie. I saw her at the grocery store the other day, and she mentioned seeing a crew at the shop. I knew better than to confirm or deny it to the old witch, but then she made some sly comment about 'hopefully there aren't any appointments going on since it'd be a terrible licensing violation.'"

Cece's face turns slightly paler—which is saying something, considering that they all have the fair skin that tends to come with the red hair gene that runs among them. "Alright. Well, maybe I misjudged that one."

"We'll need to keep an eye out for her and remind the ladies to keep their appointments quiet," Junie says.

"Not sure if she thinks driving that big, black Secret Service car makes her blend in or if she just likes the way it brings her attention." Cece rolls her eyes.

Junie sighs. "Well, maybe we won't be in a bind for much longer. I finally called Georgia."

The room falls silent, Cece and Tina looking to Junie for her to continue.

"She doesn't know everything, not all the details, just that the shop's in trouble. She's coming home tomorrow. So . . ."

In the silence Junie lets hang, she knows they all have the same thought: Maybe Georgia can fix it. With her plans or her unique ideas or probably, and most likely this time, her checkbook. Georgia is wildly successful with some swanky job in an Atlanta high-rise, just like Mama planned for her—above and beyond this little salon. Surely covering the fifty thousand dollars June's still owes to continue the renovation will be nothing to her bank account.

When Junie packed up the place, there was a whole box filled with Georgia clippings. It didn't rival the Dolly Parton stuff, but Georgia is a bit of a Whitetail hero. She always had great community service projects and won all kinds of prizes for being smart. Played softball and led the team to state—even if she did choose not to pursue one of the athletic scholarships she was offered. Musical theater, performance in general, was the one space Georgia had left for Junie to thrive in. And thrive she did, in her own way.

Cece sighs. "There's nothing I hate quite as much as pulling Georgia back into this place, but I guess there isn't much choice."

"Georgia won't mind," Tina says. "She loves us and the shop, and she knows how much it means, and her mama—"

"It's ok," Junie says, leaning over to squeeze Tina's arm. "Georgia is always calm and collected. She always knows what to do."

What Junie doesn't say is that Georgia has always filled that space because Junie couldn't. If Junie had all the answers, she wouldn't need to lean so heavily on her big sister. It only seems fitting that disaster would strike now, of all times, right when Junie felt like she was finally taking charge, taking things into her own hands and handling them. Becoming a bit of her own hero. It's probably time to simply accept that heroism is not in the cards for Junie.

"As for now, there are no weekend appointments, right?" Junie says.

Tina shakes her head. "Next ones are mine on Tuesday."

Junie nods efficiently. "Well, let's get this place straightened up a little before Georgia sees it tomorrow."

CHAPTER 3

GEORGIA

Around 8:30 p.m. Felix returns to the office, and the pizza Sophie and I ordered is long gone, the trash packed into the kitchen garbage can. We say goodbye—a hug from Sophie, a wave to Felix—and I head out.

I take the elevator down to the lowest level of the underground parking garage for the offices in our building. Few cars are left, and as I approach my Audi, it sends my guts roiling and acid creeping up my throat in shame.

This overpriced hunk of metal costs more than my annual salary. It's absurd and impossible and inescapable, and I hate every stupid inch of it. Every mechanical part, each and every screw. It reminds me of every lie I've told my family, every time I've come up short, every way I never lived up to my potential.

This car is proof of how far I've fallen.

It's the only part of my life they can see when I go back home. Junie, my dad, and the aunts. It's fake proof that I've achieved the life I was supposed to have. It's a physical example they can point to when I return home, and their friends say, *"I saw Georgia in that car of hers,"* and the aunts can continue to brag and wear their pride like a silky blouse with a loud print. I felt like I didn't have much of a choice when I traded in Mama's old Buick, the car my father gifted me on my way to college, just to show them I'd made their dreams for me a reality. That the success had come and with it a paycheck hefty enough to upgrade. Upgrade the car, certainly; I just wondered if they also thought I'd upgraded from my small-town life, from the shop. Heavens, I hope they never thought I could upgrade from *them*. That Buick had been the only family car at the time, and gifting it to me was my dad's big act of faith that planted a bowling ball of expectation in my belly. Heavy love.

I glance away, telling myself I'm scanning for strangers lurking in dark corners, because the car also reminds me of another truth: I've doubled down too many times on this Georgia Plan, and despite my dreaming and scheming and pleading to the heavens to *just go back*, there isn't a real way there.

Not truly and not all the way home.

Nevertheless, tomorrow, I will go there. In this car. But I'll always be stuck in between. Somewhere in the gulf between their expectations and my reality, between who I should be and who I can be. And all at my own doing.

I tap the remote, and the glossy navy sedan emits a high-end bleep that echoes within the cavernous garage. The door pops open with an effortless squeeze, and I slide into my liar's chariot, the buttery leather grating on my conscience. The ignition roars to life, and I drive out of the parking garage, through the streets where traffic has lightened, out of this swanky part of town, and into my neighborhood. I slide my hand over the leather steering wheel to signal a turn into a ratty strip mall, and the stack of gold bangles on my left arm jangles. I pull up behind the building and park my car with the rest of the beaters that unwealthy, overextended people like me can truly afford. I live in a dump because that's also what I can afford—once I've paid for the car.

When I walk in through the flimsy apartment door, it feels like going underground. The apartment building sits behind the strip mall, but the building itself appears to have been originally constructed for commercial use. The living room is the only room in the place with real windows, but they're covered with hippie-style tapestries belonging to my roommate, Moon. Moon is short for Moonbeam, or at least that's what she tells me, but I'd bet real money on the fact that she's probably a Brittany or Jessica on her birth certificate. Moon sits crossed-legged on our—*her*—corduroy sofa in what seems to be a trance. She's likely partaken of the marijuana she sells out of our place—activities to which I turn a blind eye in exchange for cut-rate rent.

I pass by her and make it all the way to my room, but she hears the squeak of my door as I open it.

"Georgia, that you?"

I certainly hope there wouldn't be any other strangers sneaking in while she zones out in the living room. "Yup."

She rounds the corner. "Rent? You got it yet?"

I hold up a finger and flash an apologetic smile. "Soon, I promise."

She shrugs and takes off.

It surprises me that she seems so relaxed about it, considering I've tossed and turned the last three nights over it. It's the furthest thing from my nature to miss a deadline, but a few weeks ago Junie ran into car trouble and asked me to tide her over. I didn't have anything but my rent money to give her. It's my own fault for letting them all believe I have Felix's job (and paycheck). If memory serves, Moon *did* say her last roommate would get lights-out drunk and punch holes in the drywall, so I'm hoping my more palatable behavior will buy me a grace period. More weekends than not I'm out of town and out of her hair anyway, allowing her every flexibility to host her amateur psychic readings on-site.

I waste no time grabbing my well-used overnight bag from the closet and start filling it with my go-to items. My toiletry bag stays half packed, so I lay eyes on it and toss in a few extras. I pack my comfort clothes: the softest tees, cutoff shorts, leggings, and a cozy sweatshirt for when the mountain air turns cold at night. I'm almost done with everything I can do for the evening when a text chimes on my phone.

Junie: I'm real sorry to call you back last minute, G. And even more I'm sorry that you have to keep saving me.

My heart squeezes. I believe her, and I know she feels like a screwup, even if she isn't one. She's always been so focused on her mistakes, like she wears blinders trained only to the lows. But she is so much more. Junie is bold and hopeful and moves through life unafraid of swinging big. And maybe, yes, part of that is my being here in the wings, ready and willing to pick up the mess when it eventually happens. But I do not begrudge her an ounce of my efforts.

Back when I was the driver in high school, I had to turn around every other day for a critical assignment she left at home. Then there was the time she volunteered to chaperone the Brownie troop's overnight camping and failed to plan meals or snacks of any kind. Or the countless times I served as her personal roadside assistant to change a tire or jump her battery after she left the car lights on. Even so, I am proud to be her backup.

I don't keep score.

She amazes me, and I envy her in all sorts of loving ways. Certainly, there's the little situation with her getting the big sister name and the rights to the shop, but that's not what I'm getting at. Just look at me: scared and quiet and so afraid to rock the boat against my family's expectations. I'm small and loath to admit that I've made mistakes myself, let alone to admit my limitations by asking for help. But with Junie, I get to be part of a loud life that stands up and asks for more. A life rich in appetite and delight, one that just smiles and winks at the comfort zone before taking off into the wild. It's a type of abandon that wouldn't survive inside me. It's those ways about her that I would wish for myself too.

I pick up the phone and type. I feel good, knowing I'm doing my part, filling in for our mama when she can't be here. What are big sisters for? I add a smiley face and click send.

Junie texts back a GIF of a Looney Tunes character with heart eyes throbbing, and I laugh before dropping the phone back onto my comforter. That's the other thing about Junie: Even when she takes a hit, she doesn't stay down long.

I finish up the rest of my packing and get ready for bed. Before long, I'm wrapped up with my e-reader, devouring a newly released romance from one of my favorite authors. My eyes begin to sag, and I set down the reader, check my alarm, and turn off the light.

I wake early the next morning so I have time to shower and blow out my hair. The dress code may be casual back home, but hair should always be Done.

> Done (noun): blown out, curled up, teased, shaped, or in
> some mechanical way manipulated for aesthetic pur-
> poses using hairstyling tools and/or products. See also:
> Styled.

Out of the shower, I slip into a pair of lightweight joggers and a ribbed tank. I towel dry my hair, then initiate my multistep haircare process.

It takes about an hour before my hair is finished, and then I grab my bag and head out to the car. I hit the road without looking back.

An hour later, the Audi coasts to a stop at a roadside gas station, my faithful stopping place for years now, the Pump & Pantry. It sits halfway between Atlanta and Whitetail and is staffed by friendly locals. There are only a handful of pumps, and although those were recently replaced, the main building looks right out of the 1960s with its peeling cream paint and minimal blue-and-red branding. Sort of like if the Fourth of July and an auto shop had a baby.

I hop out of the car, pop open the gas cap, and slot the pump into the metal opening. Mine is the only car at the gas station, and I take in the quiet. The sun shines directly on me, and sweat begins to gather and soaks the baby hairs on my temples and at the nape of my neck. I can just imagine how the humidity is trashing my hair, and it'll only be minutes until my porcelain skin turns insta-sunburn pink. I look down at my joggers, wishing I'd opted for shorts. The fabric stretches across my thighs. My waistline is healthy, generous—"fluffy" as Mama would adoringly say. No one in my family is thin; it's simply not important enough to us to chase. For us, food is never something to be measured, rationed, or withheld. It's a gift from above, one to flow in delightful abundance, a heavenly attempt at restitution for the suffering life requires.

My phone buzzes in my pocket and I pull it out, figuring it's Junie checking to see if I'm on the road.

It's not Junie, but it *is* June's Beauty Shop. I subscribe to alerts from their Instagram account, and my phone chirps every time they post. It's a simple way, even from a hundred miles away, to make myself feel a little bit included.

I swipe on the notification and click through to a predictably no-frills post:

> All appointments at June's Beauty Shop for this week-end (Saturday June 3rd and Sunday June 4th) will be rescheduled. Thank you for your patience!

Closed? On a *weekend?* Those days always book first and fully. Mama would pull herself into the shop two steps from the grave before she closed on a weekend. Even when the old warhorse was crippled from chemo, she'd drag herself over there, pop on a wig from our display wall, unlock the front doors, and slap on a smile. Much to our exasperation.

The sound of gas rushing into the car cuts off with a thunk, and I remove the nozzle and slot it back into the pump with my free hand. I climb back into the car and call Junie. It rings and rings, and I can picture my little sister ignoring my call. When it goes to voicemail, I hang up.

An All-Star Cuts just opened up across town, some local franchise. We pretend it's not, but it *is* competition. I know for a fact some of our clients have started taking their kids there. Rumor says they have mini TVs for each kid and chairs shaped like rocket ships. But I can't think of a way they would be a reason to close on a weekend.

I text Junie. Need to talk ASAP. Saw the post.

A sour feeling covers me. I flick through every worst-case scenario, every iteration of every terribly bad situation, trying to predict what Junie's keeping from me. When it comes to my family, when it comes to her in particular, even the little things terrify me. I guess maybe it's unavoidable when you love this big. Probably it's also unavoidable when you've already watched your mama die.

CHAPTER 4

JUNIE

WHEN JUNIE WAKES ON SATURDAY morning, the first thing she does is smile. Georgia's coming home today, and that means everything will be one step closer to being ok. She doesn't usually have Saturdays off, so she slept in, swimming in the natural depth of a late-morning sleep. Even the first appointment of the day at 10:00 a.m. is usually a stretch for her natural body clock. Georgia is certainly already on the road, a creature of habit and routine and peak morning performance.

Junie stretches and the daily shuffling of the dog along the side of the bed begins. A snout appears and a tail whacks the bed frame in an enthusiastic beat.

"Mornin', Puds," Junie says, dangling a hand over the side of the bed for her golden retriever.

Junie grabs her phone and sees the missed calls and text from Georgia. She must've seen the post Junie scheduled on Instagram. Honestly, it was mostly for Meddling Misty Prince, whose nosiness extends to every social media site, to prod June's off her radar. There weren't actually any appointments scheduled for today or tomorrow, and the plan is still a go for Tina's Tuesday appointments.

Georgia's seeing the post before she got the full explanation was simply an oversight. Junie checks the notifications and figures her sister will be here in the flesh soon enough, and it'll be better to discuss it all then when Georgia's not speeding down the highway.

Junie gets to her feet, makes a quick stop in the bathroom, shakes out her red waves, and heads to the kitchen, where she lets Puds into the backyard. She slips her feet into her garden clogs and follows him out.

The garden isn't big compared to many of the locals', but Junie adores it and keeps it weeded. She has two square raised beds, edged in railroad ties dug up from old tracks that ran through town. Tomatoes of several varieties sprawl up and across a trellis— miniature ones that pop on her tongue like delight, bigger ones she slices and uses for sandwiches, and other big varieties that she batters and fries. The zucchini has blossomed and burst out of control, and she is often seen around town peddling free zucchini to any interested party. The second bed is zinnias and sunflowers that have sprouted and climbed sky high, and now Junie greets her rainbow of blooms every morning.

"Look at us, we made a rainbow," she whispers to the flowers as she runs her fingers over them delicately.

This garden was once an overgrown yard. Junie herself cut back the shrubs at the side, pulled the weeds, and called for help to cart in the railroad ties and extra soil. It wasn't much, but she'd made it, and she was proud of it.

And that was Junie's philosophy on life: Most if not all of it can be made into a rainbow. If people just stop long enough to see it or find it or—her favorite of all—create it.

Satisfied that her plants and blooms have survived another night, Junie leaves Puds to do his business and greet the birds, and she heads back inside. After slipping off her clogs, she goes to the stove to brew her medicinal tea. Junie pops the lid off the canister and gives it a tentative sniff, hoping it's mellowed overnight, but she coughs and chokes, then sets it down. She fills the kettle and sets it atop a burner she ignites.

This tea is an Eastern remedy—or that's what the woman at the farmers market told her—and Junie's never been one to overthink a promise made by a friendly stranger. Especially now that she's Sick with a big *S*.

There's a scratch at the door, and Junie lets Puds back in and pours him a bowl of kibble. She sets it down and pats him on the head. "You're the bestest boy I've ever known," she says. Junie giggles to herself at the accuracy of her statement. She's been perennially single and entirely unbothered by it. Sure, she's dated, and in fact, to this day, she's asked out frequently; it's just that no one has ever sparked her interest and kept it. Junie believes life should be Technicolor every day, all day, and something about being tethered to another person, co-living, feels stifling.

The kettle whistles quietly, and Junie turns, flips off the heat, and makes the tea. While it brews, nerves rumble in her belly as she thinks about the state of the shop; perhaps it's also partially the promise of the hideous tea. Georgia will probably be fine about this whole thing. Right? She's so used to stepping in when things get dicey. Really, she would probably be well-suited to a crisis response job if she weren't so busy bossing people around and making her company stacks and stacks of money. Junie smiles at the idea of her big sister, Whitetail figurehead, family superstar with everything she ever wanted in hand.

When the tea is ready, Junie grips the warm mug and carries it to her favorite spot on the sofa, one that's worn and dips a little, remembering her shape. Puds joins her, curling up on the floor at her feet. She looks around at the house, the Clementine House, and notices every way she's done right by it. The new wallpaper. Tile in the kitchen. The thrifted art, the discount rugs that only look expensive. The floors that are old but kept and mopped routinely with love.

Hopefully Georgia notices. The house belongs to her, and Junie hopes to be a worthy tenant.

The deed to the house was a card their great-aunt Clementine, their grandmother's sister, played to try to settle the score for Georgia. Every firstborn daughter in the family is *supposed* to be named June—like it's a law or something, or at least that's what Junie and Georgia understood since they were girls. At some point in the family tree, the name became quite the stir. Even so, Mama wanted something different for Georgia, and she chose to give her another name and a bright future, exactly like the one she's living out. Junie was the backup June, the second choice, second string, and her appointment as such came with a mixed response from Clementine.

Junie tries to act like it doesn't bother her, the fact that she's second best. The fact that for whatever reason, Mama didn't decide she, too, was owed a life of her own choosing, and that instead Junie would be the one to take over the shop and continue the legacy. Because Georgia is, and always was, more special. Junie loves the shop just like the rest of the women do, but her personality isn't particularly well-suited to the responsibility. She wants to do her part for June's Beauty Shop, the favorite June of all to this family, because she loves it. It's just that Junie wonders if it requires denying part of herself too, growing up and possibly out of the youthful spontaneity that is like a second heartbeat inside her.

She shrugs off the thought. Even if she is mostly unremarkable, most certainly simple, she can still choose to be happy.

Nevertheless—*the house*. Great-Aunt Clementine lived in this house by herself for the entirety of her adult life. Clementine believed Georgia got shorted with the naming, and on her way out of this world, in one final act of rebellion, Clementine willed Georgia the house. Though perhaps in a twist of fate, it was Junie, a fellow single lady, who was the natural choice to take up residence. Georgia was off being a shiny up-and-coming star in Atlanta. What would she have done with it anyway?

In truth, the house has been a project for all of them, both Cece and Tina pitching in and leading the way when Junie first moved in while she attended beauty school. It wasn't quite like she could manage an actual house at eighteen.

Junie blows on the steam rolling off the mug, making sure not to inhale at risk of gagging. She sips the brew, squinting and grunting her way through it. She sets it aside and once it's cool enough, she sucks in a breath and drinks in deep gulps until she's chugging the dregs.

"*Yuck.*" The sound is throaty and heartfelt. She carries the mug to the kitchen and deposits it in the sink, opens the fridge and pulls out an icy Diet Coke.

Junie smiles at the silver can of deliciousness and does a happy dance all the way across her house, out the front door, and onto the porch, where she will sip in delight and wait for her big sister to pull up in her rich-person car.

CHAPTER 5

GEORGIA

A S I DRAW CLOSER TO Whitetail I feel the city heat lift and the fresh air of the mountains blow in. If I stopped I might spot a family of deer leaping through woods named after them. Whitetail is barely a postage stamp on the sweeping Blue Ridge Mountains, but surrounded by the rolling landscape, thick forests, and copious wildlife, it's as cozy as it is compact.

I slow as I approach the main thoroughfare of the itty-bitty downtown, Mountain Laurel Row, and after a few turns onto side streets, then back streets, I roll up to Junie's house. It's a small Victorian bungalow with delicate woodwork and dollhouse dormers. It's the perfect Girl Pad.

The girl in residence sits on the front porch looking perfectly cute and not a drop bothered. An oak hangs over the house and the driveway, a canopy of one tree, a century-old witness to our lives, and I park below its cover. This tree, the shade it affords, the cover of it, the way it buffers the worst of storms—it has always felt like Mama is still with us.

I hop out and slam the door, and the quiet of Whitetail surrounds me, only a family of birds chirping their welcome.

"Junie Bug," I say as I lumber up the creaky porch steps.

"Queen Peach." Once upon a time, that nickname accompanied Mama's hand curling into my tiny head of hair. Junie grins, and she looks exactly like she did when she was seven and I'd sneak us both a rocket Popsicle from the freezer.

This, case in point, is how I'm wound around her pinky finger. I yank her into a deep hug, inhale her, and every muscle in my body sighs into relaxation.

"It's good to see you, Georgia Louise," she says into my shoulder. When I pull back, she looks down at my chest and says, "Lookin' perky."

A laugh erupts from my belly at the inside joke we've shared for years regarding my perky, fake ta-tas. Breast cancer took our mother, and when we were both in high school, Junie and I got tested to see if we carried the gene that put us at higher risk for the disease.

Mama was young when she got sick, and testing was still fairly new, difficult to access, and expensive. Fortunately, some court ruling allowed new labs to open up shop, and I found one that—although a bit rough around the edges—offered testing at a price we could afford. The health insurance we once had through Dad's work had since lapsed, and a family-run beauty shop didn't exactly come with glossy corporate health insurance policies.

Dad worked in sales before Mama died, traveling around the Southeast pitching accounting software to small- and medium-size businesses. He was personable and likable and closed enough deals to keep us comfortable, along with what Mama brought home from doing hair at June's. But after Mama died, Dad could barely function, he was so smothered by grief. He stopped making sales calls; he could barely remember to brush his teeth. The deals slowed, then eventually stopped. After a while the company had to let him go, and after a month grace period, we were uninsured.

When my results arrived, I learned I was positive for BRCA1. I scoured the internet and learned a preventative double mastectomy would likely be recommended for me down the road. Tina and Cece left me out of it, but I know they hosted some sort of intervention with our father, yanking him out of bed and giving him a talking-to. I could probably imagine a fairly accurate script. *"Your girls need you, Rich,"* from Tina. *"Get your ass up, and do June's memory right,"* from Cece. Before long, Dad had begged a favor of a friend and landed a job at the local bank—one with health insurance. The doctors told me I could wait until my thirties to have the surgery, but I wanted to do it before I dropped off Dad's insurance. When college graduation approached I picked out my new knockers with Junie.

Her envelope had come the week after mine, and it was the answer to my every prayer when the test was negative.

I pull back to get a good look at the beautiful girl in front of me. Junie has the bone structure of a runway model—high cheekbones, straight nose, and big green eyes shaped like a doe's. A shock of red hair just like mine falls in deep waves to her shoulders and a sprinkling of freckles fans out across her nose. Not that she has a clue that she's a knockout. "And I'll say the same for you, but I think it's better than good to see you."

"Fabulous and wonderful and downright perfection come to life." She squeezes my arms and lets me go.

"Amen," I say.

Junie's golden retriever scratches at the screen door, panting enthusiastically, begging to be included. Puddleduck. He's been Junie's sidekick since he was a puppy who sat in puddles just like a wannabe duck.

Junie grabs the door handle and clicks it open. "You excited to see your auntie Peach, Puds?" She crouches to pet him, but he pushes past her and arrives at my feet.

I kneel to meet him and wrap my arms around his neck, pulling my fingers firmly through his fur. He drops to the floor and rolls right over. Puds has me, at least partially, to thank for being an only child pup, and he seems to remember. Junie being Junie couldn't bear to leave behind his three siblings three years ago at the pet adoption event and brought all four puppies home. It wasn't long before the reality of taking care of four puppies set in, and she called me for help. I put out the word and within a week, we had safe new homes for the three others.

I sit cross-legged and scratch his belly, but after a few minutes Junie nudges me up.

"Alright, Puds," she says. "If you keep her hostage she'll quit coming home."

Once my hands leave him, Puds hops up and charges over to the oak, where he zooms around the trunk in manic circles.

"He's always been *off* enough to truly fit in with us," Junie says over her shoulder as she steps inside.

"Hey now, don't talk like that about my one and only nephew," I say.

I follow her into the house, and my stomach flutters. *This is Junie's house*, I remind myself. Even if it was supposed to be mine. In actual fact, it *is* my house—at least by deed—and walking into it is like punching my ticket to *The Life I Could've Had Show*. When I picked up the keys, there was only a simple card attached. It read: *So it's never hard to stay—if you please. XO, Clem.*

If only she knew how hard it was.

Staying was never a consideration; Mama had been clear in her directive for me, and I completely and entirely bought in. I had drunk the Kool-Aid and lined up for a second serving in allegiance to Mama. When I handed the keys over to Junie, I was adamant that it was done in love and with not a single string attached, considering the hard feelings and tit for tat that so pervade our family history.

We pass through the entryway and into Junie's sitting room. "You've really done a great job sprucing the place up," I say. "Not sure if I've told you just how much I love it."

It hurts a little bit to say it, even if it's true.

Junie stands back and flourishes her arms. "I'm just glad I have someone to show it off to." She winks.

I run a hand over the embossed wallpaper. "You hang this yourself?" Junie nods rapidly. "Every pretty little sheet."

It's a charming complement to the wainscoting she painted a barely-there green a few months back. And finally the refinished floors below my feet have enough scratches to match Junie's lived-in lifestyle.

I follow her into the kitchen. "Is that a new backsplash too?"

"Almost killed me, but yes," she says. "Thanks to a lifetime's worth of YouTube videos, I managed most of it before I had to call for backup." Junie snatches a teetering stack of paperwork—bills, appointments, or something—off the counter and shuffles it away.

As if she's ever cared about hiding her clutter from me.

"I'm glad you've made it your own." I can't help but wonder for a moment what I'd have done with the place. If I'd been brave enough to give the Clementine plan a whirl.

"Clementine wouldn't even recognize it," Junie says.

"Not even for a second," I say.

Scratches sound at the screen door, and we turn our heads. Puddle-duck sits there panting.

Junie heads for the door and lifts her voice to the vat-of-syrup pet-owner octave as she addresses her dog. "What have I told you about tearing up my screen door? A new reno project will put me over the edge."

Junie moves from the door to the kitchen where something porcelain clinks. She reappears, jar of Twizzlers tucked under her arm, one she's already munching in the opposite hand. Junie crosses the living room to the sofa where she flops down and says, "Come on, let's find something trashy to watch."

"Not so fast, missy. No TV before we talk about what it is that's got the shop closed. And why I had to hear about it on the internet."

Junie holds out the candy jar. "Can I interest you in a happy stick?"

"Junie, you absolutely *cannot* call them that." I feel red heat my cheeks, and my planned lecture veering off the rails.

Junie erupts in giggles. "I only do it for your reaction." She pats the cushion seat beside her. "Come on."

I cross my arms and remain standing, only semi-seriously eyeing her. I'm the big sister, the one who is supposed to be practical and keep things proper. I'm supposed to be the responsible one. All of these things magnified since we lost Mama.

Even so, I can't help but crack a smile as the seconds tick by. Junie can read my mind, and she knows curling up with her and her god-forsaken "happy sticks" is at the tippy top of my wish list right now.

Junie bats her eyes like a cartoon character. "But it's my day off. The first Saturday in *forever*. Pretty, *pretty* please?"

I puff out a sigh that I don't really mean. "Reluctantly, yes. One episode. Then we talk business." I drop beside her on the couch.

"Reluctantly?" Junie says, eyeing me from the side.

"Ok, *fine*," I say, failing to stifle a grin. "Willingly. Maybe even gladly."

CHAPTER 6

JUNIE

I F GIVEN THE CHANCE, JUNIE would opt to fry her hair off rather than tell Georgia, now sitting right here in the flesh, the details of the problem. Junie keeps her head trained toward the television screen and flicks her eyes to the corner to get a good look at her sister. A status check. A temperature reading. A risk assessment to determine just how likely Georgia is to murder her in her sleep tonight. But when her eyes land on her sister, she is calm, cool, and decidedly unhomicidal.

Junie pulls the fuzzy blanket up to her chin.

When the credits roll a while later, it feels like only seconds have passed. Immediately, Georgia grabs the remote and flips the screen off. "Ok, out with it. What's going on at June's?"

Junie pulls herself upright and readjusts the blanket around her like armor. Puds trots over and flops down beside her; he just knows when she needs him. She pats her would-be therapy dog before she looks back up at Georgia.

Junie squeezes a tight, worried smile, and it freezes on her face as if her mind is buffering.

This fix will be an easy one for Georgia. She'll probably just give Junie the usual big sister you-need-to-think-things-all-the-way-through talk, give her inept little sister a couple of stern looks, and write the check. *Bingo, bango.*

Junie sucks in a breath. "You're going to be swatted-wasp angry about this, buuuut I'm in a bit of a pickle."

Georgia's body jolts like she slipped a pinky nail into an outlet. She arranges a schoolteacher look on her face and leans in. In any other scenario Junie would crack a joke and then tickle Georgia's ribs until she couldn't help but laugh along. *"Let me tell you all the ways we could make this beautiful,"* Junie would tell her sister.

"I guess it's more of a good news, bad news situation," Junie says. "Which do you want first?"

Georgia looks like she's using every shred of patience to keep herself from shaking the information out of her. "Just tell me the whole thing."

It's essentially the answer Junie expects.

"Yes. Of course. Well, I'd kind of prepared it as good news, bad news in my mind, so I'll just riff off that. *So*, bad news: The beauty shop is torn up, and we're breaking health codes by seeing clients in there." Junie pauses to leave space for a *Home Alone* scream that doesn't come. "Good news," she continues, "I scored a partnership with Goldilocks Haircare to rebrand and renovate the shop!"

"Rebrand? Junie, you can't rebrand the shop," Georgia says. "The brand is Dolly Parton."

Branding is what stuck out to her in this confession?

"I mean, yes and no. But the point is *how do we not* with All-Star Cuts open across town?" Junie says. "That place is newfangled—all kinds of gadgets for kids, screens and a treasure chest with a hundred varieties of slime on the way out."

"Well, you can't believe everything you hear." Georgia shakes herself upright, looking like denial in human flesh.

"I saw it with my own two eyes," Junie says.

"I'm surprised Mama didn't strike you down from heaven for step-ping foot in there. *Please* don't tell me you let them cut your hair?" Georgia's cheeks almost match her hair at this point.

"Baby, you're just one color": It's what Mama would say.

"First off," Junie announces, "if and only if Mama did make it to heaven—God rest her soul—I'm fairly certain she wouldn't get the right to strike folks down. And no, of course I didn't let those idiots touch my hair." Junie tosses her locks for effect. "I put on a wig from Tina's wig wall. Went undercover, pretending I needed to book a cut for my nonexistent husband."

Georgia opens her mouth, then stops. She shakes her head. "We're coming back to that. The mess at the shop?"

Junie squints, like she's working to remember the situation and it's not, in fact, seared clearly onto her mind. "I'd say we're missing 30 to 40 percent of the Sheetrock. And we're rocking concrete floors—which isn't in itself an issue . . . aside from the fact that they're as filthy as one might imagine considering the state of the carpet we pulled up. And then there's—"

"Ok, ok, *stop*. Back up. How on earth did you get here and why didn't you tell me about any of this? An *Instagram* post is how I found out." For the first time, Georgia looks hurt. Like maybe she's not just mad to have to fix a problem she didn't create, but in some way she feels like she should've known about a plan this big for the shop.

And addressing that point is a one-way ticket back into the nam-ing fight that, for centuries, the women in the Louise family couldn't quit having.

"The Goldilocks people reached out a while back, right as the jock hairdressers moved in, and I thought it was the answer to our prayers." *Really, it still could be.* "And it's a great deal. They'll supple-ment a portion of the renovation cost for brand positioning and cover the design costs. All we owe is $50K! How great is that?"

"Tell me about the part where it became a disaster." Georgia's knee is bobbing up and down like she's negotiating a hostage crisis.

"Well, this is where I got in my own way a bit." Junie grins, knowing full well she's doing the baby sister move she relies on far too often. "I mentioned it to Daddy—he's still running the books and bills and all—and he said it was no problem, just to let him take a look. Now, since that conversation was had, there've been a few *discussions* between me and Daddy, and it seems I may have misheard—or added a more optimistic spin to his wording in my mind. It's neither here nor there at this point, but I was so excited at the prospect that I jumped right in. I signed the deal and scheduled the demo work."

"And what about the money?"

"Well, when I went to ask Daddy Dearest to transfer the funds, he blew his lid because it turns out the beauty shop does *not* have $50K to cover any renovations. Even if it is a nice idea." Junie lets out a puff of air, her shoulders drop, and she waits for her well-deserved lecture.

"Oh, Junie Bug." Georgia drops her head into her hands and looks about as sad as Junie felt when the news hit. When Georgia doesn't make a move, Junie rubs her back.

Eventually Georgia looks up. "Let me see what I can do," she says. "And I actually mean that—no good vibes spin. I'm not sure I have that amount accessible right now, but I'll have to talk to my finance guy."

Junie nods, looking as penitent as she would have if she'd received the talking-to she deserved. When Georgia squeezes out a small smile, Junie lunges toward her and burrows herself into her sister's front, wrapping her arms around her in a way that feels like forever. "Thank you," Junie says. "I'm sorry you have to keep on saving me, and I'm even more sorry I put the shop in the mix this time."

CHAPTER 7

GEORGIA

I HAVE MY BABY SISTER CURLED in my lap and her request weighing on my mind. This is the worst I've ever felt about misrepresenting my financial status. And I've felt plenty bad. I once thought the Thanksgiving Turkey Escapade of 2012 was our rock bottom—when Junie didn't thaw the frozen turkey she'd bought, and I ended up driving around for four hours, searching for a replacement.

If only this could be solved by driving around to every grocery store I can find on a map.

I drop a kiss on top of her hair, and she looks up at me. "Can I show you the Goldilocks partnership design materials? They sent them out with the invitation to the program, so you can see what all they can do. It might help to know that your money is going someplace worthwhile."

Despite what I said, Junie is assuming I will agree to spot the money for this project. And why wouldn't she, considering the picture of my life I've sold them? If it was an actual option, of course I'd pony up the money, but I'm a woman who's behind on rent, not one who has a cool $50K lying around. "Sure thing," I say.

Junie rolls herself upright and unearths her phone from the fleecy blanket around her. She holds up the phone, the opening presentation slide displayed on the screen. "Here's the brand"—she scrolls to the next slide—"and here are their hair products."

"I know the brand," I say. "I may have moved out of town, but the hair gene is a for-life kind of thing."

Junie holds up the phone and swipes the screen repeatedly. "I'll just skip through that stuff then. Here." She stops and beams at me as she hands over the phone.

I take it and slowly look through more of the slides. The presentation is gorgeous and modern, and I see the promise in the before and afters they've included from other projects. I don't fault Junie for going after this deal; I just wish she'd done a bit more due diligence beforehand. I continue scrolling through the slides that show inspiration boards and idea banks from completed projects. Ones that could be a starting point for a design all June's own.

"I mean, look at these—they're stunning! Once we do this, not only will our customers turn their noses at the haircut jocks but we'll have tons of new interest. From the town over, then the one past that. It'll *more* than pay for itself. And you know Mama always had big dreams for this place."

It strikes me just how good of an idea—in theory—this was. A competitor moved into town, and like a shrewd businesswoman, Junie planned to up the ante. Mama would've gone for this deal too (possibly even jumped in like her daughter did), and she'd be so proud of Junie for going after it if she were here. Junie really was the right one to be made a June.

My chest pinches at the flush of shame that follows.

"I can see why you went for it. I don't think anyone disagrees that the place could use a facelift. It's just the *funds* are also an important piece of the puzzle." I pause before I ask my lingering question, knowing that what I'm about to ask for will surely bring up strong feelings. "Did they do a design board for June's?"

"Yes, of course." Junie grins back at me, and I swear it touches every inch of her, like every muscle in her body knows how to smile. "The designers are sweet and so fun and have got this whole thing . . ."

She goes on about the long, meandering design conversations, all the imaginings of big and beautiful things. It sounds heavenly, to dream in shelter like that.

She looks right at me. "Go ahead and ask. I know exactly what's on your mind."

If only.

"The Dolly decor." Junie says it like a fact.

I let the corners of my mouth twitch up. "How'd you know?"

As a young thing, Mama started covering the walls of the beauty shop with Dolly Parton paraphernalia. She adored Dolly (as every right-minded woman in our neck of the woods does). She sang her songs and collected every trinket and keepsake of the blonde bombshell within arm's reach. And she put them where she could see them most of the time: on the walls of that raggedy hair salon. Sometimes items would be framed; other times the best she could manage were a few patches of Scotch tape.

And now that Mama's gone, I can't help but cling to these objects, wondering if the memories of her will fade into nothing if these people take away her scrapbooked beauty shop decor as they make it over.

"Well, the design team thinks the Dolly stuff is actually super cute. So we're going to keep it," Junie says.

"We're keeping the shrine?" Despite this being good news, shock outlines my words.

"Not as is—but yes. She said we'd incorporate it *tastefully* . . . so I'm thinking proper frames for stuff and maybe nixing some of the newspaper cuttings from years ago. Trying to match images that'll complement the color palette. Editing, for sure."

I imagine Mama cutting those clippings with her very own hands, and my heart twists. "I'll take whatever you end up getting rid of."

"Yeah?"

"I guess I'd rather keep anything that meant something to her than see it end up in a landfill."

Junie's sigh mirrors my sentiment. "I get it."

"I just don't want the team, as lovely as they might be, to strip June's of its soul."

"You and I both know that wouldn't be possible if they tried," Junie says.

I smile to myself, knowing just how true that is. June's Beauty Shop has as much of a soul as any person walking the earth, as much as any other woman in our family. She's kept a whole bloodline of Junes as they've tended to her. She's kept them clothed and fed and honest (as much as possible, given our collective disposition). She's covered us on our worst days, like the day Mama was diagnosed, and she's held every celebration from high school graduations and birthdays to our after-hours gambling nights. She's seen us strive for our best, and she's seen us struggle. Lord, has she seen us struggle. But she doesn't judge—not once, not ever—and we're always welcomed back as is.

"Truer words—" I stop as my eyes land on her.

The way her red baby hairs fan out into a halo, the way the corners of her mouth give her entirely away. She knows this isn't good, but because it's as much a part of her as her fuzzy crown, she has hope. She's here, hoping, the way she always does, and in this moment I realize it: I may not have the cash, but I will make this right. I don't know how, but I will be the one to fix this for her.

"I promise," Junie says, "if we can get through this moment, I'll do it up right. I'll make you, and Daddy, and the aunts proud."

Make Mama proud. The unspoken words that live between us.

"There's no *if* about us getting through this," I say.

Junie smiles back up at me, and I can see how she believes me. "You could also use it as an excuse to have some time here at home.

I hate you being so far away, even if you are a Star Child. You can take a leave of absence for a 'hair emergency' or something like that."

Yes, and yes, and amen, completely and forever. It's what I want to say. I want to gush about this prospect. I want to yell and scream, *Me too, me too, me too!* But admitting I don't want the life my mother planned for me has consequences. It would mean saying goodbye to the most vivid part of her I know. I'd single-handedly be responsible for swiffering the dust that is all we have left of her.

I run a hand over my sister's forehead. "Oh, I *wish*."

Junie shrugs. "An occupational hazard of success, I guess. It was worth a try."

CHAPTER 8

JUNIE

JUNIE HAS TO WORK HARD to convince Georgia to stop long enough for some lunch at the Clementine before they head to the shop. She's already alerted Cece and Tina to meet them there a little later on. The worst possible outcome is Georgia losing it when she walks in and sees what Junie did to Mama's shop, and if this occurs, Junie will certainly melt into a puddle of regret.

But then again, what else was she supposed to do? With new competition peeling off business, it wasn't like they could milk the "retro vibe" much longer, not when the customers have spoken quite loudly and clearly on how much they like the spiffy new place across town. Junie had no choice but to do something to ensure the shop would thrive in the long run and hope one day Georgia would understand—once Junie could show her all the cards in her hand.

After the dishes are cleaned up and both Georgia and Junie are prepared to leave, they load up in Junie's truck. That's how they always do it. It's never been discussed, surprisingly so considering that Georgia's car is objectively more luxurious, but once the Audi has done the job of getting her here, it practically disappears.

The drive to the shop isn't nearly long enough to settle Junie's nerves. June's sits at the base of Mountain Laurel Row, close to where the railroad tracks touch the little town of Whitetail. The Clementine House is only a handful of turns off Mountain Laurel, so it's minutes downhill and the car's back in park.

Junie sneaks a glance at Georgia as she pulls in and stops in her usual parking spot.

Junie loves having her sister here. She can physically feel her blood pressure lower the moment Georgia rolls into town. And it's not just because of the massive ways Georgia supports her. It's because Junie loves her as her sister, and sister love isn't ordinary love. It's brighter and sparklier, and it tickles her veins when a wave of it hits her, like a giggle. Help or not, she wishes Georgia would stay—for good. They're Louise women, after all; they weren't built to exist so far apart.

"Alright, Queen Peach, you ready?" Junie says. "And we agreed you aren't going to throttle me, right?"

"As if I'd throttle an able-bodied person intending to be part of the solution here."

Together the women pause. The shop is a freestanding box of a building made of solid red brick and thick trimmed windows that've seen countless layers of paint over the years, the latest a French blue. A wide sidewalk wraps the building like a stand-in for a porch, one step up from the parking lot. It was a perch, a play space for Junie and Georgia on the weekends their mother worked as they diligently covered the sidewalk in chalk. Mama's curlicue sign, the one she picked out and hung, is still in place: *June's Beauty Shop, where a good hair day is only one stop away.*

Junie is about to ask Georgia what she thinks of the timeworn sign, whether it's cute vintage or plain sorry looking, when Junie's phone rattles in the cup holder and a familiar name scrolls across the screen: *Whitetail Breast Care Specialists.* She rushes to silence it and flip it over, the screen out of sight. It's a weekend, so it must be the automated appointment reminder call, script read in a jolting robot voice.

"Alright, let's roll," Junie says and leads the way toward the entrance.

CHAPTER 9

GEORGIA

MY INSIDES ARE A MESS of worry, but I have to push through the glass-paned door and let the slapdash bell barely hanging there bump around.

Junie is right behind me and wordlessly flips on the light.

The sight of the place cast into detail slams right into my middle, and I gasp for breath. Coming here to physically face our predicament feels like living out an episode of all the worries I've lost sleep over in years gone by. Since Mama died, I've been convinced we were in some way branded to have bad luck, destined for the short straw. Not that I really had proof. No proof until now, that is.

It's chopped up and torn up, and every shred of what it's supposed to be has been pulled out. The entryway podium, usually overflowing with the appointment book, purses, cups, customer offerings, is gone. The candy jars along the far wall (aka the Bribe Center for children in tow) are gone. Every iota of character has been stripped. The spaceship hair dryers are draped in tarps as if they're mourning, and the maroon carpet is only a memory. Mama swore for years she'd replace it with linoleum—just as soon as she won the lotto.

Not a single Dolly portrait remains.

I cross the room to the boxes on the other side.

"Anything that came off the walls went into those," Junie says.

I crouch, lift a lid, and tenderly leaf through the contents, check on each Dolly as if to make sure they're still breathing. "It's worse than I imagined," I say.

"Your stuff is there too," Junie says.

I glance over at the box beside me that has *Georgia* scrawled on it in Tina's handwriting. It's my own set of clippings, the ones Tina started tacking up around the shop when I had any sort of accomplishment after Mama died. Whitetail is not a big town, after all, so the newspaper is often willing to report on nonevents like the high school canned food drive. I often wondered if Tina thought this place was a direct line to Mama in the afterlife, that she could show me off by putting me on the walls. They're going to be so disappointed, so embarrassed, when they learn I never amounted to much. I tear my eyes away; now is not the time to digest that.

I stand and look around the shop.

Regret floods me swiftly, starting at my toes and climbing into my throat where it threatens to choke me. I avoided this place for so long, steering wide around it when I came home, convincing myself it wasn't a place for nonstylist Louises. It sat too close to my most tender pain point, the name, and Mama's intentions for me. I didn't have to come here to see my sister or the rest of them. And yet I never once doubted June's would be here—forever and untouched. I believed—*foolishly*—that it was so permanent and that my mother's memory was so potent that it simply couldn't be budged. I was sure it'd be waiting for me until the day I got up the guts to show up. But now, in front of my eyes, it's nothing like it was; it's been shorn of possibility. It's been gutted, just like I feel.

Junie opens her mouth to say more, but the front door clatters again with the arrival of a newcomer.

"Georgia Louise! You're here!" Aunt Tina shrieks. Her thin, bird-like arms wrap around me.

I lean into the hug, Mama's little sister, her version of a Junie. Tina has always made me feel loved and welcome and like I'm not entirely cast out. "Well, you know it's not like me to sit out a code red."

"Tina!" The snappy tone precedes Randy entering the shop. He looks as ghastly as he is, greasy, likely smelly—not that I ever get that close—lazy on all fronts. His T-shirt is covered in stains, and the neckline is stretched to a point I fear a nipple sighting. "I'm taking the car. I gotta see to a thing. You can text me, and I'll try to come."

Tina releases me and turns to him. "Well, how are you thinking I'll get home?" The joy that sang in her voice in greeting me is gone, and what's left is frail and apologetic.

Randy throws out his arms and gawks like a moody teenager. "I dunno, woman. That's your problem to figure out."

As though his ugliness conjured her, Aunt Cece sweeps in behind Randy. "I know you weren't speaking to my sister like that." Cece steps in front of him, and she looks ready to swing. "Right?"

Randy breaks eye contact and shuffles toward the door. "Whatever. See ya."

Silence sits in the room, Cece fuming, my jaw wide in shock, and Junie tutting and muttering under her breath. When car tires screech outside, Junie speaks up. "Enough is enough, Tina."

Tina pulls in a breath, looking frantic. "I'm sorry, Junie. I'm sorry he upset you."

Junie flashes me a look, and her eyes say *get a load of this.*

"I don't think—" I say.

"Did he not upset *you*?" Junie asks Tina. "You shouldn't put up with that."

Cece nods, lips squeezed together. I'm sure she's got a boatload of more colorful language regarding Randall the Awful, and I'm fully behind her. It's probably the one and only thing Cece and I see eye to eye on. Even though I have tried, her affection for me could fit on the head of a pin. Ever since I was a girl, she's been aloof.

Cece's chilliness, or put more kindly, her emotional restraint, makes particularly little sense considering the fact that she and Mama were twins, and Mama was well-known for hugging strangers and initiating impromptu dance parties in public. Mama *was* the lucky twin, born first, however. She elbowed her way out of the womb seven minutes before Cece to seize the name and the shop and all the hoopla that comes with it. I secretly wonder if Cece is bitter she lost out over so little.

Then again, Randy is one of those issues that unites women because he is a case study in the struggles of modern dating, an undercover bad date taken hold. Twelve years ago, when he and Tina first met, he was kind, took her out, made her happy. Next he moved into her little house with promises of a ring, a marriage, a family of some variety, pets, and construction of that white picket fence she'd always dreamed of. But since that moment, he's done nothing but sit around and take up space, not a box checked. I love Tina to bits, but to be frank, she's a complete pushover. She is so bent on making other people happy and so terrified of ruffling any feathers that she keeps her blinders on and the leech housed under her roof.

It's always bothered me, how he stole those dreams from her, but what bothers me more is that she won't stand up to him and kick him to the curb, won't demand the life she wants and deserves. Instead, she simply lets him run her life and kill her dreams slowly, one day at a time. All because she's too polite to say no.

"I used to be friends with the sheriff's daughter, if we need to call in a favor for an eviction," I say quietly.

Junie ducks behind Tina where no one but I can see her, a devious grin spread over her lips as she begins to raise the roof. I bite the inside of my cheek to prevent my face from breaking out to match.

"Mm-hmm, I don't think that'll be necessary." Tina doesn't meet my eye. "Anyway, Georgia, did you hear what happened to my wig wall?"

The moment breaks, and it's as if the four of us are reoriented to the state of the shop, the issue far more pressing than Randy could ever be.

"Tell me," I say.

The wig wall is an interesting feature at June's that dates back to Mama's time. It got most use from Mama during her chemo, and she expanded it generously as a silver lining for herself. But Dolly has also been known to wear wigs, and Aunt Tina is fond of them, so they've stayed. Tina, bless her, periodically takes the things down and shampoos them, blows them out, and styles them like pooches at the groomers. It's quite a sight, like she's working her way down her queue of bodiless clients. Wig maintenance was a task Mama assigned her during her treatment, and like the rest of us, Tina has clung to the words that woman left behind.

"Well, I'll tell you I came in here and they were pulling things apart with all those beauties still lined up on the shelf."

I glance at Junie, who's now blushing slightly.

"I didn't get a heads-up on any renovations, so I came in and very politely asked them to pause so I could please take down the wigs before they were ruined, and don't you know it, they *ignored* me." Tina huffs. "I was extremely nice about it too. I guess they were innocents, ignorant about how wigs work."

I squeeze her arm. "Thank you for taking care of those," I say. "You're right. Construction dust would've ruined every single one."

Tina smiles.

"We cleaned yesterday," Cece says. "I'm not sure it's getting better than this until it's patched back together."

I cross my arms and take stock of the place once again. "And you're sure about seeing clients."

Junie shrugs. "What other choice do we have?"

"We should hang something over the drywall holes," Tina says.

I would've snagged a few of Moon's wall "tapestries" on my way out had I known. Though entirely off-brand for June's, they're exactly what's required to do the job. "I agree," I say. "Let's spruce her up a bit."

There's no direct mention of the fifty grand we'll need to actually fix this, and I suspect the calm is due to the fact that they all assume I'll come up with the cash. But there is no quick fix to be had; this is one verifiable, unmovable problem.

"I've got a bunch of stuff at home," Junie says. "A few little rugs we can throw down in the entryway, some wall coverings. Y'all know how I am—when I see a yard sale, I just see little babies needing a home. And I love it when the babies I rescue find homes close to me."

Cece looks blankly at Junie like she simply cannot imagine relating in a single way to any of what she just explained.

"You're such a sweetie," Tina says. "Why don't you run up to the house and grab them and we'll help you set up?"

"Need help?" I ask Junie.

She shrugs. "Ok, but it's not a big job."

Junie calls out, "Be right back," and she and I head outside. She tosses me the keys to the truck, and my heart flutters. I love driving her truck. We climb in and I crank it, then roll down the windows as I tear out of the lot and let the wind run through my hair. We ride in silence, aside from Junie setting a loving hand on my shoulder and squeezing once. I idle in the driveway while she runs inside, and as promised, Junie reemerges quickly, holding a box stacked high with an eclectic mix of home decor and a tote bag on her shoulder. She drops her things in the truck bed, and I drive us back to the shop.

Once I've parked in Junie's spot, we round the truck to the bed.

Junie grabs the box. "Will you get the bag?"

I nod, already reaching for it. As I lift it, I hear the familiar clink of glass bottles. "What's in here?"

Junie looks over her shoulder at me and winks. "Provisions. For sprucing the shop."

CHAPTER 10

JUNIE

J UNIE LEAPS INTO ACTION INSIDE the beauty shop. She hands out rugs and wall hangings and drapes, barking instructions. "Hang this over there. A little to the left. Scatter these along that ledge. No, a little less uniform. Cute, nice arrangement. Let's wipe this area down first, then rug. Yes, actually no. This is better." Tina and Cece obey orders without comment, and even Georgia falls in line. Junie may not be the natural leader among the Louise women, but when she gets into her groove with something, especially something creative, the others know to let her do her thing.

Eventually Junie looks into her box, then picks it up and flips it upside down. "We did it, ladies!"

She stands back, and the others stop and look around.

"It's definitely way better," Georgia says.

"Much cuter," Tina says.

"Yup," Cece says. "But I'm beat."

Junie claps happily. "Sounds like break time. Where's my tote bag? I've got *goods.*"

"I put it in Dad's office," Georgia says.

The women pull a few folding chairs from the storage closet and arrange themselves in a circle. Junie disappears into the back office, and she takes the opportunity to pause. She's putting on a good front, but inside she feels terrible to be the cause of this destruction when there's no guaranteed way out. The sprucing looks great, but a structurally complete shop is better. The others must be sitting out there with their minds spinning about how and when the shop will get fixed.

Junie can't help but imagine how disappointed Mama would be right now. Maybe she'd even regret giving Junie the family name. Maybe she'd bench Junie and put reliable, capable Georgia in to save the day. Georgia's the sister who has what it takes.

After a few minutes, Junie takes the bag and heads back down the hallway, beginning her spiel. "I'm just so grateful for y'all helping me with this sticky situation, I brought some wine and nibbles for a little thank-you." She unloads the bottles onto a stack of plastic tubs filled with hair products, then turns the corkscrew in one of the wine corks and rips it out with a pop. "There's also bourbon in there, if anyone cares to partake. Whoop!"

Junie circles the group handing out small plastic cups and pouring the wine. Once every cup is filled, she goes back to the plastic tub stack and leaves the bottle, unpacking a box of Cheez-Its, some opened pretzels, and a bag of cheese puffs. "This is all I had in the way of snacks." She giggles at the selection.

"Cheers," Tina calls out, and she and the others raise their glasses.

They sit and sip and nibble in a quiet that soon becomes unbearable. They're all probably thinking the same thing: How does this problem get fixed? Truly the only way out is with $50,000. Junie's insides begin to wriggle and writhe, and she can't help herself when she blurts out her thoughts.

"Georgia, any word on the finances?" As soon as she's said it, Junie realizes she should've waited for a private moment to bring it up.

Georgia wriggles in her seat for a moment before she sighs and drops her hands into her lap. "Actually, I just got an email back from my finance guy, and we might need to consider some other options. From what he said, it sounds like I won't be able to get the cash out soon enough to make any difference here."

Well, shit.

"Oh. Alright. I get it," Junie says.

She doesn't get it though. Not one bit. Georgia sits there looking far too matter-of-fact considering they're in the middle of a crisis she's unwilling to remedy. This is the *shop*. *Their* shop. The one place that means a world and a half to all of them. How is Georgia not devastated at the fact that her money is out of reach? If that's even the case. Part of Junie wonders if Georgia is finally trying to teach her little sister a lesson, and if so, it's pretty crappy to do it with the beauty shop at stake.

How does Georgia not see the rest of it? If Junie and Tina can't see clients, all of them except Cece go broke. And once they're broke and closed up, that's it. They won't reopen; that's a financial impossibility.

"How much do we need?" Tina looks even smaller than she usually does with her delicate stature.

A sting of guilt rushes up Junie's throat. Tina's job here is her livelihood too. "I don't want this to be your responsibility," Junie says. It's not like Tina would have anywhere close to the funds anyhow, seeing as Randy the Moocher hasn't held a job in the decade he's been living under her roof.

"No. Speak up. What's the number?" Cece is firm.

The aunts know the gist of what has unraveled in the past couple of weeks. Obviously, they've been ringside to the destruction of the place. Junie's haste and the lack of funds. Both of them were encouraging off the bat, when Junie sold the opportunity as something the business could afford. Truth be told, they've all been a bit worried about the new salon across town, and the timing of the offer just felt so meant to be.

June was naive to think it at the time, but it kind of felt like a bone from heaven. Like Mama was pulling strings up there for them. So they wouldn't be out of business, and so their legacy wouldn't die.

But maybe it was really nothing more than an excuse Junie made to rush in.

CHAPTER 11

GEORGIA

Iᴛ's ꜰɪꜰᴛʏ ᴛʜᴏᴜꜱᴀɴᴅ ᴅᴏʟʟᴀʀꜱ."
I say it because I hate watching Junie in the hot seat, and I hate
that I can't pluck her out of it like I have more than once before. Like
when, in her exuberance, she announced a neighbor's pregnancy to
a full crowd at June's before the mom-to-be had a chance to notify
her in-laws. I swept in and swore everyone to keep it zipped. Or like
when she painted the windows of June's with a winter wonderland
scene for the holidays but forgot to check if the paint could be removed. Thankfully I was able to broker a killer deal for replacement
glass. At least the predicaments she gets herself into are lined in good
intentions.

"Look, I think this is workable," I continue. "We can figure it out."

"You don't have any bit of that amount?" Cece pushes her lips into
a sick-and-tired line.

She looks like living proof of the fact that I'm the problem here.

"I could go into it at length, but it's not going to fix this situation.
I don't have oodles of cash sitting around. Money is invested, put in
closed retirement accounts. I'm not a human bank."

I've happily gone above and beyond to help and protect Junie, but even outside of my messy existence, this is a massive ask. People can't be expected to turn this sum around on a dime. And even worse, it's all hypotheticals, and I'm still a liar.

Cece sighs directly at me, but before she can deliver a barbed reply, Tina pipes up. "I think Georgia's right. We can figure something out. When does Goldilocks need the funds?"

"Uh, like, yesterday," Junie says.

"ASAP. Got it," Tina says.

"There have to be ways to make money in this town," I add. "And the community will support us, if we let them."

"That's fine, but I don't want handouts," Junie says. "The whole idea of this was supposed to be me taking care of the shop."

"Of course, but it's not like we can keep the situation secret if the place looks even remotely like it does now," I say. "Honestly, we'll need the regulars to keep things a bit hush-hush so the licensing board doesn't get wind of it. Which I'm sure won't be an issue."

Junie gulps. "Already got that covered. But Misty Prince . . ."

"What's her deal?" I ask.

"There are several ways I might answer that, but what matters here is that she said something offhand, something catty about our current status"—Junie gestures to the construction site around us—"and hinted that we might get in trouble with licensing if we don't mind ourselves."

I roll my eyes. Misty was in my graduating class, and it seems she still hasn't grown up. Even back then she couldn't mind her own dang business, delighting when she found a way to get someone else in trouble.

"June's is as much a staple of this community as the church, let's be honest," Tina says. "Folks don't wish us any ill will."

"Aside from All-Star Cuts," Cece adds. "They'd rat us out in half a heartbeat."

"They don't count." The comment flies out of my mouth and right toward Cece like an unintentional missile.

I don't *actually* have a problem with her, but it feels like she doesn't give me a choice.

I've always wondered if—hoped—she might come around to me, seeing as the two of us aren't so different. Cece did attend beauty school, like the rest of them, but she barely passed. In fact, it took her two rounds through the program before she was awarded her certificate, and even at that rate, there was talk of Mama and Tina pulling strings behind the scenes. Inevitably once she arrived at the shop, she botched one too many hairdos and was eventually exiled to the washbasin.

Cece quit the beauty shop, and no one blamed her. She took a job working the reception desk at the auto shop a few streets over and has since climbed the ranks to general manager of the place.

Cece scoffs. "And what about their official report wouldn't count?"

"That's not what I meant. I mean, *really*, think about it—"

"Doesn't matter who—any report would send someone snooping around," Cece says.

"If you'd let me finish—"

"Will y'all *please* cut this out?" Junie says. "We've already got a big enough problem on our hands without you two at each other's throats."

I nod as I flush red. "You're right. I'm sorry," I tell Junie. "How about we get down to some real brainstorming?" I stand and look around our small circle. "Ladies, I'm heartbroken about not being able to write a check and make this go away, but I'm all in on making something work. Let's raise our glasses and get to work. The higher the hair . . ."

"The closer to God," the three of them reply.

We can't help ourselves; it's in our blood.

We tip our cups together in a silent cheers, and everyone settles back in their seats.

"We need markers, paper, a whiteboard—something for notes," I say.

"Like we've got a whiteboard lying around in the *beauty shop*." Cece says it under her breath, and I choose to ignore it. I can't be of any help if I'm snarled up bickering with Cece, who seems to be itching to get me out of her hair.

Junie hops back up. "I've got a Sharpie, and I don't know . . . I guess you can write on the drywall since we'll have to cover it for clients anyway—before it's painting time, that is."

I take the marker from Junie and give the wall a once-over.

I pop the top off the Sharpie and write in all caps, finishing with a strong underline:

GETTING BACK TO GOOD HAIR DAYS

I twirl around to show them my smiling face and ask, "What've y'all got in the way of ideas?"

CHAPTER 12

JUNIE

JUNIE BEAMS UP AT GEORGIA standing there looking like an eager schoolteacher, like she's a savior they could very much use.

"Well, naturally, there's Cards," Junie says.

"Perfect," Georgia says as she scribbles a bullet point and jots the word next to it.

"Cards" is a longtime tradition at June's wherein the beauty shop is converted to an after-hours gambling den. Mama ran the card tables during her tenure, and she told stories about her mother, another June, before her doing the same. The women set out tables, invite folks who like to play cards with a wager, and let it rip. Each table is a different buy-in, anything from a dollar to a couple hundred, depending on who shows up. The nights are rowdy and fun and soaked in bourbon and anything else with an ABV.

Tina flushes a little and takes a sip of wine. "Well, let's be careful on that one. I don't want our little under-the-table business here to affect your beautiful life in Atlanta, Miss Peach."

"Don't you worry," Georgia says, flashing a smile at her aunt. "I'd trade it all to keep this place safe."

Georgia's response is lovely and unexpected. She's probably laying it on to soothe Tina's nerves. Georgia has always been formidable like that, agile in the face of trouble.

Cece tuts at Georgia's back as she writes on the wall. It isn't Georgia's fault that Mama set her up for the life she's got, yet somehow Cece's sour about the fact that Georgia's different from the other Louise women. Like it affects her somehow. Despite all the times Georgia has left her own important work to help the family. She has never once tried to act like she's outgrown the rest of the family. Even if, in her heart, Junie knows she has.

Cece looks right at her and says, "I can play your hands at Cards. If you want my help."

Cece is a card shark if ever these parts saw one, and her offer is a generous one. Folks hate it when she sits at their card table because she wins, and she's financed more than one Caribbean cruise with her cash prizes. The woman has albums full of vacation snaps of her wearing Hawaiian shirts. Truly, Junie never believed it until she saw it with her own two eyes.

"You know, I think I have an idea," Tina says. "Y'all remember Kimmy from high school? She's constantly messaging me on Facebook about 'business opportunities at home.' I guess she sells some kind of oils that can help with ailments or moods or something. Never have given it more than a second thought, seeing as I'm already fully booked at the shop."

Even if Kimmy is certain they could be Boss Babe Mamas, Junie isn't one bit sold.

Georgia's face looks like Junie's insides feel. "We can call it a *maybe*."

"Heck no!" Cece hollers from the plastic tub stack where she's cracked open the bourbon. "Oils? Snake oil, more like."

"Ok, fine then, what about flipping a house?" Tina says. "You know I love those house shows, and it'd kinda be related since we want the money for a renovation. Have y'all seen the latest one,

Holy City Flip in Charleston? The hubby is also a total hunk, which doesn't hurt."

Flipping a house. It's perhaps more ludicrous than getting on the snake oil train. The pressure in Junie's veins rises.

"Let's keep 'em coming, ladies," Georgia says.

Junie doesn't miss the way Georgia tips up her drink as if to propel her along. She must be as disturbed as Junie.

"Lotto," Cece says.

Everyone nods. Georgia writes.

"A loan." Cece says this one more like a question. "I know someone at the auto shop . . ."

"Like, an individual guy?" Junie asks. "What about an actual business loan instead?"

"With my guy you can't ask too many questions about it," Cece admits. "And you have to pay on time."

It sounds like a broken-thumbs-and-baseball-bats-for-a-missed-payment kind of arrangement.

"I don't know about that," Tina says. "Doesn't sound aboveboard."

"And a pop-up casino is?" Cece replies.

Georgia doesn't write the loan sharking idea, and no one pushes it. "I'll save y'all the heartache of trying for a business loan," Georgia says. "If there's nothing in the bank and this asset is everything we're putting up"—they collectively take in the shop's interior—"I think our chances are slim for qualifying without getting other assets or a cosigner involved, and I'm drawing the line on that."

Junie knows what her sister is thinking about. *Who*, really. Their father and his beautiful family home with a gorgeous view of the Blue Ridge Mountains. It's not a big home, but it comes with land. The family was approached by a developer once, making an offer with a plan to raze the house and build a community of tiny houses rented to weekenders from the city. Their father declined the offer, claiming he was simply too comfortable to uproot himself, but the Louise women suspect the house is his last physical tie to June. Much as the shop is theirs. Not a one of them would risk him losing the home.

"Georgia's right," Junie says. "We don't need more wheeling and dealing—we need cash."

They go back and forth, spitballing ideas, poking holes in the ones that make it to the wall. Junie has to admit she sort of loves it, the company of them, being part of the huddle. Georgia *here*, right where she belongs, in the middle of the Louises. Her absence is the only thing about this place that has never made sense.

Junie's phone dings in her pocket, the email alert, and she pulls it out. Usually she keeps her phone on vibrate and rarely checks email, but she's waiting for some test results, the genetic testing from years back that she really didn't want to revisit but her doctor strongly suggested she dig up. Probably the company doesn't send out reports on Saturdays, but Junie has been surprised before so she looks anyway.

There is a list of emails, a couple of sale ads from her favorite retailers, a notification that the auto-delivery of Puds's dog food is on the way, and a forwarded chain email from her dad (~*Forward This to Seven Friends or Risk Thirteen Years of Bad Luck*~). God bless him. *He really needs a good friend to assure him he'll be alright to send those directly to the junk folder. Also, thanks a lot, Dad, for redirecting the promise of bad luck to your offspring.*

Cece's laughter booms across the salon, pulling Junie out of her inbox and back into the moment. Georgia is bent over holding her stomach.

"Stop, stop," she says. "You're going to make me pee my pants."

Even Tina laughs.

Junie locks her phone screen and tucks it back into her pocket. "What?" she asks. "What did I miss?"

Cece tips her cup up to finish the last drop and grins. "Georgia's got all kinds of crazy ideas keeping us laughing."

Junie's eyes dart to the list and the latest additions. *Become internet influencers.*

"Cece as an influencer? Are they allowed to curse out their followers?" Junie asks and joins in the laughter.

"Hey now," Georgia replies through gasped breaths, "anyone can do it these days. Folks from all different walks of life!"

"I'll tell y'all I'd rather sell nudes of myself than have to try my hand at internet influencing. Heck, I can barely work the camera facing outward!" Cece, unbelievably, seems to be enjoying herself.

Junie stands and grabs the wine bottle and refills the cups in the circle. She's laughing harder than she has in years. And it's not lost on her that she's standing in the middle of a scene she's longed for: all of them together, at June's. She's wondered if June's would bring them back together, and in some roundabout way, maybe that's happening right now. Or maybe it's a gift from the universe, considering Junie's situation, her wish made true.

The women drink and chat, and the edges of things grow fuzzy as the bottle grows light.

Soon enough, they have a solid starter list.

Getting Back to Good Hair Days
- Cards
- "Oils" (hard *maybe*—likely pyramid scheme)
- Flip a house (requires money and expertise no one has)
- Lotto
- Enter contests (trivia, puzzles, etc.)
- Put ad stickers on our cars (note: everyone will start asking questions)
- Complete surveys for payment
- Sell nudes (Mama would reincarnate herself for the sole purpose of ending us all)
- Become internet influencers

Inside, Junie is bubbly and thrilled in the best kind of woozy way. This whole thing is supposed to be a small disaster, but what she's feeling is anything but. It's the most at home she's felt, the most complete, since Mama died. Not that she has felt adrift or ailed in the meantime, but she has been feeling like something is missing. Amid the fun and joy she ekes from her regular days, there are little cracks that could be filled. Not ones that require it, not ones that pose a risk to the rest of her, but simply thin spaces for something else. Fissures suggesting room for more.

Maybe it's having Georgia here. Or maybe it's the power of the four of them being together, but she can't shake the feeling of how the shop seems to fade in the face of this moment. All the women, all the fun, all the love that lives inside and around it.

Call her crazy (and admittedly, she's had more than enough to drink), but Junie would rather their financial woes continue forever if she gets to keep this feeling.

"Another drink, y'all?" Cece asks.

CHAPTER 13

GEORGIA

"AND WHAT ABOUT SNACKS?" CECE'S eyes scan the shop. "Y'all must have more than Junie's crunchy cheesy offerings."

It's going far better than I ever expected. The camaraderie, I mean. Even in my wine haze, I know the options we've come up with will never—not even by a stretch—reach the $50k mark.

"I wish." Junie grips her stomach. "That sandwich hours back isn't holding up well against these drinks."

"Y'all don't keep snacks anymore?" I ask.

Tina shakes her head. "Got ourselves into an awful state having them here. All the customers would ask for *just a little bite* and the place practically became a cafe. They were like locusts."

"It was that famous cherry pie that started it," Cece says.

Tina's homemade cherry pie is a family favorite that never fails to please. It's been the center of family gatherings for as long as I can remember. Delight baked into a tinfoil dish.

"It's been forever since I had some." I let out an embarrassingly enthusiastic groan. "I'd kill for a bite of it." The flake of the pastry, the sweet and tart balanced in a divine cherry kiss. My mouth waters, and I swallow.

Tina nods. "Randy doesn't like cherries, so I always have to make two pies at a time. Apple for him and cherry for me. It's the one thing I won't compromise on for him. I love it, just like our mother made it. But that's not to say I want to eat an entire pie myself . . . so every time I'd bake one, I'd keep a few slices for me and bring the rest here."

"The number of times I had clients calling, asking, 'Tina bringing any of that pie today?'" Junie says. "They'd even cancel their appointments and ask to reschedule to a *pie day*."

Everyone loves Tina's cherry pies (Randy doesn't count—hasn't ever counted), and it has even been suggested that she open a bakery. I understand why she hasn't. It's both a massive financial risk and a break from our hairdressing family line.

"Hang on," I say. "What if we sold the pies to make some money?"

Tina drains of all color, looking as terrified as if I'd suggested a gladiator duel.

"That may be the best idea yet," Junie says after a squeak of approval.

"Oh no, I'm not sure," Tina says. "I'm just little old me. No one wants to *pay* for the pie. Part of the appeal is it being free."

"And y'all know the county fair is coming up in just over a month," Cece says. "They have a pie contest every year, and some of the contestants run booths and sell slices. I don't know how it all works, but I've fixed up the trucks of half the guys on the committee, so I can ask around and see what the deal is."

I've never seen Cece so animated about anything. Sure, the liquor probably helps on the enthusiasm front, but she looks unironically happy.

"Are y'all being seriously serious?" Tina asks.

"Yes!" Junie says.

"Of course," I say.

"Think of who else enters. I just worry—*my* pie, you know?" Tina says. "Gosh, I might throw up at the idea of embarrassing myself like that."

The three of us just sit and look at her, a silent stone wall.

"I'll need to think about it," Tina says. Her cheeks begin to flush, and she raises a self-conscious hand to her face. "I would definitely need help."

"We're here to help," Cece says. "You're the only person in town who *doesn't* believe in your pies."

I whoop and throw my hands in the air; I agree with my full body and my full voice. It isn't until after I hear myself do it that I realize it's exactly what Mama used to do—when her team won, when a hair color came out just right, after Junie and I performed a dance we made up. I guess part of her spirit lives on in me, whether or not I'm a June.

Cece freezes, staring at me.

"Geez," Junie says. "You have yourself a little seance and switch your soul for Mama's?"

Now it's my turn to blush. "Yup," I say. "Right back there in the office, so we'd best make sure Daddy sages the place in case any mischievous spirits slipped in."

"Much the company June would keep," Tina says through a laugh.

The thought of my father and his space here lifts me slightly from the delight of this impromptu happy hour. Tina and Cece are showing up for us—for me and Junie, for this shop, for our shared livelihood—like they have all along.

Rich Scott is noticeably absent.

Objectively, expecting him to appear here is unfair of me, and probably the drinks I've guzzled are amplifying what's usually only a shard of resentment. He doesn't know the scope of the issue here, Junie has not tagged him in; he is not a Louise. But he's our dad, and he should *just know*. He should feel compelled to leap into action just like he should've all those years ago. Back when he sat mired in his grief while I stepped up for Junie in ways I wasn't ready or prepared to. Back when it was really Cece and Tina doing our raising. Not only did we desperately need him at the time but even more, I *wanted* it to be him. I wanted *him* to carry us through the dark.

Despite his inaction, I loved him then, and I love him now. And I know he loves us.

It's just that part of me has always wondered if Junie and I weren't enough for him to wake up for. He's imperfect just like the rest of us. So maybe he is a bit of a Louise too.

Cece looks into the bottom of her empty cup and stands. "Well, I should get on home."

Junie checks her watch. "Is that the time? It's going to be a rough morning."

By now it's late evening, and we all need a tall glass of water, some food to line our bellies, and a good, long sleep.

"Alright, time to call it a night," I say. "Shop meeting adjourned!"

"Shop meeting?" Tina says.

"I guess it works." I shrug.

"Come on, girls, we can do better than that!" Junie says.

"What about Bourbon and Whiteboards?" Tina asks.

"Sounds a bit like a defunct rock group," I say.

Tina squints. "I see that now."

"Blowout Bar Dropouts?" I suggest.

Mama despised blowout bars—to an unreasonable degree. She called it price gouging or a monopoly or something. Frankly, there were too many twists in her theory for me to pin it down.

"It should be more positive," Junie said.

"How about some ideas from you, Miss Junie?" Cece asks.

"Good Hair Days. Right from Mama's sign outside," Junie says.

We stop and let it settle in. In silence we raise our just-about-empty cups in a wobbly toast.

"Good night, ladies. This Good Hair Day is officially adjourned," I say.

Junie scurries over to a cardboard box and yanks it open. She digs through and twirls around with what is usually the most prominently displayed Dolly Parton image, a plastic-framed "oil painting." Junie props it up atop a high stack of boxes and tips an imaginary hat. "In Dolly we trust."

"Might as well," I say. "Until the construction starts."

Junie comes to my side, and I take her under my arm into a wriggly hug.

CHAPTER 14

CECE

CECE IS DRUNK AS A skunk when Tina snags her by the arm and tugs her across the floor of the beauty shop. Georgia and Junie are knotted up together, giggling on the other side. Tina's mouth twitches and her eyes bulge like she's straining to hold back words that threaten to overflow. Georgia and Junie begin packing up, chattering about the impending jaunt home.

Tina checks that the girls aren't looking before she whispers, "This remind you of that night?" The words hiss with pent-up pressure.

Cece had the same thought, one she batted away once, then again and again as it resurfaced like a persistent buoy throughout the afternoon. How could it not? That night when their sister, June, had called them here. She'd called them together for help, to start their own redheaded revolution—a revolt from inside the city walls of the family—against the naming and the pressure from the older generations. She wanted them all truly free.

"Yes." Cece leaves it there, but she could go on. "You were busting to talk about this the entire night, weren't you?"

"How could I not be?" Tina says. "I mean, I *understand* why we can't just lay that family history on the girls willy-nilly, but I just think they would've loved to hear about their mama gathering us here, saving the day in her own way. Kinda like the girls are doing for the shop."

Cece pulls her arm out from Tina's grip as she turns away. She bites back the words she wants to say. *But did she? Did June really save the day?* Because their situation doesn't feel saved. They're in the middle of the latest Louise mess, another caused by the pressure of the name as Junie tries to do too much. June could've ended the naming, and she didn't.

June didn't save them from a thing.

"June calling us together was a onetime thing. And considering this"—Cece gestures widely to the shop—"I'm guessing we'll have to circle up at least a few more times."

"We're heading out," Georgia calls as she slings the tote bag over her shoulder.

She and Junie wave on their way out the front door.

When Cece looks back at Tina, her eyes are full of tears yet to break the seal. Cece knows exactly how they'll overflow and tumble down her cheeks, just like they always do when they talk about June. Their sister. Cece's twin. She feels the same, the hollowness that gets easier to bear but never shrinks. She's just better at hiding it.

"It's not about the number of meetings," Tina says tenderly. "And I might guess you know that's not what I meant. It's the spirit of it, that feeling running through this shop tonight. Just like June created, her very own magic. Surely you remember?"

"Of course I remember," Cece tells Tina, her chest squeezing. "Even if I'd rather not. The memories of June are all we have left, so I hold 'em tight—even if they're a little like poison."

Cece's eyes drop to the space between her feet, and despite the alcohol-induced wiggle to her gaze, she can't help but remember the maroon carpet that's now been ripped out. June despised it. If she were here, she'd be giddy over the concrete—even if it is muddy.

The hardness in Cece's chest heats and threatens to tear her. This is heartache, the hardness inside her that shows on the outside too. And finally she relents, lets the memory flood in and cover her, as she remembers that night.

June called all the Louises to a meeting. She tore into the shop in a flurry, a tiny baby Georgia in her arms. "Where are the others?" She could always get away with demanding.

As if she'd summoned them, Mother and Tina hurried through the front doors looking as confused as they were entitled to. Cece knew what June was about to say because she was with her at Grandmother Dot's house yesterday.

"Good, you're all here," June said.

Mother and Tina flitted to June's side, all eyes for baby Georgia.

"Here, let me have my grandbaby." Mother took Georgia gently in her arms and made for a hair chair, where she settled. "Now, what's this fuss about?"

June puffed out a breath, her eyes filling and her voice barely holding on as she said, "It's the name, Mama. The dang name."

Mother looked at June, and her face slackened. "Tell me everything."

"It was supposed to stop here, stop with me, all of my children free. I am supposed to be the last June." June didn't cry often, but when she did it felt like little cracks forming along the foundation of our shared life. She was supposed to be impenetrable. "Grandmother Dot, she called me to her house—"

Cece lifts her head, knowing she can't bear any more of this reminiscing, and Tina is staring into the floor herself. She is probably remembering, too, hearing the script, the blow-by-blow of June's despair.

"We'll need to tell them eventually," Tina says. "They should know why they each have their names."

Cece agrees. She always has, but there are parts that will hurt the girls, parts they might not, probably won't, understand. Though perhaps after tonight, after seeing how they've grown and matured, she should reconsider. They might be able to understand and rise above.

"They're not kids anymore," Tina says.

"It doesn't help to swim in it," Cece tells her as she makes her way to the door, then switches off the lights. "We'll figure it out. Telling them about the whole Dot situation, but it won't be tonight."

The last thing Cece wants is to upset the girls, and especially by way of Dot's drama revisited. The girls see their mama as someone superhuman, not someone to give in to threats, so she wants to tread lightly. It's been a blessing to let them see their mama as a saint and only that for all these years, a small reprieve in the face of great loss.

She knows what it feels like to have been hurt by the various issues Dot created. People seem to forget that.

Tina shrugs slowly and lets out a puff when her shoulders drop. "You're right."

They step outside, and Tina locks the door and pulls Cece into a floral-scented hug. "I love you, Cecelia."

"I love you too," Cece says.

There's always a pause in this exchange. Like a moment of silence that says, *and June too*.

The space she once took up remains in the mix.

It's a relief when Tina breaks the moment. "Randy will be here soon for me. You head on home."

"Call a ride if he's not here in ten minutes," Cece says, then turns and begins her walk home. She'd thought about calling a rideshare herself, but the mountain air has cooled off after a hot, muggy day, and she could use the space to work out her thoughts.

She can't shake remembering the thrown-together conversation they had within the same walls thirtysomething years ago, alongside baby Georgia. Back then, June, Tina, Mama, and Cece talked for hours about Dot's threats and the real options related to ending the naming, but they couldn't agree.

Cece was the only one willing to give it all up. To let Dot do what she wanted, let her keep her demands as she rotted in her miserable grave, to let the good earth reclaim the building, let the vines and shrubbery grow up and over the walls until it crumbled into ruin.

Cece would've rather set the place on fire than let it twist June to do something she stood firmly against.

But Cece was the only one who felt that way.

In the end, she went along with the others, who decided to give in to Dot's demands and assured her it would be worth it in the end. That they owed it to the next generation to keep the family business going. That reason sat in her mother's arms, peeping and cooing and gurgling in delight. What could Cece do but agree with what she was told was best for the baby? That baby girl, itty-bitty Georgia, was the best thing Cece had seen in her life.

If the women had each other, were happy and well, what else did they need?

CHAPTER 15

JUNIE

JUNIE WALKS UP THE SLOPE of the quiet road, weaving a little, with Georgia at her side. Georgia tucks Junie under her arm, and her little sister rests into her. Both of them are giggly like preteens planning a surprise party. "We're going to get this all figured out," Georgia says.

Georgia's hair catches the light from the setting sun in a remarkable sheen. "Did you get a gloss put on at the salon, Peach?" Junie asks.

Georgia stops like she's thinking back. "Oh. Yeah, I did, actually. Feels like a long time ago. When I'm home everything else melts away."

"Dang, you just have to outshine us in every way." Junie gives Georgia a wink to make it clear she's joking.

Junie smiles to herself as she looks out and up the road. The nighttime bugs are awake and chirping in a chorus, and the odd lightning bug flashes in the grass behind picketed yards. Small historic homes line this thoroughfare, and they are solidly built and well-kept. If Whitetail were the sort of place to have a postcard printed in its honor, this would be the photo of choice, the warm light surrounding and highlighting the town's best feature. In this moment, it feels like all the real ugliness of the world is suspended.

"I believe it," Junie says. She always believes Georgia—by default.

"So, Cards," Georgia says. "There's a schedule?"

Junie smirks. "What do you think we are? Barbarians?"

Georgia gives Junie a playful whack on the arm.

"Hey!" Junie grabs her arm and inspects the spot. "Good thing I have a doctor's appointment Monday. I can get it looked at."

Georgia scoffs playfully. "Hopefully they've got a surgical center on-site."

"You know me, only cutting-edge care will do." Junie waggles her brows.

"What're you going in for?" Georgia asks.

Junie tucks herself back into Georgia's side. "Just a checkup," she lies.

"I want to get going on the list of money-making ideas as soon as possible," Georgia says. "Time is of the essence here. So maybe we start planning Cards tomorrow?"

"What do you mean *planning* Cards?" Junie asks.

"The event. Surely it has to be arranged."

"There aren't any centerpieces, and there isn't a menu to speak of," Junie replies. "Frankly, calling it an 'event' at all makes it sound too formal."

Georgia tuts playfully. "Fine, but we need to start on *something* for getting the shop put back together."

She might not say it, but her urgency is a reminder that she won't be able to stick around forever. Junie lets out a slow breath. "If we must."

Georgia squeezes her like a mom would. "I know you can do it, buttercup."

Junie loves the way Georgia makes her feel. Cared for, noticed, like she's not entirely without a mother. She often wonders what it was like for Georgia—not having her own big sister. Although by all appearances it has only ramped up Georgia's competence, like she came out of the womb with some life experience already under her belt. It's hard to think about how life would've turned out differently if Mama had lived—for both of them, but especially for Georgia.

"You planning to visit Daddy while you're home?" Junie asks.

"Are you trying to change the subject?"

"Are *you*?" Junie sings the last bit.

Georgia's already grinning when Junie takes off in a skipping run. "Girl, you're a hot mess," she calls from behind.

Little does she know how much.

Junie throws out her arms like the wings of an airplane and lets the warm nighttime air carry her ahead.

"Junie, you're going to be the end of me . . ." Georgia's words are quiet between her labored breaths from jogging to catch up.

Junie won't think about endings now, not while she has her sister and this delicious moment unraveling in front of her. Not when this evening feels like a perfect beginning.

CHAPTER 16

GEORGIA

I CATCH UP TO JUNIE A block before the house. She's finally out of gas and I hope—to all things good in the world—sobering up.

"Well, helloooo there, slowpoke." Junie turns and curtsies in my direction.

I land a palm on her head and ruffle her hair as I pass her.

"Hey now, that's fighting acts, messing up hair."

She's right, but it's in good fun, and if anything warrants a well-intended hair ruffle, it's making me run after her for half a mile when the last time I voluntarily ran was while being chased. Specifically, from a local bar by a disgruntled bouncer Moonbeam rubbed the wrong way.

Junie's still chirping her complaints about me shaking the beach waves from her hair when we round the corner and head up the dusty driveway to the house. I'm five paces from the porch when I catch sight of the person standing on it. I freeze. Junie slams into my back and lets out a screech.

It's Eddie. *Eduardo Rigsby.* And he looks exactly the same as I remember him. His complexion is a deep olive, a blend of his

Guatemalan mother and his white father. Deep brown, almost black hair sits in thick waves atop his head, and like it's part of his uniform, he wears a deep smile across his face, eyes squinted. What on earth is my high school sweetheart turned lab partner extraordinaire doing back in this town? Better yet, what is he doing standing right here on my sister's front steps?

He raises a hand, waves, and calls out, "Junie, hey! I texted."

I swivel my head to look at Junie, and she's blushing sheepishly. I watch her extract her phone from her back pocket and tap at her screen, registering the notifications she missed.

Eddie moves toward us, down the porch steps. "Georgia Louise? Is that *you*?" He's still smiling. Acting like this is any amount of normal. Acting like this isn't one bit bizarre.

It's then I notice what's in his hand. He holds a well-worn cardigan, knitted together in colorful stripes and finished with mismatched buttons in front. It's Junie's favorite cardigan. I stare at it as Eddie draws closer, my frown deepening. Why would he have this?

They would have to be spending time together.

Please, no.

They can't be.

Can they?

I look first at Eddie. He looks down at his hands, and my confusion over why he has my sister's cardigan must register because he begins to fidget, almost hopping around, as if the item of clothing has become a hot potato.

"Here." Eddie thrusts the item into Junie's hands. "This belongs to you."

Eddie's eyes dart between us, and his face goes from questioning to wondering to clearly grasping the awkwardness of the looks bouncing between us. "Anyway, I'll leave you ladies to it. Junie, let's hang soon."

Neither Junie nor I utter a word as Eddie makes his exit. Eventually we turn to each other, and it feels like dancing on a ledge over nothing good.

Eddie Rigsby and I fell in love when we were kids, but like many of the good things that have come my way, I destroyed it. He is the only non-Louise, non-June, non-Dad I've ever loved. But none of that matters because I mistreated him and showed him the truth about me: I'm incapable of loving someone outside of my family the whole way. Because Mama's expectations trump it all. When push comes to shove, I will set my most prized possessions on fire—including my romantic partner—if it means fulfilling her dreams for my life.

I'll always love Eddie. Dearly and with every inch of me and more than I think I could ever love again.

But not as much as he deserves because part of me will always be wound up in this family. In my responsibility to them. My love for them, the way it pins me down.

But Junie. Maybe—definitely, absolutely, and without a doubt—she has what it takes to love a special person wholly and completely. She's got the stuff running through her.

Could it be? She and Eddie weren't ever friends. It wasn't like that in high school. She had her friends; I had Eddie. We didn't overlap aside from very minor ways, which means this is new, since Eddie apparently returned. He so casually suggested that he and Junie "hang soon" that I can only guess he's here—probably has been—for a while. Junie would've told me about a harmless friendship (because she'd have known I might not think it so harmless). She kept this from me. For a reason.

Junie's such a catch.

So is Eddie.

This whole porch situation looked, head to toe, like a moment of ease between two people grown close. How long have they been seeing each other?

I don't want the details. Not now, and probably not ever, but it's part of my role around here to fix problems. And this is certainly a problem brewing if I don't get out ahead of it, so I need to make myself ok with whatever's happening between them.

CHAPTER 17

JUNIE

J UNIE LETS THE SILENCE SIT as Georgia's frozen smile looks like it's beginning to melt off her face. Her big sister is really trying to come across as unbothered.

Junie lets out a slow, stilted laugh, her face pulled into an apologetic frown. "Eddie Rigsby's back in town by the way."

Georgia nods slowly. "I have to say, a heads-up would've been nice."

Junie wonders if Georgia means regarding Eddie's presence here in town in general or if she more specifically means here at the Clementine.

"I'm sorry. It's just with the shop, it kinda slipped my mind."

"Is this something, like, more than friends between y'all?"

Georgia looks at Junie like she believes the answer is yes. It's obvious in the hurt behind her eyes despite her stretching her face into fake comfort. Desperately, Junie wants to be honest, to tell Georgia she wouldn't *ever* run around with Eddie—especially behind Georgia's back—but her current situation doesn't allow her that truth.

Junie cannot explain why and how she and Eddie began spending time together without unloading a whole 'nother can of worms on Georgia. One that would hurt far more than thinking Junie's going on dates with harmless old Eddie. And frankly, Junie *cannot* and *will not* go there, but she could honestly promise that this is not what Georgia thinks it is.

"We ran into each other and started hanging out. He's back here to take care of his mom—really, I think she'd prefer that he just take her back to Guatemala, but that's neither here nor there. There's not that many people our age living in town."

Junie can't handle an outright *yes*, so she skirts around it. Both sides of this coin are bad options.

"Look, Junie, I think y'all would make a cute couple. I'm not upset about it. Do you want my blessing to date or something?"

Junie feels like she wants to vomit—*that's* what she wants. Well, more specifically, the relief that would follow it. But she's backed into a corner of her own making, and so she will accept this ghastly *blessing* because she must. Georgia was so smitten with Eddie, and they all expected they'd make it for the long haul. Get married and pop out some babies even.

Georgia steps closer and takes Junie's hands. "I want the best for you. You can be honest with me."

Junie drops her gaze. "Whatever you think."

Georgia beams back and squeaks with excitement. "Let me plan the first official date?"

Junie's insides are screaming out, *Yucky yuck, no thank you*, but instead she smiles and says, "Eh, that might be a little close for comfort."

She's going to have to fill Eddie in on this so he can go along with it. She can't explain it to Georgia, not yet.

Junie will say that she loves Eddie Rigsby. (She already sort of does in a different kind of way, a truth among her lies.)

She will make Georgia believe that she's head over heels.

She will convince Georgia that it's butterflies wiggling in her tummy.

She won't tell Georgia that Eddie found her at her lowest low.

She won't tell Georgia that he's become the best friend Junie has ever had.

CHAPTER 18

GEORGIA

I'M FAIRLY CERTAIN I DESERVE an Oscar for my performance earlier, but I saw the way Junie looked at him. Complete adoration. The same gaze was muscle memory of my own for the years he and I were an "us." I'd never take that feeling away from my little sister because she deserves the best, and even if it feels like it's crushing every part of me from the inside out, I'll let her have this.

Now I'm lying in my bed—Junie's guest bed—staring up at the ceiling in the dark. My body aches, exhaustion permeating every nook and cranny of it. But my eyes haven't sagged once.

A lot of what's keeping me awake is Eddie. Well, Eddie and Junie together, most specifically. I have so many questions about *how* and *why* she ever came across him. Not that I dictate what the grown woman can and cannot do, but if I were to run into a former boyfriend of hers, I'd certainly mention it to her. What if she always had a thing for him?

I love her so much, but I hate this.

I hate the way this hurts.

Quiet, thick tears roll from my eyes like little marbles set free.

One might imagine that with the love between us things would be simpler, easier.

I roll myself up to sitting and flip on the nightstand lamp. I shuffle out of bed, through the house, and out to the front porch. I settle in a rocker and soak in the moonlight. The thick trees rustle in a gentle nighttime breeze, and the warmth of it covers me like a hug. It feels like the gentle company I need while I catalog the issues keeping me awake.

The Eddie situation is only the beginning. I still have a job back in Atlanta, one that expects me to show up on Monday morning, but now that I realize the extent of what the shop needs—making $50K appear out of thin air—I know it's going to take longer than a weekend to resolve. I wish I could erase my whole Atlanta life—the lackluster job, the shoddy apartment—but I'm not naive enough to think that's possible. I need that job to support me. My entire family believes Atlanta is a well of plenty, of success and joy, for me, yet the longer I stay here, the more I put what little I do have there in jeopardy.

Telling them the truth about who I genuinely am would be not only to admit my own failures but to bring them shame too. I have been the person they brag about to customers. The mortifying clippings at June's that are still my most newsworthy accomplishments. The high school accolades Dad could list out at the bankers' lunches. If I show them what became of me, they would have to walk it all back. They would have to explain that they *didn't* have me to brag about after all.

But I can't pack up and go back to my pretending. I can't leave Junie or June's or the aunts to figure out saving our most precious possession on their own. Junie called me in for a reason. There are many things in this life I regret, but leaving my family high and dry in this big moment of need would certainly be the whopper.

I'll text Felix tomorrow at a more reasonable hour and ask him for the next week off. I'll have to call the situation a "family emergency," which for all intents and purposes it actually is. I'll add the white lie to my list of Things I Feel Guilty About. Felix has been good to me—even if the job doesn't fit inside the dreams I hold (deeply and well-hidden) inside me. I don't expect everything at June's to be fixed within a week, but maybe if we can get a plan together and start working the steps, I can leave the ladies to follow through and come back on weekends to help and check in on progress.

In the late-night air and the company of the creaking chair, extending my time here seems like the next right thing to do.

CHAPTER 19

JUNIE

Monday afternoon, Junie sits at the doctor's office in nothing but her undies and a thin paper gown tied in front. Crinkly paper covers the exam table below her, and her toes graze the cold metal step. The whole room looks gray in the wash of fluorescence from the strip lights above, but here she must wait until it's time to get her ta-tas scanned.

Again.

After finding a lump and reviewing the biopsy that followed, the doctors seem to want to rescan every bit of her and draw blood for every possible test as they generate plans for next steps.

Junie pulls out her phone to pass the time, to distract her from the fact that she's obviously the youngest woman here. All of the women, many with gray hair, looked at her with pity when she walked through the waiting room up to reception, as if she had a sign on her chest: *Barely Past My 30th Birthday.*

Junie clicks through the phone and watches a funny cat video Georgia sent and smiles for the first time since she entered the building. She'd already mentioned the appointment, one she called a "checkup," so she was able to slip out without questions. What Junie didn't mention was that she'd drive to Eddie's house so he could be her medical chauffeur per their arrangement.

Yesterday, Georgia and Junie passed the day nursing their hangovers from the Good Hair Days meeting and ignoring the awkwardness of the Eddie moment sitting between them. Later in the day, Georgia announced that she's staying in Whitetail for a week—much to Junie's delight—to help with the shop, and she'll check in with work remotely. A perk of being the boss, undoubtedly. They made a plan with the aunts on the group text to buy their first set of lotto tickets. Cash will be pooled weekly, and they will trade off who buys each week. Buyer picks the numbers and the games.

A smiling tech knocks and opens the door. "We're ready for you."

Junie follows her to the mammogram and ultrasound room, and on the way she catches sight of Eddie in the waiting room. Junie sticks out her tongue at him, which elicits an eye roll. Before long she's standing in front of the machine and opening her gown. Getting a mammogram at this juncture feels a little bit like a waste of time, but according to the doctors it's important to document where things stand as a point of comparison.

But the mammogram and its impending vise grip is not what Junie wants to think about, so she reminds herself that she has a Good Hair Days meeting to look forward to tonight. And all because of her favorite person, Georgia. Junie hasn't been able to shake the awkwardness of the run-in they had with Eddie. That night, Junie couldn't sleep. She knew Georgia couldn't sleep either because she heard her up and moving around, then the squeak of the rocking chair out front. Maybe Georgia's not as sure about the pairing as she said she was, but she has yet to mention it.

"Could you step up to the plate, please?" The tech is asking for Junie to slap her ta-tas on the X-ray plate, but in Junie's mind it sounds like a call to be honest with Georgia.

Junie nods, positions herself, and waits while the plate descends and squishes her into a pancake.

Maybe she should bring it back up with Georgia. Lord knows she'll be sleepless for days, weeks probably, if Junie's suspicions are correct. But that'd require Junie telling her sister about this deal with the breasts and the doctors and the tests and scans. It'll come, that time. It will.

"All done," the tech says.

Back in the exam room, Junie pulls on her clothes, grateful for this being over and done. She exits to the desk out front where she schedules a follow-up appointment. She turns around and scans the waiting room for her ride.

Junie plops a hand on Eddie's shoulder and shakes. He jostles upright, almost dropping the thick fantasy book that had him absorbed. He's sweet like that, Eddie Rigsby, still into magical creatures and heroes and the good guys coming out on top. And yet he's also sturdy and reliable, a true and practical force. He's someone you want on your team. The calm to Junie's chaos, very much to her relief.

"That was quick," he says. "Everything go ok?"

Junie shrugs because that's the only answer when none of it's really ok. Together they push through two sets of doors to the parking lot.

It's either the third or fourth appointment, counting blood draws, that Eddie has accompanied her to, and he's probably the very last person Junie ever expected to be by her side for any of this. Not that she expected any of this to begin with. But it all started the day Junie ran into Eddie at this very doctor's office. He'd moved home after leaving his fancy hospital professorship at Vanderbilt Hospital in Nashville and accepting a job at the local family medical clinic so he could help care for his aging mother as she recovered after surgery.

As fate would have it, his mother had a routine appointment for an annual mammogram on the very same day Junie was slapped with a breast cancer diagnosis, flashed several sets of sad eyes, and then, with a paper stack of Helpful Information, sent on her merry way. People who knew better planned to have someone come with them to appointments like these. But Junie wasn't ever supposed to be one of those people. She is young. She is healthy—or at least she'd thought she was. They already lost Mama this way. She and Georgia got tested for the faulty genes, and she was supposed to be clear.

Now it seems there may be some questions around that genetic test, which Junie has re-requested from years and years ago. Thirty is young to find a lump, and when they biopsied it, the lab reported that it was an aggressive variety. Given her family history, specifically the fast progression of her mother's illness, the coincidence seems too great to be simply a fluke. There is a possibility of an error in her own results, so Junie hovers over her email, hoping to get to the bottom of what really happened with the test. It's a good thing she made sure to always keep health insurance after experiencing life without it as a teen. It's one of the few things she can celebrate herself doing all the way right.

On that day about a month ago, Eddie saw Junie, a howling, blubbering mess, sitting in her car and did the decent thing and drove her home. Walking in her mother's footsteps, so close to Mama in the worst way, broke Junie apart on the deepest level; the injustice shook her so acutely that it felt like she was permanently rearranged. Perhaps she truly was. Eddie got her number, called to follow up, and over days that became weeks urged her to *"tell Georgia, tell someone, anyone in your family, Junie, dammit."* She thinks Eddie is alright being the keeper of her secret for now. He's not one to blow a cover, but he seems to be wearing thin under the pressure, begging Junie to tell Georgia, the fix-it queen. All the same, after the sight of Junie that very first day, he won't let her go to another appointment alone.

Eddie rolls down the passenger window from inside the car. "Junie? You feeling alright?"

"Oh! Sorry." Junie slips inside.

Once they're on the main road, Eddie clears his throat. "Ok, so what's the deal with the other night at your house? You didn't even mention to Georgia that I was back in town? That you'd run into me?"

"Of course not."

"Which I guess explains why she assumed something shady was going on." He squeezes his lips into a concerned line.

"She thinks we're dating."

The car jolts as Eddie's foot slips to the brake. "You can't be serious."

"As cancer."

Junie watches her words fall on him, and he pulls in a slow, deep breath like she's seen him do many a time now. It's the same thing Georgia does when she's trying not to lose her mind over Junie, a prayer of sorts for patience. Junie giggles—to give him permission to loosen up about all of this.

"Look. You need to talk to her. This is going too far. Can you imagine how mad she's going to be when she finds out you kept this from her?"

"I can exactly imagine it—in fact, I can almost feel it in my sickly bones." Junie adds a theatrical shudder. "Which is precisely why I'm not telling her. And she gave us her blessing to date, even said we'd be cute—which turned my guts twice over, for the record—but date we shall."

Eddie freezes and his mouth flops open.

"You ok?" Junie asks, cocking her head.

"Uh. Yeah. Yes, totally. For sure." He takes a breath. "I guess I'm just surprised that Georgia would give her *blessing*."

Even if Georgia has put this man through hell, it seems the emotional strife didn't quite burn all the way through his feelings for her.

"I mean, you don't actually want to go on a date," Eddie says.

"Yes, *actually* I do, but fake. And more than one—it has to be convincing."

"Absolutely not," Eddie says.

"Why?" Junie stops herself from pouting because he's had her back in so many ways for which she could never repay him. And because she's just now realizing how much he might be hung up on her big sister.

"Because there's no possible way Georgia's really ok with this."

Junie grins and reaches out a finger to gently poke Eddie's ribs. "You think she's still got the hots for you too?"

Eddie fends off Junie's touch and rakes his free hand through his hair like he's trying to comb out his exasperation. A flash of true hurt passes behind his eyes. "That's not my point. Though I *will* have you know that ever since she massacred our relationship, I've been retired from the dating scene. Anyway, my point here is that despite things between Georgia and me being dead, it doesn't mean she really wants her sister dating her ex. Come on, it's so weird. Even I can see that."

"She said it, so what can I do but take her word as truth?" Junie's insides squirm—she knows Georgia loves her enough to lie about this.

"Here's a compromise: You tell her we're friends but not romantically involved. Which is also true," he says. "There's already been enough hurt between us, I don't want any more at my hand."

"So she can catch us sneaking around to appointments and think we're lying to her?" Junie says. "That won't end well—"

"*None* of this will end well if you keep waiting to tell her. What difference do you think waiting will make? It won't change the truth." It's the firmest he has been with her.

The difference is obvious: avoiding inducing chaos among the Louise women once again. The difference is sidestepping more problems, sidestepping laying more requests at their feet.

"We just need to go with it, pretend we're dating, and it's precisely the cover we need while I do my treatment stuff. Let me deal with the telling people part," Junie says.

"I don't want this *undercover*." He stretches the word. "Besides, don't forget you're talking to a doctor here. There's only so long you can hide this. You're going to get very sick with treatment. You're already very sick, and it's not going away. They're going to notice something's up, so why don't you tell them on your terms?"

"I *can't*," Junie says. She pictures Georgia crushed in the wake of Mama's death. "I mean, I will, but I need to get this stuff figured out with the genetic testing first."

Eddie sighs. "What does it change? If the results were wrong or confusing or misleading, that's on the lab and their poor quality work."

The oncologist and breast care specialist both looked like they were suppressing groans when Junie told them which lab Georgia had used for genetic testing. Right before they were tested, an influx of new labs saturated the market that was previously dominated by a single company. The upside was that cheaper tests were made available to a larger group, and the downside was that some labs weren't well-prepared to serve customers and rushed to market for a piece of the pie. Apparently the company Georgia and Junie used was known for confusing paperwork better designed for the scientists manning the lab than the average Joe reading the results.

"Georgia read my result, Eddie." Junie is unmoving and serious. "I was too scared to look, so she opened the envelope. She knew it was negative right away—it was different from hers. What if it was *only* because it was different from hers?"

Eddie shrugs in reluctant agreement. "It could also be a lab error. It happens. Or it could be an awful, terrible coincidence. People do get breast cancer, often in fact, without any sort of gene for it."

All those years ago, Georgia's results arrived first in the mail. She was positive for carrying the gene, and everyone cried. Then a week later, Georgia opened Junie's envelope and glanced at the results, and the sheer elation on her face was a memory Junie held dear for years. It was a moment she revisited when she was sad. Until the appointments kicked off, and the first doctor suggested there could be a problem with the results—a lab error or an interpretation error. A mistake Georgia made in reading it. What that doctor didn't understand is that Georgia doesn't make mistakes; she's not like Junie. And if Georgia did make a mistake? And in this one very specific way? It would undo her.

Eddie lets out a strained sigh. "It's a tough situation."

Junie leans in and begs her voice not to waver. "What if Georgia read it wrong? I can't do that to her. Not when I'm already sick. That's enough. But also, what if the lab got it wrong? *She* picked the lab because it was what we could afford at the time."

She can't untangle these things, the results, her illness, the way she and Georgia love each other from inside their bones, because they're all wound up together inside her. Some of it inside Georgia too.

"*Please*, pretend date me?" Junie says earnestly. "I'm going to lose my hair."

The car rolls to a stop at a light, and Eddie looks over at her. "Is that maybe one of the worst parts?"

Junie looks back at him, and she thanks the heavens for sending her Eddie because very few people could really understand what that will mean the way he does. Junie comes from a lineage of women with salon blood in their veins. Usually, hair is what they can control with their tips and tricks. Their special kind of hair witchcraft—it is what they do. But now, in the face of this disease, that will be taken from Junie too.

"I might have to tag Tina in from the wig wall," she says casually. "But I'll add wig expertise as another hair skill as I figure it out."

Eddie nods quietly as he turns back to look at the road and drive. Eventually he speaks. "Ok, fine. I'll do it, but I'm not happy about it."

"So you're agreeing?"

Junie looks at him as he drives, and she hopes that in the pause, he'll realize it's the right choice—to let her pretend. At least for a little bit.

At last Eddie puffs out a breath. "Only for a bit. Then you need to fix this, because I don't want people thinking—"

"Are you embarrassed for people to think you're dating me?" Junie says it grinning from ear to ear as she pokes his ribs again because she knows he hates it. "That's low, my friend."

Finally his frustrated glare cracks. "Never, sweet Junie," Eddie says. "You're a doll. And not one bit of a pain in the ass."

They continue down the road, the humming engine their only soundtrack. Eddie silently reaches over and squeezes Junie's shoulder. When she turns to look, there's a tenderness in his eyes, and it reminds Junie of the way Georgia looks at her.

"Thank you," she tells him, not a hint of sarcasm.

He nods, releases her shoulder, and turns back to face the road ahead.

Soon Eddie pulls into his mom's house, and Junie picks up her car. She checks the time and decides to head straight to June's for the Good Hair Days meeting. She can't wait to get back in that bubble and away from her medical woes.

The bubble for Louises, for big hair, for drink pouring and a few crass words. Junie can't help but wonder how long she can keep it as is, unspoiled. As much as she knows her Louises would want to skin her alive for going to her appointments without them, protecting them from the heartbreak is one of the small powers she holds.

At least for now.

CHAPTER 20

GEORGIA

THE BOTTLES OF WINE IN my grocery bag clink together as I walk up to the shop, and a distant train horn blasts like it's sounding my arrival. For the most part, the train tracks running right by June's haven't caused issues over the years. Aside from when the horn sounds right as a stylist is lining up a straight edge cut. But by now the lesson has been learned: If there's a rumble on the tracks, *pause* and wait for it to pass.

Junie's already there when I step inside and cross the dull, patchy, now-medium-clean floor.

"I'm ready, ready, ready," Junie sings as I unpack my bag of wine and nibbles. She reaches past me and grabs a grape from the container I've popped open.

"Just the enthusiasm we need," I say. "But let's leave *some* of the food for the meeting."

"You say food?" Tina appears behind us. "Good idea."

Tina turns, by reflex, to hang her bag on the hooks on the torn-up walls, then goes and hangs it on the back of a chair. I screw a wine key into a cork as Cece glides in.

"I've already got a new idea for the list," she announces. She marches right over to the chairs and begins arranging them in a circle.

Junie rolls over a stray office chair. Tina and I join with wine to share in hand. "Alrighty, let's get officially started. Junie, the honors?"

She holds up her plastic cup of wine and toasts the meeting.

Cece clears her throat. "Ok, well, now that we're official or whatever, my idea is that we have a garage sale at your dad's house. Lord knows, Rich needs a clean-out."

It's a good idea. Dad inherited a ton of home items from his wealthy Connecticut family. Come to think of it, there might even be items of real value that we could sell to an antiques collector if he approves. We never really saw our grandparents on Dad's side growing up, and he never seemed bothered about it. He always said he'd left his past behind, and he was happy with the family he had here in Whitetail. As a kid I did overhear a few snippets, and after filling in a few blanks, I deduced that his parents weren't particularly interested in making the trip to Georgia, and over time, distance grew between them.

"That could work." I look around at the other two.

"Worth a try," Tina says.

I catch Junie's eye and she shrugs.

"Good thing y'all agree," Cece says. "I already told Rich we would."

I take a long, slow gulp of wine. Dad is a softie, and honestly, he'd probably let us sell whatever we pleased right out from under him. He was a good match to Mama's big personality, letting her chase her whims without complaint. After we lost her, he moved further in that direction, and for a while he was just . . . there. We knew he was hurting, surviving the only way he knew how, but it sometimes felt like he didn't care enough. Like he should've pushed back on us when we were constantly cutting and coloring each other's hair in increasingly wild styles. Like he should've said no to some of the parties Junie attended. To be very clear, I've always felt love from my dad. I think Junie feels the same too. It's just that he sort of floated out of our collective orbit after Mama, the sun around which we spun, went out. He was there, loving us as best he could; he just wasn't close.

"When?" Tina asks.

"Tomorrow clean out. Wednesday figure out pricing. Thursday sale day. I know a weekend might be better, but on account of Georgia needing to get back, I think we stick with the ASAP date and do our best."

Junie covers her mouth and speaks between bites of crackers. "Count me in. Knowing Daddy, we'll probably need as much help as we can get."

She's right. He's so laid-back that he's close to lying down when it comes to his belongings.

"You should ask Eddie," Tina says to Junie.

Everyone freezes, and Tina turns bright red.

"Sorry," Tina says. "I shouldn't have . . . Stupid old me. I'm sorry, girls. I don't want to get in the middle of this." She continues muttering under her breath about putting her foot in her mouth.

My guts churn. I guess it's time to just address it. "It's fine, Tina. All of it's ok. Let's just be adults about this, ok?"

Tina nods, looking on the verge of tears.

"Eddie will probably be at the clinic anyway," Junie says, dropping her eyes to her plate.

"The clinic?" I don't know I'm asking it until the words are already out.

Eddie knew he would be a doctor since the day his parents bought him a play set when he was three years old. I know this because it was discussed in his college admissions essay that I read five thousand drafts of back when I was his girlfriend. Honestly, the doctor thing fit him. He was fiercely intelligent, a pinch nerdy, and so loving that his worst professional transgression would most likely be attempting to donate his own organs to a patient. The local clinic is a change of plans, however. He always wanted to work in a city hospital, seeing rare diseases, having clinical trials in which to enroll his patients, working in a place on the cutting edge.

And he was good enough to snag a spot there.

"He took a job at the family practice over on Elm Street," Junie says. "At least for now, while he's home for his mom."

I don't know a thing about what's going on with his mother, and it's not really any of my business. It's been years since he and I were together, since we've had a real conversation, so it's not like I've been in the loop on family updates. Though now he's suddenly cozied up to my sister and breaking the unspoken rules of separation.

"I think we'll be fine with just us ladies," Cece says in a tone that suggests she'd rather not have to wade through any kind of boy drama.

Everyone nods in agreement.

"Might be best to keep it between us anyway," I say. "The likelihood of it being a walk down memory lane and all. Now, what do you ladies say—who's ready to throw some cash at Tina? Lotto was the first order of business today, before the new idea."

The three faces I love most in the world (yes, even Cece) crack into grins. We pool the cash quickly and melt into a conversation about lucky numbers and scratchers versus traditional lottery. Eventually we've almost drained the wine and destroyed the snacks. I intentionally brought a small amount of wine—*typical Georgia*, the others might say, but we can't all be fun Junie. We don't need Good Hair Days girls hungover for garage sale prep.

We discuss the plan for Cards this weekend. It works out well that the regular schedule falls this way, but we all agree adding extra nights might become a reality. Tina tries once more to convince us about the oils.

"I mean, they call themselves Boss Babes, so couldn't it be worth a try?"

"There's no proof of income required to call yourself a Boss Babe," Cece says. "Which is what we're in need of right now."

Tina sighs and raises a glass.

We laugh. We drink.

We find our rhythm so quickly, and I'm surprised by how worn in it feels. As if this is how we've always been. As if I never left, as if I'd never been sent out to conquer the world. This is how I always wanted friendship to feel, like somewhere I could lean into, a place I was welcome, no strings attached.

I'm just not sure how long it can last.

CHAPTER 21

CECE

C ECE WATCHES GEORGIA TOSS HER head back, and it about knocks the wind from her how much she looks like June. Georgia really has become everything June dreamed for her, the one who rose above the name, rose above the drama, rose beyond a copy-and-paste life gifted from generations before. Georgia might love this place, but she doesn't rely on it like the rest of them. She's like a chameleon who can come and go, visit awhile, fitting in wherever she lands.

It's all she could want for her niece.

When June became pregnant for the second time, she told Cece, right after she swore her to secrecy, that she'd prayed for a boy. No more girls, no more chances at a June while their grandmother was living. She wanted out of the naming game. Dot had told her that if she didn't name the next girl June, she'd deed the shop to a trust, to a distant relative, to the dang Salvation Army for their personal use, anywhere that would assure their lineage never touched the shop again.

June had cried to Cece. *"The shop's not just about me, and my hands are tied. I can't make this choice for everyone. What about Tina too? Any kids y'all have? How else are we going to make money in this town?"*

Cece pleaded with her to change her mind and tell Dot to take a hike. They would figure it out, she assured her. Times were changing.

Cece holds her anger tight. Anger about the naming and the arm-bending and the threats and the business and family all wound up together in a nest of barbs. She hates that June wasn't allowed to make her own choices, name her own children, for God's sake. Somewhere along the line Cece decided she hated the shop too. Probably because it is solid and tangible and something very real to point to in disgust, but in truth, it has always been about the choices made around it and how they made her twin sister feel. How they made *her* feel too. And the rest of the women in their family in a ripple beyond.

Cece knows very well how it feels to be a sister jilted. The non-June.

She has always wondered if Junie feels insecure in her position despite getting the name and the shop.

Cece loves her family fiercely, and she hopes Junie doesn't feel bad. When it comes to Georgia, Cece prods her away, pushing her into her own exciting life and away from the never-ending beauty shop drama. The way June wanted it. Watching her now, Cece feels her love for Georgia well up in her as a laugh bubbles out of her.

Cece may keep a guard up when it comes to most things June's Beauty Shop—perhaps because she feels like the only watchdog among them. The only one with the pulsing mistrust that conditions will be thrust upon them again, one of them forced to choose. It rattles inside her and hurts like being the one not chosen. That is what she is after all, the twin who lost out. Nevertheless, she will come to every meeting, even if she holds back.

She would be a fool to give up a single night like this with these women.

CHAPTER 22

JUNIE

JUNIE HAS SNUCK OUT OF her dad's house, her childhood home, to meet up with a boy. It's not the first time she's done it, but she'd be entirely unruffled if it was the last.

Especially since the boy is Eddie. It's like sneaking out the window and sliding down the gutter to get to a dentist appointment on time—though in fairness, both are critical to keeping her health on track.

Junie tiptoes to the vegetable garden, through the morning dew that the climbing sun has yet to burn off, and dips below the sprawling holly tree.

"Junie," Eddie whispers.

She turns and veers toward him. "Thank God."

The rest of the women are up in the attic, sifting through old stuff and choking on freshly disturbed layers of dust. Junie only has a few minutes before she'll need to get back.

"You ready for our debut?" Junie asks.

She needs this to seem legitimate, so she's staged this moment for Eddie to "stop by" and sell the story of them as lovebirds who can't stand too many hours strung together without each other's touch.

"Not sure I have much choice." Eddie's face stays slack.

"So no PDA or any of that nonsense, please, but just be nice and act like you're into me. Got it?"

"Dang, Junie." Eddie pulls her under his arm and squeezes as she wriggles. "You really think I'm going to try to plant one on you? I'm barely a willing participant."

"Fortunately, no," she says. "Thanks for saving my rear. *Again*."

Junie slips out from under Eddie's arm, waves farewell, and walks around to the front of the house. She pushes through the front door, skips up the stairs, and climbs into the attic. The basic wooden ladder creaks as she pulls herself up step by step, and as she crosses into this space under the roof, the air turns thick. It's warm from the late-summer heat baking the sparkly shingles above, and the air is hazy thanks to flecks of dust and dander the women have disturbed from their years-long slumber.

There's only a single window, set in the dormer on the front of the house. The nook could be cozy with a bit of cleaning, proper finishing, and air-conditioning.

"Thought you'd ditched us there for a minute, Junie," Cece says from behind a stack of boxes labeled *Girls Stuffed Animals 1996*. "Check this out. There's three more just the same."

"They can't all be full of stuffed animals," Junie says.

"I'd believe it," Georgia calls over. "Don't you remember that was Mama's favorite thing to buy us?"

Junie does. She remembers having so many of them lined up on her bed that she had to angle her pillow to sleep, her comfort secondary to that of her plush animals. How much of this stuff was saved because it was a treasure, and how much is simply stuff that lived in conjunction with Mama, so it was boxed up and put away? Because she's sure she doesn't need to spend hours combing through her childhood stuffed animals, not when there's so much else to be done. Not when it's going to force her to relive the last years they had with Mama.

"Y'all should definitely save those for keepsakes," Tina says.

Junie thinks Tina dabs a tear at the corner of her eye. It could also just be the dust.

Georgia calls over, "Maybe *some*." Her voice wobbles a little, then she leans back down to the box she's working through.

It's the same for all of them, finding themselves in dusty spots or with shaky voices far too often. Junie suspects every one of them misses Mama just about the same as the day she left them.

Junie is about to open her mouth to say something about it, maybe ask them if they feel the same, when Daddy calls up, "Junie, you have a visitor."

Georgia was right. This time should be Louises only—and even if the Louise name could be earned, Eddie hasn't yet qualified. Georgia knew, like she always does, that this would be an emotional crawl through things left behind. Georgia knew it would be hard.

Junie shouldn't have invited Eddie.

CHAPTER 23

GEORGIA

I SHOULDN'T BE SURPRISED WHEN Eddie Rigsby pops his head up into the attic of my childhood home and shuffles over to Junie. He gives her a platonic side hug (the chasteness for my benefit, I'm sure) and waves.

"You ladies are making quick work of this," Eddie says.

I was already shaky from the memories of Mama in here, and now he's here, and my knees are jelly, and I just want to melt and cry, but maybe I'll just scream. Not now, I can't—

Tina jumps in. "Are you up for lugging some boxes downstairs? That ladder's a bit wobbly for me."

I turn back to my boxes, tucking myself behind a row of them. I'm doing my best to be happy for Junie and Eddie, but just looking at them burns a little. I'm already being forced to revisit the loss of Mama up here; I don't need my Eddie scars resurrected at the same time.

"Eddie isn't staying," Junie says. "It's supposed to be 'Louises only,' remember? But I'm sure he could take something down on his way out."

"*Just stopping by*, huh?" Tina bites a grin. "Awful sweet."

"Stop." Junie swats at Tina playfully then slings an adoring glance at Eddie.

"For once I agree with Georgia," Cece says from the other end of the attic. "There's a mountain of work here. We don't need puppy dog eyes slowing us down."

"Let him take the heavy stuff down, and then we'll send him on his way," Junie says.

"Sounds good!" I yell from behind my barricade of boxes across the attic.

It comes out far too loud, and I stay in my hiding spot.

It feels like the sound I made gets stuck up there with us. I just hope it gets easier to watch my little sister dating the only man I've ever truly loved. Even the sound of it is absurd—something impossible by definition. But I don't have a choice, and I won't make a stink—that's what big sisters do. Sure, I probably went a bit far saying I was *giving my blessing*, like some half-wit in charge, but I also caused Eddie a boatload of hurt in the past, so who am I to deny him a bit of happiness now? Maybe karma is a thing after all.

Eddie lets the aunts load him up with an overstuffed box and shouts an enthusiastic "Good luck!" behind him as he navigates his way down the ladder.

His absence feels like a reprieve. Not that I should be lingering on my bruised heart when I was the one responsible for it. Despite my culpability, the memories become noisy in my head and the dense air around me is too much. I'm desperate for a fresh breath, a moment away from the important-unimportant stuff that my mother once touched. So I can think.

I wait a few minutes to make sure Eddie is gone, then drag myself out from behind the boxes and perch on a stack of *National Geographic* magazines. "What can I haul down?"

"I got a load of old Christmas decorations over here that no one's touched in years," Cece says. "Nothing sentimental. Just limp tinsel and cracked bulbs."

I weave my way over to her and take the box. "I'll trash this and be back after I grab a glass of water."

I shimmy down the attic ladder, balancing the light box on my palm. I plop onto the carpeted hallway with a muted thud and continue down the stairs. When I round the corner into the kitchen, I slam front first into a person, and the box launches out of my hand and flies across the room, leaving a sprinkling of Christmas behind.

My father stands in front of me. He adjusts his glasses, runs a hand down the front of his button-up, and sets his eyes on me.

"Hey, Dad." I smile, noticing he's a bit grayer at his temples than I remember. He was out for a walk in the woods when we arrived this morning and let ourselves in. "Just getting this old Christmas stuff to the trash. Might need to schedule an extra trash pickup now that I'm thinking of it."

I bend and start grabbing gnarled strings of bulbs and winding stray tinsel around my hands into Christmassy bird's nests. My father lowers himself beside me, reaches for an ornament and begins turning it for examination.

"I can handle the trash," he says. "But I'm surprised you're still here and all—seeing as it's a workday. You have a minute?" He nods at the breakfast table.

I follow him over to the table, where I place the box and sit. "What's up?"

Dad pulls a chair out slowly and takes his time getting comfortable. He smiles. "It's so good to see your face, Georgia. We're so proud of you, but we sure miss you."

"I know, but I'm here now," I say.

He nods, then places a finger over his lips, creases his brow, and puts on his thinking look. After a moment he sucks in a breath. "I'm a little worried about your sister."

I realize in that moment that I don't know how much of the situation Junie has looped him in on. Arguably, he would've asked questions about why we're setting up a garage sale of his things. I decide the safest bet is to reveal as few facts as possible in the course of the conversation. "I think she's just got a lot on her mind with the shop."

He nods. "Yes, I know all about that hullaballoo. Well, mostly. I think. Do you think she's . . . *alright*?"

I sigh in a tone I hope is understanding. "Construction in your place of work is stressful, Dad, so probably she's not her normal self. But from what I can see, she's stepping up and managing the situation as best she can."

"It's just—it's not only the shop. She seems off. Maybe she's just embarrassed about the whole situation and avoiding me, but she rarely takes my calls and when she does, she's always rushing off somewhere."

It wouldn't surprise me if Junie's trying to downplay the extent of the problem to him. She has always wanted to prove that she can stand on her own two feet. "She's working hard to fix her mistake. I don't think there's much else we could ask."

"Guess that's what I've always wanted from her." He chuckles. "Maybe soon enough she'll be handling it all and you'll be off the hook."

He says it like it's a best-case outcome for me, having no practical reason to come back, no longer being called upon to tag in. Little does he know they are some of my favorite moments.

I start to stand. "I'll keep an eye on her, but the others will have my head if they think I'm just down here shooting the breeze while they're sweating their rears off up there."

Dad pats the table efficiently. "Of course."

When I grab my box, the grocery bags on the other side of the table shift, revealing the contents. Mama's old recipe book sits beside.

"I've been trying out baking in my retirement." Dad's cheeks flush. "Learned quite a bit so far." He takes the bags and moves them over to the counter.

Dad worked at the local bank as his primary job for decades, his accounting at June's always his part-time, after-hours gig.

"Very cool. You know they say keeping active in retirement is important." I stand. "I should head up. See you in a bit."

I return to the attic thinking about my father baking. It's a swirl of fondness and sadness inside me. Because I know it's an attempt to feel close to her. He misses her just like the rest of us upstairs. It was the only directive he gave us: *Don't take anything of June's, but otherwise have at it.*

As I rise through the gap in the ceiling, the physical presence of Mama feels like a warm, welcoming hug. No wonder she is missed in the flesh.

CHAPTER 24

JUNIE

THE OTHER LOUISE WOMEN ARE pricing items pulled from the attic yesterday in preparation for tomorrow's garage sale, but Junie has taken a last-minute emergency hair appointment. She unlocks the shop and flips on the few remaining lights. In her other hand rattles a cup holder with two iced coffees from the cute place up the street that always smells like cinnamon. Hopefully it makes up—at least a pinch—for the lack of decor.

Junie sets down the coffees on the tiny workstation Tina set up for them and spritzes an air freshener that promises Spring Rain. They discussed the makeshift setup yesterday in the attic and agreed to keep the stations as clean and as cute as humanly possible. Tina even came by after she left Daddy's house and spruced it a bit more, adding a glam mirror and even pasting up a few Dolly items. Junie smiles to herself as she wipes down the chair and double-checks the station for products she'll need. She's grateful she asked the guys demoing the shop to keep both washbasins in place all those weeks ago. Without them there would be no appointments—licensed or not.

Michaela Rogers texted yesterday afternoon saying, 911 hair color emergency. She stopped in at a salon on vacation and has been wearing a hat since. Michaela and Junie were friends in high school, both involved in the musical theater community. Michaela took to behind-the-scenes work while Junie remained center stage, fighting for a prime role in each production.

Like always, Michaela walks in right on time. She calls into the space, "You said you wouldn't laugh, right?"

"Don't you remember when I tried to do my own hair for my part as Cruella de Vil?" Junie says.

Michaela chuckles. "I'm basically Cruella's sister."

Junie snags the second coffee from its perch and slips it into Michaela's hand. "Well, you've come to the right place."

Junie walks over to the prepped chair station, waving Michaela to follow.

Michaela pulls off her cap, and as promised she reveals a mottled mess that looks like someone tie-dyed her dark blonde hair. "I wanted something beachy, just a few highlights, but the girl talked me into doing some silver highlights. Anyway, I think she just bleached patches then made others gray but not in a pretty way. We were both too embarrassed by the end of the process to do anything other than part ways."

Junie frowns empathetically along with the retelling. "She should have her license taken."

Michaela shrugs. "I'm starting to wonder if she ever had one."

Junie launches into her go-to botched hair pep talk. She starts by promising that the experience will make for a great story at parties and then goes straight to tooting her own horn and explaining how easily she can fix it. Call her Fairy Godmother, she practically has a wand. Her plan is to start by making the hair one color.

"Maybe you can make me brunette for a little while?" Michaela suggests.

Junie agrees, jumping and clapping in delight, before she goes to the storage closet to dig out a chocolaty shade that will complement

Michaela's complexion. She mixes the color efficiently and wastes no
time in applying it.

"So what's actually going on here?" Michaela asks, flapping her
hands at the interior. "No offense, but this place has seen better days.
Was there a leak or something?"

Junie sighs with her whole body. "I screwed up—as usual. Got a
great deal with Goldilocks Haircare for a reno, but it turns out we
didn't have the money to finish up the project. Now we're scrambling
to make money to get this place operational—me and Georgia and
the aunts."

"Let us sponsor you!" Michaela says. "The community theater.
You know I'm over there, directing and organizing. We charge for
tickets, and the proceeds go to a good cause. We're always looking
for something local that will touch our own community."

Junie stops and considers it. They could probably raise several
grand, at least. The theater isn't small, and the seats are always filled.

"That's really nice of you—"

"Don't let me hear you say no," Michaela jumps in. "This town
loves June's. We'd probably have folks two to a seat, filling up the
aisles, getting the fire marshal called on us."

Junie giggles. This shop really does belong to the town. To everyone. All of them. But this was supposed to be her moment to prove
herself, to show everyone she was up for this job.

"Can I let you know?" she says.

Michaela nods. She knows that's not a no.

"Speaking of fire marshals—and those who aspire to be officers of
the law," Junie says. "Do you know Misty Prince?"

Michaela turns and eyes her. "I mean, I wish I didn't, but who
doesn't around here?"

Junie scoffs. "Well, she's trying to get us in trouble. Almost
made Tina cry in the grocery store, said she'd report us to the

licensing board if we keep doing hair in here while this place is under construction."

"Ah," Michaela says. "I'm going to have to cover for us in that case. She and her kids were at the pool yesterday. Of course, she couldn't help but ask about my hair—"

"Because she can't mind her own dang business for a hot second."

"And I said I was gonna come see you and have you fix it. I'll just make sure she knows you did it at your house as a friend. Not as a service in the shop."

Junie lets out a breath of relief. "Thanks. She's such a pest."

"And poor Tina. Not that it takes much to make her cry, but Misty should know better."

"Don't I know it."

"She kick Randy out yet?" Michaela asks.

"What do you think?"

"Bless her."

Junie steps back and, happy with the coverage on Michaela's hair, sets a timer to wash out. "Alright, time to let this soak in. Want a magazine while you sit, hon?"

"Nah, I'm going to do some email on the phone," Michaela says.

Junie pulls over a stool and rests on it gratefully. Although she likes to joke about it with Eddie, her bones, her hips mostly, have started to ache. It's probably from being on her feet so much plus being sick. She hasn't even started chemo yet.

Eddie will certainly make her tell Georgia and the others before then.

The truth is, Junie knows she needs to start treatment. Even if she does act like a bit of a child to Eddie, dismissing his pleas, she wrestles with the idea of telling her family each and every night. Hence the insomnia she's been battling.

She's not a complete idiot—only a partial one.

She could use their help. She could use their shoulders to cry on. She could use every tissue passed and every meal cooked as she faces down the cruelty of reliving this nightmare her family has endured once already. But how could she? She doesn't have a choice about going through it, but she does have the option to save them from the pain of watching her suffer the treatment, the heartache of every reminder of Mama. To let them sit this one out.

Because this *could* be something fixable. Maybe Junie could get through the treatment and clue them in once the storm has passed. It would be optimistic to believe it might be so easy, probably overly optimistic. At worst, naive. It's difficult to make heads or tails of where optimism ends and denial starts. Perhaps she's inventing ambiguity where it doesn't exist.

Movement outside catches Junie's eye, a figure lurking suspiciously. Her brain shuffles the puzzle pieces together quickly, and she leaps up and over to Michaela. Junie half pulls her from the chair as she whisper-yells, "Quick! Get in the back."

Michaela, thanks to her trust in Junie, follows directions and jogs into the back office, then shuts the door quietly behind her, no questions asked.

Junie pulls off the apron she had on to protect her clothes from the hair color and tosses it behind some stacked boxes. She pulls her shoulders back and marches outside and turns to look at the front window. By this time, she sees the woman with her face practically smooshed against the glass, shamelessly peering inside.

"Misty," Junie demands.

Misty turns and doesn't even have the decency to look embarrassed. Her blonde hair is big and bouncy, and if she weren't such a miserable human, Junie might complement her on it. She's head to toe in athletic wear that looks expensive—probably thanks to her ex-husband, a surgeon who still resides in Atlanta and who rumor says granted her a generous divorce settlement in exchange for her moving on and out of his life.

"I saw someone in there," Misty says. "You know you're not supposed to be doing hair while the place is under construction." She crosses her arms over her chest and saunters a few steps closer.

"First, I'm not doing hair. I was chatting about design plans with a friend over coffee." It's not *untrue*. "And even if I was, why would you care? Don't you drive to that salon in Atlanta for your services?"

Misty pats her hair. "You can't expect me to hand this mane over to *you*." She tuts. "And it doesn't matter what I think. The law is the law."

Junie shoves down a sigh. "What are you, the hair police? No one is getting hurt here. Nothing's been stolen. Why don't you go home to your brood of Chihuahuas?"

The pack of yappy dogs is as infamous as their owner.

Misty turns and begins to walk to her car. She stops halfway, like she's thought of something, turns back, and says, "I'm going to catch you red-handed if you keep this up, Junie Louise."

Junie waves as Misty cranks the car and takes off. She doesn't even correct her that she's Junie Scott. Maybe it's because they call themselves Louises.

Junie dips back inside the shop. By now it's almost time to wash out Michaela's hair.

CHAPTER 25

GEORGIA

I T'S THURSDAY, GARAGE SALE DAY. Anything halfway valu-
able from Dad's attic is displayed on the sidewalk outside June's
Beauty Shop, plus a few things Junie and I were able to scrape together
from the Clementine House. We've got music playing, food laid out,
and only then, at second glance, do I realize it's more like a party than
a garage sale.

It's a June's sale.

Truly, it's moments like these when I cannot help but believe that
my mama is alive and breathing in the bones of this little beauty shop.
Maybe it's when we come together like a brood of witches that we
magic her out of our cauldron by way of a collision of all things right.

The sun shines so brightly, and the sky is such a crisp blue. Tina
is only an outline until she's right in front of me. Her bob is perfect,
but I don't have time to complement her.

"I've got lotto news!" she squeals. "Let's circle up."

"You grab Cece, I'll get Junie," I tell her, then turn to head inside.

The interior of the shop is as wrecked as we left it, but I can hear
the quiet clinks of Junie cleaning the sink in preparation for a secret
client this afternoon.

"That's the spirit," I call over.

"It's like putting a Band-Aid on a flesh wound, but what can we do but our best?" Junie glances at me, smiling.

"Come on. Tina's got the lotto numbers, and she's tickled about something."

Junie lets out a joyful yelp. "Maybe it's the answers to all our prayers! Maybe Mama sent us a lotto win!"

I pull my delightfully optimistic sister under my arm and squeeze. "A girl can dream."

Once we step out into the late-afternoon sunshine, we're met by the hum of a lingering crowd and the gentle croon of a love ballad on the Bluetooth speaker. We posted news of the sale on our Instagram and then tapped the trusty Whitetail phone tree that's recently migrated to text. Each person knows who to text to keep the news flowing, and many even shared it on their own social media. Many people made arrangements to be here, making up missed work at another time, coverage to slip in and out so everyone can take a gander at what the Louises have set out. Because that's what this town does: They show up.

Junie smiles. "This didn't turn out so bad after all."

I tuck my head toward her and under my breath say, "Let's see how the numbers look at the end."

Tina marches up with Cece trailing behind her, and we form a small circle on the wraparound sidewalk.

"Alright, ladies, gird your loins!" Tina announces.

Junie and I exchange a grin.

Tina clears her throat. "We, Good Hair Days ladies, are lotto winners!"

Cece's expression lifts to something less than bothered. "For real? What's the number?"

"Well," Tina says. "It's not a ton. Mainly I'm taking this win as a sign from the heavens or June or Dolly—"

"Dolly Parton is still alive and well," Junie says.

"You know what I mean," Tina says. "Anyway, we won forty dollars."

Cece sighs. I feel like doing the same, but I hold back.

"I guess that'll cover food and bev on the cheap for the next meeting?" Junie says cautiously.

"That's our girl." Tina claps. "It may just be a little, but we're making our way. Now, if you don't mind, I'll be heading to the gas station to cash in. Meeting adjourned!"

Cece shoots us a look and takes off, shaking her head.

"Oh well?" I flash Junie a cringy, hopeful smile.

Junie melts into laughter. Her body is up against mine, under my arm, and I feel her shaking and wiggling. I look at her, and I hope she can see every bit of my utter delight in her all over my face.

"What on earth would I do without you?" I say.

I think this is the part about my sister, and me and her as a unit, that no one else will ever understand. My keeping of Junie is my love lived out loud. It's not a burden or an obligation; it's my adoration of her spelled out in tangible acts. I don't begrudge her a single bit because it doesn't take anything on my part to create the love. Even when I pour it out in senseless undertakings like our money-making schemes and our underground girls' meetings, it's never a bit depleted. It continues, as if it's a person as much as we are.

Eventually Junie squeezes out from under my arm and takes off between the small clusters of shoppers like the wild mustang she is, and I wave goodbye.

The feeling of her closeness stays with me, which is perhaps why I'm feeling strangely calm about the fact that I only have a couple more days before I have to go back to work. The longer I stay here, the more I feel like I'm doing work that truly matters, work that even if its progress is slow or imperceptible is moving in the direction of where I want to be.

Part of me feels like there's a bigger reason for my being here than just the ticker of the bank account shooting for fifty thousand.

I stop and close my eyes to really feel the sun on my skin. I hear the chatter of voices—our customers, I hope. I turn to the crowd and wander over to Cece, who seems to be losing a negotiation with a shark of a customer.

"That's far too low a price," Cece says.

"She's right. Absolutely too low," I say.

It's an eighteenth-century framed oil painting. Granted, the Met won't be calling to see if they might hang it in their next exhibit, but the fifty-dollar price tag (with a slight wiggle) is more than fair.

The man looks over to me. "Best I can do is thirty."

"Well, I guess you'd better be on your way," I say with a sweet smile.

He turns and huffs off, and Cece shoots me an icy look.

"I don't need your help," she says. "You may be a fancy business-person, but I also run a small business. I've got this."

Her reaction cuts me back to earth, almost so much that I feel mud between my toes. "Sorry," I say. "I was just trying to help."

From across the lot I see Eddie arrive. He stops at the edge and scans the crowd, and once he sets eyes on Junie, he makes a straight cut through the crowd to her. She leaps into his arms, and he welcomes her into a family-friendly bear hug. They rock back and forth, chatting and eventually laughing. Envy creeps into my chest in a hot burn.

Stop, I tell myself. *This is your own doing.*

When Junie finally extricates herself from Eddie's sturdy arms (which I unfortunately have experienced firsthand), she heads my way. Eddie raises a hand in greeting, and I return the gesture.

"Thanks for everything, Peach," Junie says as she passes me and enters the beauty shop.

Thanks for Eddie is what I hear.

A silver-haired lady pulls up in a wide sedan, parks, and hops out. She must be a regular, one of the appointments Junie agreed to keep. Likely one of the Silvers, the affectionate name folks use around here for the silver-haired ladies who tend to gather at churches and restaurants and sometimes walk laps at the high school track in the early morning. She lingers near the front door like she's casually leaning against the wall, then after she looks both ways, she slips inside the entrance.

Those Silvers sure do know how to follow a directive.

I smile. The Silvers always remind me of Mama. The lot of them have been tried-and-true customers at June's since forever, and they were Mama's favorites. She'd gab with them for hours, feeding and serving them drinks just to keep them and their stories flowing in her space. They're our A-list clients, if we have any.

They're also known as good shepherds in the community—cooking for funerals, cooking when babies are born, delivering flowers to the hospital.

I turn around, take three steps, and slam straight into someone. I look up and see a cosmetically enhanced face, slathered in heavy makeup and framed in blonde layers, staring back. Misty Prince.

"Misty, hi," I say, praying she didn't see anyone go into the shop, but judging from the direction she came from, I hope she's just arriving. "Surprised to see you at a *garage sale*."

Misty pulls her sunglasses from her hair. "Home for the big event? Didn't think workaholics like you took days off. And for the record, no, this is definitely not my thing." Her lips turn up at the end.

I pull a fake smile. "Any day now we'll have the shop finished and a grand reopening on the books."

Misty leans in and winks. "Reopening, *sure*. And you know the real reason I'm here is to keep y'all aboveboard. You Louises think you run this town, but there's a new sheriff now."

Misty stands and looks at me, and I wonder if I'm supposed to gasp or rush for clarification, but I have neither the energy nor the desire for it. "Alright."

I cross my arms and watch her disappear into the crowd. Once I'm sure she's not watching, I text Junie a warning, and a minute later she sends back a picture of her and her client sheltering in the supply closet. I keep my eye on Misty as she winds in and out of the crowd. Before long she climbs back up into her massive SUV with empty hands and drives off in the direction of her gaudy McMansion.

CHAPTER 26

JUNIE

J UNIE IS INSIDE THE SHOP, finishing up a trim on Ms. Luanne, as the garage sale buzzes in the background. Ms. Luanne loves to keep her short bob precise and perfect, so Junie sees her regularly.

"So they've just kinda left y'all stranded on the build? I tell you, some of the contractors these days . . ." Ms. Luanne says.

"It's a bit more complicated than that." Junie goes on to explain the rest in broad strokes.

"Well, me and the rest of the ladies at the church would be glad to host a fundraiser for you."

Junie smiles. "That's very kind. I'm a bit set on doing this myself, but I might end up taking you up on it."

Junie pulls the cape from her shoulders, and Ms. Luanne climbs out of the hair chair.

"Just as I like it." Ms. Luanne pats her hair from the bottom. "Make sure to call if you change your mind about help."

"Yes, ma'am."

As Miss Luanne pushes out of the door, another visitor grabs it before it can close all the way.

A mother and her child, about eight or nine years old, walk in.

"How can I help you?" Junie asks.

The woman looks around and takes in the half-demolished interior.

"We were just at All-Star Cuts and they said they wouldn't take my son, so I wanted to see if you could cut his hair."

Junie doesn't want the jock's secondhand clients, and she should be more careful about seeing strangers, but her curiosity wins out. "Really? I thought they had tons of openings."

The woman shrugs. "I thought so too, but they took a look at us and suggested we come here."

"You're not a friend of Misty Prince, are you?" Junie asks with a suspicious squint.

The woman rolls her eyes. "The opposite, in fact. She's the reason I got a fine from the HOA for my tree growing a branch into another neighbor's yard. It wasn't even her yard! My neighbor couldn't have cared less."

The whole All-Star setup strikes Junie as weird, but after the kid stops scratching at his head, Junie directs him to the chair. It's a quick appointment: wet, comb, and trim. She works quickly because something about this doesn't feel right, and it's probably because Junie's breaking licensing regulations with these newcomers from whom she's not sure she can expect discretion.

The mom smiles and hands Junie cash. "You're fabulous," she says. "Thank you for this. We're doing family pictures tomorrow, and I'm hoping for a decent set."

"No problem," Junie says. "We're always here. Y'all regulars at All-Star Cuts?"

What Junie hopes to hear is some nitty-gritty ugly stuff.

"Not after this." The woman smiles. "They weren't ugly about sending us on our way, but I didn't like it either. All the chairs were open, so I didn't quite believe they didn't have fifteen minutes for a boy's cut."

"I might have to agree," Junie says. "And thanks for being patient with our construction here."

"No worries." The mom waves as they exit.

Junie crosses her arms, feeling better about the situation. She's found a new client, and if All-Star wants to turn away paying customers, June's will welcome them with open arms.

The door swings back open and Ms. Sherry, fellow church lady and bestie to Ms. Luanne, steps inside.

"Saw Luanne on her way out," Sherry says. "Now, we really are serious about helping out if you want. All of us love this place . . ."

Junie appreciates these women. Truly. But she just really wants to do this on her own—well, with the Good Hair Days ladies.

"Thanks, Ms. Sherry. Come on over and take a seat."

Junie's phone chimes in her pocket, and while her client gets comfortable, she reaches in and pulls it out.

It's her email.

And her genetic testing results are in.

She types a frantic text to Eddie, telling him to meet her later at the Clementine.

Then she pulls in a deep but discreet breath and looks to Ms. Sherry in the mirror in front of them. "Same as usual today?"

CHAPTER 27

GEORGIA

I AM EXTENDED ACROSS JUNIE'S SOFA, my swollen feet propped on the arm as they pulse for relief. We sold almost everything we set out for the garage sale, so we can count on several hundred dollars. If nothing else, it's a step. For now, I'll celebrate with something delicious and comforting to eat for dinner. I wonder if Junie would prefer pizza or Chinese.

Junie rattles the front doorknob and bursts in along with a warm breeze.

I sit up, Puds raising his head where he lies beside me, and Junie startles when her eyes land on me. She almost freezes in surprise. Eddie bustles in behind her and bumps into her since she stopped so quickly in front of him. It makes sense. Junie must've forgotten I was here, and this is some sort of romantic rendezvous.

"Oh. You're here," Junie says, not hiding her disappointment over my presence one bit.

A small hurt wells in my chest, and I swallow it. "Actually, I was thinking about heading to Dad's." I won't make things uncomfortable by mentioning the dinner plans I assumed we had.

Junie nods. "Ok." Her expression is flat in a way that is unusual for her. Maybe this is the new normal of my sister dating my ex.

And honestly, out of their hair is precisely where I want to be.

Junie heads toward the kitchen where she sheds her purse, two different beverages, and whatever the last item was she had tucked under her arm. Eddie stands in the doorway unmoved. His eyes linger on me in a way that looks serious, and I wonder if he's thinking about all the ways I've hurt his feelings. His mouth drops open, and I wait for him to say something. He should be honest with me.

I don't deserve his warmth, nor his generosity. His deep brown eyes, a carbon copy of his mother's, are warm like antique woodwork. His hair is thick and just long enough to be considered shaggy.

I'm sorry is what I want to say, and now for the first time not because I think it'll win him back.

Solely because I want him to know I regret it all.

Somehow, as if he reads my mind, Eddie presses his lips together in a tight line of a smile, then drops his gaze. The way someone does right after they say *I'm sorry too.*

He follows Junie into the kitchen, and I scurry to the guest room. I shut the door behind me and take several deep breaths. It's probably the one good part about the fact that I can't stay, that I'll be out of this horrific love triangle. That Eddie and I won't ever have to awkwardly rehash any of what happened between us, not in the face of what he's created with Junie.

It's only a matter of days until I'm forced back to Atlanta, and I can get busy with forgetting about him and the two of them together.

I change my clothes quickly, stopping only to text my dad to let him know I'm coming over. Thankfully I still have my key, so worst-case scenario I'll let myself in. Who knows what social engagements my father keeps these days, now that he's fully embracing his retirement.

When I pop open the bedroom door and slip out into the common area, Junie and Eddie have presumably gone behind her bedroom door that is currently closed.

Ick. I keep moving, out the front door, to my car, inside it, and onto the road.

I think the worst part of this Junie-and-Eddie setup isn't even my missing out on Eddie or the way it highlights my shortcomings, the way I'm emotionally stunted when it comes to people beyond my family. It's the fact that I'm not getting this time with Junie, that our girls' nights at the Clementine are no longer automatic events, that she has something to look forward to and enjoy that doesn't include me.

I take a turn and head up the winding road that leads to Dad's house.

CHAPTER 28

JUNIE

JUNIE PUSHES THE BEDROOM DOOR shut after Eddie and Puds pass in. He pulls the chair out from her desk and sits.

"I don't know what to do," Junie says, pacing back and forth in front of him, jamming her hands through her hair.

Eddie pulls in a deep breath. "You have to look at the results. Whenever you're ready."

Junie continues pacing. He makes it sound so simple, which is probably easy being in the doctor seat as opposed to the patient seat. And this time it's not even just the patient seat; it's *whether Georgia missed it*. Junie has thought about it, and if the results show that she has the breast cancer gene, she won't be upset with her sister. Georgia did her best, and to be fair, she was a high schooler at the time herself. In fact, if blame is to be parsed out, it should probably be assigned to their father for not being more involved, for not waking himself up from his grief slumber for long enough to be the grown-up in the room. Georgia had to fill that role so often back then. Now that Junie's an adult, she can't believe half the things they did unsupervised while their dad floundered.

Still, none of this is about blame.

"What is this even about?" Junie demands. Eddie is the only other person in the room, but it's clear she's asking a greater power. "These doctors care so much about figuring out where this comes from, and why? So it can rip my big sister and me apart? I've already got the cancer. We're well past 'preventative measures.'" Junie throws aggressive air quotations around the two words.

Eddie sits quietly and lets her rip.

When she finally slumps onto the bed, exhausted, Eddie says, "You don't *have* to open it."

Junie perks up, eyes wide at the presumed out.

"Georgia *will* ask, I'll tell you that," he says. "So if you don't want to open it, you'll have to be prepared to tell Georgia you're unwilling to revisit the results."

Junie sits all the way up, swallows hard, and nods. There isn't a possibility Georgia wouldn't hunt down the results on her own. Sure, there's HIPAA, but Georgia would figure something out. Heck, there's probably a box, now freshly dusted in Daddy's attic, with all their medical records.

Junie grabs her phone and silently opens her email. She looks to the heavens and then to Eddie, with fat tears in her eyes. A shaky breath escapes her as her chest wavers.

"I'm right here, Junie," Eddie says gently.

Junie nods. She freezes. "Can you . . . Will you read it?"

Eddie looks into her eyes for a long pause. "Are you sure that's the right thing?"

It's not. More than ever, it's time for her to step up. Junie drops her gaze to the phone, opens the email, and taps on the attachment. It's the old test results from 2010, scanned from a printed form with the expected shading. Junie zooms in on the opening lines, struck by how unofficial the sea of sentences strung together looks. She reads the first line in bold.

No variations for genes detected.

Junie's heart leaps and she sucks in a breath. She holds out the phone to Eddie. "Look, look here, no variations were found in the genes. Georgia read it right. It's negative."

Eddie takes the phone swiftly and looks. He stares into the screen, his hand shifting up and down slightly as he navigates. Finally, he sighs and shakes his head. When his eyes meet Junie's, they glisten with the promise of tears.

"I'm so sorry," Eddie says. "This is not a negative test." He jumps up and spikes the phone into Junie's bed and growls.

Junie is frozen, and it's like watching a photo finishing in reverse. She just made the same mistake Georgia did. Right here in current day at thirty years old.

Eddie begins to pace. "They should be sued. This is malpractice. I'm sure there's already a class action—"

"Eddie." Junie's tone stops him in his tracks. "Tell me what this means."

Eddie shakes off his train of thought and settles back in the chair. Junie sees the moment he clicks back into doctor mode. "The form states that no variants were found in the genes, and although that's true, if you continue reading, they go on to explain that this is not the same as a negative result. It says they have reason to believe the sample may have been contaminated because of other aberrations in the controls. Essentially, each sample is tested for multiple markers to make sure the blood being tested is clean and presenting an accurate result. When the controls come back wrong, that tells us the sample isn't right. Sometimes it's bacteria, mishandling in the lab, even slight errors in the lab tech's steps." Eddie reaches out and squeezes Junie's forearm. "I'm so sorry, Junie. None of this is your fault. Or Georgia's. All the results paper should've said was that you needed to retest. Do it again for re-liable results."

Dread wells inside Junie. They could've known. They could've prevented her illness if she'd had the same surgery as Georgia. And it became serious so quickly. This is the answer to the doctors' confusion because this aggressive type is more likely to occur with the gene; they struggled to marry a negative result with this type of breast cancer in her family history.

Junie *can't* tell Georgia now. Her sister does a whole lot of things well, but the thing she prides herself on most is how she does things thoroughly and precisely—and how she protects her little sister. Georgia made an honest mistake, put in a position she shouldn't have been in at that age. If only Junie had just made the mistake herself, but of course she didn't have the guts to open her own results envelope.

Junie looks at Eddie. "We can't tell her this."

Eddie's face squeezes in concern. "I know what you're saying." He pauses, his leg beginning to bounce up and down as he thinks. "But can I be honest?"

Junie nods, even though she doesn't really mean it. She doesn't want honest. She wants him to agree with her assessment, no questions asked.

"It will be impossible to hide this illness from Georgia, from any of the family, at a certain point—one that's rapidly approaching. And Georgia isn't going to sit on the sidelines. Hell, she'll probably set up remote work and stay by your bedside. But what I'm saying is that she's going to involve herself in the details. So when she finds out, you have two choices. First, you can spend your treatment whispering to nurses not to mention the genetics, skirting around certain medical questions, and spending your energy on keeping up this lie—which will likely eventually come out anyway. Or second, you can be honest. You can tell Georgia that you don't blame her. That you made the same mistake yourself on the second read, even. It'll hurt, a permanent wound I'm sure. But then you can let her love on you and care for you, exactly as you'll need. You need Georgia now more than ever in your life, Junie, but you have to let her all the way in."

Tears are rolling down Junie's face by the time Eddie is finished talking. She hates all of this so much. The sickness, the genes that won't leave her family in peace, the mistake that she can't undo. But mostly the fact that she knows Eddie is right.

Junie pulls in a breath. "You're right, but I'm going to need some time to get used to the idea."

Eddie nods. "Of course."

The pair sit there in Junie's room in silence, Junie sniffling. Eventually she looks over at him. "I think I'm going to take a shower. Try to decompress a little."

Eddie gets to his feet. "Hug?"

Junie drops into his chest and lets him hold her like a stand-in brother. It reminds her that soon she and Georgia will have the same postrevelation hug, and she has to stop herself from shuddering. She pulls away.

"I'm here, ok?" Eddie says.

Junie nods, and together they walk from her room to the front door. It's a quiet goodbye, and when Eddie is gone, Junie makes a change to her plan. On second thought, she doesn't much like the sound of soaking in her misery, so she calls out, "Puds?"

The sound of nails clicking on hardwood announces the golden retriever's arrival as he emerges from her room where he had settled, his tail wagging in blond excitement.

Junie scratches his head and cups his face. "Wanna head to the garden, my best boy?"

She crosses the house to the back door, which she pops open as she slips into her clogs. Puds hops out with delight, and Junie pulls on her gardening gloves. She might be terribly sick, and she might have double the bad news to drop on Georgia, but for now, she can make something good out of the day. She looks up to the sky, covered in light gray clouds, and it begins to drizzle. Junie closes her eyes against it.

Maybe she'll see a rainbow.

CHAPTER 29

GEORGIA

I T's SATURDAY EVENING, AND IT's my first Cards night. As kids and teens, Junie and I were kept away by the aunts, who claimed Cards didn't even exist. It was done in good faith, putting space between us and an activity that was *technically* illegal. For a long time we played along, but we overheard enough to understand what was truly happening.

Once, we snuck out and spied from the wooded area behind the shop, but after less than thirty minutes of staring at the blank back side of the building, we gave up and went home. It was a terribly formulated spy plan, but we did have fun with the actual sneaking out part. In the years since, the aunts finally capitulated and admitted that Cards was for real; it wasn't like they had much choice once Junie started work at June's. But something, probably the way I felt like I didn't quite belong, kept me from joining in as well.

Tonight I have a front-row seat. The blinds are closed, the tables set, and the cash bar, my latest bright idea, is stocked and ready for customers. Really it's a long folding table I lugged in and covered with a tablecloth I found during the attic clean-out. But the bottles are lined up, cups stacked, and ice crispy in the cooler, so I call it customer ready. We don't exactly have a liquor license, but we're also hosting an illegal gambling event, so we're a little past splitting hairs on the *legality* of it all. Junie said they're always careful about the invite list, and I think once the crowd knows the proceeds are for the shop renovation, they'll be happy to continue keeping things quiet.

Cece breezes in the door and lets out a whistle as she eyes the bar. "Fancy."

I reach into my pocket and pull out a wad of cash, courtesy of my credit card's cash advance. I hand it to Cece, who pages through the bills. It's our buy-in, and Cece is playing our hands.

Tina comes out to the salon floor from the back holding a hair product with a spray top. "Did either of y'all try this root volumizer from Goldilocks yet? It says wet or dry hair."

Cece and I both shake our heads.

Tina shrugs, dips in front of the mirror, and begins spraying it into the roots of her bob. "My hair is just looking so limp these days." She pouts.

Cece walks over to the mirror and slides in beside. "Alright then, do mine too."

Tina turns and spritzes Cece's roots efficiently then tousles them with her fingers. "Oh, Cecelia, that really works on you!" She turns back and looks in the mirror. "Me? Less so."

"You look stunning too, Aunt T," I call over. I don't say that she can hardly expect at sixty to have the same volume she did at twenty. But she does. Because we're hair people, and we know that the right products paired with the right technique can defy the forces of nature.

She smiles back at me. "And you did a great job with those barrel curls tonight. Curling iron?"

Tina was always leery of the newfangled hair gadgets that came out and the large price tags that accompanied them.

I nod. "If it ain't broke."

Cece dips in front of the mirror for another look and pats her gray-streaked hair. "This is the perfect look to demolish the competition tonight. Which"—she glances at her watch—"I should get ready for."

Cece walks off with a swagger, like she's getting into the right headspace. The shop is probably looking the closest to a dive bar/casino than it ever has tonight, considering that most of the identifying qualities of a salon have been covered, removed, or plain ripped out. Part of me wishes I was seeing it in its usual state with tables set out between dryers and washbowls, an undeniably hair-related event.

Junie lumbers in the front door, dragging a massive trash can.

"How many we expecting?" I ask Junie as I straighten the bottles on the bar. If the size of the trash is saying anything, we should plan for a full house.

"Well, it's not exactly an RSVP kinda situation," Junie says.

"Alright," I say too brightly. "Just learning the ropes over here."

"You'll see," she says with a smile. "Once folks start to turn up, we just work with what we've got."

She starts a classic rock playlist, and it isn't long before guests trickle in. They don't expect military-grade planning and instead kind of filter out to whatever seat looks good. I'm surprised by some of the people who show—namely, the old librarian who runs the circulation desk with an iron fist. It seems the thrill of a bet isn't exclusive to one type or another.

Behind the makeshift bar, I pour. Bourbon, whiskey, gin, and the occasional beer, but everyone present seems intent on imbibing. The noise level grows as the crowd does, and never before have I felt June's Beauty Shop so full. Mama hummed on high just like this room does now, and it's the first time I feel like I fully understand her love for these nights. To her, the chatter and laughter, the fun and the thrill of a harmless bet must've been second nature. She knew joy like it was a phenomenon intertwined into the very fabric of her. Surely this would've been prime time for her belly laugh and fiery hair flips. I only wish I could've experienced this alongside her.

Junie stops at my side and whispers in my ear. "It's not usually this rowdy. I think it's this bar."

"Yeah?" I grab the cash box and pop it open. It's got at least double what we made at the garage sale. I hold it out for Junie to see, and I'm just about to gloat when a cackle breaks out across the room.

"What on earth," Junie says as we whip around to look.

It's Cece. She is ruddy and wobbly and slinging back the whiskey she brought for herself in a brown paper bag. Drunk as a skunk, as Mama would say. But she's at her posted table, and the players around her seem to be in the flow of the game.

"Is this normal for her?" I ask.

Junie makes a high-pitched noise that sounds like a no. "Again, it's not usually this rowdy. *She's* not usually this rowdy."

And usually Cece wins. *Usually* is what we want.

Junie grabs the bottles on my bar and eyes the level of the contents. "Yikes." She grabs a shot glass and hands it to me. "One and a half per drink, and no more. Else we'll be calling Sheriff Mike with a brawl on our hands."

"Sorry," I say. "You got it. I didn't realize I was heavy handing them."

I hang behind the bar for a while longer, eyeing my pours seriously, but eventually I loop around the tables to check on Cece. Her stack of chips certainly looks skinny compared to her tablemates', but who am I to know what that fully means? The truth is, I never learned how to play cards, nothing past Go Fish. Sure, I could've let anyone teach me poker, or taught myself with online tutorials even, but it would've felt like a sacrilege to go against our family practice. Like stealing my way into a guarded June's tradition, one that required an invite.

Once Louise women graduate beauty school and take a job at the shop, they're told about Cards nights. (Or in our case, the adults drop the pretending act.) And then they're taught the game of poker. I haven't ever stepped foot inside the beauty school, and even if the Cards nights were mentioned to me as something I could attend, I've yet to receive a single poker lesson. It's not like I've ever worked here, so I couldn't expect that. Maybe I'm being overly sensitive, but I've never felt truly invited, not when I'm not an employee here, when I didn't get the traditional beauty shop poker lesson and induction.

I'm rounding my way back to the bar table when the door blows open. Cece hollers at the doorway. "Well, this one ain't a regular." Her announcement sounds like an alarm, and all eyes fly to the newcomer. "Someone talk to him."

I, too, look over and am stopped, once again, by the sight of him now framed in moonlight on our doorstep.

He winces, sheepish, and clears his throat. "I was going to take my mom's spot tonight, if that's ok? I guess I should've called."

"Eddie?" I drop my dish towel and meet him at the door, scanning the room for Junie on my way. "You're here for Cards?"

Seeing him standing there caught out like an interloper compels me to go to him. Yes, I'm trying to keep my distance from Junie's beau, but I won't let the poor guy flounder as Cece suggests he might need interrogating. I'm not heartless, and I will always have a soft spot for the guy. Not to mention, I have some experience with feeling unwelcome at this event.

He runs a hand over his stubbled chin and his eyes flash. "I'm sorry," he says. "I figured it'd be informal."

I take his arm and guide him toward the bar like I would a regular. I pour him a bourbon straight, a safe bet, and hand it to him. "*Formal* may not be the word for it, but it's not open season. Did Junie tell you about it?"

He turns his head and takes in the activities laid out before him. He's already a foot taller than the crowd, which doesn't help his case for being an obvious newbie in the lot. "Not a word, actually. I thought it might be a little old ladies' game night."

I laugh and drop a hand onto the tabletop as I wait for him to go on. He is as cute as they come, it's simple fact, but now that I look again, maybe *cute* isn't the right word. He was once cute, back when he wore his wit and confidence like a suit two sizes too big. But now? He's grown into all of his charm, and it fits like it was tailored to every inch of him.

And it's all for Junie now.

"I heard the recording on my mother's machine." He watches my brow furrow at the mention of a machine. "Come on. You can't mean to tell me Rich doesn't have his old answering machine?"

"You got me there."

He nods slowly, like he's just now grasping the extent of his error. "There really isn't much to do around here on a Saturday night, so I figured I'd check it out . . ."

I pour myself a little drink, the first of the night, and tip it back. "You know, I don't remember a Rigsby on the call list . . ."

"You're right," he says. "Junie left a message for Gigi Ruiz yesterday—that's my mother's maiden name, so it made me wonder. Why would she use a name she hasn't used in decades for a regular old ladies' group?"

I pause to take a drink order, then turn back to our conversation.

"Part of me wondered if it was speed dating or something to do with romance—because of the name thing." Eddie laughs. "But I guess Ms. Ruiz *is* leading a double life—just not the kind I thought."

"Aren't we all in some way?" I say, surprising myself. "No one's ever *completely* all the way as they appear."

He considers it. "You're probably right."

Eddie holds my gaze too long, and in that moment all of the regrets between us swim through my mind—all of the good parts too. But I can't go there, so I drop my gaze, turn, and busy myself at the other end of the bar stacking cups that were just fine where they were before. It's then that a scream rings out.

Across the room, Cece rolls out of her chair, red in the face. My gut pinches at the sight.

"I'll be right back," I say to Eddie as I jog to my aunt's side.

My feet shuffle in leaps over the bare floor to the folding table. Junie is at my side, and together we grab and yank Cece from the floor and pitch her into her seat.

Tina flutters up to my side. "You ok?" She twitters over and over again, like a stuck record.

"What happened?" Junie asks.

"Nothing. Nothing at all." Cece brushes herself off, gathers the fallen cards, and taps them into a neat stack. "Just lost my balance for a moment. Hank, that wasn't a fair bet, and you know it!" Cece points a finger at the smug player across the table who reaches out and pulls in the entire pot. She looks so red-hot she might burst into flames.

"A word?" Junie asks as she bends down to speak into Cece's ear. She whispers, "Did you lose it all?"

Cece shrugs. She meets my eye and raises a finger right in my face. "It's you. You're the bad-luck charm. I've never lost like this before, and the only difference is you showing up here, lingering around."

The comment hits me like a punch to my chest. I stumble back from the blow.

"Cece, that's not fair. Not right," Junie says. "What is it you need? More money?"

Cece nods. "Then I'll get myself right back on track."

Junie looks to me.

All I have left is the money I'd set aside to make things right with Moon for my rent. But under the weight of the stares of these three women, in the middle of this shop that's practically an additional Louise, amid the constant hammering of expectation, it's not like I have a choice.

"Let me run to the ATM," I say.

CHAPTER 30

JUNIE

GEORGIA DIPS INTO THE BACK office, for her bag most likely, since she said she's heading out to the ATM.

Eddie sidles up beside Junie. "Is your aunt always that awful?" The tops of his ears are red; it's an Eddie-size serving of rage.

"The liquor seems to have made her meaner than ever tonight." Junie watches Cece chatting with a couple of neighbors near the bar, and she'd really like to march right up and smack her upside the head. "And just as I was thinking she'd gotten a bit softer on Georgia since we started this whole shebang."

"There's none of that tonight," Eddie says. "I'll go check on Georgia."

He's two steps away when Junie says, "Would you go with her?"

Not that Junie's in a great position to ask for *more* help from Eddie, but he might be alright with this request.

"Was already planning on it." He pats her on the back and heads in the direction Georgia disappeared.

A minute later they emerge from the back. Her cheeks are flushed like they always are when she's upset, and Eddie stays right at her side. There's something about the two of them together that seems so natural, almost predestined, as if their whole deal wasn't a ship fully sailed off the edge of the world.

They really are perfect for each other, or at least they were before Georgia took an ax to the relationship. Wouldn't it be perfect if they ended up together? Eddie's basically a brother to Junie now—having him permanently in their little Louise world would be a natural extension. It's not something Junie would've dreamed up, especially when both Eddie and Georgia were gone. But now, in a twist of fate, they're here. At the same time. Maybe it's the universe working in their favor.

CHAPTER 31

CECE

CECE STANDS AT THE BAR and pours herself a glass of water. She knows she is terrible; she never should've said that to Georgia. She didn't deserve it. It's just that the sight of her here in this infuriating beauty shop, giving the place loving looks, and getting comfy like she might easily be seduced out of her dreams by the charms of this place, its people, the fun that Cards undoubtedly becomes, she can't stand it. Cece can't let that happen.

Cece watched her twin sister, the one out of all of them who seemed beyond the grip of family influence, pushed and pulled until she bent to tradition, and it took something from June. Her delight, her will, her confidence, perhaps—not that she didn't have some to spare. Dot's relentlessness over the name changed June's understanding of the way she was loved by the women who came before her—largely and loudly, yes, but certainly not without limits. It was as if June admitted, in naming Junie, that she wasn't more powerful than this place. That though she and the rest of them loved this place like another one of them, loved the magic that occurs inside these walls, they were also bound to it, indebted to it, and subjected to its whims and wishes. For themselves—and for their girls.

The fire inside Cece starts to burn out as she watches Georgia lope out of this place with her old boyfriend. Now Junie's boyfriend? She can't keep track, and it all looks like another issue waiting to happen.

Tonight, Cece drank too much—on account of the nerves she'd worked up. In truth she wouldn't mind the bank or the haircare brand or whoever pleases repossessing this place, but she didn't want to let the girls down. She wanted to pull through for Junie and Georgia, and let's be honest—for their mama too.

Instead, she's screwed it up on all fronts, taking out her frustration on Georgia when it's herself she's upset with. Well, herself *and* her grandmother, Dot, because she's the one who turned the naming into something ugly.

Cece pushes out of the back service door and into the warm air of the night. She lights a cigarette, out of sight of the others who would take it away and stomp it. It's rebellion and self-destruction, and it matches the urges curled up inside her.

Grandma Dot once owned this shop, though she didn't start it. That was her mother, June, who opened the place in the 1930s as a basic spot for the locals to come for a haircut. Dot wasn't a June, and that fact was likely both the spark and the fuel for everything that happened. Dot's older sister, June the second, took off to California after high school. Apparently, she'd been talking about it ever since junior high, yet the entire family was *shocked* when she followed through and made plans a month before graduation. Once she bought a house out there and settled into a child-free beach bum lifestyle, it was clear she wasn't coming back to claim the shop. It was Dot's to take.

Dot's mother, June, the original one, handed it over, but she did so with some misgivings. As far as Cece has heard, straight from her mother's mouth, June saw Dot's interest as an obsession that was unhealthy and worried about what it would do to her daughter. She didn't quite foresee how her fixation might impact others in the family.

Cece walks under the light of the streetlamp and knocks the cigarette ash into a bush.

Dot was obsessed with the name, and even after she had the shop, it was as if she was holding out for her sister to give her the name too; it wasn't like she was using it. Dot eventually married and popped out babies, first four boys in quick succession until the fifth arrived, a girl she could name June. Two years later a final girl arrived, Clementine, in whose house the girls live, a surprise baby or an insurance policy, depending on who you ask. If Dot couldn't have the name, one of her children would. Or so legend goes.

Dot's baby, June the third, became Cece's mama—Georgia and Junie's grandmother. She was quiet compared to the others in the family tree but also ever-present in her support and love. She passed down the family stories and didn't spare details, as if she was preparing her girls in some way, schooling them to play the game of the family politics.

Dot didn't let a day pass without mentioning how lucky Cece's mama, June the third, was to have had three girls to help her run the shop: Cece, June, and Tina. For a while Cece figured that was how all grandmothers were—obsessive over the lineage, the family business, names. When she grew older and met some other grandmothers, she realized they weren't like Dot at all. Maybe they weren't all the active, playful adults they are nowadays, but they were softer. Kinder. Interested in who their grandchildren were, not just what they could offer.

Cece drops the cigarette to the ground and puts it out with her toe. She bends to pick it up and goes to toss it in their dumpster.

Cece never liked her grandmother Dot, but it wasn't until later, when Cece was an adult, that she truly learned to hate Dot. That was when Cece found out about the rest of what happened back then, before any of the nonsense with threatening June over naming her two girls happened. Truly, it was Dot who started this whole thing the generation before, messing with Cece's mother, June, over the twins, Cece and June, born seven minutes apart. Dot was ready to raise hell over seven minutes. Seven minutes, if you could believe it. Seven minutes for a lifetime's worth of dragging themselves across hot coals all for the namesake of June.

Their mother called them to her bedside as she neared death, a few years before June got the cancer diagnosis, and she told them the whole story. Their father, the only other person who would've been privy to this information, died years earlier from a heart attack. Cece sometimes wonders if it would've been easier simply not to know; it's another thing that makes her hesitant to tell Georgia and Junie the full gamut of Dot's drama. In some ways, it seems like an opportunity to halt Dot's influence.

As Cece turns to walk inside, she spots blue lights approaching.

"Aw, crap," she mutters under her breath. She hurries in through the back door and yells, "Five-o, y'all! Cover the tables, hide your drinks. Hell, hit the floor for all I care."

Chairs screech and the volume drops to a murmur.

Junie and Tina leap into action, pulling patterned tablecloths from a stashed bag and efficiently laying them out over the gambling.

On her way to the front door, Cece calls to the group at the bar, "Slide this in back." Three gamblers slowly guide the table, bracing the glass bottles for protection.

Cece slips out the front door and closes it behind her. The lights inside the shop turn off as the police car pulls up. When it parks, Mike Costas steps out, and Cece lets out a breath of relief.

She smiles at him. "Evenin', Mike. Anything I can help you with?"

Mike approaches, removing his hat. He gives her a look like she should already know. "Cecelia, I do my best to turn a blind eye." He sighs. "But when y'all are so loud that my junior sheriff in training drives by and calls in a safety check, you tie my hands."

Cece nods. "Apologies. We did get a little rowdy tonight."

The sheriff nods. "We've got some new guys on deck, so take that information and proceed accordingly. There's only so much I can do."

"Yes, sir," Cece says. "I appreciate the notice."

He turns and walks back to the car, then stops before getting in and says, "Just promise you'll win some money off that Hank McKeegan. Cheats at golf every weekend."

"I'm doing my best," Cece says, and she raises a hand as the vehicle pulls back out onto the road.

CHAPTER 32

GEORGIA

I SLIDE INTO THE DRIVER'S SEAT of Junie's truck, and it's the strangest feeling in the world when Eddie gets in and sits down right beside me. He offered—no, insisted—that he come with me, saying it's *just a thing he does*. I'm not sure I'm supposed to know what that means. Maybe he's developed a thing for ATMs since he and I last spoke, and honestly it wouldn't be the most surprising thing that's happened in the last week.

"Are you sure you're alright?" Eddie asks.

"Right as rain," I sing back as I start the truck and pull out of the lot.

When I catch a glimpse of him, I can tell he knows I'm faking. Mostly, I'm embarrassed that he and the rest of the crowd saw Cece's loud display of her true feelings for me. Especially when I try so hard to be responsible and reliable—all the time, but certainly for my family. It's one thing to know someone doesn't prefer you, and it's a whole other thing to have the sentiment loudly proclaimed to an unsuspecting crowd. And only slightly less, I'm worried about just how much cash this ATM will be willing to give me.

"I won't keep on at you, but Cece was awful," Eddie says. "And in *your* family? I'm surprised—"

"It's nothing new." I resist the urge to mitigate the situation, to explain that Cece is not all bad, to list all the ways she's quietly attentive.

"I know, I know." Eddie has witnessed her chilliness before. "But that doesn't make it ok. Especially when you've given up so much to be there for your family. Right now, all the planning and working, but also before." Eddie stops there, seeming to sense the dangerous territory he's approaching.

He was there for the before; he was the one most harmed by it.

This is how it happened:

Eddie and I were two Star Children in love who chose to attend the same college after high school, a distinguished liberal arts college in Atlanta that offered us both scholarships. There, we pursued science degrees. Him to prepare to apply to medical school, and me because I thought it sounded like something difficult enough for a Star Child that would make my folks at home proud, add another feather in my hometown hero cap.

Until our junior year, we'd been mostly neck and neck academically, switching out for whose grades were barely better than the other's. The competition was laced with fun and love, and more than anything it felt like a constant push toward making me my best self. But that year, we took a mind-blowingly difficult organic chemistry lab where he and I were partners. It was then that everything changed.

Every class, my chemical reactions wouldn't take. Eddie did his best to help me, coach me, guide me, *pray* me into success, but it was as if the knowledge just wouldn't fit inside my head. Eventually our final approached—my one last chance to pass the class. He'd prepped me like this was my Super Bowl, and I studied diligently.

On exam day, we worked in silence. Everything went to plan. After three hours of work, we set out our samples and waited for the chemical reaction to settle before bringing them to the professor for review. Eddie excused himself to the bathroom, and while he was gone, I sat at our bench and watched that beautiful cobalt salt form from the bubbling mix. It was the result I'd been chasing all semester. Only, the sparkly blue grains were forming in *his* dish. In mine sat a brown bubbling muck, not a mention of blue.

That one moment in that unglamorous lab I was forced to choose: fail my family or fail Eddie. If I flunked this lab, it meant getting an F in the class; it meant that my aunts who still had my honor roll certificates pinned on their beauty shop walls would have to walk back all of their pride in me. It meant letting them down, admitting I was no star. The ache to protect them from this disappointment burned in me and pushed me to consider the other option: to take Eddie's work. It was the only way to keep up the facade. My choice defined me as much as it set the trajectory of the rest of my life.

I set my hands flat on the table, checked to see that the coast was clear (premeditation), and reached out for his dish with one swift swipe. I walked that sample right up to the professor who was delighted to check off my result as correct. He'd watched me work so hard for it, after all. What I wasn't prepared for was the look on Eddie's face when I turned and watched him return to the bench.

Mortification and disappointment wound into one and smeared across the face that I loved. It didn't take long for Eddie to lift the remaining dish and check for the initials he scrawled on the bottom out of habit. Spaces were cramped and shared, and samples could be easily mixed up. I could tell he expected a mix-up, an accidental swap an hour back at the chemical hood—an honest mistake. He lifted the dish to read the initials, GLS. He looked up at me hovering at the professor's desk, and when our eyes met, I saw an awkward flash of concern as he pointed to the bottom of the dish. He thought it was a mistake.

I held his gaze as I shook my head, and his eyes flashed first with confusion and then with anger. Like a heavy tick of a clock, I saw the realization unfold across his face, and he leapt to his feet, brown sample in hand, and marched up to the professor's desk to accuse me of what I'd done: stolen his work. His face was mottled red, his brows knitted.

He looked at me seriously and paused, giving me one final opportunity to come clean.

But I was silent. I wasn't coming clean, and I needed this blue sample. To keep me as the whiz kid my family needed me to be. Even if it meant losing him.

Eddie opened his mouth, probably to call me out, demand answers, but he froze. His eyes landed on me, and disappointment flooded them. He closed his lips and shook his head slowly.

"Eddie, something you need?" the professor asked.

"No, sir." Eddie dropped the sample on the desktop. "Just a bad result—must've had an off day."

"Ah," the professor said. "Well, it's a good thing the rest of your grade is so strong. You'll still have an A."

Eddie shot me one last look, seething this time, before he marched back to the lab bench and aggressively packed his bag. He didn't talk to me again after that, as he rightfully ignored my calls, the notes I left on his car, the emails I sent. Well, aside from the occasional text response of I don't want to talk to you or Leave me alone.

I deserved it. I'd done this miserable, cruel thing to someone who'd done everything he could to help me get myself to that result. To someone who had loved me.

In that moment when I boldly stole his work, I chose my family, I chose myself. And even then, he didn't turn me in. He could've answered the professor's question by explaining the truth of what was unfolding in that moment. The professor would've believed him because his story would make sense given our separate track records and the initials *right there* as evidence. Yet he chose to let me have his work. He chose *me*.

It wasn't even a week later that both of us were called into the dean's office to meet with administration and the lab professor.

The professor had taken a second look at the dishes after we left, when he'd grown suspicious as he considered the sudden shift in performance on both ends. We were accused of cheating— everyone knew we were a couple, so it wasn't much of a leap to wonder if Eddie gave me his work, knowing he could maintain a high grade. This time I took the blame, explaining that Eddie was an innocent victim, using the initials *right there* as proof. Why would we have put our own initials on our samples if the switch had been planned? The mortification Eddie endured during the investigation was the final nail in the coffin of our relationship.

Driving to the ATM, I tell him, "I don't begrudge them my help." I already chose them. "I've accepted that I won't ever understand Cece. I just want to move past it, try to forget what happened."

"Fair." He shrugs. "Plus, I'm sure she'll be perfectly sweet when you return with more cash." He laughs. "Junie keeps going on and on about how big you've made it. I'm really happy for you."

I pull into the local Piggly Wiggly and park by the glowing ATM at the entrance.

When I glance over from the driver's seat, I half expect—all the way hope—for there to be an unease to what he's saying. The way exes try to be happy for each other, pretend, when really they'd prefer if things had just worked out between them. So it knocks against my heart when I look up and see he's entirely sincere.

"You always were so kind." I don't plan to say those words to Eddie. It's like my brain overrides my better knowledge. "*Thank you* is what I meant."

He smiles and opens his mouth to reply. But the words don't come, and I just know the wrestling happening inside his head is the same as what's happening in mine. It's just that my heart is wrapped up in my thoughts too—something I'm certain doesn't apply to him.

"It's ok." I say it to save him from the moment.

I look over at him again, and he's staring out the windshield. "Whatever happened anyway?" I ask. "To bring you back here. Junie mentioned something about your mom."

My heart picks up a little from asking these regular life questions, being this close to him, so close to our history.

"My mom's really slowed down. She needed some surgery, so I'm on leave from Vanderbilt. She'll be fine, but it might be a while before she's fully recovered. I want to be here for her because—and I learned this from you—time with our parents isn't guaranteed. Sorry." Eddie gets a look on his face like he's the one breaking the news that my mother is dead.

"Don't worry," I say. "I don't ever forget her, not for long, and remembering her is always a rush of love. Even if it does still hurt."

What I don't tell him is that Mama lives around and within me like part of her spirit was tethered to me as she passed into the afterlife. A most precious shaving of her soul. I imagine her here and talk to her memory, asking her for advice and wondering what she'd think of the situations I find myself experiencing. Over the years, I think my mind has built upon the facts of who she was when she was alive because once she died I had no choice but to extrapolate the rest of her. It was something I could do to blunt the cruelty of a life so bright snuffed out too soon. So I imagine who she would've become if she'd been allowed to stick around for me. And for Junie.

"So when she's better, you go back to Nashville?" I'm thinking about Junie and their dating, and it makes even less sense if he's only here for a bit.

Eddie pulls a tight smile. "My position stands at the hospital, but I don't know. I've gotten pretty comfortable here."

I want to tell him that in addition to his comfort, he needs to think about Junie's feelings and make sure he's not going to hurt her when he moves away. She's not leaving June's, so if he's not staying here, it's long distance or nothing.

I stare at him, a seriousness behind my eyes, and I think he understands.

"I promise I won't hurt her," Eddie says.

I feel it physically, this line landing on me. It rocks me in a lurching way that reminds me of what I lost. What I deserved to lose because of the ways I failed him. But it also grates against me because I don't believe him. He is devastatingly lovable, and if Junie has finally fallen for someone, her style will be to fall all in, right away. It's just how she lives life. So if he leaves, he will hurt her whether he thinks he is or not. Has Junie even considered this? Honestly, it's the sort of detail she usually waves off, pishposh, as something to figure out later.

I cannot get between them. I can't mention this to her. I will look jealous, like someone meddling.

"I'm going to grab that cash," I say and push out of the truck.

CHAPTER 33

JUNIE

EVERYONE SURVIVED THE CARDS NIGHT—no arrests, no tickets, no fistfights—and the following day, the women gather in a circle for another Good Hair Days meeting at the shop. After last night's fireworks, libations are purposefully absent.

Georgia calls the meeting to attention and dives right into a review of last night. "First of all, a big thank-you to Cece for playing our hand."

Cece shuffles uncomfortably in her seat, reminding everyone that she hasn't yet apologized for her ghastly behavior.

"For the night we won $1,297 at the tables, and we made a whopping $1,822 on the bar!"

"We're getting there, ladies," Tina says. She claps, looking around the circle woman to woman as if to confirm that everyone is as thrilled as she is.

Junie glances at Georgia to see which one of them will be the one to say it. Georgia swings her eyes over and gives an imperceptible shake of the head. *Fine.* Junie won't say it—that they're not even anywhere close to the number they need.

"We should go ahead and schedule as many Cards nights as we

can," Georgia says. "And maybe we can mention a voluntary donation for the shop reno?" She says the last part in an upward-lilting voice.

"No, ma'am!" Junie belts out. "No handouts."

Georgia does one of her mini huffs. "But don't you remember what Tina said before? Folks would love to help if they knew the trouble we're in."

Yes, Junie knows. The Silvers have already offered to do their thing, plus Michaela, but that's not what Junie needs. She needs to stand on her own two feet.

"I know it's frustrating, but we're doing ok so far," Junie says. "Misty Prince and her undercover threats seem momentarily calm, and we've got the sheriff turning a blind eye to Cards. We're still seeing some clients. Things are alright."

Tina cuts in. "But Georgia has a whole life she's put on hold for us, Junie."

"And she'll probably need to head back to her job soon, I'd think," Cece says. "Plus, Sheriff Mike was very clear that he's got new guys on the ground, and he can't vouch for what they will or won't report."

Georgia leans in, propping her elbows on her knees. "And we know Misty's not exactly going away. She's been this way since she was a kid; it's not like she's turned over a new leaf. Come on, Junie. June's hasn't ever truly belonged to just one person. She's a little bit for everyone. Why not let people pitch in?" Georgia doesn't respond to the fact that she's due back at work tomorrow.

She makes a good argument, though, and if Junie wasn't secretly riddled with disease and losing the battle to drum up the guts to tell her sister, she'd probably agree. She has another appointment tomorrow, and she's certain they will tell her she needs to start chemo. *Start chemo?* Junie hasn't even told her people yet. She hasn't even come to terms with it yet. She certainly has no peace with it.

"Let me think on it," Junie says.

"I'll take that." Georgia grins back at her so generously that it stops her from the inside out. Junie feels a mixture of a gratitude vast enough to drown her and a cutting pain at knowing what she will eventually set on her big sister.

"I don't deserve you," Junie says, and she knows Georgia won't understand.

"I could say the same for you, Junie Bug," Georgia says.

Soon enough the women pack up the meeting and the aunts head home. Georgia straggles as Junie tries to wrangle her to the truck so they can go. Junie's beat.

"Can we chat for a moment?" Georgia asks.

"Can't we do it at home?" Junie could handle just about any conversation if she's curled up in her spot with a bowl of ice cream.

"It's more of a Good Hair Days thing, so I'd rather it stay here."

"Fine, spill it." Junie drops into a hair chair.

"Look, I know you're set on doing this on your own, but at this rate it's going to take *months* before we've got the money to move forward. And that doesn't even account for the construction delays we know will happen. I want you to do this the way you always wanted, but also, the longer we stay open like this, the longer we run a risk."

"Risk is riding a motorcycle without a helmet or playing Russian roulette with hair color tubes," Junie says.

"Yes, Junie, it's a risk. I don't expect the licensing board to get wind, but if in the worst-case scenario they did, everything would be on the line. They could shut down the shop. We can't run things in this shape for a day longer than absolutely required. Not to mention the money we'll lose having to be picky about customers."

She's right. Of course, and as freakin' usual.

"Maybe," Junie says. The weight of her guilt wiggles in the pit of her stomach.

Georgia sighs and drops into the hair chair beside her. "Why did we say this meeting would be dry?"

"Because last night everyone was drinking at Cards, and Cece just about tried to fight you." Junie spins her chair and reaches into a supply drawer, then pulls out a bottle of bourbon. "But you and I are both on our best behavior."

"You running a bar or a hair shop here?" Georgia asks.

"Let's be honest," Junie says. "June's has never been one single thing at a time."

Georgia takes the bottle and holds it up in a salute. "Isn't that the truth."

"It's good having you here," Junie replies.

Georgia pauses, staring across the room like she's thinking. "I should probably call my boss." She looks over, and after another pause, she cracks a smile. "It's not like I can dip out now and abandon y'all."

The joy starts in the depths of Junie's belly, runs through her limbs, and cracks her face in folds of delight. It's sitting here, right beside Georgia, feeling like a million bucks, that Junie doubts she might be sick at all. This right here could power her for years—bad cells, whatever. With her sister at her side, there's nothing Junie can't do.

CHAPTER 34

GEORGIA

AFTER WE GOT HOME FROM June's last night, we went to bed early, and this morning Junie took off with Eddie. She said she'd come by the shop this afternoon, and now I sit twirling myself in a hair chair waiting for her arrival, braiding my hair in front of my right shoulder. It makes me think of Sophie. I tie the end and work my way up, loosening the braid to make it fuller. Fluffier, as Mama would say.

Late last night, racked with guilt, I reached out to Felix. It wasn't the best time, and I shouldn't have left it until the last minute, but I felt so torn it was as if the pain in my chest was an actual crack in my human makeup. He was kind. And somehow that made me feel worse.

I understand, Georgia. Family is important. We're managing ok here, but of course look forward to your return. Keep me updated.

Felix Monrovian
VP, Customer Service

I know there's only so long I can extend my absence. Especially when the other executive assistants are probably already circling in hopes of snagging the position. The higher the executive, the higher the assistant position pays, and three junior leaders have assistants who I'm sure would be happy to take a salary bump.

As I consider the idea of someone else snagging my job, it strikes me that it feels more like relief than loss.

The bell on the salon door clatters, and it's a welcome distraction from the train of thought I'm on, one that will only lead me to the same conclusion. That *here* is where I'm meant to be, meant to stay. I swivel to face the door, hoping to see Junie walking in.

"Junie here?" It's Ms. Sherry.

"Unfortunately not. I've been waiting on her too," I say. "Any way I can help?"

"Well, I just wanted to come by and notify y'all. I was in here last week, and long story short . . . I have lice."

My mouth drops open. "You're kidding."

Ms. Sherry cringes. "I wish I was. I wanted to let y'all know, but I'm also not sure where else I could've gotten it from." She wobbles a little on her feet. "Not that I'm trying to lay blame. My daughter found it on me, and she only saw a couple of the little nits—so it was very early. She's a bit paranoid about little flecks in hair since her kids got it a couple years ago. Apparently it's going around the elementary school again, and she's been checking her kids religiously."

"I'm really sorry," I say. "Junie's the one in charge here, but I agree that it's always possible we gave them to you."

She flaps a hand. "I'm not mad, honey," she says. "I just didn't want to spread it to anyone else—though a couple of the other Silvers mentioned they'd check themselves and keep an eye out for itchiness. Plus, Georgia Louise Scott, you are a Whitetail hero. You've made this town proud—no apologies necessary."

I smile, but it doesn't make it to my eyes. I'll be letting down the Silvers, too, when it eventually comes out what's really become of me.

"Can I have Junie call you as soon as she gets here? She knows more about the schedule and how it might've happened."

"Of course." Ms. Sherry turns toward the door.

"And count your next five haircuts as on the house," I call behind her.

Once the door clatters shut my professional smile vanishes, and I sprint to the best-lit mirror I can find and pull my hair apart. I check the crown of my head and the sides as best I can—I won't have any luck at the back. I take my time and slowly move through the strands.

Lice is my absolute worst nightmare. Just the thought of almost invisible bugs crawling all over my scalp and head and laying their eggs on my hair is enough to push me to the point of shaving it all off.

The lower the hair, the smaller the louse house. I could give it a whirl.

I don't find anything in my hair to suggest I've got it, but I do wonder if I need to add a scalp oil to my hair routine because my scalp is looking dry. My whole body is itchy now. The likelihood of my having it is probably minute. It's probably just in my mind, but what if it's not? It's all purely psychological. Maybe?

I pull out my phone and text Junie for the fourth time without reply. CODE BUG! CODE BUG! 911.

That, if nothing else, will get the girl on the phone.

As I wait for her to call, I go to the supply room to see if we have a nit comb hiding out in there. I'm shuffling around when my phone lights up and jiggles to life.

"Where on earth have you been that lice is the only thing to get you on the line?" I demand.

"Sorry, I was in an appointment," she says, more subdued than the frantic (even explosive) response I expected.

"Ok, well, Ms. Sherry has lice. She was really nice about it, but apparently her daughter checks her grandkids like a drill sergeant, and timeline-wise she thinks she might've gotten it from here. Do you remember the day she came in? Could she be right?"

The other end of the line is quiet, and I'm not sure if Junie is still connected.

"Hello?" I ask.

"I think I might have an idea how this happened," Junie says. "Let me finish up here and I'll come right there. Thirty minutes tops."

CHAPTER 35

JUNIE

WHAT'S ALL THE FUSS ABOUT?" Eddie asks from the chair parked over in the corner of Junie's exam room.

Junie shrugs. "One of the Silvers got lice—and probably from June's."

Eddie shuffles upright in his seat, a hand creeping up to scratch his scalp. "Just the mention of the word has me itching."

Usually, Junie would have the same response, but today she's simply not her usual self. This appointment was the worst one yet. She wants the nurse to hurry up and drop off the checkout papers so she can get out of there. The doctor kinda-sorta told her off for stalling on scheduling treatment, and he seemed more concerned about her hip pain than she expected. He says Junie needs to do chemo. Eddie says she needs to do chemo. But she's not sure she wants to do chemo because it makes it all too real. It'll force her to be honest. It'll force her to accept this miserable hand and live it.

Maybe it's the stubborn baby of the family in Junie, thinking she'll be able to stomp her foot all the way out of this diagnosis, but even that act is crumbling. She may be the Louise baby, forever saved, but she's not an idiot. If she doesn't get treatment—and fast—it's just a matter of how long before it spreads and she's on her way up to see Mama in heaven.

Junie doesn't want to die. She feels like she's just getting started. But there's also a massive shift toward the *all too real* that comes with starting down the chemo path. Less like a small spill she can dab up before the others see and more like an oil rig splayed open on national news.

"I guess maybe it's just me," Eddie says. He's now scratching all over his arms and chest.

Junie sighs. "It'd be the least of my problems."

His hands slow to a stop, and he looks her over. He grabs the Twizzlers from the tote bag and hops up onto the exam table to sit beside her. "Happy stick?"

Junie's lips curl at the ends. "Down, boy! Back in the friend zone."

Eddie's ears turn pink at the tips immediately—Junie's desired result. "Ew. That'd be like kissing—"

"Your sister," Junie says.

"Yes, or perhaps even worse. Like a nun or someone's grandmother."

Junie grabs the hood of her hoodie and turns it over her head. "Sister Junie reporting to heaven's doorstep."

"Not at that rate," he says.

Probably not at any rate, which is why Junie needs to do this treatment. In her current standing she's not sure she's quite earned a spot beyond the pearly gates. Ok, in fact, she's almost entirely sure she hasn't.

"You know, I agree," Junie says and snatches a couple of red licorice sticks.

"In which case, why don't you schedule your first appointment on the way out?" Eddie asks as he chews. "I'll block off any day you need from my clinic availability, so you have guaranteed transportation."

"And comedic relief," Junie adds.

"Junie, we have to be serious for a moment."

She knows that, but it doesn't mean she hasn't been trying to avoid it. "Do I have to?"

Eddie gives her a look that she classifies as stern teacher meets prison guard.

Junie lets out a puff. "I don't want to. Honest to God, I just don't want to deal with any of this. It's too much, too big, too heavy. Far, far too serious for the likes of someone who can't even handle a small shop renovation. I'm expected to save myself? I'm not sure if I should even try, considering my track record in making things worse."

Eddie stares into the linoleum tiles, examining the design. "And do you understand what that means?"

It's as if everyone thinks she's a complete fool. "Well, I was thinking I'd just go to Mama's Dolly Parton shrine and sing a few of her top hits and by the morning I'll be cured." She stares boldly into his eyes, but it's a hard look to hold.

"Junie, *stop*. Not now. Are you seriously considering saying no?"

She shrugs. She knows she's being childish and irresponsible and flippant, but it's all she's got left to protect her from the gravity of the situation.

Eddie tightens his jaw. "I've taken a back seat in all this so far, let you do things your own way, but if you're deciding not to do the treatment—without telling Georgia—you give me no choice." He's fully red in the face now, the licorice candy forgotten. "If you're being this reckless with your life, I will have to tell Georgia. She loves you, Junie. So do the aunts. And Rich. And me—"

"Not like that."

"Yes, today and forever *not like that*, but you're as good as my little sister at this point, so I'll be damned if I don't fight for you if you won't do it yourself."

Junie turns her head to look away, and from there she drops gently into Eddie sitting beside her. It's a physical admission. He slings an arm around her. It's quiet between them. Junie lets her new reality roll over her and seep into her pores. Inside her, part of her. She's going to get treatment. She was all along, if she's honest; life is too delicious not to stretch out for another bite. And she's accepted it: There's no way around crushing Georgia with the news—twice over. Eddie's right; he was all along.

She looks up at her friend, tears rolling in rivulets down her cheeks. "I'm going to lose my hair." A sob breaks from her.

"Oh, Junie." Eddie squeezes her. "It totally and completely sucks and I hate it for you. You deserve better."

Junie nods, drying her tears on the arm of her hoodie. "Guess Aunt Tina's been training for this day with her wig maintenance." She laughs.

Eddie smiles softly. "Can you imagine how they will show up for you? You will have the loudest and rowdiest cheering section."

"I'm sorry I'm such a pain," Junie says through tears that catch in the back of her throat.

"So big of a pain that I want to do everything we can to keep you around and giving me a hard time."

"I'm doing the treatment. And I'll tell Georgia," Junie says. "Just let me find the right time."

Eddie's quiet then, like he knows Junie is trying to make friends with this new life she didn't choose. After a few minutes he holds out the Twizzler pack.

Junie grabs one and, despite her churning guts, rips off a bite and chews.

CHAPTER 36

JUNIE

S HE SHOULD'VE EXPECTED THE SCENE before her as she enters June's, considering how well she knows each of these women.

Cece sits on a foldable chair, Tina on the floor in front of her, hair oiled to within an inch of its life. Georgia, equally lubricated, sits in front of Tina. They're like a lice-check train. Olive oil is a natural way to treat lice that has become popular in recent years because it's both effective and void of the harsh chemicals that were once widely used. No one in this circle wants her hair fried and brittle if the little bugs can be smothered and pulled out with a natural remedy.

"Well, y'all didn't waste any time," Junie says.

Georgia whips around. "Goodness gracious, there you are. I was really starting to worry about you. But also, yes, it's lice, so I'm not going to sit around on my itchy butt and do nothing."

"I haven't found a thing on Tina yet," Cece says.

"I think our chances are fairly good," Tina says. "Though it was probably a one in a million that Ms. Sherry got it from the shop."

Tina, like any good people pleaser, has held about as many short-term jobs as she has hairs on her head—and that's in addition to her

work at June's. She's just known that way around Whitetail. Someone's in a pinch, they ask Tina to step in part-time, *just until we can
get someone else.* And it was precisely this way that she ended up doing
a stint at Lice SWAT, a police-themed, professional lice treatment
team that could be dispatched to your home for a sizable fee. She
was talked into it by way of the *hair connection* (an abuse of it, by all
arguments) and took to religiously wearing a plastic hairnet while
on duty.

"You're probably right," Georgia says. "It's just as soon as the words
come out—"

"The itch starts," Cece says.

"Amen," the three women chorus.

Junie stands there and watches, taking the chance to pull in a deep
breath. Even if the discussion from the doctor's office followed her
here, it feels good to pause in a safe space.

"Tina, I can't believe you did this for work for so long," Georgia
says.

Tina shrugs. "Well, they needed someone, and then once I started,
the search for the true replacement slowed . . ."

"They took advantage," Cece says.

Georgia nods. "Sure sounds like it."

"What could I do? I didn't want to upset anyone, so I just stayed
on," Tina says.

"You shouldn't do that when it's at the expense of your own well-
being," Georgia says.

It strikes Junie that Georgia has probably suffered herself in extending help to *them.* "Precisely," she chimes in. "Time to start standing up
for yourself."

"Y'all are sweet to care about little old me like that," Tina says.

Junie rounds to the back of the train of women. "I can check you
while you work, Cece," she says. "And Georgia, you can circle back
to me once you're done."

"Georgia's clear," Tina says. "We can look again in a few days."

Cece shuffles down to share the towel-covered floor section with Tina, and Junie slips into the chair, grateful for the rest. She notices things like that now, the relief of sitting. It wasn't but weeks ago that she'd stand and walk and snip and wash and chat for the entire day without noticing an ache. That's the thing about good health: It's not appreciated until it's gone.

Junie feels the coolness of the oil running over her scalp and the loving touch of Georgia's fingers on her scalp. It reminds her of Mama. Like Georgia always does, but more this time.

"Alright, so let's talk postmortem," Georgia says.

"I'm sorry?" Junie asks, confused.

"I'm not blaming." Georgia is sincere, not defensive. "No one did anything wrong. It's just, you said you had an idea of how the lice might've started. Maybe I misunderstood?"

"Oh, *that*." Junie spritzes a nit comb with rubbing alcohol and starts to section Cece's hair. "Well, a little while back, it was . . . the day of the garage sale. A mom came in with her son. It struck me as unusual because she told me they'd been over to All-Star Cuts, and they sent them away, claiming there were no available appointments. The shop was clearly open, and it was only a fifteen-minute cut."

"Did you see the kid scratch?" Cece asks.

"Well, now that I think about it, I did, but not so much that I thought anything was wrong."

"Did you get the mom's name? Maybe she works for All-Star? Maybe she intentionally brought over a kid with lice to sabotage us." Georgia's words grow tighter and shorter.

"Hang on, hang on." Junie waves a hand. "All-Star might've been involved, but this mom was definitely innocent. I think she had no idea, and she wasn't trying to hide anything. She told me everything, that she didn't understand why they wouldn't just give him a quick cut. She said they recommended coming here."

"I bet the stylists watched that boy scratch a few too many times and lied about the appointments," Cece says.

"That's exactly what I'm thinking," Junie says. "And rather than checking the kid—or even recommending that the mom do it—they sent them over here to lob the problem."

"Oh heavens," Tina squeals. "How could anyone be so horrible?"

"Everyone knows what this means, right?" Cece says. When she's met with silence, she says, "Georgia? Are we thinking the same?"

Junie watches the two exchange a look.

Georgia clears her throat. "It means war, y'all."

CHAPTER 37

GEORGIA

I STEW OVER ALL-STAR AND THEIR sending us this client as we sit there oiling and combing out hair. All of us are focused, working diligently and quietly, and soon we're wrapping up.

I shouldn't be adding new issues to my personal docket right now, but All-Star Cuts has officially seized the number one spot on my personal hit list. I've hated them all along, as anyone in my position would, but *this*? Sending a kid with lice to another salon is akin to a crime punishable by death in International Hair Court.

Now, let me slow down. Murder is not actually an option in this case (for the record, it isn't ever), but I can't say I'd throw them a lifeline if they fell into shark-infested waters. *Fine*, no bodily harm. Just an equal amount of emotional distress.

"You want a wash?" Cece asks me.

It's enough to unfurl me from the anger tornado I'm deep within. Cece offering a hair wash is her version of an olive branch. Is there a catch I'm missing?

"A wash? You sure?" I'd planned to ask Junie, but as I scan the shop, I see her curled up in a reclined hair chair under a blanket that looks an awful lot like an emotional support item.

Cece looks at her too. "Not like you can ask her. You two hit the town last night or what?"

Junie only grunts and shuffles farther under the fleecy covering.

"If you're willing, I'll gladly take you up on it," I say. "You're still the best shampooer in town, even if you're retired."

I make my way to the shampoo bowl, stopping only to squeeze Junie's leg. Tina has been washed already and calls a quick goodbye on her way out. Soon enough Randy's signature tire screech follows, and Cece and I exchange an eye roll.

I settle into the chair. "So you really think Tina will stick it out with Randy?" I ask Cece.

She sighs. "I hope not. But I think she's building up her confidence, thanks to Good Hair Days. She mentioned her pies to me the other day, and it genuinely sounded like she wanted to try to sell them at the fair. If she can pony up enough confidence to put her baking up for judging, maybe she could get to the point of kicking him to the curb as well."

The warm water and pulse of Cece's hands relax my entire upper body. "I guess we can hope. Maybe revenge plotting against the new competition could push her further in that direction."

Cece grins. "You know I'm already brainstorming."

"And you know I'm adding it to every Good Hair Days agenda."

Cece squeezes out the ends of my long red hair and turns off the water. She wraps a towel around the damp hair. "Good as new, June."

It stops both of us. *June.*

"Sorry," she says. "You're just so like your mama."

Cece and my mama had a special kind of love, their own brand of fun, but they also butted heads their fair share. At least, that's how they used to tell the story. Whether it was the style of running the shop or the way they should support Tina or the way June should've behaved, it wasn't infrequent that they'd find themselves at different ends of the opinion spectrum. And they fought like the best of twin sisters. Maybe it was just what I'd seen in the movies, but I always imagined that twins were from birth in tune with each other. Weren't they required to be best friends? Maybe Mama and Cece were that too.

"Guess I'll take it as a compliment," I say.

"As you should." Cece rinses her hands. After grabbing a towel, she looks at me. "And before I go, I want to say sorry. The way I acted at Cards was out of line, and you didn't deserve it."

I feel a small warmth rise in my chest. "Thanks." I want to say more, really. I want to ask her the *how, what,* and *why* of her distaste for me. I want to ask for tips on making her like me. But just as much, I'm afraid that opening my mouth might break this moment between us.

"I'll let you two girls close up," Cece says. She pauses almost like she's considering reaching out for a hug, but the moment passes and she turns and heads for the door.

I enjoy the afterglow of the moment in quiet. Even though apologizing for her certifiably horrendous behavior might be the bare minimum, in a strange way, it still feels like progress.

I return to Junie's side. "Hey, sleepyhead, you feel like closing up and assuming this position at home?"

Junie grunts.

I pull down the cover. "What's wrong with you?"

"Nothing." She pulls it back up. "Just a lot on my mind."

I channel my inner Mama and rub circles on her leg. "Wanna talk about it?"

Junie only shakes her head.

"How about we get you something good to eat? Ice cream? Drive-thru fries? Your pick," I add.

"The only thing I want is impossible." Her voice is small.

"Well, that sounds like a challenge if I've ever heard one." I smile, and I hope she hears it in my voice. "And everyone knows I like a challenge."

"Cinnamon rolls."

I know the ones she means, the impossible cinnamon rolls. They aren't available for purchase, never have been. They're our mother's homemade variety, and they haven't been baked since she left us. A recipe exists over at our father's house, but no one's been brave enough to try it, let alone release the genie of what retasting it would be like. Seeing Junie in this state is enough for me to reconsider.

"You're right, that one's a little bit impossible. Especially for tonight. Let me help you to the car?"

Junie begrudgingly peels out of the hair chair and hobbles to the car on her own. I stay back to turn off the lights, double-check the locks. We ride home in silence, Junie refusing my offers to stop somewhere for food.

In the silence I worry about Junie looking so pitiful with all her brightness stripped off, and I consider that cinnamon roll recipe. What if we could use it as a remedy of sorts? Make cinnamon rolls and use them as a talisman to ward off hardship and troubles. To hold bad luck at bay. It might be worth a try, and I'd rather take on that complicated recipe than lose additional hours of sleep worrying about my sister.

I text my father before I show up on his doorstep. I don't want him meeting me in the dark with a baseball bat and his bad vision. I knock gently and wait in the warmth alongside the noisy nighttime bugs.

He opens the door with a pop. "I left it unlocked for you. Always just come right in."

The house is lit only by a few table lamps, and I follow my father into the living room where I sink into the deep sofa that feels like it hugs me back. I don't plan to stay, but something about the coziness of the space makes me feel like I could.

"Junie was having a really hard day today," I say. "She mentioned cinnamon rolls—Mama's, of course—and, I don't know, I was thinking maybe it was time to give them a try again."

If he wasn't perfectly lit by the table lamp beside him, I would have missed the way his expression lifts briefly at the very edges.

"I saw the recipe book out the other day when I was here."

"Your mama would want you to have it," he says. "Can I copy the recipe down for you? Not sure I'm ready to part with the actual book right this moment."

"For sure," I say.

Dad stands and makes his way into the kitchen, and I hear the rustling of papers and a drawer opening and closing.

"It's funny how much the smallest things can make us feel close to her," I say.

His face is earnest when he returns and hands over the paper covered in his scratchy handwriting. "Always." He stops, his eyes lingering on me as he smiles. "You've always reminded me so much of her."

It surprises me, for the second time this evening, that anyone from this little enclave thinks of me like Mama. I run a finger through my red hair. I sure try to be like her. Well, mostly to live up to her dreams for me enough not to make her dying any worse. But I don't feel like her. "Why?" I ask. "Why do you think we're alike? *How* is what I mean."

He leans back into his favorite armchair. "How much time you got?" He looks into his lap. "There are so many ways, from the red hair to the first daughter schtick. But frankly, the only thing that just doesn't quit is both of you being dreamers. Big dreamers."

My gut wrenches. Here comes the next part.

"Ever since you were a little girl, all you wanted to talk about with your mama was what kind of Georgia you wanted to be. She loved that she gave you a blank canvas, and she wanted to tour you through every single color so you knew you had options. She didn't want the same old, same old, cookie-cutter Louise life for you. I think to some extent she wished she'd had the same choice she handed you."

I sit silently, feeling like an inflatable yard decoration with a hole freshly slashed in it, slowly flattening into a lawn pancake.

"Which is why I'm so glad you've got your life in Atlanta. You've got a nice job and success. Everything you've ever dreamed of. Even if we miss you terribly and savor these weekends—or extended visits, as luck would have it."

I smile, reach out, squeeze his knee, and say, "Thank you for always supporting my dreams. And thanks for the recipe." I fake a yawn. "I should probably get going."

I stand, and he follows me to the door. Before I can slip out, he takes me gently in his arms and wraps me up. I hear him breathing deeply. "I love you," he says. "Come back and see me soon."

CHAPTER 38

JUNIE

O N THE DRIVE HOME FROM the shop, Georgia mentioned Eddie a few times—digging for an answer to what was bothering her—and Junie didn't deny or confirm the assumption that they had a tiff of some kind.

Now Junie lies on her bed with a paperback romance novel trying to get through this page without her mind wandering. She doesn't want to miss any of the story, but her life is just so loud. And distracting. Puds stirs on the floor beside her, and the sound pulls her out of the story again. She remembers when she used to think she had problems. Like a competing salon. Or an acne flare. Even Mama dying, though it was certainly a massive, life-defining problem, seems easier in this moment. At least then Junie had no hand in it. She wasn't the one who was the physical ticking time bomb.

And then there are the results of the genetic testing. Eddie hasn't pushed the discussion. He probably knows it's up to Junie in the end and she'll do as she pleases, as she always does. Plus, this morning's appointment was emotional enough, admitting that chemo was happening and then actually scheduling the first appointment on her way out. It was a lot.

Even if she was weary before, she knows she's overdue to share her diagnosis. She's only doing herself harm by holding her people at bay, not letting them flood her with their affection and acts of love. But that's something that can be addressed; a remedy can be attempted. *I'm going to do chemo. The science is so strong. Research is robust. There is a chance I might be ok.* For herself and for them all. It has never been more painful to be bound up with these women she adores than now, when she can't help but threaten to shatter their collective.

But because of the test that was misunderstood, the opportunity to avoid this whole miserable muck is gone. Georgia will be racked with guilt, and that might just be the thing, fiercer than any cancer, that stops Junie's heart. She can't promise she wouldn't rather die than set this on her sister.

More painful than all of it is this moment in front of her when she can no longer deny the truth: She must tell Georgia and tell her everything. She cannot joke or play or garden her way out of this one; Georgia deserves the full truth.

Out in the living room, sounds drift in that've become familiar, having Georgia here. Her shoes kicked off. Her purse dropped onto the entryway table with the rattle of her keys. Her flop onto the sofa. It's an advantage to having a tiny old house, an organic intimacy with the people you love most.

When footsteps approach her door, Junie leaps to turn off her lamp. She might've accepted telling Georgia, but that doesn't mean it'll be this very moment. She rolls over onto her side and pretends to be asleep. The door clicks open and the light from the hall fills the space made by the cracked door and shines on her eyelids. A soft thump of Puds's tail as he meets Georgia at the door, then sneaks out of the opening to the rest of the house. The bed sinks with the weight of Georgia as she sits gently beside Junie, who pretends to stir.

Georgia runs a gentle palm over Junie's forehead and whispers, "It's ok, Junie Bug. I've got you. Everything's ok. Back to sleep, love."

Georgia stands and tiptoes out, shutting the door with a muted click.

CHAPTER 39

GEORGIA

A FEW DAYS LATER, I SIT in the passenger seat of Cece's Jeep wearing one of Tina's wigs and holding a box of live cockroaches. I'm the only one not too chicken to do it.

"Where did you even get a box of roaches anyway?" I ask Cece.

"The auto shop," Cece says.

"Ain't nothing shady available in this town that doesn't come from that place." Tina tsks from her spot in the back seat. "Not that I have a single problem with you branching out from hair, but I think you're too good for that place."

"Well, I think *you're* too good for Randy," I say.

I can't help myself. I've been back in Whitetail going on two weeks now, and it's the first time I've let a single (direct) comment about the moocher in residence slip. It's been on my mind since Tina announced yesterday that she was officially *in* on the pie stand at the fair in less than a month now. She mentioned some preliminary planning she's been up to, part of building up her confidence, as she described it, and with every word Tina shone a little brighter. It just makes Randy a more obvious stain on her life.

"She sure turned that on you," Junie says to Tina.

She and Eddie must've smoothed things over, because they've been back to day dates and smiles over the past couple days.

"Honestly?" Tina raises her dropped gaze. "I'm starting to think you gals are right. I know you don't say it outright, but I can tell how you feel. He does take advantage. And I'm starting to get tired of it."

Junie reaches out and squeezes Tina's hand. "You deserve so much better. You're as good as gold. And Randy?"

"He's not up to snuff," Cece adds. "Whatever help you need untangling yourself, the Good Hair Days ladies will report for duty."

Our focus is stolen as we pull into the strip mall that houses All-Star Cuts, the final destination for our roaches, at least one of which I surely hope is pregnant. Aside from one shiny new storefront, the place looks mostly abandoned. Several businesses fill the spaces, but the lights look like they're off in a permanent way. Like there'd certainly be dust-covered merchandise. Like they wouldn't have change and definitely wouldn't take a card for payment.

Most of it looks like it couldn't survive today. Besides All-Star Cuts.

Their sign is double lit, brand new. The windows have been replaced with glass so shiny, it almost looks like a mirror. Inside, small lights dot the space—professional, like it's sleeping, not dead.

"Why on earth would someone open this up right here?" I ask.

Cece drives around the corner to the back alley behind the shops.

"I thought the same when I first came by," Junie says. "But I just figured corporations use computers to figure out what locations work. Not an actual person hightailing it out here to see for themselves."

"Sure feels personal," Tina says as we creep along the narrow driveway in back. "Now, what happens next with the box?"

We all look to Cece, who masterminded this stunt as payback for the lice debacle. Fortunately by now, all the Silvers have been checked and are back to regular programming. They each came into June's for their head checks, and we promised to double-check at each future haircut.

"We can't just march right in and set 'em loose," Junie says.

"Obviously," Cece says. "I was thinking we'd set it out back, where the trash is. Hopefully they'll set up camp, and every time they take the trash out it'll be a roach fest."

"Alright, here's their back door," I say. "I'll drop the package—but get as close as possible."

Cece flips her Jeep's auto lights off.

"It's midday. Turning the lights off is not helping anyone," I say.

"This is my first revenge stunt," Cece grunts back.

"Can't say I believe *that*," Tina barks in a very bold, very un-Tina manner.

"Hush!" Junie whisper-yells. "Y'all think if they hear a ruckus and a vehicle pull up out back, they won't come out to check the scene?"

By then the Jeep is fully entrenched in the intimidatingly slim alley behind the storefront, only feet from the back entrance of All-Star Cuts. Each of us is silent in the shady corridor. Nerves surge through my chest as my blood pulses in loud thumps in my ears.

Now or never.

I pop the door open and leap out, scurry to the door, and set the box down between it and the dumpster. I knock it open with my toe and sprint back to the car.

When I'm in my seat, I turn to Cece and screech, "Floor it!"

She cackles and hits the gas, barely avoiding a tire squeal that'd give us away. We take the corner hard around the side and to the exit. Finally, we make it back onto the main road and I breathe.

"I never knew mischief could be so fun!" Tina says.

I turn and release a joyful laugh from deep within.

Junie matches me.

And it strikes me: This laugh is one I thought belonged to Junie, one for people named June living their life at June's Beauty Shop.

But now I have it too. It's grown inside me during this visit, spending time among these women. It feels like a benediction of belonging. Proof, finally, that maybe I could make this home my own once again.

And because I know *this* is the moment, if ever, I say it to all of them. "At this rate I'm not sure I'll ever be able to leave this place."

"Music to my ears," Junie says.

"You wouldn't miss Atlanta?" Tina asks. "All that life you've got there?"

I think about what it'd be like if I just told them the truth. If I told them I never got a flashy job and that I don't really miss the one I settled for. If I told them I never really wanted to go, but I couldn't let Mama's dreams for me die like she did.

Maybe it might feel like relief—

"If there's anything we can rely on from you, it's that urge to go on and make something better of yourself. Even if we don't like the goodbyes," Cece says. "June didn't build you to stay."

And that decides it: Now is not my moment.

CHAPTER 40

JUNIE

JUNIE WAKES EARLY, PARTIALLY DUE to nerves and partially due to the fact that she knows her days of doing her hair are numbered. At least for now—while she has it—she will relish it. Junie showers in the bathroom she shares with Georgia and pads back to her room to dress, leaving wet footprints behind. She picks something comfortable to wear, knowing she'll be sitting in the chemotherapy chair for a good while.

When she returns to the bathroom, she releases her hair from the towel she'd twisted up and secured atop her head. She admires her damp locks, raking her fingers through them, delighted that the handful of blonde highlights Tina wove into the red months ago are still shining strong. Junie reaches into the cabinet beneath the sink and retrieves her Blowout Bombshell cream, then squeezes some into her palm, spreads it between her hands, and smooths it through her hair. She closes her eyes and lets herself feel the pull of her hands, the love of doing something for herself. *You've got this. Look good, feel good. Just like Mama promised.*

After brushing the product through with a wide comb, she pulls out a blow dryer and a thick round brush. She segments the hair and pins it up in small twists. The blast of hot hair hits her square in the face as she turns on the blow dryer, and it's a delightful reminder that she's alive and kicking. Junie pulls and turns the heavy brush up and down the sections of her long layers, twisting the brush at the end for the perfect curl. Section by section, she molds the hair into a voluminous collection of waves that frame her face.

Two hours later Junie sits in the chemo chair, and despite the fact that she's the patient, she wonders if Eddie is perhaps a hair more miserable than her. He's trying his best. He smiles. But it's strained and can't be anything but just for show.

"Do you want another pair of socks?" he asks.

He has a backpack of supplies at his side, and he diligently unloads them for Junie as needed. He bought cold therapy gloves and socks—apparently they're a preventative for complications. She's waiting on her cheery nurse to connect her drip, so she's still sitting at zero experience.

What a wild moment; it's the silence before the leap.

Eddie lays a second blanket at Junie's feet with a folded lip that can easily be pulled up. "Just in case."

When he settles into the seat across from her looking as gray as a storm cloud about to burst, she realizes what she's done. She's put too much on him; she's mined too much of his heart of gold. It should be Georgia here with her. Or Cece. Or Tina. Or Daddy.

Junie just couldn't bring herself to break the joy of Good Hair Days.

She couldn't bring herself to break her Georgia. Not yet.

"I'm sorry," Junie tells him quietly. "This is the most depressing date I could've planned for us." She tries for a smile.

"No apologies. I'm in the easy seat." He sinks down into it like he's settling in for the long haul.

Poppy, who could easily be renamed Nurse Sunshine, arrives. "Hi, Miss Junie. I'll be with you the whole way today." She smiles politely at Eddie. "Are you the boyfriend?"

Eddie's face flickers. "Depends on who you ask."

"Ooh! Do I smell drama?" Poppy giggles to herself. "Hang on, I forgot my charting tablet. Be right back."

"Look at you starting rumors," she tells Eddie. "You know I'm scheduled to come back here every other week for the next eternity, right? Let's try to keep some of our crazy under wraps."

"I think Poppy's keeping things light for your sake," Eddie says. "Oh, and we need to talk about you being sick after this. My schedule's clear—I can play the doting boyfriend in front of Georgia—even if it kills me—to nurse you back to health."

Junie grins. "We'll come back to that 'even if it kills me' part, but I won't need your help."

"You're going to be in rough shape, Junie. You can't bootstrap this alone. You need to let someone be there, and I'm happy for it to be me. I am a trained medical professional, remember?"

"Do you want to snuggle up in my bed with me and make googly eyes at me?" Junie bats her eyes with every dramatic flourish she can muster.

"Careful, or I'll be the one with the nausea." He lays a palm on his deep brown hair.

"Seriously, though, I've planned it. I'm going to be 'hungover.'"

Despite the eyebrow waggle Junie tacks on at the last word, Eddie glares back at her like he's caretaking the world's biggest idiot. And probably, he is.

"You're going to Cards tonight?" he says deadpan.

"Of course."

They wouldn't usually have Cards on a Friday, but they also wouldn't usually have it more than once a month—with November and December off for the holidays. It's part of the way the event has stayed under the radar this long. But they desperately need cash, and Cece checked with Sheriff Mike who said he's the only one on duty tonight.

"No, you're not. I won't let you," Eddie says.

His words waver at the end as he questions his authority to command Junie to do anything—in light of them being here, at the infusion center, with the Louise/Scott family clueless about what's happening.

"I don't care," Junie says. "Let me live a little. Geez. Plus, it wouldn't be a Good Hair Day if I'm not there."

She's told him the basics of Good Hair Days at this point. He's too close to all of it—and keeping too many of Junie's secrets—not to be in the loop.

Poppy returns with her tablet in hand, begins taking Junie's vitals, and charts information in her tablet. "Alright, first step done," she says. "I'm going to grab the supplies and we'll get you started, hon." Poppy takes off back in the direction of the nursing station.

"I guess you should enjoy yourself. I shouldn't be the one to stop you." Eddie sucks in a breath and then stops himself.

"Go on," Junie says.

"No."

"Fine, then I'll guess. Let's go with 'And if they're so special to you, they should know about your illness.'"

He pulls out a pack of Twizzlers. "Close enough."

Junie sighs. "You're right. I don't have a good excuse. Only a reason. Knowing she misread the result is going to send Georgia to a dark place."

Eddie nods. "I've been thinking about Georgia too. I think she'd rather be hurt than left out. Especially during a time when you could really use her help. She's a good woman, your sister. Not perfect, but she's incredibly capable and loving and actually sort of funny when she lets loose—"

Junie lets out a theatrical groan. "Good God, if y'all don't figure it out between you, I just might tie you together until you do."

"I've already told you: I don't date. Not anymore. Not to mention as far as she's concerned, I'm creepily dating her sister." Eddie looks to the ceiling for strength.

Junie shoots him a glare. "You must be the pot to my kettle, because you're an idiot."

"What?" Eddie's limbs stretch and tighten, and Junie can see he's truly struggling with this.

"Sorry. It's just that it doesn't seem that way. You both totally look like you have the hots for each other, except the one thing on Georgia's side is that she knows she royally screwed up. You're the blameless one. You could say 'Let's give it another shot' with much more authority than her."

"It's just . . ." Hurt passes across his face.

"She hurt you too badly to give it another try."

Eddie leans over his knees and begins to bobble his leg. "That's what I thought, what I planned to feel. But now she's back here, and it feels like it could, somewhere far off in the distance, be fixable. But now I'm keeping things . . . about you, about our 'dating.' I'm not certain about anything, but even if I wanted to see what could be there, I can't while I'm keeping these secrets."

It's another sacrifice Eddie has made for Junie. Passing on this second chance. She's been too absorbed with her own problems, her own drama to deeply consider it until now. She was far too quick to accept him brushing off the possibility of something with Georgia.

Junie sighs. "Ugh, I'm so sorry. Seriously."

"I know. I know you are. But I didn't want you worrying about me in this whole thing anyway. Especially about something *romantic*. That's just not that important compared to everything else going on."

But now that Junie is sitting squarely in the middle of the storm, she realizes that it truly is the rest of it that is the most important stuff. The storms will come, and no person can stop them. But the fun, the friendships, the trips, the memories, the delicious dinners in good company. Love. It's what matters the most.

"It *is* important," Junie says. "The good parts, the fun parts, the *love* we get to have in life. It's what I'm learning right here in turd storm central."

Eddie shrugs. "And you're probably right, but I want to keep this about you. Not about something hypothetical between me and Georgia."

"Well, I probably won't need you to fake it much longer. I'm coming clean with her as soon as I can. She's supposed to go back to Atlanta on Sunday, Monday morning if I can twist her arm . . . just as I'm about to need her the most."

Eddie nods. "It was really good of her company to give her two weeks away."

Junie nods. "I think she could work remote if she wanted, probably. I don't really know the ins and outs of her job, but I just get that feeling." She swats her hand. "Not that she seems to like the job *that much*. Atlanta either. Not when she's always coming home."

"Who knows, maybe she'll be able to work something out. You really think she'd be happy moving back to Whitetail, even temporarily?"

"She seems happier than ever after two weeks here. Relaxed and down to earth and unwound, even if we are chasing a fix for a torn-up beauty shop. Honestly and truly her best since she returned and kicked off these Good Hair Days. None of us are the same since, but especially her. You're the first person I've admitted it to out loud because it goes against everything Mama said, but . . . Georgia belongs here. She should be running the shop with me. Or take it herself and let me be a bohemian weirdo tending a garden and building a zucchini empire."

"Maybe," Eddie says. "But please, just tell her. I don't want to have to ruin our friendship by going over your head to tell her, and I won't be attending the next chemo alone. You decide which one of us tells them."

"You're ready to be off the hook from me?" Junie pouts.

He wavers. "There's no 'off the hook' from this, Junie. You are a royal pain that has assumed a permanent spot in my heart. I'm on your team, kid. But it's time for me to step back so your women can take over." He swallows hard. "You were born into a pack family. Y'all are made to work in a group; you've never once been a collection of individuals. And when all of you are in it together, you're absolutely unstoppable."

"I'm glad I get to keep you," Junie says. He makes her feel so loved inside his understanding. "And especially if I don't have to date you."

The nurse returns then, ready to hook her up to the IV.

CHAPTER 41

GEORGIA

D AD GAVE ME THE CINNAMON roll recipe a few nights ago, and I've been sitting on it waiting for the right moment. Not that it's an easy breezy unwrap-it-and-done type of recipe, but I want it to be a surprise for Junie. She hasn't been herself this past week, and if I had to guess, I think it's probably a mixture of the stress of knowing we're still so far off on the shop money and the adjustment to her falling for my ex.

We don't say it out loud, but I can tell we all understand that we might end up having to settle for a patch-up job rather than a glam Goldilocks makeover at the shop. Maybe patched-up is a bit more on-brand for June's anyway. Who am I kidding? Budget glam is the only brand we've ever had.

Anyway, tonight is another Cards night, and if Cece lays off the booze a tad, we could be another step closer to the goal. For now, I'm in the kitchen unloading grocery bags full of flour, eggs, sugar, cinnamon, and all the little tubs of spices and rising agents Mama's recipe calls for. Junie's out with Eddie, being cute, and said she'd meet me at June's tonight for the event.

I lean on the counter and reread the recipe. Apparently, the dough has to rise before I roll it up, and honestly, I'm not totally sure what that even is. And then I have to leave it again—another rise, she calls it. Because I didn't know how to do it the first time around, I should certainly endeavor a second attempt.

Without thinking too hard about it, I pick up my cell phone and call my father.

"What on God's green earth is this cinnamon roll rising dough witchcraft?" I ask. "Not to mention, they were all out of eye of newt at the store."

He chuckles in a low rumble. "They're not easy. That's why your mama was always so proud of them."

"So much for me surprising Junie. Not to mention I have to leave them? And by my math, they'd need to bake while Cards is happening."

It feels like another thing going wrong just for the sake of it when it would be really, really lovely if the universe would do me a solid and let me win at something.

"Why don't you come over here? We can figure it out together, and they'll be out of sight until they're ready for her."

I reload my baking supplies into the grocery bags scattered on the kitchen counters and haul them out to Junie's truck. Before long it rumbles the whole five minutes down the road to my childhood home.

When I get to the front door this time, I try the knob. It turns easily to the right, and as the door swings open, I call into the house. "Dad? It's Georgia."

I pass through the dark entryway and find him in the kitchen where he's already wiping down countertops and setting Mama's recipe book in a stand. Behind him, the coffee maker gurgles and the deep smoky scent greets me. It's almost as if we were planning this all along.

"You ready to learn?" he asks.

"Hang on, you know how to make them?" I drop the grocery bags on the breakfast table with a thud. "Before, you made it sound like you were still a beginner."

"Come on, let me show you."

Dad is like Cinderella's fairy godmother in this kitchen. He glides around measuring, pouring, sprinkling with poise and grace, swirling me into his activity like a natural accompaniment. Like he's done this so many times before. How much time has he spent baking in here? Because the new casual hobby he mentioned offhand at the attic clean-out seems anything but.

Once we have the dough put together and Dad shows me how to "set it aside to rise," we let our hands rest as well.

"Alright, so spill it. How did you learn all this?" I ask.

"Coffee first?" He holds up the pot.

"Please."

He takes out two mugs and fills them, and we settle at the breakfast table.

"A few months ago, I started teaching myself some of your mother's recipes. I've got a bit of time on my hands these days now that I'm fully retired. The bookkeeping at the shop is very part-time."

"I guess the cinnamon roll love is universal for Louises—I mean us, the family." I cringe a bit.

"I probably should've just taken your mama's last name when we married and made myself an official Louise." He laughs.

I notice the way he chooses not to be offended at my jump to ditch his last name in place of my mother's.

"You miss her," I say.

"Something fierce, every day since." He takes a swift gulp of coffee, as if to swallow the grief.

"I guess if everything else fell away, we'll always have that to bind us: her memory."

He looks sideways and nods for a moment. "It's true, but you also get to make your own path, live your own life. However you want."

"I know." I'm actually starting to believe it, that maybe the "however I want" really does apply.

I look at the time on my watch. "I should probably get going. I'll need to change before Cards."

He pops his fingers into his ears and starts humming. "Pretending I didn't hear that." He winks.

He really is good at pretending; there isn't a doubt he's one of us. It makes me wonder why he hasn't been included in Cards. Probably the same reason I wasn't. Because it didn't need to be more than it was, because I didn't ask, because he didn't ask. I'm learning that maybe sometimes in this family you have to demand a little.

I glance at the kitchen. "When do I come back for second shift?"

He leans forward. "Why don't you let me finish up?"

"No way," I say. "I can't let you down like that. I have to follow through."

He pulls a small smile. "You know, it's ok to let someone else help. Y'all have all kinds of nonsense on the docket that I'm only partially aware of. This is something I can do—for you *and* for Junie. It'd be my pleasure."

I consider it. "Only if we set another day for me to learn the rest."

He pops out a hand and I shake it slowly, a warmth blossoming in my chest. Accepting the help feels like being loved.

"I'll leave the rest of the baking supplies with you." I stand and lean over to press a kiss on his cheek.

"Drive safe, Peach," he says as we walk to the door.

"Always," I call over my shoulder as I head outside to the truck.

CHAPTER 42

JUNIE

THE BEAUTY SHOP IS BUZZING, the card tables are busy, and every Louise has a smile of some sort on her face. If Junie didn't know better, she might say they've finally found their stride on this second Cards night. And she might be the only person who knows this happy bubble of life can't carry on forever.

An hour or so ago, she and Eddie rolled in trying to look like they hadn't endured an emotionally taxing morning, and Junie suggested Eddie join Georgia as co-bartender. She specifically asked to man the poker chips, making a claim about it being her lucky spot, but mostly she wanted those two together and herself firmly parked in a chair.

Chemo was just about as ghastly as Junie expected, and she's ready to do her best to forget it ever happened until she has no choice but to suffer the side effects tomorrow.

Tina plops down into a seat next to her at the poker chips table. "Georgia and Eddie are looking awfully friendly." She says it with the largest hint of judgment she can manage.

"What would you prefer?" Junie says.

"Well, it's just— Don't you mind, honey? I guess they're not flirting, but it's hard to start a friendship when romance is the muscle memory."

"Honestly, not really." Junie feels on the border of letting the truth rip, like the pull of it is unbearable. After today, it's too heavy to hold. "I'm not sure it wasn't a totally dumb idea for me to try to 'date' my sister's ex. If 'exes' is even what we can call them—seems like there should be another term for people like them who seem made for each other."

Tina misses the air quotes Junie puts around *date*.

"Well, I never," she says. "It's not right. I'm going to go over there and pull one of them to be the 'bouncer.'"

When Junie looks over, separating them is the furthest thing from her mind. Maybe it's the chemicals they pumped into her veins this morning, but there's something just so delightful about Georgia and Eddie together. They're natural and joyful, like relishing life is their default mode when existing side by side. The way they laugh and banter and challenge each other in intellect. The effort tonight from both of them to keep their distance, not laugh or linger too long—it's obvious because it looks like work to stay away from the love that is so natural between them. Eddie looks like a fully decorated Christmas tree on his first official night, and in that moment of glory, he stops and chooses to look at Georgia. Like she's the whole world itself wound into one human body.

He adores her. Plain and simple.

Junie has been an idiot and an ass to stand in their way.

"I'm sorry, hon, I have to say something to them," Tina whispers to Junie, then pops up and marches toward the bar.

"Tina!" Junie calls after her. She stops halfway to the bar and turns to meet Junie's glare.

Junie shakes her head and mouths, *Don't you dare.*

"Just a Sprite and *nothing else, please*," Junie calls over.

Tina rolls her eyes like a surly teenager then continues *past* the bar and its two bartenders. Only then, out of sight, does she whirl around and flip the bird.

Good God, what have they done to sweet Aunt Tina?

CHAPTER 43

GEORGIA

I WAFT THE BOURBON UNDER EDDIE'S nose, then stop when I realize I'm getting too close to him. I hold it out to him instead. "Here, you do it." He takes it but doesn't sniff. "Oh, come on. Just take a whiff—you can't tell me this stuff's not quality."

He does as he's told. "Smells like gut rot and regret."

It turns out bourbon is Eddie's I-can't-drink-that-without-bad-flashbacks liquor, but it doesn't quell my efforts to convert him. "It's really hard to hang out in this place if you don't drink bourbon."

"So you're telling me if Junie quits bourbon, she's out of the fold?" He moves closer to me, and I can practically feel the warmth radiating from him. He seems to realize it and shuffles back.

"Of course not. As they say, 'A Louise is free to do as she pleases.' No one's checking her cup."

"Ah, so you're purely talking non-Louise, I see?"

I watch his lips curl into a grin I used to know so well, with lips I once had memorized. A little place inside me aches for that kind of closeness to him.

I step back and tip up the liquor in my cup. "You and I both know the Louise name doesn't have to be on a birth certificate for someone to qualify."

Ted Brunson, longtime cashier at the Piggly Wiggly across town, strolls up, a five-dollar bill in hand.

"Mr. Ted," Eddie announces. "What'll you have, sir?"

"Hold your horses, rookie." I shuffle in front of Eddie. "I'm the barkeep here."

He smiles and holds his hands up as he retreats. "Y'all two decide to give it a go again? Always thought you were a sweet couple. Anyway, bourbon neat for me, please."

I blush as I pour. I thought we were doing a good job at keeping this platonic, but if Ted assumes we're a couple again, I worry others are thinking the same. I didn't feel like I was flirting; in fact, I've been intentionally biting back the flirty comments that bubbled up in my mind. I look up and scan the crowd for Junie. I smile when I see her rocking back and forth in her seat to the beat of the song playing over the speakers. She raises her fists and pumps them, and as a customer approaches, he dances up to her. Junie jumps up and does a quick booty pop before sliding back down into her chair, looking like she's pulled a muscle.

I grin. Could this be the happiest I've ever seen her? Possibly.

Once Ted leaves, I turn back to Eddie. He's already looking at me like he's been waiting.

"Want to dip out? Get some air?" he asks.

Suddenly I'm thinking about all the other times we dipped out. From a movie night with friends to his grandfather's lake house to sit on the dock under the stars, slurping milkshakes from the drive-thru. From his mother's Fourth of July barbecue to a roadside stand a few towns over for fireworks of our own.

But we don't get to dip out like that anymore. Not when he's clearly moved on.

I want to be with him. Alone. But it would be a horrible, terrible idea.

"The bar needs to be stocked, and there's stuff in the back of Junie's truck," he says.

"Ah, ok." Part of my heart deflates when I realize he wasn't asking for my company alone, that this is purely task related, but alas, having a task to accomplish makes it acceptable that I head for the door at his suggestion.

Eddie swipes a bottle of wine and two plastic cups from underneath the makeshift bar. "I think we're also legally mandated a fifteen-minute break from this unpaid gig."

I laugh as I follow him out, leaving a good buffer of space between us.

"It's been forever since we really talked," Eddie says after the front door shuts behind us.

"Just for a few minutes," I say. "I don't want anyone getting the wrong idea." I am a rule follower by default (unless we're counting outrageously difficult science labs that push me to the very brink), but I'm even more faithful to rules that protect my Junie.

We set up on the curb out front in plain sight, a good three feet apart.

Eddie cracks the screw top on the wine and balances the cups on the concrete ledge.

"Here," I say. "I'll hold. You pour." I move closer to help.

"You don't want the Michelin-star-restaurant treatment? I was going to let you swirl it and sniff it before you send me back to the bar for something less tragic," Eddie says, looking up with a grin.

My insides curl in delight. It's like seeing him again for the first time, him like this, so *him*, no walls, beside me.

Oh my God, I've missed him.

"And you think there's anything better at the bar?" I ask.

He lets the wine glug into the cups. "Fair point."

I take one and slide back into a safe zone along the curb.

Eddie raises his cup. "To illegal gambling and the wild ways of the Louise women."

I can't help but laugh. "Bless you, Eddie Rigsby, for bearing with us."

I don't realize until a moment later that we're still staring right at each other, cups raised, untouched. A hum pulses between us like its own life force, and I remember: I was always at my best when I was with him. Even so, it has to be ignored, so I bite the inside of my cheek and look away.

Up until now, I've mostly avoided Eddie, keeping a wide berth and keeping my mouth shut. Sitting here beside him highlights just how difficult it will be to interact with him in a new way.

But for Junie, I'll figure it out.

The age-old bell on the front door of June's clatters, then footsteps approach.

Eddie and I whirl around in unison, and there stands Junie, agony painted across her face.

CHAPTER 44

JUNIE

JUNIE GETS TO HER FEET when Eddie and Georgia head out to the parking lot. She watches them through the glass door pretending so well that they can be just friends. Junie knew Georgia was capable of difficult things, and she knew Georgia loved her with a massive depth, but this is tangible evidence of just how much.

When Georgia draws closer to hold the cup, Junie wonders if she'll stay. In her head, she cheers for her to stay beside him. But of course, her responsible big sister shifts back down the curb.

The disappointment that rattles inside at the sight is enough. Junie has the power to make this right, and she's ready to step up. Or at least to make a start at it.

The clatter of the bell behind her as she steps outside makes it feel more real. She's about to confess to Georgia that she and Eddie aren't dating, that she's sick, and now there are only steps between them.

She could dart back inside and put it off another day. But she's past that now, and she'll do what she came out here for. To tell Georgia, then beg her to stay here at home. For herself, yes, and also to help lead June's. Junie knows she'll be upset with her, about the diagnosis, but she wants—for the love of everything good—to sound like she at least, a little bit, has her stuff together.

"Junie," Georgia says. "What's wrong?"

CHAPTER 45

GEORGIA

EDDIE AND I SHOOT TO our feet upon seeing Junie so distraught, and we stand there frozen, waiting for her to say something.

Junie's sad gaze is laser focused on me, heavy like a dumbbell. It's as if Eddie is invisible to her, and he shuffles back, away from us. I glance over at him, one hand in his pocket, one hand in his hair gripping the back of his bowed head. Does he know what this is about? Is Junie worried there's something going on between us? Why isn't he rushing to his girlfriend's side?

"No. It's just— I—" Junie says.

"You know we're just hanging as buds out here, right? Just a quick break before we get back to work." I look again at Eddie, hoping to make meaningful eye contact and urge him to jump in. "Right, *Eddie?*"

Junie closes the gap between us, uninterested in her boyfriend as she breezes by him, and I wonder if it would be ok to pull her close to me. I stop before I do.

Junie shoots me a grin, but now, lined in true worry, it only imitates her usual smile. "Eh. I'm kinda over him, if you wanna take a spin."

I don't even smile. Not like I usually would because nothing about this moment feels right. Nothing about her joke feels sincere. And Junie jokes can fix a multitude of ills.

"I'm sorry. Seriously, I'm not interested in Eddie," I say. "We can completely avoid each other, if that's best. I don't want you hurt like this."

Junie reaches up and cups my cheek. "You haven't done a thing wrong, Peach. It's not about him." She turns to him. "Eddie, can you let me and my sister talk, please?"

"Of course," he says. "But for the record, I do love Junie, and I would never let anything in my control harm her. Never ever."

I watch the way Eddie looks at my little sister, whom I've adored as a vocation, and I recognize it. Of course I would recognize the look of the most important thing in my life, protecting Junie. He loves her, yes, but it's gentle and sweet and lined with the fear that only comes from desperately wanting good for someone completely outside you.

Junie pulls me down to sit on the curb beside her as Eddie reenters the shop.

"Eddie and I aren't dating," she says. "Weren't ever. We were pretending."

Junie picks at her fingernails, and as a reflex I gently pry her hands apart. A nervous chuckle escapes me. "What? No. That makes no sense."

"There's a reason for it, and I need to tell you. It'll make sense. And I've been trying to find a good time to tell you this, but I knew you'd be mad. I knew you'd be so sad. I just couldn't—"

I take her hands again, squeezing them this time. "Just tell me." I try to channel my mama and all the Junes before her. "You know you can always tell me anything. What is it? More on the Goldilocks front? Because if we need to change course and just put the shop back together, that's *fine*. There's no shame in just chalking it up to not working out right now."

Junie shakes her head, and her face trembles slightly when she sucks in a breath. "It's not the shop; it's me."

My gut doubles in on itself, and I swallow the knot that instantly fills my throat. This is it. This is the moment I've known was coming. This is the moment the brief hiatus from tragedy and chaos breaks. I've tried to convince myself for years that I was overreacting, being slightly insane, but like some depraved prophet, I just knew.

"Tell me, honey. Wh-what's wrong?" I force out the words as my body resists.

"I'm sick."

"What does that have to do with spending time with Eddie?" My confusion slows my worry.

Junie stays quiet, but then it clicks and suddenly the pieces re-arrange themselves into a clear picture.

"Eddie's been doing medical care on the side for you, hasn't he? *Please* tell me you didn't let your insurance lapse." It's the big sister in me, but I've tried to hammer into her the importance of investing in her health.

"I still have insurance."

"Right. Ok," I say. "So it's about the medical bills? What do you need that costs out of pocket? Allergy testing? The price is highway robbery, but we'll figure it out. It's more important than the renovation. I get it, I really do—"

"You *don't* get it, Georgia." Junie is firm but kind. "I'm *sick*."

It's knee-jerk for me to take charge, but I will my body to be still on this curb and my mouth to stop running. I watch Junie's throat dip and release, her face fall, her reluctance to look me in the eye, and I know. Looking at her, I can see this is something more.

I raise a hand to cover my mouth as the ground seems to flip over me and spin.

Like Mama, I think. *Like Mama*, I know.

I shake my head as tears gather.

"Yes." Junie nods. "Like Mama."

My insides break in quick agony right along old fault lines. I know how to hurt this way. Yet somehow, this time, I'm not crippled by it. The heat in my chest builds and burns through me.

"And you told *Eddie*? And not me?" My voice is clipped. "You're terribly, terribly sick, and you didn't tell me?"

"He was just there that day." Even the way she says it sounds like an excuse.

He was there. I've made it my life's mission to be there for Junie, to be the one in the wings, the one listening in for the slightest need. I have thrown myself into the fire time and time again, happy to become dust for the sake of her flourishing. I have shrunk myself for her sake. And yet, *he* was there.

"What do you mean *he was there*? When?" I ask.

Junie shrugs. "His mom had an appointment the same day I got my actual diagnosis. Complete coincidence, but he was there—physically, at the clinic."

"No, Junie. *I* am there for you. I'm the one who shows up for you. Eddie? Not a snowball's chance." I stand and pace, despite nothing, not even the ground below my feet, feeling solid enough to rely on. "I've been here, Junie, sleeping in the next room, trying to save this shop, and never, not once, did you think to mention to me that you have cancer just like our dead mother?" It's not until I'm finished that I realize I'm shouting.

Junie stands and hangs her head like she knows she messed up. "I'm sorry."

And it's just about as gutting as her first admission.

I go to her, of course I go to her, and I wrap her in my arms, and I hold on like something's trying to take her, and a sob cuts up my throat. I won't let her go, not ever. Her mouth is beside my ear and I hear tears in her shaky breaths. My throat aches as I try to bite back the scream that demands to be heard, and I pull her closer. Suddenly it feels like she has an expiration date, like she might vanish from within my grasp.

"You must've been so scared, Junie Bug," I whisper in her ear. "I'm here now. I'm not going anywhere."

Junie pulls back. "I wanted to tell you, you know that. It's just, I didn't want to hurt you."

Junie drops onto the curb. I sit down beside her and wind my fingers into hers. I remember when hers were smaller than mine, and time hasn't changed the way I hold her. I wonder if we'll get to do this with ultra-wrinkly hands too.

"Tell me everything I missed," I say.

Junie lays her other hand over ours together and squeezes. "Truly, Eddie's been a godsend. He's been kind and patient, showing up on time and checking in."

I don't want to ask the next question, but I need to know the answer. "What's the plan?"

Junie tells me about starting chemo this morning, she tells me about however many times, however many weeks she'll have to go, but it's not what I want to hear. This is the punch list of bad luck, the how-to, the messy middle. This is what I want to rush through and past, blinders firmly in place. I want a guarantee, a promise, a prize at the finish line. I want the doctor to look me in the eye and tell me, "This is highly treatable. Your sister will be fine. Yes, you may take her place."

"What are the chances?" I ask.

It's then that I remember a podcast I listened to once where an oncologist talked about this question, how much she hates it, how unreliable a percentage can be. She was talking in terms of scientific accuracy, but I remember agreeing with logic all my own. It doesn't matter what size the percentage is; what matters is that you get a spot inside it. Ninety-nine percent is so promising until you become the one. I want to know my assigned seat, that I have one.

"Are you kidding? I'm a *Louise*." Junie puts on a plasticky smile that only sits on the surface.

In the silence I let sit between us, her face crumples because she's drawn the same conclusion as me: Mama was perhaps the most Louisey Louise born to earth and look what happened to her.

It's when I think about Mama, and the end, and the pain that followed and never left that I finally break. I double over and sob in heaves as I think about my Junie sick, alone, probably terrified even if she pretends she's ok. I think about all the times I went to the ends of my earth to help her, to protect her, to save her just like this beauty shop. Yet this time there is nothing to be done.

It's the very first time I cannot do the thing I've always done best: save her.

My little sister's life is just outside my reach.

Junie could die. I can't breathe.

CHAPTER 46

JUNIE

GEORGIA KEPT JUNIE UP ALMOST the entire night after their moment on the curb outside June's. Shortly after the truth spilled out, the pair left Eddie to cover for them and help the aunts wrap up Cards.

Back at the Clementine House, Georgia mostly just stared at Junie. For the whole night. She sat down in Junie's desk chair as Junie climbed into bed and wouldn't leave her side, as if cancer were a covert assassin that might strike down her little sister in one swift motion under the cover of dark. When Junie woke in the night to use the bathroom, Georgia was curled on the floor beside the bed, spooning with Puds. By this morning, Georgia was finally gone. Hopefully she got at least a few hours of sleep.

Frankly, Junie gets it. She knew Georgia would be worried. She knew she'd be protective. She's *Georgia*.

The thing Junie wasn't prepared for is how wrecked her sister is, and it was right to keep the rest of the discussion—about the old test results—for another time. Last night, Georgia's always-styled red waves frizzed into a mess that may or may not have been held up by an actual rubber band off the kitchen counter. The sobs broke from her as soon as it seemed the height of it had passed. She shook when she walked and only seemed to still once she took up her post in Junie's room at bedtime.

Junie has never, not once in her thirty years of life, seen Georgia like this.

She might've finally broken her.

Even though the nausea is starting to hit from yesterday's IV cocktail, Junie pulls herself up to go check on her sister in the guest room. Before Junie's even out from under the covers, Georgia bursts in with far more energy than someone who only got a couple of spotty hours of sleep should have.

"I'm calling an emergency Good Hair Days meeting. To discuss you." Her hair nest has grown larger overnight, but Junie stops herself from smiling at it. She needs to be extra careful with this overripe version of Peach. She will bruise easily.

"That's fine," Junie says. "I need to tell the aunts too. And Dad. Just wanted to make sure you were first."

Georgia huffs, but it's only at half power. "Well, you certainly missed the mark on that one. *Eddie* was the first, and we can't take that back."

"I'm sorry. Really I am. I should've told you right away. But I didn't want to be a burden. For once I wanted to take care of an issue like an adult, on my own."

"That might be the dumbest thing you've ever said," Georgia replies. "No person should do cancer alone."

Junie tries a tiny smile. "Never did I say I was the smart sister."

Georgia sighs and reluctantly drops onto Junie's bed. "Well, you played the part pretty well. Sure fooled me—and the aunts as far as I can tell."

Junie rolls over so she can see Georgia, and it reminds her of when they used to sleep over in each other's rooms as kids. "Be honest— were you ever really ok with me and Eddie?"

Georgia blinks her eyes closed for what feels like thirty seconds, then pops them open. "No. If I'm honest, I wasn't. But also being honest, there isn't a thing in this world I wouldn't give up for you, Junie. You've always known that."

Georgia's words are a force field around Junie. *You're loved, so loved. You're lovable.*

"I guess I have," Junie says.

"Not to mention, I wasn't even *giving him up*, was I? I chased him off long ago. Eddie and I never really had a chance, considering—"

"The past?" Junie says. "Pshh. You two want each other so bad. Seeing you together at the bar last night was the main reason I couldn't wait any longer to tell you. Keeping you apart is such a waste."

"I appreciate that. I do," Georgia says. "But the next time I see Eddie, it won't be friendly. Might even need someone there to make sure I don't start swinging."

Junie sits up and crisscrosses her legs, stares down at her sister. "You can't be serious."

"Dead serious! He lied to me about my sister being sick and took my place going to appointments and being your person. He could've told me any time. Any moment. I mean, what did he have to lose? What were you going to do? Break up with him?"

"You've got it wrong," Junie says. "I made him promise."

"These are exactly the times it's ok to break a promise."

"He didn't say anything because I begged him to let me do it in my own time."

"You don't get to make the schedule for cancer!" Georgia yells it, then flops her arms over her face to hide.

Junie rubs gentle circles on her arm. "You're right. I should've told you. I should've let you be there. I wanted you there, by the way—I just didn't realize how important it was until I was already hooked up to that IV and I realized what an idiot I was thinking bravado and Twizzlers would get me through it."

Georgia uncovers her face. "I believe you. I just got my feelings hurt—on top of my devastation. Let me help you?"

Georgia looks so vulnerable, like she's never been before. Not one piece of armor.

"One thousand times yes," Junie says. "The first thing I need you to do is have my back when I tell the aunts."

CHAPTER 47

GEORGIA

THE FOUR OF US ARE assembled in our usual circle in our usual seats in the middle of June's when Tina stands and clears her throat.

"Ladies, if I may have the pleasure."

Our chattering quiets, and we turn our eyes to Tina.

We ended up waiting an extra day to meet for Good Hair Days because Junie was so sick after the first chemo treatment. The poor girl heaved and heaved and dry heaved until she was pale and limp. I waited to cry until she found pockets of sleep, and I only ever let myself doze, just in case she called out.

I wish I could've prepared for this. I would've planned like I always do, shopped for groceries, bought her cozier pajamas, prayed for an ungodly amount of emotional strength. But instead, I'm floundering in the crisis all the while trying to digest the original news itself.

Tina claps her hands and squeals, "Happy Monday, y'all—today is *pie planning day!*" She lifts the three-ring binder on her lap and dances it around in front of us. It's professionally labeled *Tina's Pies: County Fair.*

I'd forgotten, given how Junie just turned my world upside down. "I've been looking forward to it," I lie.

I could redirect; I could tell Tina there's a more pressing issue to discuss. But these pies have her breaking out of her dusty chrysalis into a sassy Tina butterfly, and I couldn't forgive myself if I cut that short. There's no harm in letting her bask in the joy of her personal success for a little while longer. She's even come prepared with a handout. Maybe now it makes a little more sense why Junie waited so long to tell.

"Alright." Tina hops up and passes out a bullet point sheet. "At the top is the budget. It'll cost approximately four hundred dollars for supplies—I negotiated with the coffee shop's supplier—and I'll pay that up front. We'll bake seventy-five pies. At five dollars a slice, we could make over two thousand dollars on this. There are also prizes to be won, cash prizes. I know it's a lot of work . . ."

"We're up for it," Cece says. "And we'll recruit extra help."

"That's what I was hoping you'd say." Tina grins. "I'll nail down a schedule closer to bake day, but first we need a baking location and volunteers."

"Well, for volunteers, obviously all of us," Cece says. When her eyes land on Junie, she grins and says, "If Junie Bug can lay off the booze long enough to show up not looking seasick."

"*Hilarious*," Junie says.

I'm impressed by her acting skills; if I didn't know otherwise, I wouldn't suspect a thing. Instead, my mind is thinking about nothing but her and her illness, the schedule for treatment, how much sicker she'll get. *I can't protect her.* I bite the inside of my mouth to stop the tears that well in the corners of my eyes.

"Yes, all four of us," I confirm. "I'm sure Eddie would help. And Dad—honestly, I think it might be time to open the circle to him."

"But he's not a Louise woman," Cece says gently. I wonder for a moment if she feels the same as me: afraid that adjusting this precious circle runs too high a risk of breaking it. But what she doesn't know is that we'll need all the backup we can get for our next big challenge.

"I know," I say. "I guess—"

"We're not really in a position to be picky," Tina says. "So we have six of us—approximately. I wonder if I could get Sam to help."

"*Sam?*" Junie and I say at the same time.

"Yeah, who the heck is Sam?" Cece asks.

Tina shrugs. "He's the food supplier for the coffee shop, the one I worked out the deal with for the pie supplies. With all the conversations we've been having about my order, we've become friends. He's a sweetheart and has been beyond helpful. Just a quality guy—not to mention he cut me a pretty good discount."

"Don't you say he *cut you a discount.*" Junie smirks like she's wishing trouble on herself.

"Oh, stop!" Tina demands. "It's not like that."

"Sure sounds like he might want it to be *like that,*" Cece adds.

"I can't help but agree," I say. "And for the sake of the cause, it would be reckless not to at least invite this Sam to baking day."

Tina pauses—like she even has to think about it. "Ok. Alright, I'll ask. The more hands the better." She looks down and pages through her binder, but the glow that rises on the apples of her cheeks is unmistakable.

"Last thing on this subject and then my lips are sealed: Please let the record show that Randy was not mentioned once as a volunteer," I say.

Tina looks at me for a second like she's deciding whether to be mad or not. "You're right," she says. "Randy is useless." Tina lets her hands drop to the binder in her lap. "I'm sick and tired of him, and honestly, I think I've decided I want him out. I just—I just need to find the courage to do it. But I think I'm on my way."

"We're here for you," Junie says. "It's the right choice."

"I'll gladly be on the eviction squad, so just say the word," Cece adds.

"Thanks . . ." Tina swallows hard and pauses. "But back to pies—what we're really still in need of is a location to bake. None of our houses can bake more than two or three pies at once, which will take days. We need a commercial kitchen of some kind."

For a while we sit there, thinking in quiet.

"Was this afternoon *planned* as a dry meeting?" Cece asks. "In my experience we do our best thinking a little sauced up."

Junie speaks up. "Today is dry—I'll explain later. But first, I wonder if we could ask the Silvers to lend us the church kitchen? It's not quite commercial, but it's built to cook for a crowd."

"I like it," I say. "Because most businesses around here with a kitchen like that will need to be using it themselves."

"Exactly," Junie says.

"Would you mind reaching out to Ms. Luanne or any of the other Silvers and let me know?" Tina asks Junie.

"Sure thing," Junie says.

"Excellent," Tina replies. "Well, that's a wrap on pie talk for now. Junie, what was it you wanted to share?"

"Yes," Junie says. "We're waiting on—"

Before she can finish her sentence, the front door clatters open and our father walks in.

"Him," Junie says. "For the next part I need everyone here."

CHAPTER 48

JUNIE

J UNIE STANDS, PUSHES BACK HER chair, and shimmies it
sideways until Daddy has room to pull up one for himself.

She didn't ask the aunts about inviting him here, but she did warn
Georgia she'd done it. Georgia had shrugged and said, *"If ever there
was a time for it, it's now."*

Junie knows how the confession will go, how the aunts will react.

Cece shoots her an unsure look as Tina says, "Good evening, Rich."

He nods. "Thanks for having me, ladies. Promise I won't stay long."

"We're glad to have you." Georgia looks like she really means it.

Cece coughs a little then says, "Guess since Rich is here, this is
bad news. Just rip the Band-Aid off, Junie. Are we losing the shop?"

Junie shakes her head. "No. Well, I sure hope not—that's not what
this is about."

Cece's face creases in confusion. Tina sits wide-eyed and painfully
optimistic. Daddy looks like he's still adjusting to being thrust into
this circle.

Georgia clears her throat. "Need help, Junie Bug?"

Junie looks at her sister so prepared to save her. "This is one I can
handle." It surprises Junie that she believes herself when she says the

words. Maybe something about coming clean with Georgia sparked a boost in confidence. Yes, this is hard, but Junie is tough too. "I'm really sorry to lay this on y'all, but I have cancer. Breast cancer like Mama."

Tina lets out a gasp. Cece goes white. Daddy sits frozen.

"I've been going to a ton of appointments, and I started chemo a few days ago—hence me looking like a boozehound today. I didn't want to tell you, not anyone; I wanted to just manage it on my own. Eddie stumbled into me at the clinic the day I found out when he was there with his mom, so that's why we've been spending time together. No romance, no dates, just my medical chauffeur."

Finally, the feeling Junie has waited so long for comes as her chest tightens and her throat grows thick. Her breathing hitches as her eyes prickle and then burn, tears running from them. Saying these words, proclaiming the news to her family, solidifies it. It's real.

She is so very sick.

"I didn't and *don't* want to be the baby of the family; all I want to do is snap out of that and stand on my own two feet. But when I try, like with this renovation, it just doesn't work. I fail, I mess it all up, I do all the wrong things. And then I found out I was sick, and it was just another Junie Problem."

"Junie, you've never been a problem. Not once," Tina says behind tears. "I'm so very sorry, sweetie."

Georgia bows her head and dabs at her eyes, her shoulders set as if she's trying to be strong.

Cece nods. "We love you, sweetheart. Just let us help you."

Junie pulls in a long breath. "And that: help. I need to ask for it, accept it. From each of you, and from the rest of them—the Silvers who want to help raise funds, Michaela and the theater group, probably more folks once the news gets out." She laughs and it comes out wet. "Guess I can play the sickly needy woman and get our beauty shop fixed up."

"People want to help." Georgia's voice cracks on the remnants of tears. "You don't have to play any parts or any cards to get them on board. June's belongs to the whole town."

A sob creeps up Junie's chest. "I just . . . wanted to make it right before any of you had to step into this dark place."

Daddy moves to kneel on the floor beside her chair and takes Junie in his arms. "You are not a problem. This is not too much for us. We are not afraid of dark places, and we'll step inside and make a place beside you for as long as it lasts."

Junie leans into his arms and cries as quietly as she can.

CHAPTER 49

GEORGIA

I LET THE AUNTS AND DAD take Junie home after the meeting. It's their turn, for now, to dote on her and remind her of their devotion.

As for me, I pick up the phone and call my boss. When he picks up, I hear the sounds of the office, sounds that were once the backdrop to my day-to-day, ones that now sound like they belong to someone else's life.

"Georgia, so glad to hear from you," Felix says. "How are things?"

"Yeah, uh. Well . . ." I should've prepared more for this question, this conversation as a whole, as I now stumble through it. "I called to discuss work."

"Yes. I know you and Sophie have a special relationship, but I guessed that was the reason." Felix's words have a gentle teasing to them.

"Look." The sigh that blows out of me is deafening. "I'll cut right to it. This isn't good news. This situation at home, it's more than I bargained for."

"Well," Felix says, then pauses. "I don't want to lose you, but I understand how important family is. And . . . I don't know, I don't want to overstep . . ."

"It's ok," I say. "I appreciate the flexibility you've given me."

"Maybe it's the right place for you to be for now. Your voice—it sounds relaxed in a way it never was here. Though perhaps that's a bit my fault." He laughs gently. "And whenever—*if* ever—you're back in the city looking for another gig, give me a call and I'll connect you."

"Thanks," I say. "And you're right. I do need to be here." I don't explain further because I've lived through those words enough the past couple of days, and honestly the last thing I want is someone feeling pity for me right now.

Felix and I say our last goodbye and hang up. I feel relief, like an itchy appendage has been cut off. It's scary too, being jobless. Eventually it'll be my turn to confess. I'll have to tell my family about the reality of who I am, but it's not fair to saddle them with that shame-laced letdown on top of Junie's news.

For now, I'll let them believe I'm working remotely, finally taking up my job on its offer of *flexibility*.

When my last check hits my account, I'll finally settle up my rent with Moon. But I'll also have to move out soon, rather than racking up new months of charges. But that's a problem for another day.

CHAPTER 50

JUNIE

JUNIE CALLS THE GOOD HAIR Days meeting for the next afternoon with one intention in mind: activating her community to save the beauty shop. Finally, she's taking charge of her situation, even if she didn't choose all of the circumstances.

She stands in front of the women, notebook in hand, reading from the list. "So far I have the Silvers and Michaela and the community theater folks. Those are direct offers I've gotten."

"Auto guys would totally help," Cece says. "Not sure what they can do, but maybe give folks a promotion on oil changes or something. Guys work for free for a day and all labor costs go to the fund. I'll talk it over with them."

"Rosalinda said the Brownies want to pitch in too," Tina says. "Long story short, she called me for an appointment, and I let her in on the full situation here and how we need to be a little sly about appointments. She told me all about the Brownies and their community service badges and said she'd come up with a way for them to help."

"When those darling little girls go door-to-door, boy do they *sell*," Georgia says.

Daddy clears his throat. "I'm having lunch tomorrow with a couple guys from the bank. They do community service all the time, and after all the years I've put in, they might work something out."

Junie smiles. This is help that feels good. In fact, she's decided to relish every day she's not suffering the chemo yuck. Just this morning she spent the early hours out in her garden weeding and greeting the newly risen sun with Puds. She feels better now that everyone knows about the cancer—well, lighter. There's still the little bit about Georgia and the genetics test, but Junie's basking in what she has accomplished for now.

"Ms. Luanne saw me this morning at the store," Georgia says. "She was so sweet about Junie's diagnosis, wants to make a prayer shawl and add your name to their list."

"I'm not already on it? I thought any wayward soul automatically qualified." Junie laughs. "In all seriousness, though, they are the best."

"I can't believe what that jock salon pulled on them," Tina huffs.

"Hang on, is there a hair salon feud?" Daddy asks, looking like his brain is working a mile a minute to keep up. "Sorry, y'all. You have to remember, I'm new to this."

Tina fills him in, in great detail, and as she does, Junie pulls up their social media just to check in. When her eyes land on the latest post, her blood boils. "The All-Star Instagram account . . ."

Georgia pulls out her phone, navigates through a few clicks, and reads it out loud. "Reasons to patronize only licensed facilities . . ." She stops. "There's even a graphic, y'all."

"This is about us, right?" Junie says. "I'm not imagining it?"

Cece grumbles. "Think they're playing this coy."

"Ghastly place," Tina announces.

Cece looks at Georgia. "Payback plan?" The two exchange a smile that suggests they've discussed this previously.

"Tina, you have the wigs at your house?" Georgia asks.

Tina nods.

Georgia hops up. "Dad, you're off duty for the night. Ladies, let's go grab wigs, then hit the dollar store for TP. We're going to roll All-Star."

CHAPTER 51

GEORGIA

I SLAP THE FIVE-DOLLAR BILL IN the palm of the teenage girl manning the register at the Dollar General.

"Thanks," I say as I tuck the package of toilet paper under my arm and go.

My blonde wig slips as I screech to a halt in front of the sluggish electric doors. I adjust it, then swoop through and hop back into the passenger seat of Junie's truck.

"Want me to drive?" Cece offers.

She once took a race-car driving course up in North Carolina at one of the NASCAR tracks—presumably on her Cards winnings. Needless to say, the training stuck.

"I've got it," Junie says. "I don't have the energy for chasing runaway TP rolls, and I'm hoping we won't need those driving skills."

I lean my chin on top of the toilet paper package sitting in my lap and enjoy the winding of the truck through the woods. The roads aren't well lit, but it feels more like the comforting cover of canopy as opposed to anything spooky. We wind up and down hills, the brush looking blue and purple under the moonlight.

Eventually we pull onto a main road and into the outdated strip mall.

This time we don't sneak behind the storefronts; we park right up front.

"Ready?" Tina asks.

"As we'll ever be," Cece says.

"Junie, flash the headlights if you see anyone." I pop open the door and step out.

We scurry up to the store and start hanging and wrapping toilet paper wherever we can. It's a little less straightforward than TPing a tree-lined front yard. Not that I would know because I have *most certainly* never done it before. Tina winds the paper around the hinges of the front door, through the handle, and across. I make a job of stringing threads over the support beams on the awning. Cece twists hers like Christmas lights around the pillars of the awning.

When I'm done with the crossbars, I giggle to myself as I pop the mail slot open and thread in sheets like toilet paper letters.

"The sign," Cece says. "We've got to hit that too."

I stop and prop my hands on my hips. "I'm a terrible shot. Especially that high."

"Here." Cece tosses a roll that bounces off the slanted awning and rolls into the parking lot.

"Tina, any ideas?" I ask, pointing up to the sign.

She joins us. "If only we had a ladder."

I look between the three of us. "Let's get the truck. Junie!" I call out as I take off jogging in the direction of her and the vehicle.

After a quick explanation of the plan, Junie repositions the truck and backs it up in front of the awning. I climb into the bed after the truck shifts into park and Junie calls, "All clear!" through the rolled-down driver's window.

"I'm not sure that's safe," Tina says. "We need to be quick. It's only a matter of time before someone drives by."

"Junie will warn us," I say.

"I've got a great view of the road here," Junie calls from the cab.

I turn back to the awning and the work at hand, reaching up. From here I can touch the bottom of the matte black awning, but I can't quite reach to loop around the letters of the sign. I try a few times to toss a line, like a cowboy with a paper-product lasso.

"I'm not close enough. I need a boost."

"I may be sixty-two, but I think I could manage a boost." Cece approaches, lacing her fingers together and making a landing spot out of her palms.

"You're sure?" I ask.

"Go on. Let's see if those weights I've been lifting make a difference."

I place my foot into Cece's hands, and she launches me up with surprising force. In one giant heave, I latch my knee onto the front lip of the awning and reach out to pull myself onto it. Then I grab a roll and sling it across the letters. To my luck it lands perfectly across them and leaves a coily tail.

As I'm admiring my work, the awning cracks underneath me. It sends a jolt through me, and I grab on for dear life. The awning hangs at an angle, and I hang off it.

"I'm going to fall!" I cry out.

Cece's hands are firm on my hips when she promises me, "I've got you. Let go, I've got you."

If I'd been asked a year, months, even more than a few weeks prior, if I'd ever trust Cece in a moment like this, I would've laughed until I cried. But I close my eyes and let go.

She gently lowers me back to the bed of the truck.

I drop to sitting and take in the hanging end of the awning above me. I press my eyes shut, as if to reset them, and when I pop them open, Cece's grinning at the awning between us from where she's leaning on the side of the truck.

"Let me guess. Something about your life flashing before your eyes?" Cece asks.

I bark out a laugh. "Something like that *precisely*."

She pats my shoulder and then turns to Tina, who stands there with her hands clasped over her mouth with white knuckles. "We should get out of here."

The three of us step back to admire our handiwork. The awning hangs off at a forty-five-degree angle with a Georgia Louise Scott–shaped dent in the middle of it. Not that anyone other than these women here could identify the dent as resembling the curve of my backside.

Junie pops her head out of the open window. "Ladies! Incoming vehicle. Let's go!"

Tina yelps.

I yell, "Run!" as I leap from the truck bed and toward the cab.

Junie yelps at us to hurry as we pile in. Lights from another vehicle cross the shopping center as it enters the lot. Tina slams the door and Junie hits the gas, tearing off in a squeal in the opposite direction from the newly arrived vehicle. As we turn onto the main road, I look back. The vehicle we narrowly escaped is a large black SUV, very much like the one Misty Prince owns, but she wouldn't be caught dead at an All-Star Cuts, so it must be someone else.

We ride in silence until we're well clear of the scene of the crime.

"Georgia Louise," Junie says. "We never said anything about property damage."

"Yikes," Tina says. Perhaps about the damage or perhaps about the entire endeavor.

"It was an accident," I say quietly.

"Not sure the police would agree to that," Junie says.

A solid silence follows, and it's Cece who cracks first—with the tiniest giggle.

Then Tina joins in. "Oh my goodness, I don't know how or why I'm laughing because this is bad news."

By now we're all laughing, holding our bellies.

"Junie, get us home before we cause any more trouble," Cece says.

CHAPTER 52

GEORGIA

THE FIVE OF US—ME, Junie, the aunts, and Eddie (much to my annoyance)—sit in the doctor's office waiting room, and Cece pulls out a deck of cards. "Spades?"

We all declare our agreement, and the receptionist shushes us, then mutters something about this not being a sports bar. Unfortunately for her, not a one of us can control the volume of our voice, which reaches an automatic ten once a deck of cards appears.

It's been about a week since we wrapped All-Star in toilet paper, and since then we've been calling in favors left and right, hopeful of making our way to the fifty grand we need. The Silvers have agreed to host a bingo night with a raffle—which sounded at first mention like a much more aboveboard version of Cards. Dad spoke to his banker friends and they're working on setting a date for a pancake breakfast, with the bank offering a healthy sum in addition to funds raised. Michaela's production of *Grease* in a couple of weeks is on its way to polished, and they announced June's as the good cause to receive ticket proceeds. Not to mention, we have the county fair and Tina's pies to sell next weekend. I've scheduled a

Good Hair Days meeting with all our helpers next week, to gather everyone and set the tone before each small group splinters off to do its thing.

Cece shuffles the cards with the efficiency of a Vegas pro, then begins to deal.

I snatch the cards she places in front of Eddie. "*Four hands.* He's invisible for the duration of this visit."

Eddie makes a face like he's irritated, but he deserves it. I have no idea why he even came here today when I made it very clear I am furious with him. Junie, I can reconcile trying to hold it close. But Eddie? He should've known better. He should've pushed her. Sooner. Left some kind of breadcrumb for me. *Anything* before she had her first treatment, so I could've been there for her. I wonder if he even thought about me when he sat there as her only support person. Did it make him feel like he was—*once again*—superior to me?

Cece shrugs at him. "Sorry, son. Better luck next time."

"I know you're pretending you can't hear me, but I'm sorry. I was in an impossible position." Eddie rakes a hand through his hair, his eyes wide and desperate as they wait for me to acknowledge him. "What was I supposed to do? Betray Junie? Abandon her? Not to mention, I was a mess about it the whole time too. I thought I was doing the best I could under the circumstances."

"*Seriously,*" Junie says, raising a brow at me. "You need to quit this. It's childish, and none of it is Eddie's fault." It's not the first or even second time she and I have had the conversation about how Eddie should be acquitted of all responsibility.

Even Tina pats him on the shoulder like she understands, pressing her lips into a sympathetic smile. Cece's shoulders slump, relaxed. And I know they both forgive him. It's because they know how Junie is and would probably need extra hands to count all the ways they've been twisted outside their will by her. They know how disarming and convincing she can be; in many ways, it's the story of my life.

But none of them know Eddie like I do. He could've done more, crafted an argument good enough to convince her. He knows how to connect with people and speak to their reason. He's a doctor, for God's sake; what more did he need to convince her? And all that aside, he could've forced her somehow, and she would've forgiven him—probably even thanked him—in the end.

"Junie Scott," a friendly nurse in pink scrubs calls out.

All of us stand and scurry in a line behind Junie like her overgrown ducklings.

The nurse's cheer fades as she watches the lot of us continue back into the exam room area. "I'd suggest one or two folks accompany the patient," she says. "All of you won't fit, and for patient privacy, we can't have people hanging around in the hallways."

"I'm going in unless there's a police officer or a court order in my way," Cece says, already crossing the threshold to Junie's exam room.

The rest of us follow suit in a chorus of "Me too" and "Over my dead body" and pack into the small square room like sardines.

We leave the red-faced nurse to check Junie's vitals at her station and make ourselves comfortable. Before long she drops Junie back at the room and suggests *again* that some of us wait in the waiting room.

"Seriously, though," Tina says, once the nurse is gone. "We need to hear direct from the doctor what the heck's going on here. Being an oncology nurse, how does she *not* get it?"

"I tried to tell y'all," Junie says. "This would've been much easier to schedule as a call and just put everyone on speaker."

"We can always quietly talk pies while we wait!" Tina says.

"Oh, that's right, I have news," Junie says. "The Silvers were glad to schedule a baking date at the church next week, right before the fair, so everything will be fresh."

Tina squeaks. "Thank you, thank you, *thank you!*"

Eddie is tucked away in a corner trying to make himself look small, and it's a bit satisfying. "I'm a definite *yes* on baking too," he says.

There's a swift knock on the door, and the nurse cracks it open. "If we could keep things down in here, folks, that'd be great."

Tina covers her mouth and blushes. "Guess I got a bit excited."

"Speaking of which," Junie says, "any more *Sam* updates?"

Tina's rosy cheeks deepen in color. "He's coming to bake pies. He said just let him know when."

"Ooh, open commitment, even without a date," I sing. "I like the sound of this guy."

"And I spoke to Randy," Tina says. "I let him know I didn't think it was working out, and do you know what he said? 'That's fine by me—we can just be roommates,' and then the sorry son of a gun went back to his TV show."

"Well, we can go right back to your house from here and help him pack," Cece says.

Junie and I nod enthusiastically.

"He didn't even fight for me. He didn't even say he wanted to be together. He didn't care *one bit*."

"Sounds like grounds for an eviction," I say.

Tina swats at the air. "I told him he'd need to move out, but I didn't say when exactly." She looks out the window, then pulls in a deep breath. "I'll be glad to see the back of him, but it's sad, really. I never wanted it to work out this way, never wanted there to be *another man*—as scandalous as it sounds. The plan was always to do it like we discussed, to build a life together, to love and support each other. I tried, I really did, but I can't let myself be walked all over anymore."

Junie reaches out and takes Tina's hands. "I may have only learned this recently, but it seems to me like a lot of times life doesn't work out our own way. I think all we can do is make the best of the life we get, going whichever way it pleases. Even if it's not the one we wanted."

I feel a rumble of love in the pit of my tummy at Junie's words. I've been so focused on fixing and planning and caring and being unrelentingly mad at Eddie that I haven't yet stopped to think about this part. The part where Junie thinks about her illness and what it's doing to her—what it might do to her—and has to carry the fact that she will suffer, that her body, her fate, is beyond her control. It's baggage she never picked up but can't put down.

It's yet another time in the past few days that I'm faced with the reality that I can't do it for her. But this time it doesn't hurt as bad. There's something about her here today, taking charge, persisting despite her fears, that makes me wonder if she's tougher than I give her credit for.

There's another quick knock on the door, and in steps Dr. Richardson, humming to himself. He looks around at all of us before his eyes land on Junie. "Didn't leave a single one behind today, did you?"

Junie shrugs. "I spilled my guts and turns out this is what you get from my people."

He drops onto the small rolling stool, sets his folder on the counter, and turns to face us. "So you've had one chemo treatment so far, with another one scheduled for later this week. You had mentioned some pain as well that I'd like to discuss further, but first, how was the first one?" The doctor begins to do a basic exam as he talks.

"That chemo is liquid yuck, but I'm feeling way better now," Junie says. She motions at the rest of us. "Now that I've got my people on board, I'll have more help."

The doctor nods. "It's extremely helpful to have family support. Junie can expect to be sick after every chemo treatment, and she might very well get progressively worse with each. Vomiting, nausea, diarrhea. Fatigue. Between treatments there is time to recover, but sometimes it takes longer to feel better as the rounds continue. Changes in taste can occur as well."

My vision begins to blur at the edges as I hear his description layered on top of my little sister. Our Junie. It's more manageable when it's hypothetical, and it's a terribly sad thing when it happens to other people. But to Junie?

I think about her and the things that make her Junie. Her bubbly spirit, her insistent care for others, her fearless dreaming, her syrupy laugh, her fire-red hair. Her obsession with rainbows. Her garden that she seems to charm into blooming each season, rich and earthy just like the spirit inside her. Twizzlers, absurdly. And Puds, who adores her in a way that feels more human than anything.

"What about her hair?" I ask. I swing my glance to Junie, who looks like she hasn't asked this question yet.

The doctor pushes out a tight breath. "With this medication, it's likely she'll lose some, but the extent varies patient to patient."

The doctor continues into a discussion of the schedule, timing, and details about the specific medications she will be administered. Eventually he runs out of explaining. "Last thing, Junie." He turns to her. "How's the hip pain you mentioned?"

Junie nods. "It's pretty rough, and rest doesn't seem to help. Ibuprofen either."

The doctor's brow furrows as he seems to think. "Let's do a scan once you're back up after the next treatment. Get a look inside at what we can see. I think"—he turns back to the computer and begins clicking around—"yes, you had a baseline done very early on, couple months ago now, but I'd like another look."

"And what's the prognosis?" Cece asks, the bravest of us.

The doctor looks to Junie, and she gives him a nod. "The cancer is more advanced than we'd like. We found it had spread to one lymph node when we did her first scan. It's an aggressive type that's frequently seen in younger women—now that we have the genetic confirmation." He pauses. "Having hope is an important part of navigating the course of treatment. Deciding you're giving it your all. But I want you all to know that there are no guarantees. We all love our statistics and find comfort in numbers, but I make it my practice not to give percentages—in all my years of practicing, they haven't been helpful. Every patient has a different health history, different genetics—not to mention new medications and protocols are always in development and this often isn't reflected in old research statistics. At the end of the day, each patient is an individual case, and we give each person our complete effort and attention. What I will say is this: Junie's cancer is aggressive and has spread. Her treatment is of the utmost importance."

I thought I realized this when Junie told me herself, but there's something about being here in this doctor's office, with this professional speaking frankly about my sister's illness. It feels like doubling down. Like erasing the wiggle room.

This thing really could kill my baby sister.

CHAPTER 53

JUNIE

I'M RIDING HOME WITH EDDIE," Junie calls behind her as she sprints to Eddie's unassuming sedan. She slides in before any of the Louise women can corner her. All of them look like they're gasping for breath, emerging from a haunted house as they exit that doctor's office and head toward Cece's Jeep. They deserve a moment on their own.

Maybe Junie wants a moment alone too.

Up until now her cancer MO has been ignoring it, cursing it, and reinventing it in her mind, and seeing all of them react is doing something to her.

Junie has told herself this isn't a big deal. She's told herself she can beat it—which by all arguments is very possible. But up until now she has ignored the other side of it, the possibility that maybe she can't.

The driver's door clicks open, and Eddie slides into the car. He's quiet as he settles, unloading his phone and keys. He turns to the center console and begins digging through. "I'm not sure any of us knew it was so serious." He pulls out a bag of Twizzlers and offers Junie one.

"And I thought you'd forgotten," she says.

He shakes his head. "Georgia's already ticked off enough—I didn't want to fuel the fire by bringing along our traditional cancer candy."

Junie pulls a licorice whip out of the crinkly plastic. "First of all, she'd totally deserve that."

"She doesn't deserve any additional hurt right now. Even if she's being a total jerk to me." Eddie's eyes are so tender, Junie wants to rib him for having the hots for her sister. "And the second thing?"

Junie chews the bite in her mouth. "Honestly? I think I've been downplaying this whole thing in my mind. Until the chemo. And then until now. Seeing them all . . ."

"They love you, Junie, and if there's anything that can help, it's having that rowdy crowd of women on your side."

"It's also a whole lotta my favorite hearts to break." As if on cue, the Jeep passes in front of them as it exits the lot, Cece driving, Georgia shotgun, and Tina perched on the back seat.

Eddie just nods. He knows better than to argue with her, but she thinks on this point he must agree.

"I have been thinking though—about the possibility of an end."

After a pause Eddie looks over carefully. "And what've you come up with?"

"I just want to make sure I do everything I want."

"Like a bucket list?"

"Hell no. I'm not that far gone, you sicko." Junie pushes his arm. "I want to make sure I tell people what I want them to know. And as far as you go . . ." She intentionally leaves a dramatic pause, then waggles her brows.

". . . it's that you love getting a rise out of me?" Eddie asks.

Junie swats the air. "I wanted you to think I was confessing my love. Didn't go over as planned."

Eddie tosses his head back, cracking up, and Junie can't help but do the same. It breaks the tightness of all the sad things that surround her.

Finally she catches her breath and composes herself. "Georgia," she says. "I want you to know that she's the one for you."

"I heard she pretends *all* the guys she likes are invisible," Eddie says.

"Excuses, excuses," Junie says. "I have removed all the obstacles from your way, so if you don't at least try, you've only got yourself to blame."

"I told you about my no-dating pol—"

"Which we both know good and well is a cop-out. It's a guaranteed way to avoid heartache, but it's also a guaranteed way to live out the rest of your life as a sad, lonely dummy doctor. You have a long runway of life ahead, my friend. Live a little. I can promise you this: You'll realize how stupid your little *policy* is if you let this chance slip away."

He's silent for the rest of the ride to the house.

And to Junie, it sounds a whole lot like agreement.

CHAPTER 54

GEORGIA

From the porch of the Clementine, I watch Eddie park the car and walk around to help Junie out on the other side. The aunts dropped me off just a few minutes ago, and I wonder if Junie planned it this way to avoid rehashing things with them. I try, ever so fervently, to find the chilly hatred I was wrapped in before. Something about it is impossible now. Ever since the doctor explained Junie's medical situation, my angry core is all wobbly and threadbare. Perhaps it was a sham from the start. Everything has been slashed, and under the dappled light of the oak tree he looks like a handsome first responder, come to rescue us all from ourselves.

In place of my anger, my heart beats loud and imprecise. Stripped down.

Eddie pops open Junie's car door, and she pretends to hobble out, holding her back like an old lady. She even has a voice to match. "Oh thank you, young man, for helping me safely back to my homestead."

Eddie sighs as he follows a few steps behind. He pulls a smile and holds up his hands, looking right at me. *I don't know what to do with her either*, I think. I pull the heavy door open with a creak as Junie climbs the porch. The warm air flows in behind her.

"Eddie, a word?" It comes out sounding tighter than planned.

He nods and settles into a rocking chair.

"Take your time, lovebirds!" Junie yells as she swings the door shut behind her.

I let myself smile at the spunk in that woman, then join Eddie in the second rocking chair. They squeak and groan along with the deck below us as we waffle in place.

"I know I look defeated, but I am still furious," I tell him. "At least in theory."

"I know." He lets out a long breath, his face slackening.

I see his own strife, and I rock myself harder. "I'm so mad I wasn't there for her. You know that's what I do. I take care of her. That's the only thing I do right. Never in my wildest dreams did I think she'd get cancer, but even less so did I think she'd be without me at her side." I remember the other thing. "And what was the genetic stuff the doctor mentioned today? We've already been there, done that. Do you know what that's all about?"

"I do. And it's something Junie needs to tell you," Eddie says. "You might need to be firm with her to get it out."

My brows crease, and I stop myself from hitting him with "Really, again?" Instead, I sigh. "I guess she'll have no choice now that the cat's out of the bag. But it would really make this easier if you, the *medical professional*, could just explain."

Eddie plants both feet on the deck and stops. "My sharing her news wasn't the right thing to do then, and it's not the right thing for this one either."

"Keeping the people who love Junie most from her is the right thing? What did you think was going to happen? You guys were going to covertly cure her without anyone knowing?"

"I thought exactly this would happen, and I told Junie a hundred times," Eddie says. "I would never keep this from you, not if it was my choice."

He looks so sincere. I can tell the secret has eaten away at him for weeks—unlike the way it tore through me in a single moment. Different path, similar result.

"Guess you knew I'd react like this," I say. "To being left out."

Eddie nods deeply. "And so did Junie. She knew you—and the aunts—would be livid to discover she didn't tell you right away. But in her mind, I guess she saw it as keeping you away from the hurt for as long as possible. The Good Hair Days have been her saving grace, and I think she thought she'd just be blowing up all the good stuff that was left."

I can't fault her entirely because it does feel that way. Like all the good we've mined from the shop debacle has turned to dust.

"I'm just hurting. Everywhere and in all ways," I say. "And I shouldn't have been awful and rude today. That was Junie's appointment, and it should've been about her and not my feelings about you."

In truth, my feelings toward him are more than one thing. They're like his eyes that look green in one light and brown in another. My feelings for Eddie are alive and living and seem to swing in ups and downs just like palm trees in a hurricane.

It won't ever be uncomplicated.

"And I'll say it again: I never wanted this kept from you, but I was in a hard place, stuck between giving you the truth you deserved and respecting Junie's wishes for something that—as you just said—is very much about her." Eddie looks out at the road. "And Junie's not lying when she says I bugged the crap out of her to tell one, some, all, *any* of you. I told her I'd be there for her, and I will continue to be. But not in place of y'all, just as an extra."

I might blame it on all the bad news—our upcoming suffering—but I want to tell him that he's not an extra. Somewhere and somehow, he became part of the group. And even if I did ignore him today, it wouldn't be the same without him here on our team.

"And I don't know, but I tried to do what I thought you would, if you were there. Just to cover your spot until she let you in."

At that my anger is entirely eclipsed. Eddie is thoughtful, intentional in the most compassionate of ways, and it strikes me that I can't think of anyone I'd nominate as a better proxy. Eddie is remarkable at almost anything he tries his hand at (minus skateboarding, but that's a story for another day). The things he encounters, people, places, events, all of them seem improved after he leaves simply because of his presence.

His presence is a special energy, a brand of magic all his own. I've tried to tuck away my awareness of it, my familiarity with it, really— all for the sake of *moving on*. But here in the midst of all this personal tragedy swirled into us like milk into coffee irreversibly, he is exactly the kind of help we need.

I don't want Eddie to go. In fact, I want him closer.

"I believe you," I say. "And thank you. Lord knows if it'd been left up to Junie and Junie only, she might have never scheduled the initial follow-up appointment."

"Hey!" Junie's voice squeezes out of a crack in the window behind us. "I heard that!"

I whip around. "Serves you right for eavesdropping. Scram!"

Junie sighs reluctantly, and I hear the pop of the window closing all the way.

I turn back to Eddie. "You know what I mean."

He nods. "It's one of the things I love most about her."

The comment makes me swell. Knowing how to love Junie is about the closest to knowing me as is possible for another human being on this earth.

"You're the best." Tears gurgle in my throat, and though I know most of them are sad, I wonder if even a few are happy ones. Because of him. Because he really took such good care of her, took her this far.

I stand. Eddie joins me. We let our hands float close and linger.

It feels like standing beside something so big that it casts a shade wide enough for both of us. Something large enough to hold all our good parts—the jetting around Whitetail in his truck, the study dates turned movie afternoons, the falling asleep on his chest. But it also holds the rest—the hurt, *my* shame. I could reach out a pinky so easily, intertwine my fingers with his, and perhaps by extension, a little bit of my heart. If he'd have me.

His draw on me is unmooring.

But so is the fear.

"I should get going." I point inside the house. "Can't leave that mustang alone for too long or God knows what she'll get up to."

Eddie laughs, then rubs his forehead. He looks up and rests his hand on my cheek. At his touch every inch of me comes alive, and I pull in a hurried breath. He rubs his thumb along my jawline, then ever so gently he places a slow kiss on my cheek.

"I'll call you soon," he says. "To check in on everything. You included."

All I can manage is a frenzied nod as he turns and starts down the porch steps.

I slump back onto the rocking chair, and all I can feel is the patch of kissed skin, tingling. I put my hand over it—to save it, to box it up and bring it home and keep it forever.

A few minutes later I hear a car engine approach. My dad's car crawls up the gravel driveway and parks behind the limelight hydrangeas. Slowly, he exits the vehicle, grabs something from the passenger seat, and pops the door closed behind him.

As he approaches, I smell what he's brought before I can see them. The cinnamon hits my nose, and it reminds me of Mama.

"Dad," I say, when he comes near the porch.

He climbs the wooden steps slowly and sets down the platter of perfect, June-worthy cinnamon rolls before taking me in his arms.

"Those cinnamon rolls." I laugh. "I'm so glad you took over."

"It's fun for me," he says. "How's our patient today?"

I motion inside. "As well as she can be, I guess. Let's go inside and she can fill you in on what the doctor *really* said, with me to fact-check."

He was the only one of us who respected Junie's wishes to limit her number of supporters. *"I'll come to the next one,"* he'd said. *"But that means all of you Louises will be sitting that one out."* In the long run, it's probably a smarter tactic.

"I figured we might've gotten a Junie edit before," he says.

I nod. "You're not wrong, but I'm sure she can be bribed into full truth with all of these cinnamon rolls. You made them perfectly for her." The comment catches in the back of my throat, but I don't think he hears it. The moment of us baking together feels like a lifetime ago, considering all that has unfolded since, and only now do I see how it's maybe the closest I've been to him in a long time.

"Both of you, honey," he says. "These are for both of you."

CHAPTER 55

JUNIE

Junie is glad to be back at June's after seeing nothing but the inside of the toilet bowl for the past couple days. It turned out the second chemo treatment wasn't any easier than the first. *Surprise, surprise.*

She and Georgia are alone at the shop, setting up for the very first *community* Good Hair Days meeting they were lucky enough to squeeze in before the Fourth of July holiday tomorrow. Cece needed a little bit of convincing, but it didn't take long before it was made obvious that there was no choice but to fully embrace the people willing to help. Georgia unloads drinks onto a table as Junie sets up the snack trays. This time the options are a little more well-planned—purchased, in fact, rather than scraped from the pantry at the Clementine. Sparkling water, sodas, fruit and veggie trays, some cookies and pretzels.

"While we're here alone," Georgia says, "I've been meaning to ask you about what the doctor meant—at the appointment we came to—about the genetics. Is there some new technology or something?"

Junie's hands stop, her eyes focusing on the tabletop before her. She knew this moment was coming—should've known Georgia isn't the type to let an offhand comment slip by—she'd just wanted to delay it as long as possible. In the pause Junie considers her options. Lying is an option, if not a great one, and honestly, she feels like she's finally righted the big untruths she perpetrated. The idea of going back there is heavy. But being truthful doesn't feel right, not right now, not before this special meeting. Junie pulls in a breath.

"Yeah, it's something I wanted to explain to you," she says, turning to face Georgia. "It's just— It's kind of a lot. And I don't want to go into it right before this."

Georgia glances back, a hint of worry in her eyes. "Ok. I get that. But is everything ok?"

Junie smiles to herself. "Oh, Peach. I am where I am with this illness, and I'm not sure anything is 'ok.' Genetics or not, it doesn't change the next steps, what happens going forward."

The tightness in Georgia's face releases. "Alright, well, I guess that makes sense. I do want to hear about it, though."

Just as Junie nods, Tina waltzes in past the torn-up drywall like the queen of France and props her hands on her hips. "Y'all want to know what I just told Randy?"

"Only because of the way you walked in here," Georgia says.

Cece lopes in behind Tina looking weary, as though she already heard the story on the way over.

Junie cracks the top of the sparkling water bottle with a fizz and pours it into small plastic cups. It has a bold fruity flavor that seems fun enough to rival wine. She holds one out to Tina. Tina's bob is styled in beachy waves, and Junie wonders if Tina finally gave in and bought one of those Beachwaver irons of which she's been equal parts enthralled and suspicious.

Tina accepts the cup with a grateful smile. "I told him he needed to be out by the end of the week—or there'd be hell to pay."

"'Hell to pay,' huh? Nice one," Junie says. It's definitely not the right time to ask about the Beachwaver.

"About time," Cece adds.

Soon the community members trickle into the dusty bare-bones shop. First come the Silvers, all smiles, gray curls, and sweet perfume. They hug and chat before visiting the refreshments and finding their seats. Michaela rushes in five minutes late, her top covered in what might be the remnants of her toddler's dinner. Daddy and a couple of well-dressed men arrive looking the most nervous of the visitors. The Louise women welcome them intentionally.

Georgia stands, raises a glass, and calls the meeting to attention. "Thank you all for being here! We are thrilled that you're willing to help us get June's Beauty Shop back up on her feet." She goes on to discuss the branding deal with Goldilocks Haircare, sparing no detail, and outlines the target numbers. "After the meeting we will email the renderings Junie has received from the brand so y'all are fully aware of where your efforts are going."

In the digital image, the floors are covered in a warm wood LVT—the most practical material for a hair salon and much grander than any linoleum Mama dreamed up. The walls are painted a deep cream and the hair dryers are replaced with retro peach versions. The hair chairs will be recovered to give them a new lease. The wig wall remains, but the rickety plastic shelving is gone and chunky wood shelving is in its place. The pièce de résistance, the Dolly shrine, is intact—only by the grace of God and not possibly anything else—because it's gorgeous. Their precious Dolly clippings are framed in an assortment of textures and thicknesses and composed into a gallery Mama would've fainted over. The place looks like the color pink come to life—once it grew up and got a job and a mortgage.

Junie stands at Georgia's signal. "Yes, and we've already under-taken our own fundraising endeavors. We have amassed a little over seven thousand dollars between our family garage sale and two *fund-raising evenings*."

A titter spreads among the group. Everyone knows about Cards—even if it feels safer to talk around it. Despite its local notoriety, Junie wonders about pausing on more Cards nights now that Sheriff Mike's new deputies are out on the roads.

Ms. Luanne from the Silvers raises her hand. "So as y'all know, we've got a bingo event planned at the church next week, and all of our friends and their friends are coming. We're also working on setting up a bounce house event for the kids in town. Sherry has been chatting up the guy who runs the inflatable rentals."

Ms. Sherry waves and pats her hair, as if acknowledging her wiles that give her sway. "I'm close to finishing the agreement, but we might get as many as five inflatables for a few hours. I figure we can sell tickets and even do a snack bar if we have the time."

"What a fabulous idea," Tina says.

Junie lights up on the inside at the idea. "We should also have a thirty-minute *adult* bounce. Just saying!"

The Silvers erupt in chatter and laughter and more than one mention of a broken hip.

Michaela chimes in. "I might only have one toddler, but I can assure you all the families around here would show up for that event."

"Assign us all a job," Georgia says to the Silvers. "We're all available as staff."

"Even me," Junie chimes in. "Unless it's right after a treatment day."

The looks that folks turn upon her surprise Junie. They look so sad and forlorn, so unlike how she feels on the inside. Georgia let everyone know what was going on with her—well, the basics—apart from Michaela, whom Junie told herself. They worry, most likely. Truly the treatments are a bump in the road—even if they are weighty, full-body-rattling bumps that put her down for days.

"Don't look so sad, y'all," Junie says. "We're going to save June's!" She looks around at the group. "Who's next?"

Georgia shakes out of the sad moment. "Oh. Yes. Dad?"

Daddy clears his throat. "Thank you for having us. I'm here with two reps, Darius and Lucinda, from Whitetail Bank. We are already in the process of planning the pancake breakfast. Whitetail Bank has agreed to sponsor the event with an eighteen-thousand-dollar check, thanks to their community enrichment program. June's will be this year's recipient. And many thanks to them for pushing up the selection process by a month or so to accommodate our schedule."

Everyone claps, and a few "oohs" escape at the generous amount.

"We're so appreciative," Georgia announces.

Michaela takes over next and describes the show. "Over three nights, we sometimes amass as much as ten thousand dollars in ticket sales, depending on interest. And we have a donation box for our cause in the theater lobby. I don't want to overshoot, but this could really make a dent."

Junie can't help but squeal and clap in glee. The math is coming together despite the odds. This should be manageable. And to think she wanted to do it alone.

Tina clears her throat. "And also, we'll be selling my famous cherry pie at the county fair this weekend! We probably won't break into five figures like the rest of y'all, but it's promising to be a successful event as well!" The pride that flushes over Tina and out of her as she speaks is palpable. The same woman who at the first suggestion of this shrank like cotton in a hot wash.

"I've got a commitment from the auto shop that they'll run the oil change special, but we'll have to wait and see what amount it turns out. Already had a couple guys volunteer some free hours too," Cece says.

The rest of the meeting includes the creation of a calendar of fund-raising events, small breakout conversations to iron out details, and meetings set for each event's planning. Junie feels overwhelmingly taken care of; she doesn't even have many follow-up tasks on her list, other than to attend the events and bask in them. To laugh and enjoy and focus on getting better.

Letting everyone in was the best choice she has ever made.

CHAPTER 56

GEORGIA

W E SPEND THE FOURTH OF July baking festive treats at the Clementine before we head to Dad's house for burgers on the grill. He has a perfect view of the fireworks from his deck that sits above the treetops, and we gather there and delight in the colorful explosions like never before. With Junie's condition, the simplest things like fireworks and a juicy slice of watermelon have a special magic.

Two days later, I step up to the long metal prep table in the White-tail Episcopal Church kitchen, where we've been instructed to gather for today's pastry-making day. Given the number of pies we need for the fair, we plan to make pastries today and then assemble the pies and bake tomorrow. I'm here today, but Junie and I will be absent for tomorrow's festivities due to her scheduled MRI. The sweet Silvers were quick to offer themselves as subs.

"Girls, come meet Sam," Tina says.

Junie and I share an excited look and walk over side by side.

Sam is smiling (of course he is, with Tina interested) when I hold out a hand. He's about a foot taller than Tina and his dark brown eyes match his complexion. He wears a golf polo tucked in, with a belt, and a polished pair of loafers.

"Nice to meet you," I tell him.

"You must be Georgia," he says. "Tina's given me a profile on every Louise woman." He reaches his hand out to my sister. "And are you Junie?"

"Did she share the manual on how to handle us too?" Junie asks, laughing.

"Oh, I figured it's only fair I should learn on the job like everyone else." Sam winks.

He's passed the first test: decent—or better—sense of humor. "Well, welcome," I say. "Hope you like hairnets."

"I'm an old hand at them," Sam replies. "Don't forget I'm in the industry."

Just then the rest of the crew barrels in—Dad, Cece, and Eddie.

Dad and Eddie introduce themselves to Sam, and Cece greets him with a nod.

"Cece, did you two already meet?" I ask.

"You think I was going to let her get tangled up with another moocher? You know how it is between sisters."

"Touché," I say.

I pop the box of hairnets on the tabletop. "Here. Everyone line up and grab a net."

"Do we *haaave* to?" Junie pats her fiery blowout. I know her hair is thinner. Because I know hair, but also because I've seen the locks of it in our shared bathroom. In the trash mostly, but hints of it in the shower and on the floor. She cleans up after it, but I'm not sure if it's for the sake of being a good roommate or out of her own embarrassment.

"Certainly doesn't come natural to us," Tina says out of the corner of her mouth to Sam.

"Fine, I'll go first," Sam says. He pulls a single hairnet out of the box and pops it right on. "See, I didn't burst into flames or anything."

Tina immediately giggles, far too enthusiastically, as her cheeks light up in a shiny pink. "Oh, alright then!" She snatches one and pops it on.

Cece crosses the room and takes her own without a word.

"Team uniform, huh?" Eddie says as he grabs his own. "Count me in."

Once hairnets are in place, Tina assigns us in pairs to a baking station set up with flour, salt, shortening, and little bowls of ice water. My insides flutter when she assigns me and Eddie to the same station. He cozies in beside me and whispers, "I was hoping for you as my partner."

Tina claps her hands and begins barking directions. I sure hope her expectations are realistic, because I think Dad is the only baker among the group of us kitchen minions she's assembled.

We begin mixing flour and shortening, Tina checking over our shoulders to make sure it's blended.

"Next, add the shortening in small chunks, then pulse the food processor," she announces.

"Where did you get all of these?" Junie asks.

"Where do you think? The Silvers," Tina replies before going back to checking our work.

I look up at Eddie. "Ok, she's telling us to drizzle the water in." I'm nervous, and I feel a shake in my hands. I just can't tell if it's because of my perfectionist nature that makes me want the pastry to turn out right—or because of the company beside me.

"Want help?" Eddie asks, and he wraps his hands around mine before I can respond.

I feel the warmth rush into my cheeks, and I grin as we drizzle as a team.

"That's enough," Tina says.

We jump apart.

"Enough *water*." Tina grins at us, one at a time. "As for the other stuff, have at it."

Eventually Eddie and I turn out a batch of decent pastry. Once Tina tests the texture, we form it in a disk, wrap it, and place it in the fridge—per Tina's detailed instructions.

We keep at it for hours, and between the lot of us we make the number Tina wants. It's enough to make the full batch of pies, plus a surplus in case of emergency—or a bad batch she didn't weed out. Dad and Sam take off early for a meeting about the bank's pancake breakfast. As it turns out, Sam offered to donate supplies for the cause. Cece and Junie finish their quota quickly, and the two head home for extra rest. Even if her spirit is at max level, Junie's body is beginning to sag under the weight of treatment.

"Can I ask y'all to finish up here?" Tina asks. "Any extra supplies, you can stack in that open cabinet. Hand-wash your food processor, and smaller items can go in the dishwasher. Just start it before y'all head out."

"Yes, ma'am," Eddie calls over. "You can count on us."

Tina winks and mutters, "I sure hope so" under her breath as she turns and pushes out of the swinging kitchen door.

Eddie and I begin wrapping up the supplies. "Look at us, a regular old pastry powerhouse," I say.

He grins back. "Well, we've always worked well together. This just might be the first time in hairnets."

"Empire now expanded to pastry." I throw a chef's kiss.

He laughs. "Junie does that too, but I like it better on you."

I prop a hand on my hip. "Just so you know, she took it from *me*."

"Potato, po-tah-to," Eddie says over his shoulder as he carries the dishes to the sink. "You two are more alike than you'll ever know. At least from what I've seen since I got back."

I stop and consider the "since I got back" part. "I guess the fact that you and Junie weren't really dating makes your whole 'temporarily here' thing make more sense. I was already mad at you for breaking it off with her once you decided to take off back to the action."

"Hey there, no one said I was in a rush to go anywhere. What about you? Is Atlanta calling?"

I sigh. He already knows that the news of Junie's illness changes everything, but he doesn't know I've decided to stay. None of them know that I'm *not* employed in Atlanta or that I'm *not* working remotely. I'll be here for as long as Junie needs me. I cannot see a future in which she's undergoing treatment and I'm anywhere but by her side. But staying for real requires so much coming clean. That's what I want, but the more I see the family circle around a struggling Junie, I wonder if my laying that truth on them would be a load too much.

"I'm still figuring it out—but I want to be by Junie's side through all of this." I glance over at him. "You aren't bored? Hanging out around Whitetail, taking Junie to appointments?"

Eddie shrugs. "I like it here. I guess I thought there was so much more, so much better out there, back when we were competing for top grades." He shoots me a wink. "Don't get me wrong: The hospital's great, but other than that a lot of that life felt like it belonged to someone else."

His explanation sounds like someone breaking into my brain and reading off my experience like a script.

"Huh," I say.

"Hard to relate?" He laughs. "I won't be offended."

"Actually, not completely," I admit. "There's nothing quite like being surrounded by my people here."

I turn and start carrying the sealed flour and salt to the cabinet. Eddie carries the shortening container behind me.

"You'll figure it out. You always do," Eddie says.

There's a moment when my lips part slightly, no more than a millimeter, and stay that way. I consider saying the unsaid between us.

What it might be like if I told him that I truly and absolutely have yet to figure out pretty much anything, and the things I thought I had figured out have mostly become small disasters. What would it be like if he knew that most things about my life—aside from my loved ones—are completely wrong? Aside from him.

The taste of the truth on my lips is delicious. And for a moment, in light of all the real and serious things we're facing, being entirely honest looks manageable, like we could leave my lies of omission as nothing more than small inconveniences.

I clap my hands together. "Should we tackle the dishes?" I don't wait for an answer, and Eddie follows me to the sink where I start the water. Soon it's full enough, with a bubbly topping, and Eddie squeezes in beside me.

The warmth of just our arms touching resonates through me, and I let myself enjoy the feeling of being close to him. After a few minutes of washing, Eddie clears his throat. "Look at me for a second?"

I turn, expecting a serious question, about the lab, Junie's health, but he swipes some suds onto his finger and boops them onto my nose. A laugh bursts from me and I follow suit, but I run my full hand through the bubbles and plant it on his head.

Then I take off, fearing retribution, and Eddie follows.

"You can't possibly outrun me," he calls out.

I don't even really try, and I slow, letting him catch me from behind, wrapping his arms around my waist. I giggle and wiggle, pretending to try to escape him. In my writhing I end up turning, and when I stop, his eyes are fixed on my lips. Is he thinking about kissing me? I am all the way thinking about us kissing.

He leans in and cradles my cheek. I feel warm and melty and if I were less buttoned up I'd groan a little. The basics of being cared for by Eddie Rigsby fry my insides.

He's closer, and I'm not sure if it's me or him or both of us closing the gap.

Our lips brush together, and the thrill rushes through my middle. My hands wander behind him, and I pull him into me. I let myself, for the first time since we fell apart, want him. I know I don't deserve him, I won't ever; he is too good. But I never stopped wanting him.

I lean into the kiss his lips first suggested, and Eddie pulls me closer.

"Another thing we're exceptionally good at," Eddie says in a pause.

I smile against his lips, but only briefly before rushing back in because I hate the break it creates between us. I run my palms up his back to his neck where I lock my fingers together, hanging myself on him right where I could stay for a lifetime. Maybe in some way, I want to send him that message. *Keep me.*

Slowly Eddie's hands run from my back to my thighs where he lifts me effortlessly. He breaks the kiss when he turns and sets me on the prep table behind me. He stops and cups my face in his hands, and he pauses and takes me in, his eyes beholding me like a thing of consequence, a thing worthy of his adoration. My eyes search his face. For what I can't be sure. Probably confirmation, proof, *anything* to protect me from the hope coursing through me as my insides beg this moment to stay. Not to vanish like it feels it might devastatingly do.

I pull in a breath to ask him, to make some sense—but before I can speak his lips press back into mine. My mind goes blank, and I let every fiber inside me unravel into the magic of us interwound. I heat from deep inside.

Maybe love doesn't need to be put on a bullet point list after all.

Suddenly the kitchen door rattles, and we break apart. Looking up, we see it's the cleaning crew.

I feel my face flush as I slip discreetly from the prep table and turn to head for the sink. "I can't believe you just kissed me while I was wearing a hairnet," I say.

Eddie joins me at my side. "Means I really meant it."

CHAPTER 57

JUNIE

Junie's MRI appointment is at an imaging center about an hour away, so she and Georgia get into the truck early Friday morning to make it on time. The drive is quiet, both of them sleepy, sipping coffee from their thermoses. Junie isn't sure how to feel about today. She's not worried; it just feels like one more box to check along the way. But that fact in itself makes her wonder if she should. Worry, that is.

When they arrive Georgia parks the truck, getting a spot relatively close to the entrance, and they walk through the automatic doors that slide open at their approach. Georgia takes a seat in the waiting area and gets on her phone, checking work email presumably. It hasn't been lost on Junie that Georgia hasn't had any issue so far with staying in Whitetail, working remotely. She's wondered if maybe it'll be zero hassle for her to stay, taking care of her little sister as she gets better.

"Fill these ones out, and don't forget the back." The receptionist slides a clipboard across the desk. "And I'll need your insurance card and driver's license."

Junie hands over the cards and accepts her stack of forms with a smile. She drops into a seat next to Georgia and completes them. Before long, she's called back and directed to a changing area. There, she slips out of her clothes and into a gown. She leaves her items in a locker and proceeds to the MRI room, where she's eventually slotted into a big white tube and told to be very still while she's scanned.

The cheery tech hits the button for Junie to slide out of the tube a good while later, and when Junie sits up, she sees the mess of red hair left behind.

"Oops," she tells the tech. "Occupational hazard, I guess."

The tech smiles. "Don't worry, doll."

Junie's breezy air falters once she's alone in the changing room, shedding even more hair as her shirt passes over her head. She takes a final look at herself in the mirror. *It won't be forever*, she tells herself. *You've still got it, Junie Bug.*

Georgia wasn't allowed back with Junie, per center policy, so she's been sitting in the waiting room for almost two hours. When Junie returns, Georgia looks up with a smile. "All done?"

"Let's get going. I need to call an emergency Good Hair Days." She marches off in the direction of the exit.

Junie is already out the door and at the truck when Georgia catches up, clicking the key fob to unlock. Junie slips into her seat, and Georgia climbs into the driver's seat. Junie is grateful that Georgia doesn't jump right on top of her and instead starts the truck and drives for a good fifteen minutes before she speaks.

"What's the emergency?" Georgia asks. "Not that it matters— we'll be there."

Junie looks out the windshield, determination in her gaze. "I don't want this to be sad," she says. "It's time, but I cannot bear this being some twisted weirdo funeral sort of thing."

"The genetic test?" Georgia asks. The way she says it gives away the fact that she's been thinking about it and wondering. Ruminating probably.

Junie shakes her head. "That's not what's on my mind." She laughs. "Actually, it's what's literally on my mind-slash-head-slash-brain."

Georgia glances over briefly before looking back to the road.

"It's time for the hair to go," Junie says. Her words are warm, gentle, matter-of-fact, and remarkably light. "I need y'all to be there with me. I need y'all to cut it short—Tina probably—and then I need a wig from the collection."

Georgia pauses, swallows deeply, and nods. "Of course. We'll be there. One thing, though. Are you sure you don't want to go to a specialty shop? You know it's just a little bit of a drive to Atlanta, and they've got places that can fit you precisely, not June's 'most sizes fit some' situation."

Junie shakes her head confidently. She's already thought this through and made up her mind. Taking charge, she might say, of her own hair, her own life, and perhaps so much more beyond. One day.

"I need it to be fun. A bit of a party. We need to go out on the town afterward."

Georgia's mouth lifts a little, a barely there smile. "I would expect nothing less from a Louise."

CHAPTER 58

GEORGIA

Back at the Clementine, Junie heads for the shower "to wash off the medical juju and all," as she says. I call the aunts—Tina first, who doesn't pick up. Then Cece, who answers, clanging and chatter in the background.

"Hey, how're the pies coming?" I ask.

"As good as can be expected considering how chatty these Silvers are." Cece lowers her voice toward the end of the sentence. "But we're done and cleaning now."

"That's great news. Because we need an emergency Good Hair Days. Junie needs us."

"She says jump, we ask how high."

"Does three-ish work? I know it's going to be tight, but I don't want to make her wait."

"What's really happening, Georgia Louise?" Cece's words are loving and heartfelt, and she's as tender as she can be when it comes to dealing with me.

I let out a breath. "She needs to cut her hair. Tina needs to bring the wigs and prepare to do the cut. Junie doesn't want it mopey, so no sad puppy looks or tears. And she wants to go out afterward."

I hear only the sounds of a kitchen for a moment. "Say no more. See you at June's as close to three as we can."

Just over an hour later, Junie is freshly showered and dressed in a flowy top and jeans. She and I push into June's, and Tina and Cece are already waiting, wearing Dolly Parton–inspired wigs from the shop collection. A speaker is set up with a bopping party playlist, and the aunts have brought donuts, popcorn, and drinks. They've decorated one of the hair chairs, wrapping pink feather boas around it with glitter scattered on the floor.

Junie stops at the sight and pulls me into a side hug. "Thank you," she whispers in my ear.

"Now, we know your mother, God rest her soul, would have our heads for the glitter on the floor, but we figured if there was an occasion that calls for glitter, it's today," Tina says.

Junie giggles as she closes the gap between her and the aunts, pulling them into hugs one at a time. "And I trust Georgia told you: This ain't something sad. Ok? No tears, no blubbering. We're playing dress-up, alright?"

"Message received," Cece says seriously, then breaks into a dance routine that is entirely out of character. She's trying.

Junie plops into the hair chair and says to Tina, "You know what to do. But let's do the scissors, no trimmer."

"As you wish, my queen," Tina says with a bow. "Would you like a donut while we work?"

"Why the hell not," Junie says.

The reality of the moment hits when Tina cuts a large lock from Junie's hair and it hits the ground, mixing in with the glitter. It's heavy even if we will it not to be. Still, in light of what we're making out of this moment, I assure myself it could be worse. I now fully understand how this would be ten times more difficult if we were huddled around, teary and sobbing, as our beloved lost her hair.

Tina cuts and snips, and Cece and I keep the music running and spirits light with an array of ghastly dance moves that Junie laughs at, reflected in the mirror in front of her. We hand Junie drinks along with too much food, but it's not necessarily for consumption. The food and drinks we ply her with are more like offerings at her altar, our acts of love laid out because in moments like these, there is nothing about the depths of our love we're willing to leave unstated.

It doesn't take long before Tina is finished, and Junie looks striking with her short-cropped hair. It's not buzzed; it's styled into a super-short pixie. She turns in the chair.

"Junie Bug, I know it's not your first choice, but you do look really great," I say.

"I hope you're not trying to talk me out of my wig," she says. "And by looking at yours, Georgia, you and I *both* need to pick one out."

Tina helps Junie pick a wig, and again, she rocks it. It's a shoulder-length chocolate-brown number styled in modern brushed-out curls. It makes the green in her eyes pop. Junie admires herself in the mirror, and though there is a hint of sadness, she looks confident. Like she can manage. And like she knows she definitely looks good.

Tina wrangles me into a blonde wig that washes me out, but I don't argue. She's baked pies all day, two days in a row, styled Junie, and now I'm asking her to fit a wig? Please, I can see to myself.

"Alright, ladies," Junie announces. "Let's get cleaned up, then it's dinner and the honky-tonk. We're celebrating life."

I sweep the floor. It feels appropriate considering my rank among the present company, all of them with more hair experience than me. I don't mind, and if I'm entirely honest, it actually feels good to be part of it. Really and truly a June. I don't even need the name—I just want in.

In some ways I feel like I've already been accepted, but this small act of service, sweeping up Junie's red locks swirled in glitter, feels like *a moment*.

CHAPTER 59

JUNIE

COMING HERE TO THE SADDLE, Whitetail's one and only dance-hall-slash-bar, was the only option on a Friday night in this town.

"Stop gawking at the cowboys and come dance." Georgia yanks on Junie's loose arm, and she's jolted in the direction of the dance floor.

The crowd kicks and steps in line, and Georgia shuffles her up front.

"I don't know how to line dance!" Junie yells over the pop country thumping through the speakers.

Georgia swats the air as she slams into the patron grapevining beside her and mouths, *Sorry!*

Cece is parked at a high-top with Tina flittering at her side. Junie waves at Tina, who hurries to her side.

"Three left, kick, turn, spin," Tina calls as she dances the steps perfectly in time, clapping out the beats.

Junie looks at her, astonished and impressed, but of course, of all of them, Tina would know the steps. She takes Junie's hand and helps her move along with the crowd, collision-free.

Junie hits a grapevine the next time and lets out an excited scream.

She keeps studying her aunt, and by the end of the song she's got half the moves down. She doesn't remember the last time she had this much fun, for fun's sake only. This is living. And Georgia too. She's freestyling off to the side, looking thrilled and confident. She's spent too much of her time working, chasing, performing, excelling—come to think of it, this might be her first time to stop to enjoy herself.

Soon the music dulls, and Cece waves the others over to her table. She unstacks four plastic cups and pours from the pitcher of sweet tea.

"Oh, Cece," Junie says. "Why don't you get yourself a splash of bourbon in there?"

"This'll do for now." Cece lifts her glass and pats her wig. "Feeling brand-new in this."

The rest nod, clink cups, and sip as they sway to the music.

Suddenly, Tina yelps. "That son of a—" she snarls.

Everyone turns to look at what has her all hot and bothered. Randy the Worst is leaning on the bar, slurping on a longneck beer and chatting up Tallulah Franklin, one of the sweet nurses from the hospital.

"That man's rarely up to any good," Georgia says, then rolls her eyes.

Tina is growing redder every second.

"Guess he's out shopping for a new woman willing to house him," Cece says. "Tina, how do you want us to handle this?"

Tina takes off marching in his direction. The others follow, prepared to intervene only as far as required to keep her out of legal trouble.

She stomps right up to Randy. "What on earth are you doing here, chatting up girls? Trying to find the next innocent young thing to mooch off of?"

"Oh, it's not that!" Tallulah scoffs, like the thought of her entertaining romance with Randy is laughable. "*Really.*"

Tina turns to her. "Go on, honey. Find your friends. Don't waste your time on this guy. *Trust me*, I've already wasted years."

She twists back to Randy. "You're seriously here hitting on other women? Tell me I'm seeing things."

He shrugs. "You said we were over."

"But you haven't moved out."

"You know that'll take time," he says.

"Time's up." Tina snatches the beer right out of his hand. "I guess you used my cash from the jar to buy this? So it'll be mine?"

He has no reply.

Tina eyes the bottle for a moment before a smirk spreads across her face. She lifts the bottle and tips it upside down over his head.

The Louises stand there and watch in awe as the frothy liquid runs over his hair to his shoulders and down his arms. A few giggles erupt at the bar. When the bottle's empty, Tina shakes out the last drops on him.

"Get yourself out or your stuff's going on the curb."

CHAPTER 60

GEORGIA

CLEAR BLUE SKIES AND A steady breeze—perfect weather for the county fair. Whitetail and the towns around have shown up and dressed up for the occasion. I wear a plaid shirt, knotted at the top of my high-waisted jeans. With boots. Of course, boots. I have a cap on my head—an excellent alternative to a hairnet—but it allows my red hair to spill out and down my back like a flag marking me a Louise.

The breeze carries children's giggles and shrieks from the game booths across the path to the livestock section well-known for its noxious fumes. Music surrounds us as it travels over from the stage that's been erected out of scaffolding and jazzed up with Americana bunting. Even the sun seems to be twinkling to the beat.

Tina deserves a day this delightful.

Since the gates opened, Junie, Cece, and I have been slicing pie, slinging plates, and swiping cards for payment at such a pace that we've barely looked up.

Tina, the face of the operation, is planted in front of the booth like a cable TV saleswoman.

"Hey there, Michelle!" Tina calls to one of her friends. "Let me show you around the booth."

Tina sweeps her arm around Michelle and begins telling her the story of her mother's mother's mother's mother putting together this pie recipe. None of us is sure how much is fact versus family folklore that has seeped in over the years.

Countless times, people arrive at the booth with the same script: "*I was told I couldn't leave before I try this.*"

Tina is thrilled every time she hears it.

And I am too. Not because I want people to like the pie but because Tina finally believes she has something real to offer. The person Tina was when I first rolled back into town in my overpriced car is now mostly a memory. Maybe that version of me is a little bit gone too. Well, all the best parts of Tina haven't changed, so maybe it's actually that she turned up the volume on *Tina* right after she brushed off her self-doubt.

"Georgia?" Tina calls over. She comes around the side of the booth with a customer in tow. "This lovely lady would like to buy a *whole pie*! Can we accommodate her?"

"No problem." I'm more than happy to sell her the whole thing considering it'll be one less to slice up and plate. "Ma'am, can I wrap it for you?"

The customer nods. "That'll be just fine."

Once she pays and goes on her way, Tina dips behind the booth.

"Y'all, can you *believe* the success?" she says, struggling to contain an excited yelp. "Everyone seems to love it."

"Maybe you'll believe us the next time we tell you you've got a winner on your hands," Junie says as she pulls Tina into a slow hug, a physical *I love you.*

Junie looks grayer than she did this morning, and I make a note to pull her aside and suggest she take it easy after we're done here.

She wears the same chocolate-brown wig today, and although she looks beautiful, it's a reminder of reality. I'm planning to pin her down at some point soon and ask again about the genetics. It must be something minor, since we already dealt with that years back, but a part of me knows she's avoiding telling me rather than simply waiting for the right moment. I know my sister well, and I have *deep* experience with her avoiding the things she'd rather laugh her way around. It might not be at the top of my daily agenda these days, but eventually, one day, I might want to have kids. One day she might too. So it's something important to understand.

"We believed in the pie, and also in you," Cece says.

Sam shuffles over from his post at the bagging station. "Tina, you really outdid yourself," he says. His eyes hang on her, sincerity filling them. The twinkle is so honest and obvious, I can tell it takes a lot when he pulls them away.

Tina blushes, looking up at Sam from underneath her eyelashes. "Well, thank you. And I appreciate all your help around here."

Tina's gaze reaches beyond her beau as she registers us beside him. "And you ladies as well, of course. It goes without saying, we couldn't be doing any of this without you. Not without the Good Hair Days and the ladies that make it."

It's just as I'm soaking in our collective praise that my father walks up. "And *man* who makes it," I say, knowing the rest of them will agree with me.

"I overheard at least three people talking about the pie on my way in," Dad says. "I wouldn't be surprised if you're in the running for first place in the contest."

Tina smiles, but I also notice her gulp. More than forty pies are entered, even if only a handful are also being sold at stalls. Because selling at the fair isn't a prerequisite for entering the competition, and everyone's mother, grandmother, aunt, and uncle think their pie is the best in a hundred-mile radius.

It's a real competition, but Tina's pie is also a real contender.

"We'll see," she says. "Honestly, just this day itself has been beyond my wildest dreams."

Before any of us can reply, several teenagers appear at the front and assemble into a loose line. "Ma'am, is this the cherry pie?"

"You're in the right place," Cece announces, and the lot of us get back to serving.

We have enough pie left to serve only a few families more, and then we're forced to hang a Sold Out sign. When would-be customers arrive, watching their faces fall in disappointment is a letdown but also a *tiny* bit satisfying.

"You really could have a thing on your hands here," I say to Tina. "We could still be selling if only we had more pies."

"Maybe one day you'll have your own bakery," Junie says with a playful elbow nudge to Tina's side.

"But I've only got one menu item," Tina replies. Her face squeezes a little, like she's being caught out.

"Maybe not a whole bakery, then," Sam says. "But from someone who knows a little about food distribution, you could certainly sell *these* pies."

Tina swats at the air. "Oh, pie-in-the-sky dream." She giggles at her wordplay. "Not that it isn't fun to dream a little."

"I think by now we can all agree with that more than we thought was possible," Cece says. "It only took a couple weeks and a bunch of Good Hair Days, and look at the lot of us."

My eyes find Junie, and I hope in that moment that all of the possibility thrumming among us lands on her. That somehow it might wind itself up and give her that second chance. That fate, and love, and the heavens, and anything else that's willing to listen to a bunch of beauty shop women would just give her a pass.

"I mean, they haven't even announced the winner yet," Junie says. "Don't sell yourself short."

Tina grabs her watch face and says, "Probably not for at least another thirty minutes or so I'd guess. So we should all grab a break, check out the other stands, and say hello. We'll gather up together for the announcement."

Cece and Dad break off, chatting between themselves, and Tina and Sam head off in the direction of the refreshments stand, probably for another glass of the lemonade Tina was enjoying earlier.

I slip my arm into Junie's bent elbow. "You feeling up to a face-off at the Fish Bowl Toss?"

It was our favorite game when we came here as kids, and we spent hours and all of our spending money lobbing temperamental ping pong balls at fish bowls, hoping to sink one and win a prize.

Junie grins. "If I ever say no, you'll know something's *seriously* wrong."

We walk across the grounds arm in arm to the fair games. To our luck, a small gaggle of girls are just wrapping up at our game of choice, and we slide in. The attendant is a bored teenager absorbed in his phone. He barely notices us walk up.

"We'll take a full bucket, please," I say.

He nods, accepts the money, and hands off the bucket of balls before going back to his phone.

"Youngest goes first," Junie announces, dipping her fingers in and snagging the first ball.

I fake-sigh. It's fun to pretend I'm exasperated when really I just love having my little sister at my side. She might look somewhat different these days, but what makes Junie Junie has always been the magic that runs through her insides.

Her ball predictably hits the rim and darts off to the side.

I take a turn, methodically lining up my shot, one eye closed.

Before I can shoot, Junie laughs and calls out, "Come on, just have some fun with it!"

I turn to look at her, wink, and let the shot go out of sight. I look back and it scatters across the board. "That would've been so cool if it went in."

"I think we can leave the prizes for the kids anyway," Junie says as she takes her next shot.

Her words jog my memory again, about my lingering questions concerning our shared gene pool. "That reminds me." I take a ball from the bucket. "Tell me about the news you got on the genetics front. I know you're clear, and I obviously have the gene. But we should know about other variants for future . . . endeavors."

"*Endeavors*? Like, kids?" Junie looks at me like I've suggested she adopt a zoo animal.

I take my shot. "Yeah, kids. You might want to have them. And if this is *another* gene issue I might have, I'd like to know too."

Junie takes her ball and stops, propping a hand on her hip. "You're thinking about having kids with Eddie, aren't you?" She waggles her eyebrows in a way that makes me flush with embarrassment. "Aww, you little lovebirds."

I cough and splutter in surprise.

"Gotcha!" Junie cries as she explodes into a celebratory jig.

"*Stop.*"

"Why?"

"Because it's not even like that."

"Are you sure? Because I think it's very much *like that*."

"June Scott, you have never met a button of mine you didn't love to push."

"Apologies. It's why God made younger siblings after all." Junie throws up her hands in mock acceptance. "And so I do as I must."

We fold over, giggling, and I wrap her in my arms. I pop a kiss on the top of her new brown hair and pull back. "You're not getting out of this conversation, though."

When Junie looks back at me, there's a flash of something serious in her eyes. Just like when she told me about the shop. When she told me about her sickness. I should be worried, but there's nothing I can imagine that could rock me like her diagnosis.

"Three more shots first?" Junie asks.

Again, a common thought runs through my mind: Doesn't she know by now it's impossible for me to say no to her?

"Why not."

We quietly take three shots each. We don't make a single one. Neither of us seems to notice.

"Excuse me," the teenage attendant says, propping a sign at the front of the game. "It's my break, so I'm going to put up this Closed sign. But feel free to finish your bucket."

"Thanks," I tell him, and he takes off.

Only a few balls rattle in the bucket anyway.

"Alright, so what's the news?"

Junie turns to face me, and her shoulders drop, along with her gaze. She opens her mouth, but nothing comes out. When she finally pulls in a breath, she says, "Promise me you won't be mad."

"Well, I don't think— I mean . . ." Concern wells up in me. "Please, Junie, just tell me."

Junie looks at me, and defeat crosses her face. "I'm so sorry."

"What? *What* are you sorry about? Stop all of this and tell me."

She looks around, and the crowd has cleared around us, probably moved toward the stage where the contest winners will be announced shortly. Once she sees we're mostly alone, she nods and swallows hard.

"I'm going to tell you exactly what happened, and I want you to know that I don't blame you, not one bit. You and I both made the same mistake, and we were just doing our best." Junie closes the gap between us and takes my hands in hers. "There's no other human to walk this earth that I love the way I do you, Georgia Louise. The results we got back then, all those years back . . . The lab was too sciencey and not regular-folks proof. Their result letters looked like lab printouts and they were confusing."

My face folds into lines. I remember reading the top line clearly. Admittedly, not much past that because the sheer joy that erupted inside me made reading impossible. It was a new lab, yes, but somebody would've stopped them if they weren't reliable. Right?

"I read it, Junie. They said 'no variations detected.' Did they make a mistake?"

It was possible. Labs are run by humans, and even if they are excellent, people are imperfect. Heavens, do we know something about imperfection around these parts.

Junie examines the ground before she looks back up at me. "It did say that, and Eddie said the way their letter was laid out was atrocious. They went to market too soon, and we needed a doctor to interpret the results for us."

"If that's what it said, why can't we read that for ourselves?"

"Because it said other stuff too," Junie says. "It should've been clearer when sent to patients."

"So they sent us the wrong information?"

Junie shakes her head gently. "We just needed to read the rest. The controls on the test were off. It was a bad test. Eddie said it should've just said 'Contaminated sample, please test again,' something like that."

An icy cold I've never felt before runs through my heart, and nausea wells up as my head starts to feel light. It couldn't be. No. We missed something. *I* missed something.

"I misread your result."

Junie sucks in a quick breath. "But when I re-requested the results and they sent them to me, I read it the same exact way you did all those years ago. I'm thirty years old, and I might not be a rocket scientist, but I am decently competent. It's not your fault."

"You're sick now, and it's *my* fault. It's all my fault . . . All I've ever wanted to do was keep you safe and protected after Mama, and look what I've done." Tears run. "And here I stand, all the bad tissue cut off, plastic boobs and not a worry in the world. My God, Junie, how can you not blame me?"

Junie nods rapidly. "You've protected me in every way you could. You have saved me countless times." She runs a gentle hand up to cup my cheek. "You are saving me right now. Look around at what's happening here, at the shop, with all of us Louises, Daddy joining in, forgetting there ever was bickering about the name. None of this would exist without you." Her eyes glisten with tears, but she continues as if they're not there; Junie is being brave for *me*.

Her love and her forgiveness feel like hot pokers pressed into my shattered heart. She's trying to fix the devastation I laid upon her. *How could I?* How could I have let this happen? How could I not have suggested a second opinion, a backup test? Me, of all people. I shouldn't have overlooked a box to check on the list of big sister responsibilities.

"I will never forgive myself for this, Junie. I'm *so* sorry."

My legs feel wobbly as I stand there trying to find some sort of solution inside a corner of my mind. I'm not sure I've ever felt so desperately like a failure.

The announcement comes over the loudspeaker: "Please gather at the central stage for the announcement of prize winners. This includes livestock, pie baking, and the children's art contest."

"We don't have to go," Junie says.

"So I can let someone else down?" I say, my words laced with anger. Anger at myself.

I turn and gently pull my arm from Junie's grasp, walking in the direction of the stage. I don't deserve her anyway.

"Wait," Junie calls from behind me. She catches up and slips her hand into mine, squeezing. "At least let me walk over with you."

CHAPTER 61

JUNIE

J UNIE AND TINA ARE AT June's a handful of days after the county
fair, and Tina is still carrying around her brassy pie trophy, the one
for first place. Today she's set the trophy up on a box stack, pulling it
down to shine it with a cloth while she waits between clients. Junie
is in the middle of trimming Susie Worley's hair—she's a lovely local
woman who works every other day at the pre-K down the street.

"How am I on length?" Junie asks Susie in their reflection in the
mirror.

"Great," Susie says. "You always know."

Junie adds a few last snips and begins blowing out Susie's hair.
It doesn't take long, and before she knows it Susie is sending her a
payment on Venmo and taking off out the door.

In the pause Junie turns to Tina. "Between you and me, I'm starting
to wonder if it's in Georgia's best interest—for her own well-being—to
head back to Atlanta," she says. "And I never would've imagined myself
saying that."

"Well, a lot has changed recently . . ." Tina says.

Junie drops into the empty chair and lets out a puff of breath.
"She's just in rough shape. I think I might need to send Eddie in."

"That bad, huh?" Tina says.

Junie had filled in the rest of the family on the genetic test and the events surrounding it in the days since the fair, so Tina didn't look surprised at the news. "It's typical of Georgia, though. She can't make a mistake on anything. Let alone something like that. About *you*."

Junie lets the quiet sit between them. She's had so many versions of this same conversation with Tina, Cece, and Daddy over the last few days, it's starting to feel like talking in circles.

There's a knock at the door, and Tina calls out, "Come on in, Luanne!"

When no one enters and a few moments later a second knock comes, Tina and Junie exchange a confused look, knowing Luanne would have walked right in—especially by now. Junie gets out of the chair, and together they head for the door. When Tina pulls it open, a short, thin man stands outside. He's wearing a medium-brown suit and small wire-frame glasses, and his stringy hair could definitely use a cut.

He extends his hand. "Leonard Bulstead. I'm from the State Board of Cosmetology and Barbers. I was hoping to come in and look around."

"Oh, hi," Junie says, stepping out alongside Tina and pulling the door shut behind them. "We're actually not open right now—temporarily closed. The shop is under renovation, so we're not seeing clients."

Leonard pulls a face. "There was a report that business is still being done at this establishment while it's under construction."

Junie gasps in faux horror. "Oh goodness, no! I'm not sure *who* got that idea."

Leonard nods briefly and his face seems to relax. He scans the outside of the building and walks over to the front window, where he peeks in.

Tina clears her throat. "We'd obviously never cut hair in a construction zone." She pulls a hand to her chest.

"This station that's set up—it looks operational. I'm going to have to go in."

Junie breaks into a theatrical sob and looks to Tina. "I guess I'll have to tell him."

Tina falters for only a second before jumping in. "If you must." She adds her own sigh for dramatic effect.

"I'm undergoing treatment for cancer." Junie brings the back of her hand to her forehead like she's seen done in the old movies. "I needed my aunt Tina here to cut my hair off because it started falling out." Junie slides the wig side to side. "See? Not a stitch of it mine. But thanks to my mama—God rest her soul—I have my pick of all these wigs she collected and then deeded to my aunt here."

When Leonard looks away, Junie tucks away the pair of scissors that was sticking out of her apron and winks at Tina.

"Oh, I'm so sorry to hear that," Leonard says, pulling at his collar in discomfort. "Wow, I think I really put my foot in it. Of course your own aunt would help with that. And it's not business." He looks straight ahead, like he's doing the math on the situation.

"Yes, sir," Junie says in the saddest tone she can muster. "I'm also quite frail these days, so I'm certainly not up to working, being on my feet, walking around and standing for long periods of time. And my poor aunt here has been at my bedside night and day."

Leonard's face leaps with shock and a flash of guilt. "Goodness, yes, of course you wouldn't be working."

Junie coughs dramatically and heaves.

Even Tina steps back a little at the deep guttural sound.

Leonard practically jumps back. "Is she ok?" he asks Tina.

Tina rushes over and pat-pats Junie's back. "There you go, honey." It's almost like she's burping a baby, but Leonard doesn't ask questions.

"My apologies for the intrusion," he says. "That'll be it for me."

Junie leans on Tina dramatically as if for support. "Thank you," she says.

Leonard takes a few steps back. "I simply cannot believe someone would report a sick woman." He tuts. "What a disgrace."

Junie nods. "I'm not sure, sir. Probably someone with a heart of ice." She smiles but tries to make it look tired.

He walks to his car, and Junie and Tina wave as he pulls out of the lot. By the grace of God, it is thirty seconds later when Ms. Luanne pulls in from the opposite direction. Junie is in stitches when their client climbs out of the vehicle.

"What's all this about? My hair can't be in that bad of a state," Luanne says as she approaches the shop.

"Junie just scared off the licensing board guy," Tina says.

"I have to be able to use it to my advantage, come on!" Junie continues giggling. "I should ask Michaela about a role in the next production."

The three women tumble into the shop laughing at the good luck and Junie's quick thinking.

Junie's first thought after the coast is clear is how fun it will be to tell Georgia the story, but then she remembers how Georgia is doing, that this will likely not get the laugh it should. She stops and texts Eddie to see if he can go talk to her, help her, use his skills to swing her out of this funk.

Before she's even started on Ms. Luanne, the reply comes in.

Eddie: Of course.

CHAPTER 62

GEORGIA

WHEN JUNIE COMES HOME LATER that afternoon and tells me about the surprise visit from the licensing board, she laughs. I want to laugh. Some small part of me tries. But all I feel is fury, deep and buzzing inside.

We stand together in the Clementine kitchen as she recounts it one line at a time.

"So I just totally played it up, even put on my feeble old lady voice I usually reserve for Eddie," Junie says, looking like she's about to slap her knee. "The guy was such a softie. He didn't even make us let him inside. Bless him, we could've had all six chairs lined up with clients mid-cut, and he would've been none the wiser."

"Well, it's good he left, but have you stopped to ask yourself how he got there?" I ask.

Junie sighs and throws up her hands, like it's water under the bridge. "Who cares? Probably Misty, but he took off and he won't be back."

"Probably Misty? No, *definitely* Misty. How are you not upset about that?"

Junie reaches over and pops open her candy jar. "Maybe it's being horribly sick or the fact that we've got real problems, but I'm zen on this."

"You don't care?"

"Of course I *care*, but I'm not about to waste my energy on Misty."

If I were in my right mind, in any sort of good space, I would applaud Junie for her maturity. For being the bigger person. But not today.

"I'm going over there," I announce, then cross into the living room and gather my things.

"Georgia, you're in pajamas," Junie calls out behind me. "Let's think this through."

I snatch my keys off the counter, the ones for the fancy car, and I hold my phone in the other one. "Celebrities do it, so why can't I?"

"When did you last wash your hair?" Junie says, trailing my march to the door.

"Recently? I don't know. I don't really care." I push out of the door and skip down the steps.

When I reach the car, I dust some pollen and tree dander from it before yanking open the door.

Junie stops me with a hand on my shoulder. "Just don't do anything stupid."

"Do I look like someone who is going to do something stupid?" I don't give her time to reply and tell me yes before I slide in, shut the door, and start the car.

I'm not willing to admit it to her, or to myself, but I'm absolutely someone who might do something stupid right now. Perhaps not only might do but am likely to do.

I know exactly where Misty's house is because it's the only McMansion in town—thanks to her divorce settlement with her surgeon ex-husband. It's gaudy and too much. But people like her won't ever feel like they have enough. Not until they take enough from others just to feel like they've got an upper hand on all fronts.

The drive takes ten minutes, and I turn into the driveway and park. I march up to the miniature castle, not an ounce of my gusto lost on the short drive. I knock. I don't even wait a reasonable amount of time before I knock again. And again.

Eventually a flustered Misty arrives behind the cut glass windows that dominate her double door entrance. She yanks one of the doors open. "Georgia." Her words carry a hint of disgust. "What are *you* doing here?"

"You called the licensing board on us is why I'm here," I announce. "How dare you."

Misty crosses her arms over her chest as she levels a sneer at me. "You vandalized my mama's new salon. The cute one across town."

My eyes must pop wide in disbelief. "*Your mom* opened All-Star Cuts?" I scour my mind for a memory of who her mother is. All-Star hates us, and so does Misty, but she's so high glam, my mind struggles to connect her at all with a family-friendly franchise.

"Sure did. All my mama is doing is opening up a small business of her own, and you and your Louise cronies try to bully her out of business."

I scoff. "*Hardly*. She—or her cronies—sent us a client she knew had lice."

"And why do you think she did *that*?"

I throw out my arms. "To start a haircare feud? That's the only rationale I have, so you let me in on whatever else there is."

Misty tuts and rolls her eyes. "You're a liar if you tell me you don't know about the beef between your mom and mine."

I swallow, my anger faltering momentarily. "Misty, my mama died when I was thirteen years old. Apologies, but I didn't exactly spend my last moments with her asking for an annotated list of her sworn enemies." I feel freshly shaky and watery at the memory of Mama, of yet another revelation of something bad. "It's been one thing after another these days, so you might as well lay it on me."

Suddenly I wish I'd changed out of these ratty pajamas that don't smell to me but likely only because I smell the same way. I wish I'd brushed out my hair, tossed it up in a clip at minimum.

Misty uncrosses her arms. "Your mama was a bully, just like y'all. She treated mine awful. Ask your aunts for the details." She grips the edge of her door, halfway to closing it. "So if that's all, I've got a smoothie to blend."

She shuts the door without a response from me.

I turn around and head for my car. I don't necessarily believe Misty; she's far from a reputable source, and especially so as she seems out to get anyone with a minor vulnerability. But the way she looked when she said those things, I could tell she believed it. From what she's been told, she's learned to hate our mama, June Louise, the woman whose personality has become more of a deity among us with her death. A woman whose word is as good as religious doctrine to us. A woman whose wishes directed me to a place where I've twisted myself into something unrecognizable, a shape that hurts, just to follow her will. Because of Mama's wishes, Junie has run the shop, something she likes but probably doesn't adore in the way she does other fanciful things like her garden. Because of their sister, the aunts have guarded us and tended us, putting us ahead of themselves. Tina, keeping that wig wall that sat unused for decades.

But maybe Mama was also human, and maybe there's a kernel of truth in what Misty said.

The higher ground always seems to become slippery under Louise feet.

I hit the road and head for Cece's house.

CECE

Cece is used to being left alone, unnoticed perhaps, in her cabin-style home tucked off an out-of-the-way road and up a twisty driveway. That's why she's surprised when she spots Georgia's fancy car snaking up toward her. She steps out onto the deck, afternoon coffee in hand.

She leans on the rail and calls out once the driver door pops open. "Georgia Louise, do my eyes deceive me?"

Cece means the words even more once she gets a full look at Georgia. She's wearing wrinkled pajamas, looking like she was just spit out of a spin cycle, haggard with hair her mother would insist on fixing—*first things first.*

Georgia throws up her hands. "I know I'm not your preferred niece, but I'd hoped you'd take pity."

Cece's heart squeezes. She could probably be softer with Georgia. "Come on up. No Louise woman will ever be turned away from this house."

A smile passes Georgia's face, and it tickles Cece. She's always loved the way both girls delight in being called a Louise by their aunts—even if their actual name is Scott. Being a Louise is a way of life, not a name you have to own. Names have already done their number on this family, so the Louise one will be open to anyone in their circle.

Georgia climbs the decking steps and stops in front of Cece, who sets down her mug and opens her arms. Georgia falls into them, and she is heavy like someone desperate for rest. Cece wonders if she's still doing that job remotely and, if so, *how* she's doing it. All the same, it's not the priority now that the genetic testing debacle is out.

Georgia breathes in and out in deep gulps that fill her belly and press the women closer. Cece relishes it as a moment to have Georgia close, one she doesn't have to hurry her along from toward her next big thing.

"Come on," Cece says. "Let's get you inside and a cup of coffee in your hand."

She grabs her mug and leads her niece inside to the sofa, where she leaves her. After a few minutes, Cece returns and Georgia is curled in a ball looking like she wants the world to leave her alone.

The mugs let out a muted thud as Cece sets them on the coffee table. Georgia looks up at the sound. "If I ask you a question, will you tell me the truth?"

Cece sighs, and they exchange a knowing look. "The truth gets a little squirrely around here, doesn't it? I think your sister didn't want to hurt you with that news."

Georgia sits herself upright. "That's not what I'm here for. But for the record, you're right, and I'm not upset with her. On that front, I'm entirely upset with myself and will be forevermore."

"Forevermore? *Really?* We have to do that to ourselves?"

Georgia stifles an eye roll and then mutters, "It's what I deserve." She finds her voice. "But I'm here to talk about Mama."

Cece perks up and reaches for her coffee. She holds out a hand for Georgia to continue.

"Was she a bully? Because long story short, Misty Prince called the licensing board on us, and I went over to her house—like this, mind you"—Georgia drags her hands up and down her sides in demonstration—"to confront her. She basically said All-Star is her mom's franchise and that my mama bullied hers. And I have never heard such hogwash coming out of her aesthetically enhanced lips. I could—"

"Well," Cece says, "your mama wasn't a saint."

Georgia scoffs. Yet her tone is uncertain when she says, "How dare you . . ."

Cece holds up her hands. "Please. You want this info or not?"

"Story of my freakin' life," Georgia chirps. "I guess I'll take it, Lord help me."

"I know the woman—now that I think about it—Cynthia Stonewall. What with Misty keeping her married last name, I didn't put them together. Cynthia went to high school with us, but really your mother knew her better. June and Cynthia were rivals. In hindsight, it was silly. They both ran for student council, but there could only be one president. They both wanted the prize for best homecoming decorations, but only one hall won. They both wanted to date the same guy, but although he might've entertained it, they couldn't share. I imagine had they competed less, they might've been friends. But . . . your mama, just like she always did, took it too far."

Georgia sits quietly listening, her face giving nothing away. Perhaps she's yet to be convinced.

"There was one night where Cynthia was on a date with the guy June wanted. She'd been sore over it for weeks—though no one could be sure if she really wanted the *guy* or just the *win*. So June hears that Cynthia and this guy are heading down to the creek behind the shops."

Georgia's face finally cracks into a curious frown.

"She recruited her meanest gal pals, and they staked out the creek. Turns out, the lovebirds climbed uphill to the deeper part, and they caught them skinny-dipping. June and her crew took their clothes and their shoes and left them high and dry. In the moment, I'm sure they thought it was a prank—for June it was certainly *revenge*—but it wasn't until the next day that they realized the extent of what they'd done.

"Cynthia and the boy had to hike back to town covered with whatever they could scavenge, sopping wet and shoeless. They were teenagers. Mortified. And Cynthia's father was a minister at the Baptist church. It turned out that once he got wind of the skinny-dipping, he sent her off to some terrible 'camp' for troubled kids to be 'corrected in their ways.' It went so far south that all the girls involved were racked with guilt—your mama included. But just as the pendulum swung and knocked Cynthia off her throne, your mama was labeled as a bully for a while."

Georgia leans in. "*Mama* did that?"

Cece nods. "Yes, honey, she did. She made a mistake, and it turned out to be much bigger than she planned. She was human. She messed up."

"It just doesn't seem in keeping with her, you know? Are we sure? Mama just seemed more sensitive than that. Like she'd be able to take the higher road, that she'd have better insight."

"This is what happens when people die," Cece says. "We forgive them their faults by forgetting them."

"She did have faults, I'm not denying that—"

"Which ones?" Cece asks.

Georgia stops in her tracks, her lips pausing in the shape of an O. Her eyes flit around as if the list should be close at hand, but eventually they stop and she looks to the ground in defeat.

"See?" Cece says. "It's ok for you to love your mama like crazy and think about all her good parts—because don't get me wrong, she was wonderful and incredible in all kinds of ways. But she was also real life, human and flawed, just like the rest of us."

"I was so young when she died," Georgia says.

Cece nods. "We wouldn't have told you any of this then. And frankly, you and Junie reminding us of all our favorite parts of June— either by talking or by showing us—has been a balm all these years."

"I've been trying to live up to her example all this time." The earnestness and true belief drips from Georgia's face. "I've treated her words and ideas like some divine final word. I forgot that she was only a person."

"And she was an incredible, insatiable, irresistible person at that, Georgia. We don't have to dull her. But you owe it to yourself to acknowledge that your mother made mistakes, and you can too. She wasn't perfect, so you don't have to be either."

"I wouldn't be letting her down?"

Cece slaps her leg. "You remember June as the woman who told you to eat your veggies and stay out of the middle of the road. I remember her drunk and arguing with the guy from the auto shop over the price of her oil change. You remember sweet bedtime stories and gentle tuck-ins. I remember her cussing over dead houseplants. All of them are true. All of us have both."

"She wasn't perfect. What a thought." Georgia sounds like she's trying for a sarcastic lilt, but it comes out sounding much sadder. Like news she could've used a decade earlier.

"She'd want you to have a full-spectrum life too. Do what fills you up, be kind to your sister, love your daddy, but also don't kill yourself for the sake of someone else. You deserve the main meal, not the leftovers."

"Do you think she'd forgive me for misreading Junie's results?" Georgia's lips quiver.

Cece rushes to wrap her arms around her and wills herself to become her sister come to life. "I am as sure of that as I am about anything in this world. June wouldn't blame you. She would tell you that you don't need to be forgiven. Now, she'd probably already be on-line searching for the home addresses of the people running the lab, cussing and yelping as she plotted some revenge. Again, she wasn't a saint."

Georgia pulls back, finally nodding slightly, as if she's starting to believe it. "With every year, the weight of being the big sister, the responsible one in charge, grew. It started with Mama's memory and it ran like fire in a dry field. But from here, maybe it can be some-thing else too. I can be lots of things and still make Mama's memory proud."

Cece nods deeply and doesn't stop as she begins to speak. "You've done more for Junie, more for this family than is reasonable to expect of any one person. It's why we wanted you to have the life you wanted for yourself, Georgia. You were a high schooler who took on the task of making genetic testing happen for you and your sister. Don't you see how much that already is? And as much as I hate to admit it, if you hadn't, it might not have been done. At least not for years until we all got our heads on straight and finally got around to remembering it—not to mention the time and effort it'd take to figure out how to get it. You did your best, and it was more than we could've asked."

Georgia looks back at Cece, relief finally in her eyes. "I think I'm starting to understand that."

CHAPTER 64

JUNIE

AFTER GEORGIA CAME HOME FROM Cece's, she showered, and Junie sensed it was the start of things getting better. And to think, of all the members of this crew, Cece was the one to soothe Georgia's wounds.

A few days have passed since, and it's Saturday morning with zero percent chance of rain in the forecast. A perfect day to cover the high school practice fields in bouncy castles and bouncy slides and bouncy corrals.

Junie busted her behind to help the Silvers put together today's Bounce Party, and despite persistent pain, she's determined to enjoy the day. She'll manage with ibuprofen and Twizzlers. Truly, it feels good to help, and she's the leader of the Snack Squad, the volunteer team selling snacks from under the pop-up tent. She always imagined that letting folks in to help would be like stepping back and putting her hands up, like showing them all of her failings, all of her shortcomings, so they could fix them. But instead, it's truly been a hand up. No one has let her off the hook, and no one is treating her with kid gloves because of her illness. Sure, they ask what she's physically and mentally up for doing, and they encourage her to rest as needed, but not one person involved thus far has made her feel inept.

Maybe it's been her all along, the one making herself feel incapable.

Junie unloads the bags of chips into their respective bins while a few ladies from the church set up the candy rack. One of the Silvers' husbands is bringing a popcorn machine, due to arrive in the next ten minutes. The A/V guy has a family-friendly mix playing at a reasonable level from a handful of speakers scattered on the outskirts, and the Silvers are decked out in matching pink collared shirts and white tennis skirts. Junie might want to be a Silver when she grows up.

Georgia slides up in front of the makeshift booth. "Hey. I've got first shift counting heads on castle three, but I wanted to check in on you. Snacks good?"

Junie nods and smiles. "Yup! Can I count on seeing you during the adult bounce?"

Georgia smiles. "Eh, against my better judgment, I'll commit to ten minutes." She turns and takes off toward her post, the hint of a smile on her lips.

Junie and her snack staff stay busy for the next hour or so. Turns out, kids walking past a well-stocked snack bar are immediately and insatiably hungry, their parents groaning about finishing breakfast less than thirty minutes earlier.

She watches Georgia in the pauses. She's over on the other side of the field counting heads, calling out reminders for "shoes off." The seriousness with which she takes her role is palpable even at a distance, but her demeanor changes when Eddie Rigsby walks up.

CHAPTER 65

GEORGIA

I'M ABOUT TO CALL FOR a switch out to allow the kids waiting in line to have their turn in the bounce house when a familiar voice speaks from behind me. "There a height limit on these things?"

I'm already grinning from ear to ear when I turn to look at Eddie Rigsby. "You, sir, will have to wait for the adult bounce that will commence at 11:00 a.m."

"Will I see you out there?" he asks, stopping at my side.

"You and Junie in cahoots or something?"

Eddie lets out a laugh. "I mean, no, but I'm also not surprised if she's pried a commitment from you already."

"If she wasn't my little sister," I say, jokingly shaking my head.

"Speaking of which," Eddie says. "Now that everyone is doing the whole 'being truthful' thing, I did receive an SOS text from Junie regarding the new info she shared in hopes I could help cheer you up."

The sadness hits me again as I remember the facts he's referring to, but they are no longer paralyzing. "It was . . . is? . . . I don't know. It's devastating. But . . ." I remind myself, *You are human, you did your best—the people you love want you to live beyond this.* "I'm doing my

best to make peace with the fact that I can't go back and change it."
I swallow the sadness that sits in my throat.

Eddie tucks his hands in his pockets and nods. "It's the tough part
about being human. Not being able to go back and change the past."
His eyes linger on me and I feel my insides flutter, knowing we're
both thinking about our shared history. "And for what it's worth, I
think acting in good faith counts for a whole lot."

I nod. "I'm starting to believe the same. It's just, you know how I
am. A tad black and white at times. All this stuff with Junie and the
family, it's just very gray with all sorts of shades."

"*You?* A tad black and white?" Eddie looks off and frowns. "Not
ringing a bell. You sure we're talking about the same person?"

I whack a playful hand into his middle. "Oh, cut it out."

He throws an arm around me, and by reflex I turn into him, giggling. It's my favorite muscle memory. It's the part of loving him
that never left, despite my best efforts. I think about the kiss in the
kitchen, and I savor the pressure of his arms around me. I wonder
in the most optimistic of ways that were once entirely out of reach:
Could there be a road back?

"Hey, we're waiting over here," calls a child-size voice.

"Sorry!" I call over. I shoot Eddie one last look. "Here I am slacking
on my duties." I disentangle myself and head for the bounce house,
where I rotate kids in and out.

Eddie follows. "Hey, I was wondering, did Junie get her MRI
results back yet?"

I shake my head. "It's been just over a week. I think her doctor
scheduled an appointment for next week to go over results."

"Let me know if I can be of help with any of that. As always."
Eddie looks at his watch. "And speaking of Junie, I should head over
there for my shift at the snack shack."

I laugh. "Watch out, I hear she's running a tight ship."

Eddie drops his eyes and shoves his hands in his pockets. When he looks back up, he seems to be talking himself into—or out of—something. "Hey, before I go."

My insides lurch in anticipation of another Bad Thing. I frown.

"Oh no." Eddie holds up a hand. "Good thing." He pulls in a breath. "I know this is not your priority, and there's a million more important things in your life than me, but I just wanted to put it out there, no pressure, but maybe, would you want to get together? Be open to it? Consider it for a day when you're not overwhelmed, and I—"

"Yes." I can feel the smile crinkle every fine line life has gifted me thus far. "Can we call it what it is?"

Eddie nods, blushing slightly. "I'd love to take you on a real date."

I want to close the gap between us, leap into his arms, and kiss him for far longer than we got in the kitchen. But gaggles of elementary schoolers surround us, ones who are already waiting very patiently, and I am unsurprisingly not one for public displays of affection.

"You are a bright spot right now"—I look at him, feeling hopeful—"in the middle of a terribly tough time."

"Anything I can do to make it a little more bearable," he says, then offers a lopsided grin.

I smile and look away. I might be thrilled at the idea of dating Eddie Rigsby again, but it's fresh and the butterflies are swarming.

"See you around," I say, immediately wondering if that sounds too much like something one pal says to another.

"Sure thing, *bud*," he says, confirming my suspicions, and he winks as he turns to go. "Thanks for making my day."

CHAPTER 66

GEORGIA

THE NEXT DAY, JUNIE AND I are sitting on the sofa at the Clementine debating which *Real Housewives* cast is the most entertaining, and she's hammering home her final arguments for the Beverly Hills crew when the front door bangs open.

Tina tumbles over the threshold, hiccupping between sobs. "Girls, I need reinforcements."

I set down my coffee mug and rush to her side. Junie shuffles in on her other side.

"It's Randy. I told him he needed to leave—*now*—and he told me to get lost. Laughed in my face and told me to *make him*."

"Let me call Cece," I say. "We can help."

"But isn't that the problem?" Tina looks up from where her head was set in her palms. "Here I am marching around planning massive bakes and pouring drinks on people, and all it takes is a few harsh words from Randy to level me. This is who I am."

"You better hush about that," Junie says. "You are a pie-baking, beer-dumping, no-nonsense woman."

Tina looks down at herself. "I'm not so sure."

"Truly," I say. "Don't let him take anything else away from you.

Randy being a scumbag doesn't mean a thing about you. He's mean and lazy and probably ticked that you're finally standing up to him."

Tina swallows hard and puffs a breath. "You're right, girls. So right. To hell with him." She pulls us into her sides for a group hug. "And you're living proof that part of your mama will always be around."

When she releases us, I look between them. "Am I clear to call Cece?"

"You betcha," Tina says as she hops in excitement and claps her hands.

Junie and I throw on tennis shoes and I grab a ball cap, and the three of us head to the truck.

Cece picks up on the second ring. "It's time," I tell her. "Randy."

"Be there in five," she says and hangs up.

I'm cranking the engine when Junie asks, "Don't y'all need disguise wigs for this? Kinda feels like a wig expedition." She pats her own locks that she's styled into a cute half-up twist.

"Pretty sure he'll know it's us, honey," Tina replies.

Junie shrugs. "True, but wigs make everything more fun."

I whip the truck out of the driveway, and the oak flutters in the rearview.

The four of us plow through Tina's front door, and Randy leaps off the sofa.

"What are y'all doing here?" he asks. Like he has any right.

"Time's up, son," Cece announces.

Tina passes out black garbage bags to each of us. "Randy, you best tell the girls what you're taking with you or it'll be up to them."

"This way?" Junie asks, already halfway down the hall to the primary bedroom.

Randy skips behind her to catch up. "Hey, slow down." He whirls back and bends over to plead with Tina. "Honey, please don't do this. You know I love you. Let's work this out."

Tina crosses her arms, looking like she's thinking it over. *Don't even consider it. Stop. Keep this eviction going.* If I could telepathically send these messages straight out of my mind and into hers, I would. But this is Tina's deal, and I trust her. She's got this.

"You know what's interesting?" Tina asks Randy, then goes on without waiting for a response. "This is the first time since I mentioned you moving out that you've tried to fight for me. And I don't believe a word of it. You were peachy keen to suggest living as 'roommates,' and now the moment we're here to physically remove you from my house, your heart's miraculously in the right place. Sounds a little too convenient to me."

"After all this time, you won't give me another chance?" Randy asks.

Tina blinks once. "You're already on the last chance. In fact, the last chance was two chances back."

"That's right, time's up!" I announce. "Come on." I wave for him to follow us.

When I glance behind me, I see Tina's got her glow back.

The packing doesn't take long. Most everything in the house belongs to Tina because Randy never cared enough about making this place a home to contribute to. Of course, that also would've required him to get up off his tail and work a job.

We fill six garbage bags with the clothing and toiletries that are his, and I don't see anything else.

"Take a couple last laps to grab anything that's yours," Tina calls behind Randy. "Then we'll help you to your car with the bags."

Randy looks around nervously. "Guess I'll grab a hotel till I can figure something out."

Tina flushes a little, and I can tell she feels bad about the idea of Randy riding out time at a hotel. We all know he can't afford it.

"I gave you plenty of notice," Tina says. "I told you this was happening, and rather than make a plan to get a job or stay with someone else, you planned to just bleed me for as long as I'd let you. If you were working on finding a place or even applying for jobs, I'd be willing to work with you." Tina sounds kinder than I would be when she says the last thing. "But now it's time for you to stand on your own two feet. You can do it. It just won't be with me."

I let Tina be the one to help him out with his bags. She's so good at this. All we need to do is fall back and let her close it out. She stands in the drive and waves as he pulls out, and when she spins around to walk back up to her quiet little house, she cracks the widest grin.

"So long, Randy the Worst," she says. "You ladies want to order some food and rechristen the place while we wait on the locksmith?"

Of course, she already has him scheduled.

Tina the Queen.

CHAPTER 67

JUNIE

LATER THAT WEEK, JUNIE IS back at the oncologist's
office, this time with only Georgia at her side, as opposed
to the entire crew. She has her third chemo treatment tomorrow,
the "Friday special," as she's taken to calling it. At least she has
Michaela's production of *Grease* to look forward to on Sunday
evening, once she's upright and feeling closer to normal.

She's back in the exam room, sitting on the table where the patient goes, the thin, crinkly paper already a balled-up mess. Georgia
sits in the chair by the window.

Junie shifts and the paper rips (not for the first time). "What does
this stuff even do? The wind blows wrong and it's a crumpled ball. I
don't see it protecting any surfaces."

Georgia looks up from her phone, where she's probably reading
work emails. "You'd think by now someone would have come up with
a better solution."

There's a brisk knock on the door, and Dr. Richardson enters. He
nods. "Good morning, Junie. And is it Georgia?"

Both women say hello, and the doctor settles on the rolling stool
and logs into the computer that's mounted to the wall.

"So we've got some results today. But to start, how are you doing? How are you feeling?"

"Tired. Still some pain." She points to her wig. "I ended up cutting it all off because watching it fall out in clumps was worse."

Dr. Richardson pivots on the stool and nods, an empathetic look on his face. "I've heard the same from many other female patients."

"She's been active, though," Georgia chimes in. "Participating in some community events, spending time with family and friends."

"That's great," Dr. Richardson says. "So—let's get to the results. Junie, I'm going to pull up the scans and show them to you as we discuss." He clicks on the keyboard and eventually images pop onto the screen. He pulls in a deep breath. "Now, this MRI is a helpful tool because it can look across the entire body to check for spread of the disease, and since you had one very early on, we have a point of comparison."

Junie nods, a serious look on her face.

"What we had hoped to see was no spread of the disease. Unfortunately in this case, Junie, we can see from the images that the cancer has spread. Specifically to your bones and your liver. And this is likely the cause of your pain. I'm sorry it's not better news."

Junie sits frozen, and the doctor lets the silence stand. This isn't what she'd expected. Not at all. She was planning for this to be fixed up. "How is that possible?"

"Although every patient is different, the variety of cancer you have is aggressive. It can move quickly. Especially considering the genetics and the type, it adds up. Even if it's not the outcome we would hope for."

It adds up? Not one bit of this situation *adds up.* A thirty-year-old woman with her whole life ahead of her cut down at the knees by a disease she was supposedly already declared free of decades earlier? That one family tree must carry so many versions of this sad story? That someone who relishes every crumb of life is thrown into the fire?

"I did everything I was supposed to," Junie says.

Dr. Richardson nods. "You did. And it's not your fault."

"So what does this mean—for my treatment?" Junie asks. "I'm supposed to go to chemo tomorrow. Is it the same plan?"

Dr. Richardson nods. "Continuing with the chemo is a good idea. We will also scan more regularly, and I'm going to consult with the other oncologists in the practice to see if they have different recommendations based on this spread."

More words are exchanged, but Junie is stopped, frozen. This is bad. It certainly sounds bad.

In the moments that follow, she feels like she's unpeeling from herself, like she's leaving reality. Despite the magnitude of this news, it's at the core of who she is to not give up. She will make this ok. She'll force it into the shape of something manageable, something alright, something palatable.

CHAPTER 68

GEORGIA

THE TIME FOLLOWING JUNIE'S MRI results is blurry—from tears and hurt. Naturally, I feel responsible for the entire situation, and it feels like steps back after making some progress on accepting the reality of what happened all those years ago. Still, Junie tries to be optimistic. She sings as she bakes muffins that afternoon.

"What do you expect me to do instead, Georgia? Curl up and wait for it to get me?" she'd said with a smudge of flour on her button nose. *"I feel like muffins, so muffins I'll make."*

We ate the muffins and watched television, and I watched her whenever I could catch her not looking.

Friday we went to chemo, and Junie chatted up her favorite nurse and brought her new crochet project. She's taken to wearing a rainbow beanie she knitted herself—one that has a bobble sitting at an adorably jaunty angle—now that she's lost her hair. She even brought the container of muffins and shared them with the staff. The other patients, too, though none of them accepted.

The fact that Junie is coping so well makes me proud, and it also makes me feel so weak. Maybe it's strength she possesses—certainly she does—but I think what's at play here is her delight in living. She simply refuses to be miserable about the life she's got because having one at all has always been a miracle to her. She is miraculous. Like a unicorn to match her beloved rainbows.

Perhaps if she's the rainbow, that makes me the rain. The inevitable misfortune through which the sun must shine to make magic.

Saturday was a mess of sickness and couch lying for Junie, and I leaped to my feet at every creak of the floorboard. *"Give it a rest, Georgie,"* she groaned from inside the toilet. *"We both know I'm not moving that fast or light these days."*

Dad came for a shift of Junie aftercare and sent me to bed.

This morning, Junie wakes with a twinkle in her eyes, even if she moves slowly as she passes into the kitchen, where I stand making breakfast.

"'Summer lovin', happened so fast,'" she sings, swinging her hips beside me.

Tonight we're heading to *Grease* at the Whitetail Theater, and Junie is going in costume as Sandra Dee. At her urging I agreed to a slicked-back ponytail and a black leather jacket to go as her Danny. I've planned to pencil in sideburns as a special surprise.

"You sure you're feeling up for it?" I ask.

She scoffs. "I would drag myself there even if I had to bring my own throw-up bucket." There's a weariness to her swagger that I hope she knows she can accept as well.

I don't want to dim her light, but sometimes I want to remind her that this is the time—if ever there was one—to complain and moan some. Even so, I don't want to rain on her joy. Not if it's working for her.

I smile back. "Let's catch up on our reality TV today, and we'll be in good shape for the evening. You get comfy, and I'll bring you a tea."

"My favorite tea. Not the medicinal," she says.

"Like I would do that to you," I say. The stuff smells like fish left out in the sun.

Junie pulls a blanket over her on the sofa and scrolls her phone. "Good news," she sings. "I just heard from the Silvers, and the bounce event made just over three thousand dollars!"

"Those Silvers sure do know how to organize an event around here," I say.

Junie grins. "Not to mention, the snack shack lady was quite on top of things—or at least, that's what I'm hearing around town."

I laugh. "She stole the show, to be honest. Let's hope she doesn't do the same tonight at the *actual* show."

"And then there's $1,200 from bingo," Junie reads from the screen. "So added to the $7,100 we had, we're now at $11,300."

"We're making progress," I say.

When I look at Junie, when I hear these numbers, everything feels a pinch better. My sister, if nothing else, is helping me see the good that continues to exist in this life. She points out the things that even the horrible parts can't touch. Like how the Silvers are showing up for us in action and in love.

Hours later, I begin the process of slicking back my hair, and Junie disappears into her room to change. I laugh at my reflection in the mirror as I draw on extra-long sideburns with eyeliner. I slip into the black pants, white tee, and shiny loafers we planned out in advance. With the leather jacket slung over my arm, I head back to the living room.

Junie cracks her bedroom door. "Drumroll, please!"

I lean over and drum on the coffee table.

Junie pops the door open, and the big blonde curls are the first thing I see. She stops, pops her foot, and pulls her own jacket open, revealing the skintight black getup right from the screen. I notice that she's thinner from treatment, but I push the thought away. Instead, I whistle and whoop.

"I don't know about you, but I'd say we're ready." I motion to our costumes.

"All I need is the candy cigarette," Junie says.

As we wait in the theater lobby, everyone fawns over Junie, and soon she's pulled across the room from me, flitting between her fans. By now the news of her illness is well dispersed among the community, and the "June's Reno" donation box in the middle of the room is seeing a steady flow of visitors. Music from *Grease* is playing over the speakers, and everyone is chatting and laughing. It's exactly what we need.

Eddie arrives, and the sight of him approaching me looks like the last piece slotting into a puzzle. It's been just over a week since he asked me on a date, and we've been texting regularly between his routine check-ins on Junie and the shop. Maybe it's that we've now acknowledged our mutual interest, but Eddie never seems to miss an opportunity to show up somewhere he knows I'll be.

"Never thought I'd say this, but you really know how to rock a pair of sideburns," he says.

"I know my way around makeup a little. Must be in the gene pool too."

Eddie's face flickers with something, and I wonder if he's thinking about Junie's latest results; I wonder if he has things he wants to say about them. I wonder if he knows things doctor people know but doesn't want to say anything about them.

"I'm glad I caught you alone," Eddie says.

I pray he doesn't ruin the magic of tonight by talking about the illness.

"I really just wanted to let you know two things," he says. "One, you're the most beautiful woman I've ever seen with sideburns. And two, I asked Michaela to switch my ticket to next to yours so we can count this as our first date."

It's the furthest thing from what I was expecting to hear, and like reflex, a smile unfolds across my face. Between his responsibilities at the clinic and mine to Junie and the fundraising for June's, it has been difficult to pin down time for us together.

"Look at you making things happen." I stand there grinning at Eddie like a total fool.

He is exactly the sort of fun I need.

The bells chime in the lobby to let the crowd know it's time to take our seats. Eddie loops his arm in mine and escorts me in. I look over my shoulder and lock eyes with Junie, flocking in with a chattering group of friends. She winks.

CHAPTER 69

JUNIE

ABOUT A WEEK LATER, IT'S the Saturday morning pancake breakfast hosted by Whitetail Bank at the local community center, and it is the first of these fundraising events where Junie feels like she needs to be on her best behavior. A lot of old white men with comb-overs attend, so she wears a dress that buttons up right to her throat. She can't help but point out the high correlation between comb-overs and banking professionals, and Tina busts out in laughter as the rest of the crowd chews in dignified silence.

Aside from one close call where Cece almost confronts one of the bankers about a contested hand at Cards, the women don't cause a ruckus. Eventually all of them shake hands with the bank owner before piling into their cars and meeting back up at June's.

They tumble into the shop buzzing on maple syrup and coffee and begin arranging chairs in a circle.

"Eighteen thousand dollars is what the guys said," Junie announces. "Let's add it all up and see. We *have* to be getting close."

It's not that Junie particularly wants this brand of fun, the saving June's fun, to end, but—especially as she gets sicker—she does want the shop fixed. It's important and necessary, and even if the thrill of chasing the fix has been fun, it's the grown-up thing to do.

She doesn't want to have to scare off Leonard from the licensing board again.

Georgia pulls out her phone. "I've got the running tally. So we had the $7,100 from our two Cards nights and garage sale. Then $3,000 from the bounce event and $1,200 from bingo. Michaela's show ended up bringing in $12,000. And the $22,000 total from the bank." She pauses. "That's $45,300 total!"

Tina whoops. "We're there! Just about!"

"Don't forget to add in the $4,000 from the oil change promotion the auto shop did," Cece says. "They let me know the total just yesterday, so that's $49,300 total."

Junie grins, looking around the shop, imagining what's to come. It feels right that this place is being saved by everyone, the entire community. She can't remember why she thought it was so important that she do it on her own, but now she knows that this shop belongs to all of them. Especially as she continues to get treatment, and possibly get sicker, it'll need to be covered by more than her.

Cece clears her throat. "So, Georgia, what does this mean for you? Will you head back to the office in Atlanta? Anything you had in the fridge is probably moldy."

Georgia looks at her, and Junie can tell from the look that it would take a force of nature to pull her sister away from her. Not that she wants Georgia to stay against her will, but Junie needs her. She wants her big sister here for the treatments and to be her buddy and confidant at the Clementine. But if Georgia wanted to return to that life, she wouldn't stop her.

The bell on the front door jangles, and Daddy pops in. "Ladies? Room for another?"

"You know what," Georgia announces. "This is perfect. Come on in, Dad. I've got something to tell everyone."

CHAPTER 70

GEORGIA

NOW THAT CECE HAS POSED the question, now that I've realized I won't ever be the perfect Star Child I've been trying to be, it feels inevitable. Even if there is a part of me that won't completely, not fully and entirely, give up the quest to meet the expectations my mother left behind for me, I'm already marred with mistakes. And every time one of these mistakes has been revealed to these women, my people, my family, they seem far less bothered than I expect.

Forgiveness is quick for them. So very unlike my own is for myself. I'm trying to learn from them, still.

I say a silent prayer to Mama. *Please don't be mad. If they love me as is, like this, current state, no repairs, could you too?*

"Here it goes." I stop for one final look around the group. "I lied. So many times, y'all. I'm not the VP of customer experience; I'm his secretary—a fairly good one, but still. I— The car I drive." I massage my palm into my forehead at the absurdity of it now that I prepare to say it out loud. "I can't really afford it. I pour my paycheck into it, so it looks like success. I live in a junky apartment and barely do anything outside of work. Nothing about my life is glitzy or glamorous."

Junie's brows lift in concern, but without an ounce of doubt I can tell it's all for me. *Poor Georgia.*

Tina squeaks. "Oh, sweetie. But why?"

"Why else? *June,*" Cece says. Her arms are crossed, but her eyes are gentle. She's really been putting in an effort with me.

"Let me finish," I say. "Cece is right. All I wanted was to live up to Mama's vision for me. For her and for everyone else. Because if I was just sitting around here being underwhelming and shooting daggers at my baby sister because she got the shop, how would that be? It would be another loss. And then everyone loved me so much for being good at things, bragging around town about how I was a softball star or won an academic scholarship to college. I was able to make y'all proud and admitting it all went off the rails meant forcing you to admit you didn't have much to brag about to begin with. I didn't want to let you down like that, or embarrass you either."

Tina cocks her head and shoots me a sassy look. "Sorry to burst your bubble, honey, but we mostly did that for your benefit—talk you up and everything. See, I brag about all of y'all *regardless* of whether it's warranted or not because I love ya and want you to feel good."

Cece smiles. "Remember when we talked up June at the talent show in high school, Tina?"

Tina nods. "She was really quite a terrible singer, but she loved it, and so we loved her for it. Anyway, there wasn't a person I saw around town that I didn't tell, 'You just wait for my sister to win first prize.'"

"She wouldn't have ever in her wildest dreams won," Cece says.

"Not without an act of God," Tina says.

Dad shakes his head, his face folded into an earnest smile. "Wish I was here for that one, but I can attest that her singing skills were not touched by the hand of God in the time I've known her."

I let out a puff. "So y'all weren't proud of me to start with?"

Tina and Cece shake their heads fiercely.

"'Course we were!" Tina gasps. "It's just, we were proud of you because you're ours, you're *you*, not because of any one accomplishment or the other."

Cece shrugs. "We were excited about anything you were excited about. Didn't need to be one thing or the other for us."

I let out an exasperated groan all for myself and my jumping to conclusions. "So no one's embarrassed by me?"

Cece and Tina scoff, looking at each other as they swap looks.

Dad comes to my side and wraps me in a hug. "I'm so sorry you felt that way. You don't need to be bigger, better, not anything but you."

I pull back. "But that hasn't really ever been the deal." The room falls silent. "Mama gave me this name, against tradition, and with it all this pressure to go beyond this place. This shop but also this town. I felt like beyond the family. When all I really wanted was to stay, to be part of the group. And these past weeks here, I've been pretending to work, but I left the job to stay. I could go back, but"—I look around slowly—"even if Junie wasn't sick and I didn't want to be at her side in every step, I'm not sure it's possible for me."

Tina leaps up and takes a turn to hug me. "I can't believe you struggled all along. You didn't let us help you. You know we would've. We'd want to. Always want to." I let the warmth of her arms around me slow my racing heart, calm my racing mind.

When Tina finally releases me, Junie is looking at me, happy tears in her eyes.

"All I've ever wanted, all I've ever wished for, every birthday candle wish, every time I saw 11:11 on a clock, every stray eyelash I blew onto the breeze, it was for my Georgie to come home," Junie says. "I wished for us to live in the Clementine together, like we're doing now, but permanently. I wished you would go to beauty school and come work at the shop. Or just be a businessperson, but come home and run the shop. Come home and *not* run the shop, whatever you needed to be *here*. If it takes a June to call the shots, to rename something, to remake tradition and expectation, then so be it: Georgia, there is no place on earth for you like right here, among us, welcome. You are free, like every Louise."

Happy tears threaten to fill my eyes to match my baby sister's, and in this moment I wonder if all of us got it wrong. About Junie too. She wasn't ever floundering or rogue or disorganized or *struggling to follow through*. She was as mighty as she is here in her beauty shop declaration, standing up and filling the shoes our mother left behind that have sat cold far too long.

She's a leader too.

"Alright," Cece announces. "Now that we're spilling the beans, I'll go next."

CHAPTER 71

CECE

CECE WAITS FOR EVERYONE TO find their seat after Georgia's confession. She feels for the girl and frankly had not a clue she was pretending about so much. She feels a bit foolish now, what with how she pushed her away all this time.

"Georgia, first of all, I'm glad you told us the truth, and like the others I'll say you're welcome here any and all days. And you're free to choose as you please." Cece pulls in a breath. "And I'm sorry for being a bit harsh—ok, plenty harsh—about you sticking to the June plan. I only did it because I thought it was your plan too."

"Thank you," Georgia says.

"Next order of business: this June naming nonsense," Cece announces. "It's time we put it all to bed."

"Finally," Tina says.

Rich looks on nodding, and when his and Cece's eyes meet, he asks, "Should I go?"

Cece shakes her head. "You're considered a Louise by now too. You stay as long as you like.

"Now, this naming nonsense has been a curse on this family since your great-grandmother Dot," Cece continues. "You two are the latest generation hurt by her dramatics. We wanted to keep y'all out of it for as long as we could."

"Great-Grandmother Dot," Junie says, looking puzzled. "Was she the one who moved out to California or something?"

"No, honey, that was *June*," Tina says.

Georgia squints in confusion. "Another firstborn who didn't run the shop? Hang on, how did I not know about this?"

Cece sighs. "We intentionally glossed over it. And to be honest, y'all didn't ask, so we didn't bring it up. You had enough on your plate with losing your mama, and Rich going dark for a while there. Georgia, I think you had a family tree project once, and we just said Dot died when we were babies."

"*If only,*" Tina mutters under her breath.

"Wow, ok. Tell us the rest." Junie flops back in her seat at the revelation.

"Whoopsie there!" Tina reaches out to support her. "You a little wobbly, honey?"

Junie throws on her feeble granny voice. "Oh, the weight of Louise family lore is too much for these brittle bones to handle." She cackles in delight.

Cece lets a beat pass because she's not sure the girls have any idea what she's about to tell them. She's kept this from them to make sure they knew their family, their home, as a sturdy, reliable place. For years, she feared anything that might rock them. They'd already endured so much.

"This is about why your mother, June, named you two the way she did," Cece says.

"You knew this whole time?" Georgia asks.

"We didn't want to keep it a secret from you," Tina says. "But y'all didn't need to hear it as girls. Now it's time for it to come out in the open. And with the shop having a fresh start, maybe we all can too."

"Your mother didn't want to name *either* of you June," Cece says.

"So she picked a new name for Georgia, but once our grandmother, Dot, who owned the shop at the time, caught wind of it, she threatened June. She said if your mother had another girl, she had to name her June, or Dot would disinherit the lot of us—June, me, and Tina. Give the shop to anyone outside the family tree."

"But why did she care so much?" Georgia asks.

"Dot was obsessed with being a June because she wasn't one," Tina said. "Simply put, she was jealous, and she let jealousy consume her."

"I tried to talk everyone out of it," Cece says. "I'd rather have let June do as she pleased—as we all agree Louise women should do—and wave this place farewell. But your mother . . ."

"She had a big heart. Like both you girls," Tina says. "And she didn't feel it was her place to lose the shop—for everyone, and y'all to come—for her own wishes."

"Poor Mama," Junie says.

Georgia nods, swallowing hard.

"So neither of you two are *chosen* or *unchosen* or really entirely meant to be one which way or the other. You're just part of us, and you chose all the other parts." Cece sighs. "Georgia, I think your mama worried a lot about you feeling passed over, so she talked up your name as an opportunity. She loved you as is—accomplishments or not. In hindsight, being honest was probably a better approach, but she did her best."

"Life may have to keep hammering me over the head with the lesson," Georgia says. "But I'm starting to believe that all we have to give is our best."

"And Junie," Cece says. "You're not a backup or a runner-up. Heavens, June wished you were a boy to save you from having to catch the family hot potato."

"I'll admit, 'hot potato' sounds sort of fun," Junie says. "Like a musical artist."

A short laugh flies from Georgia.

"And by the way," Cece says, "*I* am the firstborn daughter, not your mother."

Junie lets out a gasp.

"How on earth?" Georgia says.

"Yes, another vote for *how on earth*," Junie says.

"It's the second layer to our family nonsense in the closet. I was born first, but there was a mix-up at the hospital. The nurses thought our mother said Baby B was to be named June. I was Baby A, born first."

"I'm so sorry." Junie says it like it's her fault. "I'm sure Mama felt awful that she took it from you."

Cece sighs in reply. "Please stop before I have to whack you upside the head and risk messing up that glossy hair piece. You're missing the point. I'm not mad. I'm not upset. Lord knows my hair skills would never be up to running a salon, and I wouldn't be happy doing it. But let me get the rest out: Our grandmother Dot—once again—found out about the naming mix-up between me and your mama, and she tried to force our mama to switch our names." Cece laughs.

"I can't picture June as a Cece. Anyhow, our mama lied. She told Terrible Dot she'd switched the names, and Dot never knew the difference. We were newborns and barely distinguishable, but especially so for someone who didn't spend much time with us. Dot just thought she got her way, even if she did put our mama through the wringer in the process. Naturally, our mother supported June in naming you Georgia or anything else she wanted."

"But it still hurt, right?" Georgia says. "Missing out. Even if it's silly, it never feels good to feel like you weren't picked."

Cece sees herself reflected in Georgia's eyes; so much of them is the same.

"What I'm saying is that it *shouldn't* have hurt," Cece says. "That we didn't need to do the naming. That we're all Louises regardless of our names. That it takes more than one person to run the shop, and whoever wants to pitch in should—and however their skill set allows. Like the past weeks have shown us, this shop needs everyone to operate."

"So how were things between you and Mama?" Georgia asks.

"I never held anything against her, and I think part of her felt guilty—"

"I know the feeling," Junie says.

Georgia reaches over and pulls Junie's hand into hers and squeezes. "I know neither of us is planning to have babies anytime soon, but what do you say? We'll just let the shop keep the name forevermore?"

Junie smiles. "Best idea I've heard today."

Tina's mouth bursts open in a sob. "I knew you two would be the ones to make this right. To change the path of the family."

"And don't break your word to each other on it." Cece looks at them seriously. She believes them, and she believes in them. "You can both make your mama the proudest she could ever be—by being the fresh start she wanted."

Junie holds out her pinky finger.

Georgia twists hers into Junie's.

"The higher the hair," Junie says.

"The closer to God," Georgia says.

And Tina and Cece (and perhaps most remarkably, Rich) reply, "In Dolly we trust."

CHAPTER 72

GEORGIA

D ESPITE THE NATURAL CLOSURE THAT came from the Good Hair Days meeting and all its confessions, I struggled to sleep that night. I should've been light of guilt and heavy with exhaustion from carrying it for so long, but one thing kept nagging in the back of my head.

Misty Prince.

Now that the noise of my secrets and the issues between us Louise women have been quiet, it's All-Star Cuts yammering all night long.

I text the ladies early the next morning and ask them to meet at June's. I arrive first and pop open the overstuffed supply closet. After a few minutes of digging, I uncover the Goldilocks brand box they sent, and I snag a stray box cutter from nearby and slit it open. Inside, products of all varieties are stacked together—precisely what I wanted.

I pull out my phone and text Tina.

> Got any of those big wicker baskets you used for the church raffle? Could you bring one?

Yes ma'am, Tina replies. Not sure what on earth you're up to, Peach, but I guess I'm a part of it.

Before long, Cece pulls up with Junie, whom she stopped for on her way. Tina arrives moments later toting the basket. I take it gratefully and begin loading it with Goldilocks supplies.

Cece crosses her arms and looks at me. "Care to let us in on what we're here for?"

I stop my hands and stand straight. In my hurry I forgot I hadn't yet explained. "Sorry." I pull in a breath. "We have one final wrong to right—so to speak."

"*Another?* I'm starting to think this family has a lifetime of skeletons we're responsible for," Junie says.

I shrug. "I think it's the last big one. Misty Prince and All-Star."

Junie scoffs. "We don't owe them a thing!"

Tina raises her brow.

Every one of us knows the connection between Misty and All-Star and the beef with Mama since my confrontation with Misty. Including *Junie.*

She groans. "Fine. But I'm not happy about it. What's even the plan?"

"We're going over there to All-Star, and we're going to deliver a gift basket of our Goldilocks products. I don't know if Misty will be there, but if she's not we might have to trek over to the McMansion again." I stifle a shudder. I may understand the feud and I may want to put it to bed, but I would still prefer to keep my distance from Misty and her overgrown residence. "Anyway, this is where we start."

"A peace offering," Tina says. "Great idea."

Cece grunts.

"I'll take that as agreement," I say as I toss the last few items in the basket. "Who's driving?"

We end up piling into Cece's Jeep, perhaps fittingly since it's what we took on our first jaunt to All-Star to unload the roaches. The ride is quiet, and after winding through the woods, we pull into the parking lot. A few cars are parked in front of All-Star, and among them is Misty's hulking SUV. We file out of the car silently and head for the entrance.

Halfway there, Junie whispers from gritted teeth, "Anyone having second thoughts?"

Tina giggles and swats in Junie's direction. "Can you imagine if we took off now? We'd reignite this thing like a bonfire."

"It's the right thing to do," Cece says, though her tone suggests she's not enjoying it.

I keep my eyes trained forward and march to the door. Inside, I'm met with the familiar smell of a hair salon, fragrant and warm, and the receptionist looks up at me with a smile.

"Good morning." Her eyes go to the basket in my hand. "How can I help you?"

I raise it slightly in a hugging motion. "Is Misty here by chance?"

The receptionist nods and lifts the phone to her ear. "Just a moment, and she'll be right out."

I hear the clopping of high heels before I catch sight of Misty's signature blonde blowout. I can tell the moment she lays eyes on me because her step falters. Her eyes are pressed into a squint as she approaches, and she crosses her arms slowly as she stops beside the receptionist's desk.

"Louises," she says. "And to what do I owe this pleasure?"

"Hi!" I jump in with a sweetness I have to work for. Really, I just know the women at my sides are holding in their comments— *Pleasure? Your face sure says something else*—and I want to block any opportunity they might have to deliver them.

"What is it that y'all need?"

I raise the basket. "I—*we*"—I take a step back to put myself in line with the others—"brought this for you. To say sorry for the misunderstandings, for my coming to your house, all the *things*."

Misty's face softens as she pauses. Her eyes flit quickly to the awning outside and back.

"Honestly, I didn't know about any of the stuff with our mama and yours. Not that any of us is responsible for that, but I understand why you don't like us." I hold out the basket. "This is for you, some of the products we have for your use. It's all great quality stuff."

Misty takes the basket and looks it over. There's a hint of suspicion remaining in the way she appraises it, but she's not scowling like she would've been weeks ago.

"Thanks," Misty says. "If I'm honest, I'm sort of ready to be done with it all."

"We are too," I say.

Junie and Cece nod along beside me in agreement.

"Definitely," Tina says. "Not a great use of anyone's time."

A quiet moment follows, Misty's eyes locked on mine. I pull an unsure flat smile. And when she mirrors me, I know it's the best version of a peace treaty we can manage.

We say our goodbyes quickly, and I shepherd my women out of the hair salon before we can make a misstep that might tank our freshly minted truce. We load back into the Jeep, and as we drive away, Tina sighs. "Your mama would be proud of you for doing that."

I smile to myself. I believe her.

I glance into the back seat at Junie. She pulls a face that gets a stern look from Tina. "You're right," Junie says. "But you know it wouldn't be a sincere olive branch if we enjoyed having to do it."

"The girl speaks the truth," Cece calls from the driver's seat.

"Fair," I say. "It still counts. Even if we have a bit of an attitude about it."

CHAPTER 73

GEORGIA

EDDIE AND I ARE THE only people over the age of fifteen in the arcade, but it doesn't bother us one bit. We stopped first for a large bag of popcorn before strolling through the aisles of games, assessing which of the offerings are new and which are unchanged. I didn't mention it to the ladies earlier, but this was what helped me get through the apology tour with Misty, the promise of this evening's date.

We used to come here, to this arcade, when we were kids—before we even knew each other, while we were friends, and after. It's strange to be back here with Eddie, but at the same time something about this place feels outside all that. Like the stuffed animal you carry through life, until you put it in a box marked *Special! Do not toss!* Even when life inevitably changes around it, it's reliably the same.

"*Pac-Man?*" Eddie asks as we stand shoulder to shoulder at the machines with rolling neon lights and computerized blips and beeps.

"Why else would we be here?"

"Just checking," he says with a wink.

Of course I remembered.

Eddie stretches his hands one finger at a time, then shakes himself as he approaches the machine. I catch a glimpse of the curve of his lower back as his T-shirt lifts and drops. He's softer than he used to be, loosened from the natural athletic tightness of youth, but it stirs something in me. I can't pin it down, but like the rest of him, it has aged well.

"Don't eat all the popcorn." He turns and settles his gaze on the machine before hitting the start button.

"No promises." I pop a few kernels in my mouth.

I cheer for Eddie as he racks up points, and I quietly enjoy the concentration furrow that settles between his brows. Much like me, he takes most endeavors seriously—on occasion a bit *too* seriously. I call out encouragements and clap, but eventually he runs out of lives and *Game Over* scrolls across the screen.

Eddie spins around and lets out a breath. He catches my eye as he steps aside and holds out a hand. "My lady?"

I glance down at the popcorn in my hand, considering whether I want to hand it off.

Eddie takes a step closer. "I *will* promise not to eat all of your popcorn."

I look up at him and grin. "You really are too good to me." I reach up and set a tiny kiss on his nose as I transfer the bag to his hands.

He shrugs. "If those are part of it, I have to say I'm more than happy with this arrangement."

I dust off my hands on my jeans and prepare to start the game. Less seriously than Eddie, I jump right in and hit the button to begin. I do my best, but I look back over my shoulder at Eddie. "You made this look easy. I'm *so* rusty."

"Hey now, eyes on the road, miss."

I laugh as I sling the ill-fated Pac-Man around the screen, and then Eddie slides in behind me. "Help?" he whispers beside my ear.

I nod as the rest of me shivers.

Eddie's hands slip around mine, his head set atop my shoulder as he navigates the Pac-Man toward the pellets of food. I don't really try—with the game—because the man wrapped around me is too distracting. The warmth of him so close is something I thought was forever lost to me, so I revel in it. Pac-Man be damned.

Before long the game ends.

When I expect Eddie to step back to release me from the small gap between him and the machine, he doesn't. It magnifies the feeling of him and his sturdy arms around me. I turn and shoot him a grin smooshed right there between him and the video game. I run a hand up his neck into the back of his hair.

Eddie leans down and dots kisses from my collarbone up along my neck, sending me into a full-body shiver. When he gets to my ear, he stops and whispers, "Looks like my plan worked."

Surely his plan doesn't stop at the little pecks, and in that moment I'm not sure I care what was or was not his plan. I close my eyes and pull him to me and into a deep kiss. We stay there, and I wish we were somewhere less public.

Eventually I pull back, and when I open my eyes, he's grinning.

"Yup. That was the rest of the plan."

I laugh as I swat him playfully, and we break apart.

Eddie snatches the popcorn from a table behind us and hands it to me. "Want to grab a drink too? We can let some of the kids get a chance on this."

"Perfect," I say and begin in the direction of the refreshments counter.

We order two sodas that come out quickly and pay.

"Want to sit for a minute?" I ask, nodding down at the popcorn and drinks between us.

"Probably for the best," Eddie says. "I'm not sure many of these games can be operated with the forehead."

We head to a high-top off to the side and slide onto tall stools. I set the popcorn between us, and we sip our icy drinks.

"So how's that firecracker of a sister of yours?" Eddie asks.

"A little better today, I think—*hope*. She's got another scan later this week to check on the status of things."

Junie has been struggling over the past week or so since our big hurrah over practically closing the fundraising goal. She had another chemo treatment, and it knocked her down like she hasn't ever been before. The pain in her bones has increased, and her appetite is down. The doctor prescribed her a serious painkiller. She tries to keep from taking it, but she needs it. She wears her wig less frequently, opting for the rainbow-striped beanie. She's even asked me to check on her garden and weed it for her.

It's the reason for the gaps between Eddie and me getting one-on-one time together—I don't want to leave her. Of course, in true Eddie Rigsby fashion, he understands and checks in. Dropped off an obscenely large batch of Twizzlers the other day.

The worst days are those when she won't even munch on one of her happy sticks.

At least she still laughs when I make that joke for her benefit.

"This type of treatment is brutal," Eddie says. "So what about you? I figure you're sticking around for her treatment . . . at least?" His eyes linger in a hopeful way, and I wonder the same for him—if or when he'll go back.

"Can I tell you something?" I ask, knowing very well I might be undoing this lovely date.

"Uh, sure. I mean, unless you're giving a critique of my personality. Or of my fitness level—it's been tough without a gym membership here."

I laugh. "No, none of those. Actually . . . it's that I'm moving here permanently. Once we find a good day, Cece and I are going to go pack up what I've got in Atlanta and move me into the Clementine."

Eddie's eyes shoot wide. "Wow. Good for you. I mean—it *is* good, right? Hopefully you're not feeling family pressure to do so."

I slip a popcorn kernel into my mouth and chew in silence, allowing myself a beat. "It's definitely good. Eddie, I lied to them and everyone here about my work. I had a decent job that I was alright at, but I didn't have oodles of success or anything. Also, I have to return this car I can certainly no longer afford to lease."

His eyes crease in confusion. "What do you mean? Do they know?"

I sigh. "I wanted to be who I thought they wanted me to be when they just wanted me to be happy. I know it sounds like a riddle, and it definitely felt like one living it all those years. But we're finally *talking*—since I've been home."

"So you pretended to have a high-paying job all to make your family happy?"

I shrug. "Can you believe how awful I am?" The question is not entirely serious when I say it, but it allows the option of him agreeing wholeheartedly. "I put all my money into that car, all so they could think I had a life I didn't. You remember—they put me on this pedestal, 'Whitetail Local Defying the Odds,' and I didn't know what to do when it didn't work out."

"Plus the name," Eddie says. He's well aware of the drama—aside from the latest details Cece shared.

I nod. "I'm really sorry. Because I lied to you about this too, even if it's only been for a handful of weeks now. I've been letting you believe it."

He smiles back tentatively. "The pressure of the Louise family is like a force of nature. I'm glad you finally surfaced. Found your way out."

"So you're not walking out on this date?"

"Not even close."

There's a moment between us where our eyes linger. I've put this first issue out there, and in the quiet between us, I wonder if we're both thinking about the other issue. The much larger one from all those years ago.

"I guess while I'm at it, I should keep going. I'm also sorry for everything that happened before. You were right not to take my calls back in college." I glance away. This is the real meat of what stands between us.

But I don't want to let this wait. I want this resolved, us agreeing to move past it. Because if we can't, and us dating is only a bit of fun to him, I don't want to delay the heartbreak that would be mounting. The longer we wait to call it quits, the more it'll hurt.

Eddie sighs as he wipes his hands on the flimsy napkin from the dispenser on the tabletop. "I was hurt. Really. It messed me up for a while, and I struggled to date—"

"I'm sorry. I shouldn't—"

"*Georgia.*" Eddie's eyes are kind but firm when I look up and meet them. "Wait for the but."

I nod once and listen.

"*But*—seeing you here over the last few weeks, with your family, and coming back here myself . . . It's just highlighted how much time has passed, how you've changed and how I've changed. Neither of us is who we were at nineteen years old . . . *Thank God.* We've got perspective."

I let out a breath. "I'm not sure I'd recognize that me."

"Eh, I wouldn't go too far." Eddie gently reaches over the table, places his finger under my chin, and tips my head up so we're eye to eye. "There's still a lot of the best parts of you left. And now that I've had a front row seat to y'all saving June's, I think I finally understand. What it means for you—and the rest of your Louises—to show up for each other, to do right by each other. Enough to make yourself someone entirely unrecognizable if it fills a void for another."

"It's love, but it's like a fine chain that knots and clumps so easily."

Eddie nods. "I knew you felt bad, wanted to take it back and all that. But the way you know how to love someone? It's remarkable. It's like no other person I've met."

I smile tentatively. "And it's just like you to see something beautiful in the middle of a big old mess."

He leans in. "It's so easy when you're the one I'm looking at. And for the record, I wouldn't be here with you if I didn't think we could get past it. You can ask Junie, but I thought about it forever, knowing I needed to have a decent feeling that we could make this right before I even asked you out."

I drift toward him, and inside I'm cursing the table sitting between us.

He grins. "And as it turns out, I've decided to stick around here too."

"No way."

Eddie nods. "Yes way. I mean, I'll be getting my own place. I love my mom, and she's a big part of me staying—wanting time with her, to be here if she needs help, another surgery—but the roommate thing is getting *very old*." He laughs.

"That's . . . *amazing*. It's amazing."

"I think I've realized that sometimes a change in plans can be a good thing. It doesn't always require some sort of failure—like I thought it did for a long time—maybe just a change of heart."

I grin. "This town isn't that bad after all, right?"

The corners of his eyes squeeze into a fan of lines as he looks at me. "Definitely not from where I'm sitting."

CHAPTER 74

JUNIE

JUNIE REALLY HAS BEEN HAVING a harder go of it in the week since she and the Louises dropped off the apology basket at All-Star Cuts. She can't remember much she's accomplished since then. Well, she did have that MRI she needed, not that she counts it as a highlight. Those would be her garden, her dog, and her family.

She might be slower and in more pain, but she's determined to live her little life as best she can. Puds follows her from the bathroom where she's put back on her Sandra Dee wig from the *Grease* night. It fits fairly well, and something about wearing it gives Junie a little oomph in her step. She laughs at her reflection as she smears on a red lipstick perfect for a night at the theater, date night at a steak house, or a visit to her beloved garden with her golden retriever. Important undertakings.

She's almost to her back door when she hears a knock at the front door. She almost doesn't answer. Everyone in town is dropping off gift baskets or casseroles or their mama's mama's herbal remedies for gout (never mind that she does *not* have gout or even any condition gout-adjacent). It only amplifies her love for her sweet community, so Junie figures a quick hello might be good for her heart.

She pops open the door, and there stands a pack of small children. At second glance, it's all girls and they're dressed in brown sashes laden with badges hand-stitched to them. A chaperone stands back at a distance and waves when Junie notices her.

Junie smiles and waves to the adult before looking back down to her miniature visitors.

"Well, hello, friends." She pops a hand on her hip. "I would've worn my own sash had I known y'all were coming over."

The girl in front smiles, less a few teeth. "Ms. Junie, are you a Brownie too?"

"What kind of brownie are we talking? One that bakes up nice with the chocolate chunks?"

The girls break into giggles. Then after a moment they begin elbowing each other until the same girl, presumably their leader, speaks up. "We've got cash. For you."

Junie laughs. "Oh, girls, I'm not going to take your money."

A tiny blonde one pipes up from the back. "Oh yes, ma'am, you will! We worked hard for this."

The tallest girl of the bunch, a redhead with freckles, speaks. "Ms. Junie, we know about your beauty shop, and we fundraised for it. Plus, we don't get our badge unless we *actually* give you the money. It wouldn't be right to lie and take people's money for ourselves."

Junie's insides just might melt into something sweet and sticky at the pureness and sincerity of this small and mighty crew. She squats, squeezing her hands to her chest. "My goodness if y'all aren't a fabulous blessing landing on my doorstep right in the nick of time."

A few of them carry a large box from behind the group, between the small crowd, and hold it up. "These are a special order of cookies we got for you too."

Junie takes the box and examines the gorgeous hand-drawn decorations on the outside.

"We decorated it with glitter stickers and rainbows," the lead

Brownie says, then holds out a slip of paper. "Here's a check for the money."

Junie gently accepts both. "Rainbows, huh? I have to tell you girls, rainbows are my absolute favorite."

There is a chorus of "Me too," "Unicorns too," and "Especially if they glitter."

Once the goods are handed off, the gaggle of Brownies wave goodbye, disperse, and scramble back to their leader at the bottom of the driveway. It must be Rosalinda, who offered her help weeks ago.

In truth, Junie is grateful for the donation. Her medical bills are starting to stream in, and she and the other women had finally agreed to accept her dad's offer to cover the $700 gap remaining to reach $50K. His offer allowed her to contact Goldilocks last week—during a pause in her vomiting and nausea—to schedule a transfer of funds so construction can resume. Now, work is scheduled to begin next week.

Junie carries the box to her kitchen table, and when she looks down at the check, the number rocks her in delight.

Maybe it's the universe or the power of this small town that cares or even Mama pulling strings up above, but the precise amount the Brownies raised for June's Beauty Shop is $700.

CHAPTER 75

GEORGIA

I T's BEEN OVER A WEEK since the arcade date with Eddie, and I feel like I've shed a heavy, itchy coat now that we've talked and I know we're both looking beyond the hurts of the past. That we're giving this relationship a real go again. It's not a guarantee of anything specific in the future, but it is a second chance.

I think about him as I pull up to June's Beauty Shop in Junie's truck. Construction has been under way for a few days, and I want to see it with my own eyes. Even with all the effort that went into raising the money and all the time the shop felt out of reach, my mind hasn't shifted construction out of the "impossible" category. Also, I know Dad is already here overseeing the work, and I have a refund check for him.

Well, I don't actually have checks, so Junie and I drew one (just like we would've as kids), and I sent him the money electronically. I just want to hand it back over to him physically because making our progress into something tangible right now makes it better, fuller. Especially while Junie's struggling health-wise.

When I pop open the door to the shop, the drywall is up, not a rip, hole, or tear to be seen, and the crew is beginning to prep the floors. Dad hovers in the lobby area perusing a packet.

He glances over when I enter. "Hey, isn't it looking great in here?"

I nod. "I can't believe how fast it's moving now after being stalled for so long."

"I'm in touch with the guys every day. We've got a great crew, which certainly helps."

Seeing him in action—here for this shop, for his girls, and very likely for the memory of his late wife—feels like he has finally and fully come back to us. As our dad, the man he was before we lost Mama.

"Thank you," I say. "For all you're doing. And here." I hand him the floppy slip of paper.

He glances at it and smiles. "What's this?"

"I sent you the money, but it was a fun project for me and Junie. You can probably guess which components she's responsible for."

"Oh, I'm going to say the glitter border and the rainbow-marbled shading."

"Bingo. We wanted you to have your seven hundred dollars back."

"Come on, honey. I don't begrudge y'all the money. You raised a massive sum, and I've got this to give."

"I know, but that's not what it's about. Junie and I have agreed that we want everyone who stepped up in the community to get the hand in it they offered. Those Brownies worked hard, and between you and me, they're a rowdy bunch who just might pack a punch if you pushed them to it. Plus, you're already part of the crew."

He sighs but not unkindly. "If you insist."

"I mean, there are no guarantees we won't need to call on you in the future." I toss him a wink and a grin.

A deep laugh comes from his belly. "Hopefully nothing of this scale, but moving forward, I hope I'm a first call when any of you need help."

I nod slowly, and our eyes stay fixed.

Dad clears his throat. "I could've done better back when y'all were young. I could've been better. When we lost your mama, it crippled me, and it took me a long time to figure out how to get up."

I reach out and squeeze his arm. "It's ok. We were all just doing our best. Not to mention, you're here *now*, and that's what counts."

As soon as we had the money and Junie reached out to Goldilocks to restart the planning, she looped in Dad. From there he, as the person with true financial experience, was naturally included in continuing conversations. And as Junie has become sicker, he's really stepped in to keep the progress moving. The design was already complete, and Junie has been spending her days on the sofa mulling over cream wall paint samples. They are taped up around the Clementine and rotated based on time of day and the way the light hits. It's an outstanding task she is taking to heart.

"I'm lucky to have you. All of you," he says.

"Me too," I say.

"Everything ok at the house? With our littlest Louise? No results yet, right?"

I lean against the fresh drywall. He's talking about the second MRI Junie had late last week. "It's peaceful. Junie is slow and not herself—aside from the personality component that's impenetrable. No results yet, but last time they called and scheduled an appointment so the doctor could explain in person. But she's still in the garden some. Noodling over the paint choice for the walls. Cece and I are working out a date for her to come help me move out of the apartment in Atlanta."

Dad smiles. "Well, I like the last part. You don't want my help?"

"You know, I think it could be good for us. Things are better between us."

He holds up his hands. "Well, I know better than to interfere with you wonderful women."

A crew member walks up, and we stop talking to look at him.

"Sorry, y'all, but we're going to need the space." He gestures to the floor prep. "We need the whole floor free, and—"

"We're in the way," I say. "We'll get out of your hair."

The crew member smiles. "We know you're ready to get back to business, so we're working our fastest."

"Bless you all," I say, taking Dad by the crook of his arm and pulling him out the door with me.

CHAPTER 76

GEORGIA

C ECE AND I SCHEDULE MY Atlanta move-out for Tuesday of the following week. Moon was understanding about my quick departure, considering the circumstances, and as luck would have it, she found a replacement roommate within a few days of my call. Timing-wise, this day works well so the next tenant can get moved in the following day.

When Tuesday morning rolls around and we stand assembled—Cece, Junie, and me—at the Clementine, it feels like anything but good timing.

"The doctor can see her today, so she needs to go," I tell Cece.

They just called this morning; Junie's latest scan is in and they have an opening for an appointment.

Cece has a U-Haul rented and sitting in the driveway, there's another person waiting on the room, *and* I've scheduled the return of my idiotic car for today. But Junie's pain is worse, and she's supposed to have chemo again on Friday, but honestly, she doesn't look like she can withstand it. Checking in on the MRI results could help—especially if they show the cancer is shrinking. It might make going on with the chemo feel like the right thing.

"We'll get it all done in one day. If we leave now, we can finish and be back . . . probably just after dinner. You're the one who said you didn't have much," Cece says.

She's right. And I don't have much stuff. It will go quickly. Quite honestly, I'm only going back to return the car and clear the place out. I'm not particularly concerned about the items or belongings there; I never bought anything of real value, never truly settled in. Part of me pretended it would always be temporary because that's what I wanted it to be.

I turn to my sister. "I don't want to leave you to go on your own."

Junie grins from underneath the beanie that's become her uniform. "I've got Tina and Dad, Peach. I'll be far from alone. Plus, I want you to go turn in your keys so you officially become a *permanent* resident here." She shimmies her shoulders in delight, and I can't help but feel it a little too. "I'm a big girl," Junie assures me.

She is. Junie, as much as I once delighted in it, does not need saving. At least not by me and not from her life. She is astounding, as if her joy has its own heartbeat.

"I believe you," I say. "So I guess Cece and I will go take care of this."

Cece throws an exuberant thumbs-up. "And not to worry—if the doctor messes around at all, Tina will dump a drink on his head."

Junie giggles. "We'll stop for a Big Gulp on the way just in case the moment arises."

I pull my little sister into a hug. She feels smaller in my arms, but in my mind she's grown into a giant. It's a strange contradiction, but I ignore the way my mind tries to make it fit into the outline of our past. How can I do anything but delight in the way she's grown?

I release her. "Text me as soon as you're done with a full update."

"Yes, ma'am, *bossy pants*," Junie says, and swats me on the rear as I turn to go.

I smile to myself as I leave the house, Cece at my side, and slip into my ball and chain of a car I can't wait to be rid of.

Two hours later, I'm sitting at the car dealership signing the paperwork required to return the leased vehicle. At first they lay the sale on hard, offering a discount to sign a new lease with an even swankier vehicle, but as soon as I drop the fact that I'm now unemployed, they happily move on to sorting the return paperwork.

It's a relief to drop the heavy fob into the salesperson's hand and meet Cece back at the U-Haul that idles in the lot. We hit the road, and I call out directions as we go. Fortunately traffic is light, thanks to the time of day.

When we pull up, Cece's eyes are wide. "You weren't kidding, Peach. This place really is a crap hole."

I laugh, and I let it flow. Looking at it now that I'm on the outside, I have so much affection for that version of me. She really was doing what she thought was best. But choosing to live here? When the Clementine was available rent-free? She really did get it wrong. If I could meet her on the street, I would wrap her in a tender hug and assure her she will make it home.

This time I'm quick to forgive myself. Quick to remind myself that I did the best I could at the time.

"I have to admit, my current digs are quite the upgrade," I say.

"I'm sorry I helped push you into this," Cece says.

I nod. "Consider it water under the bridge. So does this mean we can be friendly?"

Cece scoffs, a laugh behind it. "You don't consider *this* as friendly?" She hops out of the driver's side of the small cab.

I follow suit, and as we walk to the small building, Cece slings an arm over my shoulder and pulls me in. "If friends is what you want, friends is what you get. But in full transparency, the Cecelia version of friends may not be as fluffy as the kind between the rest of y'all."

I look up at her and smile. "Well, I'm in luck, because rough around the edges is just how I wanted it."

CHAPTER 77

JUNIE

AFTER HER APPOINTMENT THAT DAY, Junie makes sure she's in bed by the time Georgia gets back. Tina and her father went with her to the appointment, and she sends them home as soon as they're back, claiming she needs a nap. What Junie really wants is just a few more hours to herself before she has to explain. She's felt like she's been getting sicker over the past few weeks, and that was made clear at the appointment today. Despite the chemo, the cancer has spread.

Today the doctor didn't hold back when she asked for his professional opinion about her condition, and she was so grateful because it was the permission she needed. Her scan did not look good. The cancer showed up larger in her bones and has spread to her lungs. The chemo doesn't seem to be working, and the blood work they pulled before the MRI was concerning as well. She is scheduled for chemo in a few days, and at the bottom of her guts, Junie doesn't want to go.

It's entirely different from when she didn't want to do it the first time around. Her reluctance is not because she's afraid, not because she wants to deny her reality, but quite the opposite. She has fully accepted what this means.

When she asked the doctor, he didn't say she should stop chemo. But he also didn't blanch when she asked about it.

He said the chemo has not shrunk the growths, that the cancer has grown and spread. That the treatment has no guarantees either way, and it's up to her.

Neither she nor the doctor pretended like the outcome was looking good; neither pretended like their early optimism still fit into this picture. Neither pretended that this wasn't in line with the progression of this specific disease.

The next morning, Junie is up first. Most likely due to her 6:00 p.m. bedtime and the fact that Puds spooned her all night. She goes to the fridge and pops the tab on a can of Diet Coke and slurps. She wanders out to the garden, and there is a slight chill to the air. It feels like a promise from fall—*be there soon*. For now, thanks to the battering heat and routine thunderstorms of summer, her garden is green. She harvests a few zucchinis. Puds runs out, and she stoops to pat him.

"Now this is the good life, my good boy," she says.

She pulls a few weeds, then settles into a wooden slat-back chair. Junie turns her head to the sky.

Not long ago she could work out here for hours without even thinking about this chair. Still, what a miracle that she can walk to and through her garden. She's determined to delight in what remains.

A couple of hours later, and with many rest breaks in between, Junie arrives at June's in her truck and parks as close as humanly possible to the door. Her eyes well with happy tears when she sees the progress. The walls are new and complete. The floor is now shiny LVT. She taps it with her foot and manages a quick boogie before dropping into a hair chair stashed against the wall and covered in plastic wrap. It lets out a crinkly thud to welcome her.

Her phone buzzes with a text.

Dad: Hi honey, sorry to bother you, but the crew is
ready for your paint selection. They want to get paint up
before any of the lighting fixtures or decor is placed. I'm
happy to take over on that. Or Georgia, I'm sure. Don't
want to pressure you.

"Ha," Junie says out loud to herself, alone in the middle of her
mama's—no, all of their—beauty shop. "Little does he know."

She lifts herself up and slides a few paint chips from her back
pocket. It's down to three front runners: Winsome Dove, Fresh
Porcelain, and Marshmallow Fluff. Junie holds them out in a fan
and carries them around the room, pausing for angles. She had an
idea of her favorite, but now here in the shop, it's obvious.

She settles back in the chair and texts her father. Marshmallow
Fluff. Just ask at the hardware store, and they know the brand.

An answer pings. Final answer?

He always did love that game show. Junie types back: Final answer.

She watches the dots scroll, and then his response pops up. You
win the million-dollar prize! You're still a million bucks, Junie Bug.

The phone pings again, this time Georgia: Where are you? Then:
Did you drive alone? And finally: Calling now.

Junie silences the phone and gets up. She needs to talk to Georgia
about this face-to-face, and to be honest, she's ready to get back to
her sofa. She'll face her sister at home.

CHAPTER 78

GEORGIA

WHEN JUNIE WALKS BACK INTO the Clementine, relief floods me. Objectively I knew she was probably fine, but she hasn't driven herself in weeks, let alone jetted around running errands. She's been chaperoned and generally lying horizontal.

Junie goes right to the couch and curls up.

I squeeze in beside her and pull the blanket over her. "Where you been, Bug?"

She looks up at me and grins. "I wanted to see the swatches in the shop, you know, with the light there."

"I could've taken you," I say. "I'm here for that kind of stuff."

"I'm not so sure with the way you slept in today," Junie says, grinning. "*I* was starting to worry, in fact. Georgia Louise up later than 6:00 a.m.? Not in *my* lifetime."

I laugh. "Honestly, I think it was finally being done with Atlanta. The job, the car, the apartment. Closing the door on it and coming back here is such a weight off. It was like the sleep you get on the first night back in your own bed after a long trip away."

"Like coming home," Junie says.

I nod. "But enough of that. How was the doctor? Do they have a new miracle drug to put you back together in a day or two yet?" I look at my little sister and smile. She is so precious, and now I get to be here for the foreseeable future, not a single plan to leave.

Junie shuffles up to a sitting position. "Look, it might not be the news you were looking for. And now that I'm acting like the grown-up I am, I'm not going to try to joke my way out of it." Her hands emerge from the blanket, and they feel bony when they wrap around mine. "I'm not doing well, health-wise. The scan was not good. It's spread, bigger in some places. So the chemo I've endured this far hasn't worked. I told him, the doctor, how I'm feeling, how the pain continues to come and I'm leaning heavily on those meds I know are the big guns."

I resist the urge to jump in. To argue her points. But I trust her. I do, so I will sit quietly and let her speak.

"I'm supposed to do chemo again in a couple days." Junie swallows, then meets my eyes earnestly. "But I don't want to. And not because I don't want to fight or I'm trying out the whole denial thing again. But because when I'm honest with myself about what's happening with my body, I don't want to waste what's left. I barely make it to the garden. I can't even take Puds around the block. My heart and my soul are still so good, though, and this life that I've got, I want to live it. I don't want to spend a week in bed from this treatment, only to barely have a couple days of eating something before doing it again. And he said it again—the doctor said chemo is no guarantee."

The pain starts in my chest and shoots out from there to the very tips of me as I realize what she's telling me. My body aches as it braces for what's to come. "So this means . . ." My voice catches.

Junie nods. "My body has already made the choice. I don't think it's really up to me anymore. Not that part at least."

The *choice*? No, this isn't a choice; it's not a choice if there's only a single outcome. Angry tears prickle my eyes, and I curse the world for dangling this love, *her*, in my life only to wrench it away. This miserable science for doing something but nothing of value. For wasting our precious time and letting me down, letting all of us down. For failing Junie.

For being so very human in light of a person so extraordinary.

Is nothing all we've got for the most remarkable among us?

My arms are around her, and I pull her in so tight. I scramble to memorize every bit of hugging her. The shape and weight. The smell of her.

"I can't lose you." Even before the words are out, I know they're as powerless as a sieve holding sand. My demands won't change the truth. Sobs start in the depths of my throat and erupt in sounds I've never heard myself make before.

I will lose her.

"Forgive me this one, Peach, but I might have to die a little to live what I've got left," Junie says.

She is asking for mercy, for a gentle hand. For permission to rest.

I pull back and look into those eyes that are desperate for my agreement, and I am torn in half. How can I agree? How can I say, "Yes, let's stop the chemo," when I would settle for fragments of her? I would settle for the scent of her on a breeze if that's the best I can do. When every part of me wants to keep *something* of her.

Junie lifts the corners of her mouth, a suggestion of a smile, and even now, weeks into chemo, and in the face of devastation, she is beautiful. Not beautiful like a supermodel or even a well-designed beauty shop, but beautiful like a human who can see the world in its very best light from inside her own worst case. When she's losing. When she's ending. Junie has always been magic, precious, like the truly beautiful things of this world. And much like them, much like hope and holiness and the promise of a repeatedly rising sun, she cannot be owned or kept or held.

All I can do is nod as tears stream down my cheeks.

"Ok." The word is a wisp.

Maybe part of me wondered as we've watched her decline if the treatment wasn't working, but another part of me knew to expect her to get sick and then sicker. I desperately want to fight and scream and claw to get her life back. I don't want to give in to this. It's never been my style; I would kill for her second chance.

But it's her. It's Junie, wonderfully herself. And at least for a while longer, she's here.

I take my baby sister's face in my hands. I look into her eyes intently. "I promise I will follow your lead."

Junie's face cracks into a smile and lights up in a way I now realize has been absent over the last few weeks. Being so unlike herself must have taken its toll on her too. Her relief, now painted across her face, cuts to the core of me, and I cannot help but realize in this very moment that she will be the greatest love story of my life.

Nothing will top her.

I wouldn't allow it.

I pull her into me, and she makes no move to go. Eventually, she wriggles, and even though I keep my arms in place, Junie extracts herself and looks at me.

"Thank you, Peach," Junie says. "You always were the best big sister. *Now*—first order of business: I need some *wheels*."

My brow folds in confusion.

"A wheelchair. I need one if I'm going to be out on the town. And if we can get one with flames down the side, that would be best."

There she is.

CHAPTER 79

JUNIE

JUNIE SPENDS THE NEXT TWO weeks surrounded by the people she loves the most, enjoying herself. She gardens, crochets, and pets her dog a perfectly unreasonable amount.

She lives.

Sometimes she cries too. How could she not, feeling the reverberations of this life inside of her, the way it shakes her awake as she lives one moment at a time, knowing it won't last. She won't last.

Tonight they're having a traditional Friday night slumber party at the Clementine.

Junie is on her throne of a couch, Tina on a fluffy pallet she and Georgia constructed on the floor after dragging the coffee table out of sight. Cece sits in the high-back armchair looking the most restrained of them all—besides the lavender wig cut into a bob she wears on her head.

Tonight they all wear wigs, and at Junie's request they're colors of the rainbow. Junie is in bright pink, long and straight to her waist, Georgia in baby-blue curls, and Tina in a fire-red shoulder-length.

Georgia wanders in from the kitchen, but the smell gets to the living room before her.

"Mmm, salty, buttery popcorn," Junie calls to it like it's a dog capable of heeding a command.

Her appetite has returned a bit since she stopped the treatments, and it's been a gift. Her taste is better too, so she can taste the red flavor of her Twizzlers. She and Georgia have been meal planning. Georgia shops and cooks, but they've tried new things and stuck to old-time favorites alike. It's so nice to see her big sister settled, her shoulders sitting at a normal height.

Georgia has finally set down her armor and gotten busy having a regular life.

"Cece, open your mouth. Lemme see if I can make it in with a piece," Tina calls over.

Well, at least as *regular* as is possible among a crew like this.

"I'm not about to let you choke me to death," Cece says. "I'm fully capable of feeding myself."

"Y'all quit bickering," Georgia says. "Or you're going to force me to start a game of truth or dare. Or worse, mani-pedis." She grins at Cece, who reflexively pulls her hands into her sleeves.

"Not if I can outrun you," Cece says.

"Junie, honey, what did you want to do? Watch a movie? It's been a while since I've seen *Steel Magnolias*," Tina says.

"Didn't I walk in on you watching it last weekend?" Georgia asks.

"Yes." Tina nods deeply. "Like I said, it's been a while."

Junie laughs. The spirit that circulates among these Louises is like an energy source. She wonders for a moment if she might run on it when the lights inside her eventually go out. It's like a magical fairy tale designed just for her; maybe that's what heaven will be like.

Junie considers Tina's question for the evening. "What I want to do is make a big memory."

Georgia pouts. "I thought we promised no sad stuff."

Cece grunts. "Oh, let her have it."

Junie clears her throat. "Excuse me? If y'all are done, let me finish."

"Whatever you want, honey," Tina says, patting Junie's leg from her perch on the floor.

Junie waggles her eyebrows. "Let's streak the green."

She's met by a chorus of groans and gasps.

Streaking the green in Whitetail is an activity typically reserved for rowdy teenagers or drunk adults who don't know better yet. Not once in Whitetail history has a streaking incident gone unrecorded. Inevitably, someone sees. Someone walking a dog, or dropping off an early delivery, or driving the garbage truck for the restaurant dumpsters. So if a resident decides to streak the green, he or she is inherently agreeing to become the talk of the town until the next big piece of news drops.

"Are you sure, Junie?" Cece asks. "I'm less asking about the naked part and more asking about the running part."

Junie throws her a look that says, *You think I didn't think of that?* "Georgia's going to push me."

"What? So I can spend *more* time *naked* traversing the green? We all know the maintenance of that area is spotty at best."

Junie erupts in giggles. "Precisely. But don't worry, I'll be shielding you partially in my chair."

Tina makes the sign of the cross and mutters under her breath about forgiveness for her sins. "Alright, well, y'all better let me stop by the house for my robe. You know I'm not spending a second more than necessary out there naked."

Georgia throws her hands up. "Why the hell not. I guess now is the time if ever."

Cece quietly gets up out of the chair and walks toward the door.

Junie clears her throat. "And where do you think you're going?"

"I thought we were all going to get our robes." Cece grins, and Junie feels the mischief in the air.

"As you were," Junie says with a nod.

Thirty minutes later, the women are back at the Clementine,

outfitted with robes and naked as the day they came into this world underneath them. Rainbow wigs intact.

They stand in a circle, and Georgia raises an uncapped bottle of bourbon.

"The higher the hair," Georgia says.

"The closer to God," everyone replies.

The bottle travels the circle, each taking a hearty swig. When it arrives at Junie, Tina reaches out and snatches the bottle.

Junie levels a look at her aunt. "*Really?* What difference is this making in the long run?"

Tina sighs as Junie tips the bottle, then wipes her mouth on the sleeve of her robe.

"It's about to be the best Good Hair Day we've ever seen, girls," Junie says. "Let's load up."

Ten minutes down the road, and the women are huddled together beside the truck parked parallel to the green. Cece unsnaps the wheelchair and rolls it onto the grass for Junie.

"I cannot believe what you've got us doing," Georgia says to her sister, positioning her robed self behind the chair.

Junie pulls off her robe and plops herself into the chair. "You're welcome, Peach. Now drop the robes, ladies, and let's get to it."

"On three?" Tina asks.

"You got it," Cece says. "One . . . two . . . *three!*"

Fabric flies, and the women dash across the grassy knoll in the dark night. Laughter flies from them and the blur of flesh they create. Georgia moves the wheelchair over the grass with unbelievable aptness.

"You done this before?" Junie asks her sister, cackling.

Georgia can barely push words through her giggles. "As if you wouldn't know so by now."

They get to the edge.

"Mercy, I didn't think about having to double back," Tina yelps.

Cece whips back in the direction of the truck. "And what did you think would happen?"

Georgia and Junie are last to make it back, and their aunts hold out their robes for them.

"Well, did we do it?" Junie asks as they load themselves and her wheelchair back into the truck, shading their faces in case of on-lookers.

"What's that?" Tina asks.

"Make a memory."

"Not a one of us is going to forget that anytime soon," Georgia says, pulling her robe tight across her. "Just as it should be."

CHAPTER 80

JUNIE

ABOUT TWO WEEKS AFTER JUNIE convinces her Good Hair Days girls to streak the green, she gets the call from the construction crew. Well, her father got the call, and he diverted it to Junie saying, *"This one's for her."* The shop is complete, walls in place and painted, flooring secure, can lighting installed, mirrors replaced, hair chairs dolled up. Junie puts out a call to gather her people. It's time to see June's in all her renovated glory.

They meet in the parking lot. Cece and Tina are the first to arrive, and they greet Junie and Georgia with wide waves as they pull up. Soon, Rich and Eddie join them. Georgia unloads the wheelchair onto the curb and helps Junie into it. She hasn't been out much in the past weeks, mostly sticking close to the house and her garden.

Junie wanted to invite everyone who helped, all their neighbors who pitched in, but there will be a grand reopening hoopla for that.

This part is for family only.

"I'm not sure I should be here," Eddie says, looking around at the group gathered.

"Pishposh, buddy. We've taken you as our own whether you like it or not," Junie says, reaching out from her seated position to squeeze his arm.

He and Georgia have been sneaking off together and canoodling, and Junie has relished every bit of watching the feelings between them rekindled. More than once she's spotted Eddie sneaking out of Georgia's room looking tousled and red in the face.

Georgia pulls him into her and smooches him exuberantly. "You're welcome here."

"Alright, well, enough messing around. Let's see the place," Cece announces, clearly having had enough of the googly eyes and excessive politeness.

Georgia positions Junie at the front, and the others form a loose line behind her.

"Y'all ready?" Junie calls over her shoulder.

The others call out an enthusiastic *yes*, and she leans forward, turns the doorknob, and nudges the door. It swings wide open, and Georgia pushes her inside.

It feels like the world pauses when Junie passes onto the edge of the main floor where she can see it all. Like the moment in a solar eclipse when all the birds stop singing because it would be rude to interrupt a moment so divine.

June's Beauty Shop. She's back. Back and grown-up, glowed-up, reinvented just like Junie and the rest of this gaggle of Louises— Louises, that is, by birth or by their own decree or by extension because being a Louise is about living, not a stupid little name.

The Marshmallow Fluff walls are delicious, and Junie pats herself on the back for that one. And Dolly Parton. She's *here*, and just like the design promised, she's sprinkled tastefully around the place in a way that makes her presence more fun than scary. The decor details are put together like toppings on an ice cream sundae. Fluffy towels, light and bright drapes. Even the carts have gotten a refresh with trendy rose gold details.

The mirrors are new and have inset lighting that's modern but glam. Shiny glass jars of clips and scissors line the vanity area, and even the Goldilocks branded section fits right in.

This reveal is the final piece for Junie's heart to be at peace: seeing how her good intentions gone awry have been made right—and with the helping hands of so many people who love her, love this family and this shop.

Georgia leans down from behind. "You did so good, Junie Bug."

Tina leaps out from the group and squeals as she skips across the floor to her refreshed wig wall. She runs a hand along the thick wooden floating shelving with an "ooooh." The wigs have been edited down to a smaller selection, and the team even created a beautiful "look book" to show the other wig options Tina has in storage, though she's now short a few that Junie has taken off her hands.

Cece beams from ear to ear and lets out a whoop. "Look at those fancy basins." The porcelain shines, and the brass hardware adds a fun, trendy element. "Would've been nice to have that when I was around."

"Don't you worry," Tina says. "You're welcome to pick up a basin shift anytime you'd like."

"You ladies really knocked it out on this one," Daddy says. He looks around smiling, and it's the proudest Junie can remember him looking. He slaps Eddie on the back in celebration.

"I have to agree with Rich," Eddie says. "Big congrats are in order. I'm probably going to sound like an idiot asking this, but is there going to be a reopening party?"

"*Grand* reopening," Georgia adds. Her eyes glitter when she looks at him, and she floats from behind Junie's chair to intertwine her hand in his.

Junie's heart swells at the sight of them. She laughs when the thought hits her, and then she says it out loud. "Hey, Eddie, remember when we dated?"

Eddie half laughs, half scoffs. "Still firmly in the long-term memory. No worries there, friend."

Tina looks over warmly. "I never would've fancied ourselves coming so far in this short a time."

Junie giggles, and when she should stop, she keeps on. The laughter comes from her belly, the depths of the little that's left of her skin and bones. Life may not always be happy endings, not for her, but this scenario with June's and the Louises she loves? It is the best case within her life. The life she's had might be worn-out, but it's worn-out from her putting it to very good use.

She has no tread left on the tires of her life, but she's put on miles of exploring, of being loud and sometimes difficult, of being honest and doing her best.

She has worn holes in the socks of this life from dancing at every whim.

She has made it beautiful, as much as she could in a world that is admittedly ugly and harsh as well.

She could not picture a more beautiful sight than this hole-in-the-wall beauty shop made new, filled with her beloved people, after a very big storm.

Tears run. Because she wants to stay in this moment forever, but it won't last and neither will she. But then again, the best things in life never do. All of it is fleeting, which is perhaps a prerequisite to magic.

She has known such magic here.

CHAPTER 81

GEORGIA

IT'S ONLY A WEEK LATER when I call Junie's doctor to ask for home hospice. The plan for them to swoop in when she began to struggle has been agreed upon for a while now. A tender team of nurses and home health aides slip in and out quietly, administering medications to make her comfortable. They are sweet and kind but move around in a way that says they know this time isn't about them. They bring a hospital bed that we switch out for Junie's regular bed, and I decorate it with a swath of feather boas.

Junie calls the staff who visit her "angels with the good stuff."

I stay by her bedside, the rest of the family rotating in and out. I set up a makeshift bed beside her. I bring her Twizzlers she doesn't really eat, and we watch reality television. Puds is anxious and paces; I give him all the attention I can manage.

It's when Junie stops making jokes that I know the end is near. Her appetite slowly disappears, and she begins to sleep for much of the day. I put on the shows she loves, and I wonder if she can hear them. I wonder if the sound of them will tempt her back, if I could convince her to stay for a few more minutes. I don't remember when I started measuring my life in minutes rather than the greedy days, weeks, even months I was once so willing to consume without a second thought. I so desperately cling to each and any moment I get. She's not herself, but I'm happy with fragments or crumbs of her because it's better than nothing.

It's better than having to accept it being over.

That the little sister who has always lived in the very center of my heart, the person whose well-being is and always has been at the forefront of my mind might just simply . . . stop. That her phone calls will stop. That she won't be here to live in this house that she has made cozy and so very *her*. That she will leave a dog who adores her confused and alone.

It's impossible.

And where does it leave me? Who can I even be without her? So much of me exists only in relation to her.

The doctor comes this afternoon, and everyone is here. Cece and Tina, Dad and Eddie. Me. I ask him how much longer, and he says it's impossible to know. Some patients look like they're close and live weeks longer. Others slip away faster. He doesn't stay long.

All of us are circled around a sleeping Junie. Tina fluffs and tucks Junie's covers. Eddie adjusts some of the monitors for no obvious reason other than to have something to do for her. Dad crouches beside her and runs a palm over her forehead, whispering about how he loves her. Cece stands beside me, and I wonder for a moment if she's the person looking out for me.

When I glance over at her, she reaches out and rubs my back. "You're doing so well for Junie."

I swallow at the pinch of tears threatening and nod swiftly. "My best."

We linger for a while, quietly for the most part, occasionally sharing fun stories about Junie. After about an hour or so, Dad pulls a buzzing phone from his pocket.

"Looks like there's a bad weather alert," he says. "Tornado watch and a big storm coming through."

"We should all probably head home before it hits," Cece says.

The others murmur their agreement and begin gathering their things. The aunts and Dad go first, and Eddie lingers.

He crosses the room to me and pulls me into a long hug.

I let out a deep breath and for the first time today, I feel my shoulders relax, my breath settle. I stay there in Eddie's arms and let his strength hold me up. I don't want to talk, and he seems to understand because he doesn't move or flinch. He remains steady and solid for me, like he's always been, and like I so very desperately need right now.

Minutes pass. Precious minutes spent in his arms, and I feel like I'm being recharged. Like I'll have enough steam for the next leg of keeping watch.

Eventually I pull back. "Thank you," I whisper.

Eddie nods. "Do you want me to stay?"

I glance over at Junie in the bed. "No. You should go. But thank you for asking."

He nods and drops a gentle kiss on my forehead as he squeezes my hands. "I'll talk to you tomorrow."

I hold on to the tips of his fingers as he pulls away, and before he goes I tell him: "I love you, Eddie."

He grins. And the first thing I think is how Junie would love this look on his face. "I love you too."

Eddie's gone for fifteen minutes before I hear the thunder rumble as promised. It's a comfort to know they'll all have made it home safely, and Junie and I will be cozy and safe at the Clementine. I go to the chair at her side and perch on its edge, and the rain rattles at the windows, the wind whistling. I sit for a while and listen to the power of the storm outside, and it feels less lonely to know that we're not the only ones sitting in the middle of unrest. I find Junie's hand in the covers and grasp it gently in mine. I talk to her, like I've come to do routinely here in our little house.

"Thank you for bringing me back home, Junie. Really, I'm not sure where I'd be without it—floundering for sure and pretending. I'm so lucky to be your big sister. Really, it's the best job I've ever had. The only one I've really enjoyed, if we're being honest. Anyway, I'm thinking about maybe going back to school for hair, so I can help Tina with appointments. I don't know. Maybe yes. Maybe no. Maybe just part of me is a little scared. Aren't we all?" I laugh a little, trying to imagine the joke Junie would crack. "I just wish you could stay too."

I sit quietly for a while longer, the thunder quieting as the whistling winds blow the storm onward. I think about Junie and everything I want to tell her. Everything I want to somehow cover in advance so it'll hurt less when she misses it in real life.

Junie's eyes flutter open. They are glassy and pale, staring across the room, but eventually her eyes make it to mine. Her lips move. "Peach."

My heart lifts, explodes really, if I'm honest, at this morsel of her offered up at my feet. "Junie Bug." My hands squeeze hers and I lean in closer, over her. "The others just left; I might have to lie about you being awake."

She's only spoken a few times in the last week.

"Storm," Junie says. Her words are papery, like they've been made out of borrowed time. "*Please*, check my garden."

My brow crinkles. "I can't leave you now. You're awake."

Junie's eyes close then open, like she's drifting back off.

Her eyes close, and she's back asleep. And like the—*her*—big sister I am now and forevermore, I heed her call. Like the sucker I am, I pull her covers up, and I walk out into the house, through the living room and into the kitchen. I glance briefly out the window, Puds wagging at my feet. It may be a fool's errand, confused words from a hazy mental state, but I go. Because it's Junie who asked.

At the back door, I see the storm is mostly passed. I slip into Junie's clogs and open the door. I take the two steps down, and it's otherworldly outside. Over to the east are the dark gray and blue clouds, and over the garden and over to the west is a golden twilight, warm light scattered by the drizzle left in the air. I walk through her planters, check her birdbath, even look at the gutters, and not a thing is out of place. I walk the outskirts and check the fence, glance around for downed branches. I stop in the middle and prop my hands on my hips for a final look.

It's then that I glance back up.

A textbook-perfect rainbow in colors red through violet streaks across the sky with such vibrance that a gasp escapes me.

It couldn't be. Could it?

But *how*? How could she know or see?

And then I realize. I *know*.

Oh, Junie.

I spin around and sprint to the house, up the steps, blood rushing in my ears. The back door hangs open behind me. The clogs come off as I tear through the house to get to her.

No. This can't be. She wouldn't, not when I was gone.

But she would, she very much would.

When I return to her room, the monitors tell me I was right. The signal shows her heart is not beating.

She's gone.

She left when my back was turned, slipped out quietly in one big act of mercy.

And she left me with a rainbow.

CHAPTER 82

GEORGIA

THE WEEKS AFTER JUNIE DIED are blurry and lived very much minute to minute. Home health comes and removes the medical equipment. Once it's gone, it almost feels like it might've all been a dream without the physical evidence before me. Tina and Cece take shifts sleeping on the sofa. Dad sits in the armchair and nods off. Eddie comes too, but he follows my lead. Sometimes I'm up for seeing him, and sometimes I want to be alone. I cry. My eyes swell.

Part of me feels like she's closer somehow when I'm alone. Maybe really it's in the quiet when the Clementine creaks in a particular way that sounds like her coming home. The way Puds gets excited to see a friendly stranger approach, and it looks like a joy only she might evoke.

Between all of us, we keep the garden alive.

Today is the grand reopening of June's Beauty Shop, an event we have discussed and debated at length. Mostly it was the others assuring me that having it is the right thing to do. And me throwing an argument at them that might stick. *It's disrespectful, too soon, too loud, too fun for a time like this.* But I know on the inside they're right when they say it's what she would've wanted; it's been weeks, and the shop needs to open. I hate the sound of that phrase, by the way, *what she would've wanted*. It's nothing but a reminder that we won't have more time for her to change her mind. What I wouldn't give for her making one last change of plans, diving into another raucous adventure. I know June's should be celebrated, reopened; it's just that it will hurt to do it without Junie.

I shower, towel off, and wrap myself in a robe. I know better than to put a stitch of makeup on my face before I do my hair; I have avoided doing my hair at length since I lost Junie. I have air-dried it, ignored it, tossed it into countless thoughtless, meaningless pony-tails. But today my hair will be Done. For her.

I stand in front of the mirror that should still be hers, that showed her face for years, and I unwind the towel from my head and release the red curtain of hair. I look down to pump a leave-in conditioner into my palm and work it through. My hair is so long now, and I wonder if Junie would be urging me to get a trim if she were here. I look at myself as I brush the length. It is so thick and long, and tears spring up, then rush and roll down my face with every sweep of the brush. It's too much hair, it's unworkable, just like this life without her that is too thick to wade through. I pick up the blow dryer I don't remember plugging in, and before I start it I turn on the hot rollers to heat. I rough-dry the hair with my fingers, and as I do, my tears slow.

Look good, feel good. I tell it to myself like a promise, and I have no choice but to believe I can make a difference to this life that feels empty. Even though I know better by now than to think my mother can impact the tides of time, I invoke every ounce of her. *June's Beauty Shop, where a good hair day is only one stop away.* It's enough to get my hair in the rollers.

As I apply makeup for the event, I realize it's the first time in weeks, save Junie's service that I attended in a haze. I slip on a royal-blue dress that is comfortable and makes my eyes shine. I feel stronger when I step back in front of the mirror, release the hot rollers, and douse my hair with hair spray.

Before I head for the shop, I stop outside of her bedroom. Since they removed the hospital bed and drips and returned her bed to its place, we've all tiptoed around it. Even my purse hangs on my shoulder in a way that gives me an out: *I'm already on my way.* My fingertips reach out and the door pops open and swings back. If it could talk, it would say, *Look at me, making it easy for you. It's ok to remember, Peach.*

I step inside, and visiting her room put back together again is like stepping back in time. Like saying hello again.

I squeeze my hands to my chest, and like I do as habit, I talk to her out loud. "I miss you, Junie Bug. You should be here today, but you're not. So I will do it."

I close my eyes as the pain of longing for the impossible cuts through my middle, but I will myself to feel something else. I remember Junie. *We can make this something beautiful.* I have made it my mission to live this—for her, and for me too. There never was any promise that beautiful things wouldn't hurt at times too.

I step over to the bureau she painted a bright teal, and sitting on top is her jewelry collection, complete with costume earrings, bohemian crystal pieces, even glittery hair clips befitting a woman much younger in age. But that was the thing about Junie: She was so good at being more than one thing at a time.

I slip a ring on my finger, a bracelet on my wrist, and a clip into my hair.

"Thanks," I whisper to her. "This is what I need to get over the hump."

And I push out of the room and head for the beauty shop.

Ten minutes later, I park in the lot at June's and wait. My heart beats quicker than usual, and my throat is tight. I'm surrounded by cars, which means the community has come. Despite my urge to crank the truck and drive it back home to hide at the Clementine, it's time to take the step.

"Look what you're making me do on my own," I whisper to an imaginary Junie.

Probably she'd pop me gently on the rear and say, *You're a big girl. Keep it hoppin'.*

I can't help but smile as I climb out of the car. Maybe her memory will fuel me further than usual.

When I step into June's, it's as stunning as it was when we came for our first reveal. The aunts have probably been back since, and Tina has probably seen a client or two in the time between. Especially when my eyes land on the Silvers and their neat bobs, I know she's been at work. The shininess of this place hurts a little in the face of how I feel on the inside.

Eddie approaches me with a big smile, two drinks in hand. "I have options. Wine or Diet Coke. I didn't know what you'd feel like, but I also wanted to have a drink waiting for you. And there are juice boxes available, and no one is checking that only the kids are taking them."

I smile. "How thoughtful." I take the Diet Coke. "And you wouldn't be embarrassed to stand beside me sipping on a juice box?"

"I am nothing but proud to stand at your side, whatever your drink of choice."

I laugh to hide the way I blush. All of my feelings are intense these days, and they all sit so close to the surface. I don't want to cry or scream or dissolve into a mess. I'm a swirl of intensity.

He pulls me into him and instantly I feel my shoulders drop. I could stay here, sleep here, arguably live here in the sturdy place his embrace creates. I pull back and kiss him tenderly before burrowing back into his chest, like it might undo all the difficulties that exist in the world that surrounds us.

He pulls back. "Seriously," he says when I meet his eyes. "You should be really proud of the way you've navigated all of this."

I nod as the tears fill my eyes and spill down my cheeks. "Is *that* what I'm doing? Navigating it?"

Eddie unwraps his arms from me and takes my hands. "It's ok to miss her. I miss her like crazy—and I was only her fake boyfriend for a couple weeks."

I pull a hand back to wipe the tears. "At least I got those over with." I roll my eyes at myself. "And I wondered if I might get through this with no tears at all."

"Tears will always be a reasonable response. I'm not sure a day will come when they won't apply."

I nod. It feels good to hear someone say what I've felt: I won't ever get over losing her. *Tears will always apply.* It feels good to know that someone else realizes they will be forever changed and that time won't heal the hole. Life might get easier. I hope it will. But now I have someone else saying the same: The part of me that broke when I lost Junie won't ever be fixed, even if I'm still living.

Tina floats up. "You're here. Wonderful! We'll start the program."

I squint. "Program?"

Dad rolls out a projector, and the crowd parts. He clicks it on as the group falls silent. *Welcome to Our Good Hair Day* scrolls, a fun pop song playing in the background.

The crowd claps, and I look around at everyone gathered. The Silvers have shown up strong, and beside them Michaela is trying to wrangle a wiggling toddler on her hip. Even a few of the cast from *Grease* showed up in costume. The Brownies are here, a few in uniform and a few with glittery dresses and high-glam looks, dragging parents behind them. People from the bank are here. Some of Cece's colleagues from the auto shop came, and Sam stands dotingly at Tina's side. That might even be Sheriff Mike in the back.

"Now if I can have your attention," Dad announces. "Before we lost our Junie, she and I planned a little surprise for today."

He clicks the video to life, and there sits Junie on the screen, alive.

She grins wide, and I know they must've done it before she got really bad. She wears that rainbow-striped beanie and Puds is curled up beside her.

"Happy Good Hair Day!" Junie announces. "I'm officially back from the grave." She giggles. "Just kidding. That's probably very blasphemous, but anyway, I'll already have my assigned seat in the afterlife by then. So perhaps . . ."

My dad clears his throat in the background of the video, and Junie makes brief eye contact off-screen.

"Yeah, you can just edit that part out. Don't need the whole town knowing I'm a hot mess . . ."

More rumbling from Dad's off-camera voice.

"True. I'm fairly well-known around these parts, you're right, and no one should be surprised. Anyway. Start it here when you show it, okay?"

Junie rights herself on-screen and smiles. I can see the sparkle in her eyes, and I almost feel it in my bones when she says, "I know this is going to be the best day. Thank you to everyone who pitched in and helped me—*us*—make this thing right with the shop. It is beyond anything I dreamed, beyond what our mama would've dreamed up. And it's thanks to you all. This place belongs to you too, so thank you for celebrating this place with us today. You are the MVPs. I miss you all already."

Junie pauses and looks to Dad off-screen. "Maybe you could have Tina and Cece throw some Twizzlers up in the air after it clicks off. Or glitter—though maybe not on the brand-new floors. Whatever, just something with pizzazz."

And Dad cuts the video.

The crowd erupts in cheers. Tears are dabbed and hugs exchanged.

I guess I didn't have to do it entirely without her. Despite the brief comfort, the moment the screen goes black feels like waking up from a favorite dream, knowing even if I will myself back to sleep, it won't be there waiting for me in the dark.

Eventually my aunts find me, and I lean into deep, long hugs. I make it to the refreshments table and choke down a Twizzler for Junie. I nibble and realize that I haven't tasted food in weeks, but now, here, it settles full in my belly like comfort. I go back for a second plate. The Silvers come by and each has a story and a hug to share, something cute from the week, a favorite memory of the shop, of Junie, even of our mama before her. Promises to restock the freezer that's already overflowing with casseroles I haven't touched. Even one brave Brownie walks up to me, her fellow troop members hanging back and eyeing us.

"I'm really sorry about Ms. Junie. She was really nice and seemed pretty fun for a grown-up."

Warmth blooms in me, and I bend to her height. "Thank you for saying that. And you're right—she was way more fun than the average grown-up."

Tina sits at the computer Cece set up at the check-in desk, and she books appointments as people leave. Several promise to call and schedule. Sam writes out appointment cards that he hands off to each customer with a smile. Eventually the crowd thins, and it's just the aunts and me left.

"We'll be doing so well with this new business. Even better than before the reno," Tina says.

"I guess people are invested here even more after they helped save it," Cece says. "Might even need to hire another stylist eventually."

I didn't plan to mention my ideas out loud, not yet, but with these two, I figure why not. "Maybe not so fast. It's just—I've been thinking about going back to school for hair."

Tina squeaks.

"Now, I don't want us to get ahead of ourselves, because maybe I won't be good at it or maybe it's too much to take on now on top of losing her. But it's on my mind."

Cece pulls me into a side hug. "Good for you. And if you flunk out, you're in good company with me." She winks.

"What I know is that we can all contribute here with whatever skill set we have. Everyone can be helpful," Tina says. "I guess that's my way of saying you've got a job here."

I smile. "Thanks, Tina." I turn around for another look at the place. "It really did turn out incredible."

"Mm-hmm," Cece says.

Tina nods.

I feel a surge of pride. It's quiet and thin, wispy, but despite its stature, it rushes into me and is so unfamiliar that it's like something brand-new. It's different, and I wonder if—*hope*—it could be a promise. Of what's to come. Maybe there is good to come inside these walls.

GEORGIA

Two Months Later

WHEN I WAKE IN THE morning, the first thing I do is reach down for Puds. His tail thwacks the side of the bed, and I roll out of it and follow him to the kitchen, where I pour him a bowl of kibble. He'll get a piece of the bacon I make for breakfast later too. Both of us are making great progress on gaining back the grief pounds we've shed.

It's cold this morning, so I pull on a heavy overcoat before I slip into Junie's clogs, my feet in thick socks. I wander out to the garden to check on it for her. Long gone are the lush greens, the abundant vegetables, the flowers that bring butterflies and the buzz of bees. But still, I come. Still, I check. Long ago, I cut back the brittle branches after reading some gardening blogs online. Still, I will keep watch over the winter. Maybe it's for me, too, a meditation on my love for Junie.

It felt good to watch the garden die as fall turned to winter, a physical example from the earth of my insides curling up in my own pain. It felt right that her garden would mourn Junie too. And right as it was, alongside it also sits a belief in the depth of my belly that it may be gone in the version that once existed, but it will come back anew. It's a promise that though this garden will sit dormant and icy for the next few months, it hasn't forgotten me. *Us.* It's an example we can all rely on to show us how to come back too.

If we're willing to first endure the winter.

Once I'm satisfied with the condition of the garden and now fully awake from the chilly morning air, I head back inside and start making coffee. I make eggs and toast and the bacon Puds sits so patiently and waits for. I sip my coffee before I do the dishes.

I shower and do a quick cleanup on the house. I shuffle aside the legal paperwork I received last week from the class action suit against the lousy genetic testing lab. Researching it and getting us on the list of plaintiffs was Eddie's grief project in the weeks after Junie passed. Anything we get in a payout we'll put back into our community, help someone out who needs a hand up. Just like the community helped June's.

I stop to check a text from Eddie confirming our dinner plans for this evening. He just accepted a position as the medical director of the clinic and officially resigned from Vanderbilt. He's staying, and I've even wondered if maybe, one day, he and I could live here in the Clementine together. It's a *someday* thing for now. I set down the phone and open the fridge to count the juice boxes, double-check the pantry for snacks. And then comes the chime of the doorbell.

"Good morning, Ms. Georgia," the Brownies announce as they push through the door, remove their shoes, and line them up neatly.

"How many today, Ms. Rosalinda?" I ask, stepping out onto the porch.

"Seven girls today. I just dropped four." Rosalinda looks then points at another car pulling into the drive. "And here come the others. Once word got out that you were having them this week, everyone changed plans to make it."

"These are my best Saturday mornings." I smile, and I feel it run into the rest of me.

I step back as the new arrivals rush up the steps and past me into the house.

"What can I say?" Rosalinda says. "You have a gift. The girls adore you."

"Excuse me, Ms. Georgia," the leader of the Brownies, whom I now know dearly, Reese, says. "Can we *please, please, please* do braids first?"

"You girls know I can't say no to hair!" I play like it's painful to admit, and the girls love the act.

I wave Rosalinda farewell, and she heads off to greet the other parent driver before leaving.

Reese whips a large box from behind her. "Good. Because we brought supplies."

The group erupts in giggles and squeals and requests for pink or glitter or clips with unicorn hair.

I spend the next few hours braiding seven little heads of hair. Big French braids. A few baby braids. And some just want clips. We laugh and chat, and I hear all the gossip from the elementary school—not that it makes much sense to me at almost thirty-three. When I first volunteered to take some Brownies shifts from Rosalinda, it seemed like coincidence that what they always wanted to do was hair. I do theirs or they do each other's.

And for the longest time I thought it must just be the trend. Or their ages.

But today, as I hear this house come back to life with the patter of these small feet, their giggles and shouts and well-meaning demands, I do wonder if there is any celestial way possible that Junie sent them for me. That she put them in my path to urge me to say yes, to listen to their woes and triumphs, and each and every time be reminded that I am still a big sister.

That I can be that part even without her. Even if it's different.

I can remember her now without crying every time. Not most times yet, but some. It's progress.

I even signed up to start cosmetology school.

I'm doing it, living, step by step.

Braid by braid.

I'm doing my best, and to be entirely truthful, for now that's all I can ask of myself.

"Ms. Georgia?" Reese asks. "Can I tell you something?"

I nod. "Of course."

She runs her hands over my hair, examining it from root to tip. She grips my cheeks in her hands and grins. "You are having a *really* good hair day."

ACKNOWLEDGMENTS

GOOD HAIR DAYS IS A book I dug deep to write, one I love, and one that stretched me. I'm so thankful for the people who walked this path to publication alongside me.

To my readers, thank you. Without you, there would be no books!

To my editor, Laura Wheeler, thank you for pushing me to take this book to the next level. Your insights and good catches are forever saving me. As I've told you before: thank you for pointing out the toilet paper stuck to my shoe before I walk out of the bathroom. I am so proud of this book that we built together, and there isn't a doubt in my mind that these Louise women, who I love so dearly, wouldn't have the depth and sass they do without your contributions.

To my agents, Margaret Danko and Kim Perel, thank you for always having my back, pointing out the potholes in the road before me, and constantly looking at the big picture of my career. I'm so lucky to have you in my corner. Particularly so when you're also so much fun. Let the dreaming continue.

To Jodi Hughes, thank you for another meticulous line edit, for your patience with my vague timing and misplaced commas, and your humor. Thank you for polishing this into a final product worthy of these wonderful readers.

To Caitlin Halstead, thank you for stepping in and shepherding this book through so much of the behind-the-scenes tending required to bring it to publication, and thank you for answering a zillion of my questions. I'm so glad we've gotten to work together on this one. To Savannah Breedlove, thank you for the sleek formatting and your keen attention to detail. The interior of the book is a beauty. To Halie Cotton for your hard work to create the beautiful cover.

To Colleen Lacey, Taylor Ward, and Jere Warren for being my go-to marketing and PR team. Thank you for all of your support, for always being so on top of my questions, and for all of your work behind the scenes. You are true pros. To the rest of the marketing and PR team, Nekasha Pratt, Kerri Potts, Margaret Kercher, and Patrick Aprea, thank you for all you do and especially so in creating resources and holding office hours where I've been fortunate enough to learn from your expertise.

To Amanda Bostic, thank you for your leadership and your continued support of my stories and their transformation into books.

To Sarah Berke, I adore you (not that it's news). You are a heartbeat within my writing career, and I would not be where I am without both your practical and emotional support. Thank you for all of it: the reads, talking me off the ledge and out of my head, and sanity checking my ideas. But mostly for your friendship, for being you, and for always being an example I look to proof of genuine and good humans existing in the world. I'm so lucky to know you and to call you a friend.

To the authors who I've met along the way and now call friends. Kimberly Brock, thank you for your sharing all of your wisdom and insights, being a listening ear, and for being a friend inside what can be such a tough industry. Jennifer Moorman, for all of your help and advice, for your encouragement and enthusiasm, and for all of your positivity that extends to those who know you. Elizabeth Bass Parman for the tips shared and for cheering my books on alongside your own. Colleen Oakley, for being the very first author to agree to blurb my debut and for your warm welcome into the author community.

To the independent bookstores who have shown up to partner with me for book events, thank you for being the vibrant bookish hubs our world so needs.

To BTP and each fabulous member for making my book a traveling ARC, and for posting with such delightful enthusiasm. It is groups like yours that are the true lifeblood of the book world, and we authors are beyond fortunate to have you. Thank you for your friendship and support.

To all of the book bloggers who have shared my books, told a friend, or written a review, thank you.

To my family and friends, thank you for stepping in and helping. To my husband for all your support, for being a true partner, for creating time for my work to happen within our family system, and of course for guerilla marketing and flame emojis online. To my parents for taking the kids so I can do events and for following along so lovingly. To my friends, thank you for giving my life depth and fun and for cheering me on as I branch part of my life out in a magical new direction.

DISCUSSION QUESTIONS

1. Which female lead did you relate to more, Georgia or Junie, and why?

2. Who was your favorite supporting character and why?

3. The town of Whitetail, where the Louise/Scott family lives is a small, close-knit community. Could you imagine yourself living here? Why or why not?

4. The Louise women have extremely strong bonds between them (despite their history of white lies!). Do close relationships, either with family or friends, always require full honesty? Is it ever ok to lie to a friend to protect them?

5. June's Beauty is a family business that both provided for the women in the Louise/Scott family and drove wedges between them. In your experience do family businesses bring people together or divide family members?

6. In the story, Georgia moves away from home to pursue a "bigger" life beyond her small town. Did you leave the town you

grew up in or do you still live there? What reasons contributed to your decisions?

7. Hair is clearly very important to the female line in this story. In your own family, are there any special traditions that bond the generations? Or any skill sets that seem to run in your family?

8. One theme in this story is that being honest and telling the truth will lead to freedom and peace. Is there a time you saw this play out in your own life?

9. In the Louise/Scott family birth order holds a lot of importance as to what roles each person plays in the family as well as what opportunities they've historically gotten for work at June's Beauty. How did your birth order among siblings (or growing up as an only child) impact who you became?

10. When Junie made the difficult decision to end her treatment, how did you feel?

FAMILY TREE

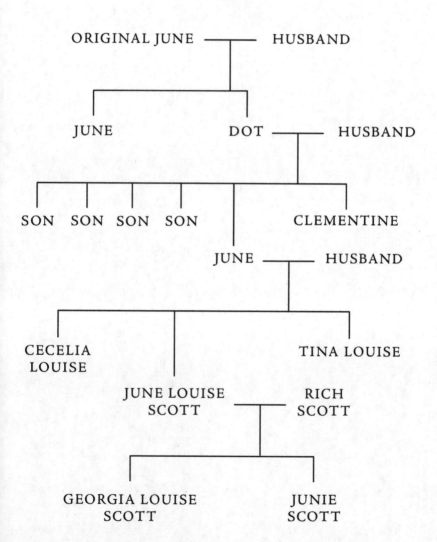

ORIGINAL JUNE —— HUSBAND

JUNE   DOT —— HUSBAND

SON   SON   SON   SON   CLEMENTINE

JUNE —— HUSBAND

CECELIA
LOUISE   TINA LOUISE

JUNE LOUISE   RICH
SCOTT   SCOTT

GEORGIA LOUISE   JUNIE
SCOTT   SCOTT

FOR MORE FROM GRACE HELENA WALZ

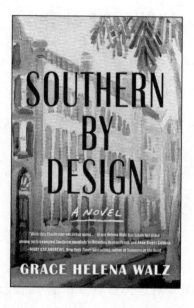

"A story of second chances and long-lost love as atmospheric as the Lowcountry itself, this is a positively charming debut from a stand-out new voice. Add it to your TBR list immediately!"

—Kristy Woodson Harvey, *New York Times* bestselling author of *A Happier Life*

Available in print, e-book, and downloadable audio

ABOUT THE AUTHOR

Photo by Lisa Liberati Photography

GRACE HELENA WALZ received a master's degree in social work from the University of Houston and has worked with children in foster care, as a medical social worker, and in a mental health capacity. She currently resides outside of Atlanta, Georgia, with her husband and two young children. She writes women's fiction in the moments between sticking Band-Aids on scraped knees and coordinating pint-size social engagements.

Connect with her online at gracehelenawalz.com
Facebook: @gracewalzauthor
Instagram: @gracehelenabooks
Pinterest: @gracewalzauthor